Untold

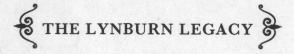

THE LYNBURN LEGACY

Unspoken

Untold

Unmade

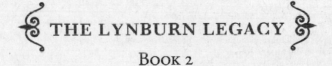

Untold

THE LYNBURN LEGACY

BOOK 2

SARAH REES BRENNAN

EMBER

Text copyright © 2013 by Sarah Rees Brennan
Cover and interior art copyright © 2013 by Giorgio Fochesato/Getty Images
Map copyright © 2013 by Theo Black

All rights reserved. Published in the United States by Ember, an imprint of Random House Children's Books, a division of Random House LLC, a Penguin Random House Company, New York. Originally published in hardcover in the United States by Random House Children's Books, New York, in 2013.

Ember and the E colophon are registered trademarks of Random House LLC.

Visit us on the Web! randomhouse.com/teens

Educators and librarians, for a variety of teaching tools, visit us at RHTeachersLibrarians.com

The Library of Congress has cataloged the hardcover edition of this work as follows:
Brennan, Sarah Rees.
Untold / by Sarah Rees Brennan.
p. cm. — (The Lynburn legacy ; bk. 2)
Summary: As Kami Glass and her friends continue to battle the sorcerers of the Lynburn family in the sleepy English town of Sorry-in-the-Vale, friendships and families are torn apart.
ISBN 978-0-375-87042-2 (trade) — ISBN 978-0-375-97042-9 (lib. bdg.) — ISBN 978-0-375-97995-8 (ebook)
[1. Magic—Fiction. 2. Magicians—Fiction. 3. Family life—England—Fiction. 4. Journalism—Fiction. 5. England—Fiction. 6. Horror stories.] I. Title.
PZ7.B751645Unt 2013 [Fic]—dc23 2012029991

ISBN 978-0-375-87104-7 (tr. pbk.)

Printed in the United States of America
10 9 8 7 6 5 4 3 2 1
First Ember Edition 2014

Random House Children's Books supports the First Amendment and celebrates the right to read.

For Susan

Who can make about a thousand beautiful things I could
never dream of making, and also write faster than I can.
(Where's the justice in that?) Who is the life of every party
and also makes a party in a living room:
basically, who is a joy forever.

Here's to you, Suzy Q.

Contents

PART I
IN THE DARK

And lonely as it is, that loneliness
Will be more lonely ere it will be less. . . .
—*Robert Frost*

Chapter One

The Scarecrow Trials

WELCOME TO SORRY-IN-THE-VALE. IT'S A MAGICAL PLACE (AND WE MEAN THAT LITERALLY).
BY KAMI GLASS

Let's not front. We all know magic is real.

You know. Or it's time you knew. It's time someone told you.

I always said that every town has a story, that even our sleepy Sorry-in-the-Vale must have one. I was so sure that I could find a story hidden somewhere under the chocolate-box prettiness of our town. I thought finding a story would be like bird-watching in the Vale woods, waiting for bright eyes and a burst of wings. I thought it would be like finding gold.

It wasn't like that at all.

I was searching for a story, and then the Lynburn family returned to the manor above our town: the sisters Lillian and Rosalind, their sons Ash and Jared, and Lillian's husband, Rob. They had been gone seventeen years, but as soon as they returned there was blood in the woods.

They were not here long before a girl died.

The Lynburns are sorcerers. I have seen magic with my own eyes. I saw Jared Lynburn turn himself invisible. I saw Ash Lynburn make objects fly. I saw shadows come to life, and come for me.

It was neither Jared nor Ash Lynburn who killed someone. Jared Lynburn may be, in this reporter's completely unbiased opinion, the most infuriating idiot in the land, but he was not responsible for this. Lillian, Jared, Ash, even Rosalind are not the ones who want to make Sorry-in-the-Vale again what it once was: a place where the sorcerers were our lords, demanding our blood as their right.

Rob Lynburn killed Nicola Prendergast. She was my age: she was seventeen. We were friends when we were children. I do not know how to talk about her death, that she died so a selfish lunatic could have more power, but I know I must. There are people in this town who already know the secrets of Sorry-in-the-Vale: people who are not talking and not acting because they are afraid. But hiding from the truth will not make it go away.

The Lynburns aren't the only sorcerers. They are the leaders, but there are others. There are police officers who are sorcerers. There are teachers who are sorcerers. There is magic on every side. Rob and Rosalind Lynburn left Aurimere House two weeks ago, and we know Rob was recruiting sorcerers to kill with him months before that. He has not been seen or heard from since he left, but that means nothing. He is a sorcerer and can walk unseen, gathering more sorcerers to him and making his plans.

We have to plan too. What can we do to fight magic? What power do we have?

Knowledge is power. Knowing this is power: me telling you this is power, for me and for you.

Try to be as strong and know as much as you can.

The sorcerers are coming for our town. Let's be ready for them.

"Well," said Kami Glass to herself, staring at her computer screen. "That doesn't make me look mad as a bucketful of hedgehogs at all."

Then she checked the time on her computer, saved the document, and made a grab for her bag and her orange jacket with the lace cuffs. It was Halloween, and if Kami didn't hurry she would be late for the Scarecrow Trials.

＊　＊　＊

The sun was setting in crimson slashes and gold ribbons over Sorry-in-the-Vale. Night was falling and Kami had a lot of scarecrows to get through.

"I hear in the big city, girls dress up like sexy witches and sexy vampires and sexy Easter bunnies, and go to parties where they do all sorts of scandalous things," Kami said. "Lucky you and me, we walk around our town looking at our neighbors' gardens and remarking 'My, that's a good-looking scarecrow' to each other. I guess this is why our natures are so beautiful and unspoiled."

"My, that's a hideous scarecrow," Angela drawled. "Are we done yet?"

"No, Angela," Kami said patiently. "This is our first scarecrow. I'm going to write an article on the tradition of the Scarecrow Trials, and I'm going to put a picture of the winning scarecrow on our front page so everyone can say to themselves 'Fine figure of a scarecrow.' For the preservation of our sacred journalistic integrity, we have to see *every* scarecrow in town."

"I can't figure out how I got roped into this mess," said Angela, who looked all scarecrowed out. "Obviously, I've made some very poor life choices."

Kami fell silent. She had roped Angela into much more than the Scarecrow Trials. She was the one who had told Angela that she heard a voice in her head, and that the voice was a real person. She'd drawn Angela into her investigation of the murder and magic in Sorry-in-the-Vale. She had caught the attention of Rob Lynburn, sorcerer and murderer. Kami knew it was due to her that Angela had almost died in the woods two weeks ago.

Kami and Angela were on the west edge of town, at the top of the steep slope of Schoolhouse Road. Kami looked down at the old yellow cobblestones shadowed with the coming of night. She traced the line of the road with her eyes, to the sloping roofs and spinning weather vanes of Sorry-in-the-Vale, then to the woods waiting beyond.

Kami did not know how to talk to Angela about that, or how to tell her she was sorry. Misery and uncertainty kept flooding through her, tides that had been turned back all her life by a secret voice. Now the voice in her head was silent.

Angela, her brilliant dark eyes almost hidden by her veil of black hair, gave Kami a sidelong glance. Angela looked annoyed, which was her default, but Kami could see a hint of concern lurking underneath. She knew that her new hesitance was freaking Angela out.

"You know what?" Kami said with a grin. "Mrs. Jeffries at the post office tried to slip me a little somethin' somethin' to praise her scarecrow in *The Nosy Parker*. It's shocking how corrupt the Scarecrow Trials have become. What about honor, Angela? What about the craft?"

"How much did you get?"

"Well, okay, she slipped me some free stamps," Kami admitted. "Still, my first bribe as a journalist. I'm feeling pretty fancy." Sorry-in-the-Vale didn't have a local paper, and Kami had been proud when she saw people without kids reading the paper she edited, aptly titled *The Nosy Parker*.

At least she was succeeding at something.

Kami and Angela stopped at the Greens' house, one of the few old houses not made of golden Cotswold stone but of granite and slate. It was a gray crumbling edifice that seemed bound together by the dry brown briars of climbing roses growing over it. The Greens' scarecrow was lopsided on its stand; its yellow gloves, stuffed fat with straw, seemed to wave feebly at them.

Kami clicked her tongue. "Poor effort," she said, taking a picture with her phone and making a note to that effect in her notebook. "Might scare off a few thrushes. Possibly a pigeon. But it's not a hardcore scarecrow."

"I'm uncomfortable checking out scarecrows," Angela said. "I don't swing that way."

It was Kami's turn to give Angela a sidelong look.

That was something else they hadn't talked about. Kami had found out secondhand that Angela had tried to kiss their friend Holly. Kami must have been more or less the worst best friend in the world if Angela had not felt like she could tell her that she liked girls.

"Have you . . ." Kami cleared her throat. "Have you had a chance to talk to Holly?"

"No," Angela snapped. "Been chatting much with Jared?"

"We often have special moments where I come into a room and he immediately leaves," Kami said. "I treasure those times." She swallowed, the knot in her throat as sharp as if she had swallowed a rose, the thorns raking on their way down.

"I don't mean to—to make you feel bad," Kami added, hating that she had to say it. Words felt so clumsy when she was talking about feelings and not facts. "I just wanted you to know that you can talk about it. If you want."

"I don't want," Angela told her flatly.

They followed the curve of the road until it became Cooper Lane, fringed by pale buildings and dark trees. Kami concentrated on the scarecrows going by and scribbled: "Write in your notebook to avoid this awkward moment!"

Angela said, after a pause, "But I know I can."

Kami nudged her, which, considering their relative heights, meant that she elbowed Angela in the thigh. "Life sucks sometimes."

"Thank you for that amazing journalistic insight," Angela responded, very dryly, and Kami felt a little better.

Cooper Lane turned out to have an eclectic mix of scarecrows, from the traditional cloth and straw to the experimental: there was one scarecrow with a balloon for a head, and one made of papier-mâché. Kami liked the scarecrow in the pink flowered hat at the Singhs' because there were so many scarecrows that were clearly guys. Kami felt ladies should represent in the scarecrow movement.

"A papier-mâché scarecrow is cheating," Kami observed judiciously as they passed through the town square at the end of the High Street, heading toward Shadowchurch Lane. "And the cardboard cutout scarecrow was just sad. Enough to make a true scarecrow connoisseur weep." She was mostly talking to distract Angela from the group of guys standing at the foot of the statue of long-ago town hero Matthew Cooper. In the middle of the little crowd, Kami glimpsed Holly's golden curls.

Kami quickened her pace, and they soon arrived at the church and Shadowchurch Lane.

It was almost twilight, the sun a bloody smear on the horizon, the pale blues and greens of the sky fading into gray and indigo. Across from the stone horseshoe-shaped archway of the church entrance was the Thompsons' house. Their garden was fenced, unlike most gardens in Sorry-in-the-Vale, the black iron bars making a shadowy cage of their front lawn. The scarecrow that stood in that cage wore a black suit. The sack that was its face had been whitened with chalk, and it glowed in the darkness.

"Vampire scarecrow?" said Angela.

"Undertaker scarecrow" was Kami's verdict. Her voice came out less assured than she wanted it to.

The next house belonged to Sergeant Kenn, the police officer Kami had talked to after Nicola Prendergast was murdered. The same police officer she had seen coming to help Rob Lynburn the day he tried to kill Angela. Kami slipped her hand into the crook of Angela's elbow and held on.

Since the Kenns' house was beside the church, the church spire cast a black triangle on the ghost-gray grass. The scarecrow on their front lawn was slumped on its wooden frame, its black-hatted head hanging. Something about the way it was slumped, the fact that the body was a little too realistically proportioned, made a chill crawl down Kami's spine. It reminded her of someone dead. But she was being ridiculous. She was imagining things because of whose house this was. She could see the straw sticking out of the scarecrow's cuffs. Keeping hold of Angela and drawing her along, Kami set one foot in the dark wet grass and stooped down, peering to see the scarecrow's face.

In the shadow of its hat, the scarecrow's eyes shone, not with the glint of metal, but with the wet gleam of something alive. Kami's fingers clamped down on Angela's arm. There was a flicker of darkness, the gleam of the scarecrow's eyes vanishing for a moment, and Kami realized what had happened.

The scarecrow had blinked.

"Angela," Kami said in a low, extremely calm voice. "I think it might be a good idea to run."

The scarecrow began to move, sliding its stiff arms off

the wooden frame where it rested. Kami watched with paralyzed fascination as it stretched out a leg and took a step toward them.

"Kami," Angela said, in an equally low, calm voice. "I think it might be a very good idea to look around."

Kami looked and saw that every garden on Shadowchurch Lane was stirring into life. The undertaker scarecrow in the Thompsons' garden was already off its wooden frame and climbing the fence, its round pale face shining like a small horrible moon, coming through the darkness at them.

The air was filled with the whisper-like rustle of straw. Behind them, Kami heard screams and the sound of people running. She let go of Angela's arm and grabbed hold of a branch from the Kenns' yew tree. The bark rasped cold and harsh against her palms, and Kami wrenched at it as hard as she could until it snapped off in her hands.

Angela walked, empty-handed, across Shadowchurch Lane to meet the Thompsons' scarecrow. She kicked it in the stomach. That did not wind it, or even make its stride falter. Another scarecrow came tottering down the road, bleeding a trail of straw, making straight for Angela. Kami ran out into the street wielding her branch.

Angela whirled and grabbed one of the Thompson scarecrow's arms. It ripped its own arm off and launched itself at her, so light it seemed like it was flying. Angela launched herself right back, with no finesse or any of the self-defense moves Rusty had taught them, just fury and clawing, as if she planned to shred it to pieces with her bare hands.

The new scarecrow Kami was keeping at bay with her branch was getting braver, its sackcloth feet shuffling in the mess of straw it was bleeding, feinting first one way and then another. It had a turnip for a head, which was wagging obscenely at her as the scarecrow lunged. Kami stared into the dark hollows of its eyes and got an idea. She stepped forward, advancing even though every muscle in her body was urging her to cringe away, and jabbed her branch as hard as she could into its grinning face.

The face shattered, turning into vegetable pulp as she hit it again and again. The scarecrow's hands touched her, rubber gloves filled with crackling straw fumbling at and catching her throat. Kami forced back a scream and struck until the turnip fell off and the scarecrow tumbled down into an inert heap of straw and cloth.

Kami whipped around still clutching her branch, with a cry on her lips for Angela. But Angela had seen what to do already. She was crouched on the road, ripping at the creature's neck until the sackcloth gave way with a horrible tearing sound, and Angela rose to her feet with its chalk-whitened head in her fist like a trophy.

Her eyes met Kami's and she dropped the head. Kami reached out with her free hand to grab Angela's. It was only when she found Angela's palm clammy, and Angela held her hand back hard, that she knew Angela was scared too.

Then she heard a choked-off scream, and both their heads turned. Kami thought of the screams and running she'd heard behind them. In the square. She should have known Holly wouldn't run anywhere but to them.

Holly was still in the square, still in a crowd, but the boys were gone and the crowd she stood in now was a jostling, rushing crowd of scarecrows. Kami saw Holly's bright crown of hair disappear among them, swallowed up. Angela's immediate race forward was checked when the scarecrow from the Kenn house lunged in front of her. Kami ducked down and scythed its feet out from under it with her branch.

At least, that was the idea, but instead the scarecrow's straw legs sagged forward, bowing instead of falling. This still gave Angela plenty of time to dodge around it.

"Go," Kami said. "I've got this."

Angela hesitated for an instant, then nodded and ran, her black hair streaming behind her.

Kami had told her to go. She had not expected to feel quite so abandoned and alone, the only human left on a street full of horrors.

The light from the Kenns' windows gleamed in their scarecrow's eyes, and Kami saw they were marbles that had transformed into something that glistened as if they were made of the same stuff as human eyes but stayed small, swirling colors at their center.

It had a plaster face that had turned waxy and a little flexible. Kami saw its mouth move infinitesimally, its grin stretching. It flexed its hands in black gloves, and Kami heard tiny wooden pieces click inside the leather. Rob Lynburn and his sorcerers had made all these creatures come to some semblance of life. Kami had known as much already. But this scarecrow was specifically designed to last longer, to be more capable of hurting her.

It was horrible that there were lights on in the Kenns' house. She wondered how many people were awake in the other houses along this lane, knowing nothing or hiding in fear, or standing at the windows watching the chaos they had created.

A hand touched the back of Kami's neck, so terribly light, like a glove filled with nothing but air. Kami spun, trying to keep both scarecrows in her line of sight and jabbing her branch at the new one.

It was the scarecrow in the pink sun hat. Kami felt a little betrayed.

She hit it and the branch caught on the ruffled material of the scarecrow's dress. Kami stabbed the branch in deeper and then yanked it out, ripping the scarecrow in two.

The Kenns' scarecrow grabbed at her arm, its grasp firmer than the other scarecrow's, feeling slick and strangling-strong on the bare skin of her wrist. Kami wrenched away and saw that there were other scarecrows very close now. One with a little whittled wooden face, its nose a knot in bark, was suddenly at the Kenns' scarecrow's side like a henchman.

A couple of houses down, there was a dark shape lying splayed in the grass. Kami felt her stomach turn, cold and sick, as she realized it was a scarecrow so badly made it could not stand.

It was crawling to get her, on its belly like a snake.

Kami dived for the scarecrow with the wooden face. The Kenns' scarecrow crashed into her, heavier than a scarecrow should have been, as if it had a wooden skeleton buried underneath its straw, and caught her off-balance.

Kami fell heavily onto her side, elbow catching the edge of the pavement. The Kenn scarecrow's leather shoe slammed down toward her face. Kami rolled to avoid it, and ended up flat on her back in the wet grass of the Kenns' garden. The scarecrow's waxy face and living marble eyes glistened above her, impassive and terrible, and Kami lifted her branch in both hands to ward it off.

In the black shadow of the church spire, light was born. First an orange glint ran along the dark wood of her branch; then Kami caught the sharp smell of smoke and heard a crackle nothing like the sound of straw.

Kami kept tight hold of her branch as light raced along it, sparking between the forked ends, and watched it burst into burning life. By the sudden light of fire, she saw there was someone with her in Shadowchurch Lane.

Jared Lynburn, one of the sorcerers. Rob Lynburn's nephew, the real boy she had once believed was her imaginary friend.

He was standing back, arms crossed over his chest, watching her. His face was mostly shadowed but the stark line of the scar on his face was white as moonlight, firelight catching the sleeping gold in his dark-blond hair and setting twin lights burning in his pale eyes.

The boy who used to live in her head.

But not anymore.

Kami lifted herself onto her unhurt elbow and plunged the burning branch into the Kenn scarecrow's body. Its coat caught alight, and Kami scrambled to her feet as it scrabbled at the branch with its leather gloves. She shoved the branch into its straw breast and watched it burn from the inside out.

She was not surprised when she looked for the scarecrow with the wooden face and saw its face already a charred ruin. She *was* surprised when she looked across the street and Jared was gone, twining shadows and moonlight where he had stood.

Firelight burst in the corner of her eye. Kami turned and looked down the street. There he was, a shadow passing through forms bright with burning. Some of the scarecrows writhed as they burned in a ghastly parody of a dance. Jared stopped at the garden where the ill-made scarecrow lay, a humped-up shape in the grass. Kami watched him looking at it, weakly rolling in the grass as it burned, and thought she saw him smile.

She could have followed him. He would not exactly have been hard to track, what with his blazing path of destruction and all. But Jared obviously did not need her help. Angela and Holly might.

Kami turned away from him and ran, clutching her burning branch, down to the town square.

Angela was standing beside the statue of Matthew Cooper. Holly was sitting at the base of the statue, short skirt riding up her purple tights as she put her boots back on. Beside her was a metal sign from one of the High Street shop fronts.

Standing diffidently on the other side of the statue was Ash Lynburn, Jared's cousin and Rob's son, his camera around his neck and piles of cloth and straw all around him.

"How'd you do that?" Kami asked. It was the first thing she had said to him in two weeks, since the day she found out his father had persuaded him to spy on her, and almost persuaded him to kill Angela.

Ash blinked and smiled at the sight of her. "It's easy," he said. "You just undo the spell put on them in the first place—it's like undoing a knot in your mind."

So setting them on fire and watching them burn was an entirely unnecessary and insane thing to do, Kami thought. But she did not say that. Instead, she said, "Everyone all right?"

Angela nodded. Holly looked up and smiled too, her smile shakier and thus more real than Ash's. "I'm okay," she said. "I see you are too. I also see you have a weapon that is on fire."

"I'm badass like that," Kami said, putting the branch down on the cobblestones. It was still burning. She had no idea how to put it out.

"My mother's up by the woods, dealing with the gardens there," said Ash, as if Lillian Lynburn was trimming hedges rather than killing scarecrows come to life. "Jared's—"

"I saw him," Kami told him shortly. She jerked her head toward the road past the church, and the burning trail Jared had left. She went to sit at the foot of the statue beside Holly.

Holly linked arms with her. Kami leaned in close, sharing warmth as they looked around the nighttime square and past it to the rest of their town where there were still fires burning and straw men moving through the dark.

They had known it was coming: Rob Lynburn's first move to terrify the town into submission, to make it a place where sorcerers ruled again, where they could kill for power and nobody would stop them.

They didn't know who most of Rob Lynburn's followers were, but some people who didn't follow him must have seen what was happening. Nobody had come to help. Kami shivered in the night air, and felt Holly shiver too.

When they saw someone walking toward them down the High Street, they both jumped.

Angela ran past them, and when she reached her brother she punched him in the shoulder. Rusty's shirt was torn; he put an arm around his sister and looked at Kami over Angela's head. His often-sleepy hazel eyes were bright and intent.

"Cambridge?" he said, using his silly nickname for her. "A scarecrow just tried to choke me. I don't wish to seem overly inquisitive, but do you have any idea what on earth is happening?"

Kami looked at Holly and Ash, who were both silent and totally unhelpful. "Well," she admitted, "I might have some idea."

"You'd better tell me," Rusty said.

Kami looked around the square at the remains of scarecrows in the moonlight. "We'd better go to your house first," she said. "It's not safe here." She didn't know if *anywhere* was safe. She didn't want to go home, so there was nowhere to go but Rusty and Angela's place. She wasn't welcome at the Lynburns'.

Kami lifted her eyes to Aurimere House, which stood outlined against the sky. Its windows reflected the lights of fires burning all over her town.

Chapter Two
The Heir of Aurimere

"So to review," said Rusty, two hours later. "Magic is real. The Lynburns are sorcerers who founded Sorry-in-the-Vale as an ideal place for sorcerers to soak up nature, which gives them their, ah, magic powers. But not as much magic as they get from killing people. Rob Lynburn killed Nicola Prendergast, and we can't go to the police because at least one member of the police force is one of Rob Lynburn's sorcerers."

"Also because the police might not find our story particularly convincing," Kami put in.

She scrutinized Rusty. He was sitting on the other side of the kitchen island from herself, Angela, and Holly, resting his elbows on the granite surface. He was back to his usual self, all traces of his former alertness wiped out, big shoulders at ease and eyes heavy-lidded as if he might just go to sleep. There was never any way to tell what Rusty was thinking.

"And the imaginary friend you've had all your life—the voice in your head—was actually Jared Lynburn, who is also a sorcerer," Rusty said. He shrugged. "Well, I did think there was something weird going on with him. And the fact that you guys were sort of . . . wearing *woo-woo* mental friendship bracelets meant he had more, ah, magical power, and you could use it."

"I could use it better than he could," Kami said. "He's a sorcerer, and I was a source—the link between us meant I was a source of magic to him. But I broke the link between us."

"Right," said Rusty. "So you don't have, ah, magic powers anymore."

"Can you stop prefixing magic powers with 'ah'?"

"I'm not ready to drop the prefix," Rusty told her. "If you like, I can switch prefixes. I'm happy to go with 'um, magic powers' or 'er . . . magic powers.' Whichever works best for you ladies."

Angela leaned across the table. "Rusty, I already beat up four scarecrows tonight. Do not push me."

"Okay," said Rusty. "So, we have three people with magic powers on our side: Lillian, Jared, and Ash Lynburn. And Jared and Ash—or, as I think of them, Sulky and Blondie—are still sorcerer trainees. On the side of evil are sorcerers in double digits, and aside from Rob; Jared's mum, Rosalind; and Sergeant Kenn, we don't know who most of them are."

"*Yet,*" said Kami.

"Wow," said Rusty. "Bet family reunions are going to be awkward for the Lynburns from now on. Also, I have lost a certain amount of faith in the police force."

It was possible Rusty thought this was all an elaborate practical joke. Kami looked at Holly and Angela, hoping for backup. Angela scowled and Holly seemed uncomfortable. Maybe Holly didn't want to look like a lunatic in front of a cute older guy. Or maybe she was uncomfortable being in Angela's house.

The Montgomery house was never a comfortable house to be in at the best of times. Kami looked around at the shining kitchen island, the coffee machine she thought might unfold to be a robot butler, and Rusty, who seemed to have relaxed himself into a coma. She could not imagine a less likely place to tell someone about magic and be believed.

"You saw a little of what they can do tonight," Kami said quietly. "There's much more. There's so much worse. Rob killed Nicola. He tried to kill me and Angela. We have to find some way to stop them, because there isn't anybody else who will. If you don't believe me, it doesn't matter. If you won't help me, it doesn't matter. I know what I have to do."

"You usually do," Rusty said, and smiled lazily at her.

Holly reached out and squeezed Kami's hand. "And we're with you," she said, her voice subdued but firm. Kami squeezed back.

Angela turned her gaze to Rusty and said, "That's right. We don't need you, you useless lump. In fact, you'd probably get in the way."

Rusty placed a hand on his heart. "Without the love and support of my family, I would not be the man I am today. I'm with Cambridge too, of course."

"You are?" Kami said blankly.

"A scarecrow tried to kill me. I don't see anyone offering me alternative explanations for that," Rusty drawled. "I believe you. I'll help you. I'm with you. But it's a lot to take in all at once. Could someone maybe fix me a snack? I think it would really help me process."

Angela threw a roll of tinfoil at Rusty's head. Holly started to laugh, and Rusty got up and fixed himself a snack, spreading tuna salad on bread with the air of a serf being worked unto death. Kami started to talk more easily, and Holly and Angela joined in, telling Rusty about going to the shut-up Monkshood Abbey, where Lynburns had committed murders two generations ago, and talking about seeing magic in the depths of the woods and the heart of their town.

Rusty was on their side. He believed her, and Angela and Holly had spoken up for her, been there for her despite the awkwardness between them. They could all be there for each other.

It was a relief to tell someone and be believed. Kami wanted to tell the world. For now, she could feel her team coming together. She could believe that her plan would come together as well.

✳ ✳ ✳

Ash had scoured the town for his mother and his cousin half the night, trying not to think about what might happen to them if they were caught alone by his father. He trudged up the slope to Aurimere House, his camera beating a rapid anxious tattoo against his chest with every step, and heard his mother's voice as he opened the door.

So they were both back safe. He doubted that either of them had been desperately concerned about him.

It struck Ash as almost unbearably strange sometimes that they were in Aurimere at last. For his whole childhood, it had been the promised land, the one thing his mother and father agreed on. He'd known that once they found Aunt Rosalind, they were going home. Where he belonged, where they all belonged, where they would never suffer again. "Our house," his parents had called it. "Our town."

Except he hadn't understood that his parents meant different things by "our town": his mother meant they had a responsibility to care for it, and his father that they had a right to rule it.

It had seemed easy enough to reconcile their different views when Aurimere was nothing but a dream. Both his mother and his father had told him, always, that they weren't like other people: they were better.

He had spent his life knowing he was the heir of Aurimere, that Sorry-in-the-Vale was waiting for his return. He had spent his life wanting, so badly, to please them both.

His mother's and father's different views had ended in Ash seeing Angela chained on a quarry floor and knowing his father expected him to kill her. Now his father and his long-awaited aunt Rosalind were his enemies, and the only friends Ash had left did not trust him. He pulled his camera off from around his neck. He didn't know why he was still carrying it around: it had been weeks since he saw something so beautiful and right he wanted to record it. He left it on the hall table and climbed the broad wooden staircase, heading toward his mother's voice, which was coming from the general direction of the portrait gallery. His mother had not spoken much to him since she learned that he had picked up one of the golden knives the Lynburns had used long ago to shed blood and gain power, and almost used it.

Ash walked softly toward the gallery, past the door that led to the wing where they all slept, hesitating only when he reached the gallery entrance. The doorway had been carved in stone at a time when people were shorter than he was, and he had to duck his head slightly.

The gallery had a ceiling like a chapel's, the curves of the walls meeting in an arch. The walls themselves were bright with gilt frames surrounding the faces of dead Lynburns. Two living Lynburns were standing in one of the alcoves, on either side of its dark, narrow, diamond-paned window: Jared was leaning against the stone, face turned toward the night. Ash's mother never leaned against anything. She stood with one hand half outstretched toward Jared.

Ash hung back in the doorway. He felt short of breath and was not sure whether it was guilt, or whether he simply did not wish to be heard.

"Perhaps you do not entirely understand how the Lynburns work," said his mother.

"Perhaps," Jared said, mimicking Mom's English accent, an ugly edge to his voice, "I don't care about anything to do with the Lynburns."

Mom was unruffled by what Ash would've thought she'd consider blasphemy. "You are one of us. Sorcery is in your blood and bones. You can't be anything else. You can't escape from what you are."

"Oh, really?" Jared asked. "My mom ran away. Holly told me that her uncle ran away as well. Of course, maybe he wasn't running from magic. Maybe he was just running from you."

Ash had never heard anything special about Holly's family, never heard his mother mention them. She ignored the mention of them now.

"So is that what you're going to do, run away?" his mother asked. "Strange. You are many things, but I would not have said you were a coward."

"Sorry for bringing it up," Jared drawled, not sounding sorry. "But I wouldn't have said you were an excellent judge of character. Based on the current evidence."

Jared is wasting his time trying to make Mom flinch, Ash thought.

"Because my husband is a murderer, my sister a weakling, and my son such a coward he almost became a murderer too?" Lillian asked.

Ash felt sick. He'd known this was what she thought of him, but hearing her say it was worse than he could have imagined. He wanted to speak, to protest, but he stayed silent. Because she was right, and he was such a coward.

Jared was smiling, but his smile looked twisted. His eyes and scar were pale reflections in the dark glass. "That is what I meant, yeah. What a family. 'One of us'? It would be better if there were none of us left."

"But neither Rob nor Rosalind nor Ash is the leader of the Lynburns," Mom said. "I am."

"No offense, Aunt Lillian," Jared told her, "but I'm not crazy about you either."

"Rob is older than I am," Lillian went on, and Ash found it terrifying how little they were actually communicating, how they refused to respond to each other even as they talked. "Rosalind was born before I was."

"Fascinating," Jared said in a monotone.

"The heir of Aurimere is not chosen by age or direct descent," Ash's mother said. "The leader chooses the strongest heir, the Lynburn who will be the best leader. That's why I was chosen. And that's who I would choose. You could lead after me. You could have Aurimere."

Jared looked amused. "And why would I want it?"

"Because you want to be anything but what you are now. You want to be so strong that nothing can hurt you. You could be the heir. You could be someone that anybody would think was worthwhile. Think about it."

His mother's voice was forceful now, no longer cool: Ash could almost see the dream she was conjuring up, the vision of being a leader, the shimmering promise of Aurimere above their town.

It wasn't his dream, not anymore.

Ash saw the glint of Jared's pale cruel eyes in the dark glass differently now, saw the lift of his hooded lids and registered a certain focus. If he could see Jared's reflection in the glass, he realized, Jared could see his. His mother was unaware of his presence. But Jared knew he was there.

"Sure," Jared said, still smiling that little, twisted smile. "I'll think about it."

Ash ran then, stumbling as if he was drunk or blind, through the home of his dreams and out into the night. He ran down the path into the dark woods, until he could no longer see the lit windows of the manor on the hill. Then he sat at the foot of a tree, head in his hands, and wept.

Everything was meant to come right, once they came home.

Chapter Three
Broken Homes

THE SCARECROW VANDALS
by Kami Glass

You are probably all, dear readers, wondering what occurred in Sorry-in-the-Vale on Halloween night. It is only natural that masked attackers and random small fires across town might inspire some curiosity.

"What on earth is happening?" asked a witness to these events (Rusty Montgomery, age 20, who insisted on not remaining anonymous and also wished this paper to record the fact that he is single).

Let me tell you what was happening.

"Are you sure this is a good idea?" asked Holly.

"I am not going to tell lies in *The Nosy Parker*," said Kami.

Ash was staring at the pictures on his computer screen with the fixed gaze of someone who was not seeing anything, and had been doing so since at least seven on this Monday morning, when Kami had arrived, coming straight from Angela's house to school. Holly, who had arrived at eight, was looking extremely doubtful about her gallant leader's dedication to truth.

"So you're going to say that evil sorcerers made the scarecrows come to life and attack us?" asked Holly. "Won't that make everyone think we're—I don't want to sound harsh here, but—completely and hopelessly insane?"

"No, no, no," said Kami. "A journalist has to make editorial decisions. Nobody can report everything. If you try, you'll only end up giving people false impressions. Like the one you mentioned about people thinking I was completely insane."

"Oh yeah," Holly said. "False. Totally."

Kami waved this aside with a sweep of her hand. "So one must judiciously edit reality in order to convey to people the, if you will, soul of the truth. The *true* truth."

Holly did not look entirely convinced by this brilliant logic. "So, uh, what are you going to write?"

"That the confusion of last night, by which I mean the regrettable incident that spoiled one of the cherished traditions of our town, is thought to be due to the actions of a group of malcontents who clearly do not honor said traditions, or understand the real spirit of Sorry-in-the-Vale. We, and by 'we' the humble writer hopes she can include all the readers of this article, can only hope that the people of Sorry-in-the-Vale will soon drive this evil-minded faction away."

"Wow," said Holly, looking gratifyingly impressed. "So anyone who knows the truth will read it and know you're basically spitting in Rob Lynburn's face. Aren't you worried he'll take revenge?"

Kami was about to tell Holly that she knew no fear in

the pursuit of justice, when Ash tore his eyes away from his computer and spoke.

"Like my father's going to care about what a teenage girl writes in a school newspaper," he sneered.

Kami waited a beat too long to respond to him, and realized that she had been waiting for the usual reassurance that Jared would send her any time she ever felt unsure. She'd always thought she had so much more confidence in herself than this. Well, she had to learn more confidence. She had to rely on herself now.

"The truth is never stupid," she said, trying not to wonder if she sounded stupid. "Every act of defiance counts. Every call to arms that people hear matters. I believe that. And your father is a proud guy. He won't like anyone calling him names, even in a school newspaper article written by a teenage girl. And I take petty but huge satisfaction from that."

People don't talk much about that sort of thing around here. And they would never write it down. Someone had told her that once. Everyone in this town was hiding things, so nobody knew enough, and everyone was scared.

Kami was not going to be part of that.

"He's not going to *read* it," Ash protested. "We have to do something else. We have to do something big: we have to stop him."

"Someone's going to read this," Kami said. "It's worthwhile. But yes, we have to do other things as well, and I have ideas about what. I just think we should talk about them when we're all together. We've got Rusty on our side now too. You go to your mother, and to—Jared. Tell them we all need to talk. Tell them I've got a plan."

Kami tried to say Jared's name as if she could not have cared less. She couldn't do it, could not stop the catch in her voice before she got out his name. She felt a wash of humiliation go through her when Ash rose and left without a word.

There was no comfort for her in her mind. She had to swallow pain down and pretend. "What's wrong with him?" She was certain that her casual tone did not sound very convincing. But Holly only looked distressed.

"Well," Holly said. "Well—it's probably Jared."

Before, she had always known if Jared was all right. Now anything could happen to him and she wouldn't know.

Kami looked up at Holly and said, painfully, "What's happened to Jared?"

Holly looked so sorry for her.

"What's *happened*?" Kami demanded, and her voice shook. "Tell me."

"Nothing," said Holly. "I mean, he's all right, Kami. I promise you. It's just that I imagine Ash is upset that Jared left home."

"Left home?" Kami asked. "Left Aurimere?"

Holly looked alarmed, possibly because Kami sounded slightly hysterical. "Yes. It's all over school," she added, which did nothing to help Kami away from the path of hysteria.

Kami grasped the edge of her desk, and used it to stand up. "Where did he go?"

* * *

She was running too fast and completely against school rules when she almost sent Amber Green, a girl she sometimes sat beside in English class, flying down the school steps. Kami grabbed Amber by the scarf and prevented her own arrest for haste-motivated manslaughter.

"Sorry, so sorry, but I can't stop," Kami said. "I promise to bring some of Mum's cookies to school and share them with you. Don't think of it as a present. Think of it as a bribe for your silence."

"Don't bother," said Amber.

Kami blinked. "Ah, I see. Making a hard bargain for some caramel squares. I have to admire your tactics."

"Were you working on your little newspaper?" Amber sneered.

"Uh," Kami said, stunned for a moment because Amber had never spoken to her like this before in their lives. "Uh, 'little,' really? Like, you're literally belittling the newspaper? Not going with anything more imaginative than that? Sure, I was working on my little newspaper. Good luck trying to make me feel small."

She made a move to go past Amber, but Amber's hand shot out and grabbed her wrist. Her grip was tight enough to let Kami know she really meant it.

"Rob says he doesn't want any more of your pathetic li"— Amber swallowed the word, and Kami felt an obscure sense of satisfaction—"your pathetic stories about him in the paper."

"I've been considering this new headline," said Kami, "but I'm worried it's a little juvenile. Tell me what you think. 'Rob Lynburn Is Not the Boss of Me.' Yes? No? I guess he's the boss of you."

Amber's eyes narrowed: green sparking in the hazel, like something stirring in the woods.

"Cease loitering on the steps, girls," Ms. Dollard, their headmistress, said sharply as she walked up to them. She gave Amber a push between the shoulder blades.

Amber jumped almost as if she had received a tiny electric shock. Actually, *exactly* as if she had received a tiny electric shock.

"Don't bother the other students, Amber," Ms. Dollard added.

Amber glanced at Ms. Dollard, at Kami, then all around. Her shoulders were hunched: she looked afraid. "But what am I supposed to tell him?" she hissed.

"Tell him thanks," said Kami. "Now I know another one of the sorcerers on his side."

Amber recoiled at the word, as if Kami had waved a cross in front of a vampire, as if all the sorcerers of Sorry-in-the-Vale thought their secrets would never, ever be told. Kami noticed Ms. Dollard flinched too.

Amber glared at Kami and scurried up the steps into the school. Kami turned back to her headmistress.

"So . . ." She tried to think of the best way to phrase *Are you a minion of evil? If so, please don't give me detention!* "Whose side are you on?"

"I like to think of myself as a free agent," Ms. Dollard said.

"Well," said Kami, "consider our side. Just say no to human sacrifice! Excuse me, I have to go."

"Kami!" Ms. Dollard called as Kami darted away. Kami walked backward and waved, but kept going. "Kami, school is starting now!"

"Um," Kami yelled back. "I'm really sorry! I have to, um, go get something of mine. It's in the pub!"

Now that she had told her headmistress that she was skipping school to go to the pub, she felt it was well past time to flee.

* * *

Kami had been to the Water Rising dozens of times. She had gone to the Sunday carvery with her parents, and been given her first real drink there at fourteen by an indulgent Martha Wright. Kami was used to strolling up the gentle slope of the High Street and having the white-painted Tudor building come slowly into view, with its black latticework and the shutters open.

She was not used to throwing herself through the door in search of a lunatic. Kami stared wildly around the dim interior of the pub. The wood of the rafters in the ceiling and the top of the bar was old, and so were some of the regular customers sitting at the bar. It was Kami's impression that there were fewer customers than usual. The ones who were there looked distinctly apprehensive.

Fred and Martha Wright, who owned the Water Rising, were both standing behind the bar. They looked terrified as well.

This situation had "impossibly crazy," which was to say Jared, written all over it.

"Don't panic," Kami told Martha. "I will handle this. Is it all right if I leave my schoolbag on this stool?"

Martha nodded, though she looked very dubious about Kami's handling abilities. Kami put her schoolbag down, cheered by seeing a copy of *The Nosy Parker* lying on the bar, and headed into the next room, ducking her head to avoid bags of dried herbs hanging from the doorframe.

There were a couple of elderly women sitting at a table. One had an empty glass. Jared had just gotten hold of it. The lady clung to it for a moment, but Jared seemed set on taking it away. Kami had never seen anyone clear tables in a menacing fashion before.

"Jared," she said, and he gave her an unfriendly look over his shoulder. "Jared, I need a word."

"I'm working," Jared said curtly. "You done with that?" he asked the other lady. He sounded as if he was demanding her money or her life rather than a glass.

She mutely surrendered a half-full glass of gin and tonic.

"I severely doubt she is done with it," Kami said. "Give it back to her right now."

"I'm done with it," the lady said in a low voice. "Honestly."

"I'm going to have to insist on a word," Kami said.

Jared set down the drink. "Be right back." He turned away from the table, to what appeared to be the ladies' intense relief, and came toward Kami.

"Let's talk outside," she said, and heard the hateful new uncertainty in her voice.

Once outside, the November wind cut through her blouse. She stood on the doorstep and hugged herself, sorry that she had forgotten her jacket. Jared in his thin T-shirt gave no indication that he felt anything but annoyed.

"You should be in school," he remarked.

"So should you!" said Kami. "You're the one who's a year

behind! You absolutely cannot afford this kind of academic recklessness."

"Fred Wright called the school and got me the day off so I could learn the work," Jared said.

"Which brings me to my first and most important question: What the hell do you think you're doing?"

"Working," Jared said. "I asked the Wrights if I could work in the pub for room and board. They agreed."

"You're seventeen! This is not only ridiculous, it's super illegal."

"It's possibly not the most super illegal thing a Lynburn has done this week," Jared pointed out.

It was so strange to Kami, how little she could read him. It was like coming to a door that she had always run through before, to find it locked and barred.

"Why did you leave Aurimere?" Kami asked, her voice small.

"My aunt Lillian made me an offer I had to refuse," said Jared. He looked forbidding.

Kami knew that expression, and remembered the feeling that used to go with it: he was unhappy. "So you ran away from home," she said. "To become a tavern wench."

"I'm not a tavern wench," said Jared. "That's not a job." His voice was slightly less stern than before, as if he was taken aback.

"It sounds like you're a tavern wench," Kami told him. "Fleeing persecution, you have to take up a menial occupation to keep body and soul together. But at least it's honest work, though as you labor, many predatory customers make advances and offer indignities."

"One can only hope," Jared responded.

Encouraged, Kami reached out a hand: Jared flinched away. He always did that. Kami didn't know why she kept forgetting. "Jared. You realize the Wrights only agreed because you're a Lynburn and they're frightened of you."

A muscle in Jared's jaw twitched. "What do you want me to do?"

"Jared," she said again, her voice softer. "If you needed help, you could have come to me. Don't you know that?"

Jared gave her that new look, winter-gray and cold, as if he hated her. "I wouldn't come to you for anything. Not for any reason."

That stopped her. Jared turned away and opened the door to go back inside.

"Wait," said Kami. She didn't have the chance to force her voice steady, and it was humiliatingly obvious she was on the point of tears. "If that's how you feel, why set my branch on fire last night?" It was a dumb question. No matter how little he cared about her now, Jared was hardly going to let her die. She braced herself to hear as much.

Jared stared at the door. "I thought you would like a weapon better than a rescue," he told her, and ducked inside.

Kami had to stay outside, because that did make her cry. If he still knew her that well, then how much he hated her hurt even more. He seemed like such a stranger, to the point where she wondered if it had been the link she loved, and never him at all. If she had never loved him, if it had all been the link, this shouldn't hurt.

She should be able to cut him out of her life, the same way he had her.

Kami blotted her tears fiercely on her sleeve and went inside to collect her schoolbag. She did not spare Jared another glance.

* * *

After school Kami found her father making chocolate pasta in the kitchen. At this time of day, her mother was usually still working at Claire's, the bakery and restaurant she owned, so her father tended to make dinner, but dinner rarely looked like this. "How is my best girl?" her father asked.

Kami observed the concoction in the pan. "Considering moving out of home."

"I can't say you're not being provoked," said Dad, and stirred in more chocolate. "But it is Ten's revolting favorite, he's been sick, and we're having it for dinner, because eating the disgusting things a family member mysteriously craves is part of love and togetherness, and because I am lazy and have no clean pans to make other food."

"That is such a touching sentiment," said Kami. "It gets me. Right here."

Her father laughed, then saw her expression and stopped. "Speaking of moving out of home," he said, "I couldn't help hearing about the Lynburn boy."

"He's got nothing to do with me," Kami said. "He wants nothing to do with me," she added. Her throat went tight. "We were never dating. I wish you'd get that dumb idea out of your head."

Kami's father was pretty easygoing, but he would not normally have been okay with Kami talking to him like that. Just now his black eyes were watching her, a little narrowed and more than a little concerned. He reached out and rested his knuckles against her cheek. "I can't help it, the dumb ideas, they just come to me," he said, voice tender. "You all right?"

Kami closed her eyes for a minute. "Yeah." She opened her eyes. "Do I have chocolate on my face?"

"You do," said Dad. "It's all over. Total mess. Sorry about that. Go wash your face, and maybe go up and say hey to Ten afterward. He seems bummed about missing the Scarecrow Trials."

Kami hadn't realized that she'd been hoping maybe, when she came home, Dad would have seen something like Rusty had. Something that would make him believe if she told him about magic. Something that would stop Mum lying.

"Did all of you miss the trials?" Kami asked.

"Ten got sick when your mum had already left, so Tomo and I had to stay in," said Dad. "Did you have fun? I hear there were vandals."

"Yes, Dad, vandalism is always fun."

"It is the way I used to do it," Dad informed her. "I was a true artiste."

"I'm sure," said Kami, and went upstairs to wash her face. She felt better with the chocolate and any last trace of tears gone, and was able to go into Ten's room smiling, ducking the model airplanes he had hung up around the place.

Kami stopped smiling when she reached her little brother's bed. Ten was sitting up, arms around his knees. Both knees and arms were covered with his spaceship-patterned sheet. He was always serious, their Ten, the only one of the three Glass children who did not look Japanese, the introvert who was scared of people and had a love of encyclopedias. His face looked white and pinched. Behind his glasses, his eyes were huge and dark.

"Kami," he said, on a quick raspy breath, as if he'd only just been able to let it out.

"Hey, little man," Kami responded, and sat down on the bed. "I heard you've been sick."

Ten huddled further into his bedclothes, like an animal burrowing into a hole. He looked very small. Kami felt a pang of protectiveness. She reached out to touch his shoulder and offer comfort, trying not to baby him. She could still cuddle Tomo, when she could catch him, but Ten was ten—unfortunate though that was, name-wise, this year—and had made it clear that he was too grown-up for hugs from anyone but Dad.

To Kami's surprise, Ten immediately shuffled his bedclothes toward her and curled into her side. Kami laid her freshly washed cheek against his hair. "Ten," she murmured. "You must feel really bad."

Ten whispered, "I'm not sick."

Kami paused in the act of stroking his thin, pajama-clad back and felt him quail against her. She made a determined effort and resumed stroking, keeping her hands and voice steady and gentle. "What do you mean?"

"I was never sick," Ten confessed in a low, reluctant voice, trying to lean into and shrink away from Kami at the same time. "Mum asked me to pretend to be sick, so we would all stay inside for the Scarecrow Trials."

Mum had done a lot, had done the spell that linked Jared and Kami together, to prevent Dad from finding out about magic. But Kami would not have thought she'd do this.

"I see," said Kami, and tried not to sound upset or scared. She kept her arm tight around Ten.

"I thought maybe it would be all right to tell you," Ten whispered.

"It was," Kami said with all the conviction she could muster. "It was absolutely all right. You did absolutely the right thing. I'll talk to Mum and work this out. Don't worry." She rocked her little brother, and made him a promise she hoped she could keep. "I'll take care of everything."

PART II
THE LYNBURN WAY

For all night long I dreamed of you:
I woke and prayed against my will,
Then slept to dream of you again.
—*Christina Rossetti*

Chapter Four
Meeting

Kami had not been sure Lillian would agree to meet, but she did. Ash carried word back that his mother would come to their planning session against Rob Lynburn's sorcerers that night. Kami dressed up for a business meeting, in a ruffled black dress that came with a silvery-gray waistcoat and a skinny tie, but she was still incredulous as she and Angela made their way to the Water Rising.

The private parlor in the Water Rising had been made considerably smaller to accommodate the pool table in the adjoining room, and a little dark corridor now lay between the doors. This meant she, Rusty, and Angela almost ran into Holly, who was lurking outside the parlor.

"Hi, Angie!" Holly said, then hastily transferred her attention elsewhere. "Kami, Rusty. I'm glad you guys are here. The Lynburns are all in the parlor being terrifying."

Kami pushed open the door to reveal the parlor of terror. The room was crammed with jostling furniture and what looked like a jumble of things the Wrights had decided didn't go in the bar. All three Lynburns were still wearing their jackets and scarves, as if they couldn't wait to leave. It struck Kami as especially crazy that Jared had his leather jacket on, since he *lived here now.* She supposed now that he'd run away to live in a bar, bad fashion decisions were the least of his worries.

Jared was slouching against the low windowsill and smirking, seldom a good sign. Ash was sitting in a high horse-hair armchair, which of course he made look like a throne. Lillian Lynburn was standing at the ornate Victorian fireplace that dominated the furthest wall, looking extremely displeased to be there. She looked even more displeased when she saw Kami.

Holly slipped past Kami, and Kami saw Jared's and Holly's eyes meet. Jared's smirk looked slightly more pleasant for a moment, and he jerked his head in her direction. Holly went over and joined him, perching on the window seat so her curls were brushing his shoulder. Jared and Holly had always gotten along. The idea of them as a couple had occurred to Kami before. It just hadn't hurt like it did now.

She'd never be beautiful like Holly or Angela. She knew that.

"A Prescott," Lillian said, eyeing Holly with disfavor. "Bad blood. At least there's some magical talent in that family, but they do not tend to be trustworthy."

"I trust Holly," Kami snapped, angry with herself as well as Lillian. "We've all got to stick together and trust each other. We're a team."

"A team," Lillian repeated, disdain overflowing in all directions. "So on this team we have, besides a Prescott, the former source who is now entirely useless."

"You'll be surprised," Kami informed her. She took a few

steps to the cracked black leather sofa and sat on it. Rusty and Angela sat down on either side of her.

Lillian ignored this. "And two complete strangers who I believe are newcomers to Sorry-in-the-Vale."

Angela said nothing, but curled her upper lip at Lillian. In a disdain-off, Kami knew where she would have put her money.

Rusty smiled. "We haven't been introduced, have we? I'm Rusty. *Enchanté.*"

Kami glanced at him and mouthed, *"Enchanté?"*

Rusty just grinned at her.

"Rusty is a dog's name," Lillian remarked in her most quelling voice.

"It's Russell Montgomery the Third, actually," said Rusty, still grinning. He leaned back against the sofa, putting his arm behind Kami's head. "But I'd be obliged if you keep that bit of information to yourself."

"I don't imagine any of us cares enough to remember," Jared said.

Kami shot him a furious look, but he refused to meet her eyes.

Rusty grinned at him too. "They call me Rusty because I have a fetching red glint in my lustrous dark hair."

"Yes, all right," Kami said, intervening before Lillian could actually expire from annoyance at their feet. "We may be straying off topic."

"The topic isn't my stunning good looks?"

"Devastating though they undoubtedly are," Kami told him, patting his knee, "no."

"Shame," said Rusty.

Kami fixed Lillian with a bright smile, full of team spirit. "So," she said. "Let's get planning."

"I don't want to plan with useless creatures who have no magic," Lillian snapped. "I came because Ash said Jared was going to be here. I came because I want my nephew to drop this ridiculous farce and come home."

"I will never go back to that tomb," Jared informed her, every word clipped and precise. "You can rot there worshipping the Lynburn name and all the moldering Lynburn bones. I don't care. I'm going to help destroy Rob and everyone allied with him, and then I'm going to get out of this town."

Kami looked over at him again, as if her gaze was a compass always swinging north. The one thing she could read from his face was that the burning pallor of his eyes meant he was miserable. But his eyes looked like that all the time now.

"Destroying Rob," said Lillian, "will not be so simple. That little trick with the scarecrows was only his first move. He is going to terrorize the town into supporting him. His goal is to make them all aware that magic has come back to Sorry-in-the-Vale, real magic. He wants to rule by fear: to have them so maddened by dread they turn against the Lynburns of Aurimere and to him."

There was an appalled silence. Lillian's words hung in the air, seeming to open up a dark vista in that little white room.

Kami cleared her throat. "Good analysis of the other side's goals, Lillian. Now let's discuss how to foil the enemy at every turn."

Everybody stared at her as if she was speaking the

language of aliens from a strange and far-off planet, emphasis on "strange." Except Jared, who was staring out the window.

"Right," said Kami, undaunted. "So a girl in my class called Amber Green, and our headmistress, Ms. Dollard, are both sorcerers. Amber's with Rob, but we could use Ms. Dollard."

"I never trusted Amber," Angela remarked darkly. "Only the evil are that enthusiastic about volleyball."

Holly hid a smile behind her hand. Kami decided to ignore this valuable volleyball-related input. "What we need are more names. We don't know who the other sorcerers following Rob are. We don't even know who in the town is a sorcerer. Lillian can tell us which families magic runs in, and we can check out the likeliest suspects. Any sorcerers who are on Rob's side, we need to identify. Any sorcerers who aren't, we need on our side."

Lillian's mouth curled in a way that was very reminiscent of Jared. "You can't find them, and you can't stop them," she said. "So your plan is to make some lists."

"For a start," Kami said. "There are several strangers in town I have my eye on. We need to watch the newcomers. And we need to find out where Rob is. I went back to Monkshood Abbey—where Rob's parents lived," she added for Rusty's benefit. "And I didn't see anything. I've been watching the inns and the homes of the people who I thought might shelter him. But he can become invisible, of course."

"Oh yeah," said Rusty. "That's very inconvenient. But very cool."

Lillian's eyes narrowed. "How do you know that? Have you been looking at the Aurimere records?"

"I saw Jared do it," said Kami. "He made himself invisible and me too. We broke into a swimming pool and didn't want to be caught in our . . ." She stopped before saying *underwear.* "But that's not important at this time. There are Aurimere records? Can I see them?"

"Certainly not!" Lillian snapped.

"We have to learn," Kami argued. "We have to find a way to protect ourselves against magic. I want everyone to train to fight people physically"—Rusty and Angela perked up as one—"but there must be ways to shield against magic."

"I'll tell you how," Lillian said. "Do not put yourself in the path of sorcerers."

"Since that's not happening, do we have an option B?" Kami inquired. "The way I see it is, we have to know exactly who our enemy is and work out exactly how to fight them: it's the only plan that will work."

"Let me tell you *my* plan," said Lillian. "*My* plan is to kill Rob, and anyone else who continues to defy me once he is dead. How many times must I point out to you that you are useless?" Lillian asked, using her voice like a knife, and twisting it. "This is a matter between sorcerers: this is a question of magical power. Any use you could possibly have had, you lost when you broke the link between my nephew and yourself. You cost us a great deal of power that day."

"So is there a way to get us more power?" Ash asked. "A way that's not—not Dad's way?"

"There is a way for Jared to gain more power," Lillian said, looking at Jared rather than Kami or her son. "It is very dangerous."

Jared absorbed her words in sullen silence, head bowed

and shoulders bunching under his jacket. At last he asked, "What would I have to do?"

"There is a ceremony a sorcerer can go through," Lillian said. "One must go down to the depths of one of the Crying Pools, and come out reborn. At the bottom of the pools there is—"

Jared glanced up, his face looking younger suddenly, and shocked. "Gold," he whispered.

Lillian gave a tight little smile of satisfaction. "So the pools have been calling out to you," she said. "I thought they might. Not as a human would mean gold. But yes, in a way. There is power to be found there, a ceremony you can perform to enhance your own power. Complete the ceremony and you can see into the heart of the woods. You might gain the power to wake the woods again. And you would have the magic to remake a link that was broken. To have a source again."

"No," Jared said, his voice full of loathing. "I won't do that."

"I simply thought, as the young lady seems so anxious to help—"

Kami felt a chill run through her. She could have the link back, have him back.

Jared said, still in that disgusted voice, "No."

Lillian spread her hands, as if to say *As you wish.* "If you do this," she said, "you will have more power than any sorcerer in Sorry-in-the-Vale, save two. Only Rob and I have completed the ceremony."

"*I* could do the ceremony," Ash said suddenly, his voice cracking. His eyes rested on his mother, obviously hoping for her approval. "I want to do it," he said, his voice getting stronger as he went on. "I want to help. You can count on me."

"Absolutely not," Lillian told him. "You wouldn't live through it."

Ash leaned forward in his chair. "And why not?"

"How many people have died trying to complete this ceremony?" Kami asked, her voice rising.

"Rob would have died, if I had not linked myself to him and shared my magic. The ceremony calls for courage and determination," said Lillian. "Without those qualities, the sorcerer who goes through the ceremony will not survive."

The implication was very clear. Kami saw Ash flinch.

"Sure," Jared said, sounding tired. "I'll do it."

"You most certainly will not," Kami said in protective terror, at the same time Ash demanded, stung, "Why do you think Jared has a better chance of surviving than I do?"

"She doesn't," Jared drawled. "But I'm not much of a loss, am I? I'm a half-breed: isn't that how you put it once, Ash? Not really a proper sorcerer at all. And nobody cares much if I live or die. Why not risk it?"

"I care," Kami said loudly, and found herself the sole focus of everybody's attention.

They all looked sorry for her, she thought. Except for Lillian, who looked faintly contemptuous, and Jared himself, who looked away.

"Well," he said, "I don't."

"I think Jared has a good chance of surviving the ceremony, or I would not suggest it," Lillian said. "I am not in the habit of recklessly throwing away my resources."

That made Jared let out a sound almost like a laugh,

though it seemed to get stuck in his throat. "Why, Aunt Lillian. You old softy."

Lillian ignored this as she did everything she did not like. "And who says," she asked, "that you're a half-breed?"

"My father was a lot of things," Jared said, and Kami remembered all the things Jared's father had been, before Jared threw him down a flight of stairs in the dark: violent and hateful, all the things Jared thought he was too. "But he wasn't a sorcerer."

Lillian's voice rang out in the hush. "Who says that he was your father?"

Ash started, not Jared.

"Look at Ash," Lillian continued, not even seeing how her son flinched. "Look at yourself. My sister was in love with my husband. She was pregnant before she ever left Sorry-in-the-Vale. I think your father was a sorcerer. I think your father was Rob Lynburn. You can talk about leaving this town, about leaving Aurimere. But you can't get rid of yourself, no matter how much you want to. There's magic in your blood. Every drop."

Jared was looking down: not at the floor, Kami realized, but at his own hands, knuckles linked together and bone-white. He stood up and crossed the floor to Lillian in two strides. She tilted up her face to look at him. Their eyes met.

"Is that supposed to change something?" Jared asked softly. "It doesn't change a thing. Either I already killed my father, or I'm going to kill him soon." He turned away from Lillian and left the room, banging the door behind him.

"Well done, Mother," Ash snapped, and left too. He might have been following Jared or just fleeing; Kami couldn't tell.

Lillian regarded the rest of them with composure, as if they mattered to her not at all, because they were simply human and she was infinitely superior. "We will return momentarily," she announced, and departed, closing the door with a decisive little snap.

Those left stared around at each other. Holly was openly dismayed. Kami could feel Angela's stiff muscles against her own body, though her face betrayed nothing.

"This is all very intense," Rusty said, giving Kami's shoulder an encouraging little shake. "The Lynburns are better than cable."

Kami stood up. "I have to go after him." She couldn't stand seeing them look at her sympathetically again, so she didn't look. She just left, and they were all too kind to point out the obvious: that he didn't want her.

Kami went through the corridor and into the bar. At the pool table, a couple of older boys were standing around looking at her strangely. She went into the next room, where Martha Wright gave her a look of appeal from behind the bar.

There was no Jared or Ash in sight. Kami opened the door and took a few steps into the street, white building and yellow street both turned gray by night and rain. The street was empty except for the thin, freezing rain slicking the cobbles and seeping through her clothes. Kami went back inside and walked slowly to rejoin the others.

She crossed the floor of the pool room, ignoring the staring guys again, and opened the door to the corridor leading into the parlor. It took her a moment to realize there was someone else in that small dark corridor.

He was standing against the wall in the shadows. The only light was the stripe cast through the door Kami had not quite shut behind her; the iron doorknob was still pressed against her palm. His face was shadowed, but in that pale strip of light, she saw the gold glint of his hair and the line of his body, shoulders squared and arms folded.

"It doesn't matter," said Kami. She let go of the doorknob and reached for him. Miraculously, he did not flinch. He let her fingertips rest against the worn leather of his sleeve.

"Listen," Kami whispered, braver now. "I don't care what Lillian says, or what anyone says. It doesn't have to matter. You don't have to hate yourself. I know you. Better than anyone. Don't I?" She felt sinking disappointment when he uncrossed his arms and her hand fell. She was certain he was about to move farther away.

But he moved nearer. Surprise ran through Kami at that simple action, his warmth so close to her chilled body. His breath was a whisper of heat against her cheek. As she swallowed in the dark, she felt his fingers lightly touching the collar of her dress, trailing back to the nape of her neck.

Then his hand closed tight in her hair, and he pulled her in against him and kissed her. Kami arched up against him, sliding her hands up along his chest, feeling muscle move under thin cotton against her palms. She clenched her hands and held on tight to the fabric of his T-shirt, knuckles pressing into the lines of his collarbone.

She kissed him, pulling him down to her, as his fingers tugged at her tie and her body drew in closer to his with each tug. She felt the material give, the buttons pulling free so her collar drew open, and he slipped his hand just inside the warm space between her collar and her throat, his fingertips curling against her skin.

His other hand was stroking her hair, pulling at it a little too much but with a frantic attempt at gentleness. He was pressed against the wall and she was pressed against him. She was finally close again, inside a circle of warmth, his leather jacket around her and his body against hers. She was almost close enough.

The door to the pool room opened, and Kami tore herself away, throwing open the door of the parlor and hurling herself inside. She found herself blinking in the impossibly bright lights. When the dazzle cleared, she saw everyone looking at her curiously. Holly was leaning across to Angela, as if they had been talking at last, and Rusty looked as though he had just woken up from a nap.

Kami resumed her seat on the sofa in complete silence, and found out who had opened the door to the pool room as Lillian walked into the parlor. Lillian, naturally, had not a hair out of place and gave no indication that she had witnessed any torrid corridor encounters. Kami watched her walk calmly toward the mantelpiece, and jumped like a hare at a gunshot when the door opened again.

Ash walked in.

Kami had not noticed before that he was wearing a leather jacket. His was black, and looked a bit newer than Jared's battered brown leather one, but she hadn't been able to see colors in the shadows.

Oh no, Kami thought, *surely not.* Life could not be that ridiculous or that cruel. It could not be true.

Ash met her fixed stare and offered her a smile, shyer than his usual smiles. Kami forced herself to smile weakly back. It wasn't one of her best efforts, but Ash looked pleased. He went back to his chair, glancing at her and smiling again.

Then Jared marched into the room and headed straight for the window seat. Once he was at the window, he leaned against the glass and looked out at the night.

So if Kami did the making-out mathematics, and weighed the chances of it being the guy sneaking looks and smiles at her, or the guy who was keeping up his perfect record of stonily ignoring her . . .

Kami sat stricken. She could not imagine what expression was on her face, but she saw Angela giving her an odd look out of the corner of her eye.

Rusty leaned in to her, settling his arm around her shoulders again. "Everything all right, Cambridge?" he murmured.

Kami said numbly, "Never better."

Chapter Five
As You Wish

Jared did not look at Kami, and Lillian would not listen to her for the rest of the meeting. Kami could not face the idea of going home and confronting her mother about her lies after the Lillian Lynburn Sorcerer Appreciation Hour, so she figured she would go stay at Angela's again tonight. She whispered the suggestion in Angela's ear as they were getting up to go, and when Angela nodded Kami pulled her out of the room fast.

"What are you doing?" Angela complained. "Are you trying to make me jog? You know I think people who jog should be shot at midday."

"Why at midday?" Kami asked absently.

"There's no need to ever get up at dawn," Angela told her. "Not even to shoot joggers. We're going to leave my brother behind, Kami; he is one of life's born saunterers."

"He knows his way home," Kami said callously. "Failing that, he's a personable lad—some kind lady is bound to take him in and treat him well." She was dragging Angela down the cobbled street, but she heard the door of the inn bang shut. She looked determinedly ahead, pretending she found the High Street fascinating.

"Miss Glass," called out Lillian Lynburn. "A word?"

Kami stopped and turned. She felt relieved—she was better equipped to deal with Lillian right now than either of the Lynburn boys—but she was also puzzled. "A word?" she repeated. "We were in the same room for two hours and you barely let me speak."

"As I said, I have no interest in my fight against Rob being a team effort," said Lillian. "I only came here because my boy asked me to—and he only asked because he knew it was what you wanted."

"Yes," Kami told her. "This evening was all my dreams come true. I can never get enough of people looking down their noses at me. You do it beautifully. I wish you had two noses, so that you could look at me down both."

Lillian shut her eyes briefly, as if she hoped when she opened them she would behold a world in which people never said ridiculous things.

"I want to make a bargain with you," she said. "You're keen to be the intrepid girl reporter, aren't you?"

"Golly gosh yes," Kami replied. "Awfully keen!"

Lillian also refused to acknowledge sarcasm. "You want to do research and reconnaissance and have every little scrap of information you can dig up, as if poking your nose into things is bound to help matters. If what you want are the Aurimere records, you can have them. But they won't do you any good."

Kami realized that Angela was holding on to her hand, so they presented a united front.

"Why would you want to give me access to your records if you think I'll be so useless?" Kami asked.

"I'll give you what you want in exchange for what I want," Lillian said. "Talk to my boy. Tell him to come home."

"Jared?" Kami asked, disbelief making her voice come out almost soft. "You want Jared back?"

She was going to ask if that meant it had been Jared who asked Lillian to come here, and why he would do that. She was going to ask why Lillian thought Kami could persuade him. She was going to ask why Lillian wanted him back—if a person like Lillian really loved anyone, if Jared could have that much from his family.

But Lillian's eyes narrowed as though she could read Kami's mind and was preemptively finding all her questions offensive. "Do we have a bargain," she asked, "or not?"

Kami did not even have to think about it. "Yes," she said. "We do."

Lillian needed to hear no more, and had no truck with common non-sorcerous habits like saying goodbye to people. She turned and walked up the street, toward her manor on the hill. There was still light rain falling and a wind blowing: there was a gust that blew all the raindrops aslant, and in that movement of night wind Lillian vanished.

A second later a light was shining in one of Aurimere's windows.

* * *

Kami had always slept in Angela's bed during sleepovers. She wondered if she was supposed to feel different now that she knew Angela liked girls. After all, she wouldn't have shared a bed with Rusty.

It didn't feel different. Kami wondered if she was being

a bad friend even thinking about it. She certainly wasn't worried that Angela fancied her at all, given that Angela was ridiculously good-looking and, examining the current Holly evidence, went for likewise ridiculously good-looking girls.

Still, Kami was restless, lying in the four-poster bed with the gauzy hangings. Angela thought the hangings were dumb, but Kami secretly coveted them in all their pretty, pretty princess glory. She levered herself up on one elbow and traced one of Angela's red-flowered pillows with a finger. "Angela," she whispered, "are you asleep?"

Angela, lying on her back with her eyes shut and her hands folded like Snow White in a glass coffin, said flatly, "Yes."

"Because I'd like to talk about our feeeeeeeelings."

"I wish I was dead."

"Angela, you don't mean that."

"Kami, I do. And do you know why? Because then you might let me rest in peace."

"I really wouldn't count on that. The thing is," Kami said, "you used to mention guys. I mean, you used to say things like you'd only date college guys. Wait, is it guys too? Because that's fine. I mean, anything's fine. I just want to know. I want us to be able to talk about it."

Angela opened her eyes and looked up at Kami, her gaze dark and clear. "No," she answered, quietly. "No, it isn't guys. Not ever."

"Well . . . ," Kami said. "That's good."

Angela's eyes narrowed, not sleepy now but almost angry. "Is it? Why is that good?"

"Why wouldn't it be good? I love you," said Kami. "And

this is who you are. It would be a shame if you were any different."

Angela turned her face away. Kami saw her throat move but could not tell if Angela was upset, angry, or something else.

"If you don't mind my asking," said Kami, "why pretend? With me, I mean."

Angela kept her face turned away. "I can't talk about stuff like that."

Kami knew that much. Angela and Rusty's parents, when they were there at all, talked a lot but never about anything that mattered. Rusty was able to replicate their superficial chatter and charm, and Angela rebelled against it by being spectacularly rude to almost everyone she met. But neither of them ever talked about anything that really mattered.

"You never used to either," Angela continued after a pause, sounding accusing.

"I always had someone else to talk to," Kami said in a low voice. "But I'm sorry if I haven't been open with you—if I've made you think you can't be open with me. . . ."

"That's not it," Angela said. She sat up, grabbing one of Kami's pillows and shoving it under her own head. "I knew I could tell you. I knew you'd be supportive. I knew you'd be proactive about it and try to drag me off to gay clubs."

"Oh, we could totally go—" Kami began, and Angela looked appalled.

"Let me make myself clear," Angela said. "I'm a lesbian who hates people. I don't want to go anywhere hoping to meet someone, because the idea of mixing with a bunch of strangers makes me want to be sick. We live in a small town.

My parents are awful. I just didn't want to deal with the hassle of any of it. I thought, once I left Sorry-in-the-Vale and went to college, I'd meet someone and then I'd tell you. When it was worth telling you. I didn't expect to meet anyone I'd like here."

Only she had.

"I won't tell anyone," Kami promised. "I won't push you into anything."

Angela raised an eyebrow.

"I'll try not to," Kami amended. "I'll try to be less pushy. I'll just be kind of nudge-y instead."

"Then I'll try to talk about my feelings," Angela said. "Maybe I will indicate that I have one feeling. Once a year."

"Deal," said Kami, and hesitated. "Do you mind that I'm still friends with Holly?"

"No. *I'm* still friends with Holly. I just—it just hurts, because I was stupid, and I ruined things, and now everything is awkward. I wish we were all still comfortable. I want to put everything back the way it was." Angela paused. "Is that what you want?"

To put everything back the way it was, when Jared still seemed to care about her.

She'd always thought the truth was important. If he'd only cared because of the link, it was better to know.

"No," said Kami slowly. "I don't know what I want." She paused. "I thought Jared kissed me tonight."

"You thought?" Angela repeated. "Like, you had a kissing hallucination?"

"It was in the corridor," Kami said. "It was dark. I thought it was Jared but it might—it might have been Ash."

Angela blinked. "Excuse me? Might?"

"One of those mistaken-identity makeouts," Kami said defensively. "They happen."

"Oh, sure," Angela replied. "In Shakespearean comedies, all the time."

"You are full of cruelty and mockery," Kami said. "My heart breaks to think of the day I entrusted you with the fragile flower of my girlish friendship."

Angela obviously wanted to laugh, and was holding back. Kami appreciated it.

"Ash, huh," said Angela.

"I know what he almost did to you," Kami said. "I'm sorry. I would never have done it on purpose."

"It happens," said Angela. "So I hear. Look, he almost did something really bad, but he didn't. He helped me escape instead. I don't like him, but I barely like anyone. You can make out with him if you want. I mean, you seem as if you could use some cheering up. Didn't you like him before?"

She had. It seemed like so long ago, when Ash had come into her headquarters and she'd thought he was the most beautiful boy she'd ever seen in her life. He still was.

"Is he a terrible kisser?" Angela asked in a practical way.

"No," Kami said disconsolately. "He's a good kisser. He kisses like a minx. Like a minx on fire."

"That doesn't sound good." Angela looked at her, half amused and half concerned.

Kami lay back on her one remaining pillow. "I really thought it was Jared," she said to the shadowed ceiling. She'd wanted it to be, but she didn't know if she'd wanted it because she wanted him—or if she'd wanted to feel like he cared about her, in any way at all.

It was the most ridiculous situation in the world. She couldn't blame Angela for not being able to take it seriously. It was just that she missed Jared so much, and couldn't seem to stop. She missed who she used to be when she had the link. She missed being sure of herself. She missed the whole world, the way it used to be. She didn't know what she wanted, except to stop feeling like this.

"College, I'm telling you," said Angela.

Kami laughed softly. "If you want to get out of this town so badly, why are you willing to face down sorcerers to defend it?"

"Basically because sorcerers are jerks," said Angela. "And because they tried to hurt you, and they tried to hurt me, and I will not let anyone do either."

"Thanks," Kami whispered.

They lay side by side, staring up at the ceiling where the gauzy fabric that Angela despised cast shadows flirting with moonlight. They were silent so long that Kami thought Angela had fallen asleep.

"Maybe I was a little scared to tell you about me," Angela said at last. "But even while I was scared, I knew I was being dumb." She rolled on her side away from Kami, decisively ending the conversation. Kami smiled at her best friend's back.

* * *

Aurimere, Kami thought, was extremely chilly in the morning and extremely intimidating all the time. This room in Aurimere House was one of the oldest parts of the building, something like a feasting room or a great hall with a fire-place big enough to roast a wild boar in, a curved ceiling like a church but with painted rafters, and rough stone walls. Part of one wall had been taken out to put in a window that stretched from floor to ceiling in hundreds of small yellow panes, the kind of glass that had always been clouded because that was how glass was made hundreds of years ago. The glass transformed the winter garden of Aurimere: turning dead grass into a bright carpet, dipping every bare branch in gold.

Lillian called it the Counting Room.

Kami had been afraid that Lillian would shut the door of Aurimere in her face, especially since it was so early that she had left both Angela and Rusty still catatonic. But Lillian had answered the door in her robe and then had, albeit with an air of weary resignation, led Kami into this room. Here she had shown her a large table, dark wood in the shape of a half-moon.

"Uh," Kami said, "very nice. Antique?"

Lillian, possibly the only person in the history of the world to pull off being condescending while in a faded pink wrap, began to open up sections of the tabletop, sliding compartments with swift, silent efficiency. "All of Sorry-in-the-Vale used to come pay tribute to us," she said. "These are records from four hundred years ago until thirty-two years ago, when our power was broken."

Because Lillian's parents, the Lynburns of Aurimere, had gone to stop the Lynburns who lived across the valley in Monkshood Abbey from killing people. They had succeeded, but Lillian's father had died and Lillian's mother had remained an invalid the rest of her life. Lillian's mother had taken the Monkshood son, Rob, into her home. And now there was the same battle to fight again.

"So it's like a rent roll, in a way," Kami said, hand hovering over compartments, curious but aware she had to be careful.

"Except the sorcerous families never gave us money," said Lillian. "We traded in favors and rituals, blood and marriage. So many sorcerers intermarried, it is hard to keep track. But it is a place to start, if you must insist on making a list of those who might be potential sorcerers. I think the list will be too long to make any material difference. But you are free to waste your own time." She gave Kami a nod and left the room.

"Well," Kami said into the echoing silence, her voice small, as if pressed flat by heavy stones. "Splendid." She dragged up a chair, its back topped by carved hands on either side. She sat down, despite the feeling that those two hands might fasten on her shoulders at any moment, holding her captive there. She pulled her trusty notebook out of her bra, took a folded yellow slip of paper out of one compartment, and read the words written on it in a crabbed black hand: *Gytha Prescott: bought protection for her children by offering herself as a sacrifice.* The date on the top of the page was 21 December, 1821.

Kami was on her second notebook page of dates and names when she heard the door of the Counting Room swing gently open.

"Morning, Kami," said Ash, in his most charming voice.

Kami kept her eyes fixed on her notebook. She was sure

that her ears turned bright purple with embarrassment and gave her away. "Morning," she said, clearing her throat.

"I was wondering if you could maybe use some help."

Fatalism settled on Kami. Things were the way they were, messed up and absurd. She couldn't change that, and she had an investigation to carry on. "I could," she told Ash. "Pull up a chair."

Ash did not seem disturbed by the creepiness of his own chair, though he was so much taller than Kami that the wooden fingertips were actually brushing both his shoulders. Maybe to a Lynburn, it felt like a benediction.

Kami had decided to look on him as a potential source of information rather than a potential source of extreme kissing-related embarrassment.

"Hey, sorcerer boy," said Kami, tapping the page of the book she was reading. "What does 'house-warding' mean?"

"Cutting a man's throat on the first stone laid of a new house, and burying him under the threshold."

Kami stared at him. Ash went scarlet.

"I'm sorry," he said. "That record's from 1902, isn't it? It was probably an animal's blood. And if it was a sorcerer's house, the warding would be more specialized."

Kami thought of the spell her mother had done with Jared's mother, Rosalind, using blood and hair. Using her mother's own hair. "Could you prevent someone from coming in?" she asked. "If you have their blood or their hair, you can make a special spell directed at them, right? Have you done that, to keep Rob out of Aurimere?"

Ash hesitated. "Yeah."

"Do it for Angela and Rusty's house. Do it for Holly's. Do it for mine."

"I can't," Ash said. "Not to keep another sorcerer out. He'll use magic against the spell. My mother has to use a certain amount of power to keep Aurimere safe all the time. If we wanted a stronger spell, we'd have to kill for it."

"Because death is a source of power," Kami murmured.

"So's life," said Ash, the dull flush still in his cheeks. He fixed his eyes on the ledgers. "It depends on what way you choose to get power."

Kami's face must have spoken for her, because Ash burst out, "It didn't seem so bad, at first."

Kami raised her eyes from her notes. "The killing didn't seem so bad?"

"It was just animals," Ash said. "Father-son hunting trips. I wanted—he wanted to spend time with me. It felt like there was nobody like us in the world. Neither of my parents let me make friends with people at school, and we moved around so much."

"Until you moved back here," Kami observed, her tone cutting. "And your father told you to watch your cousin's source. So on your first day, you made a mad rush to join the school paper, and you did a good job of pretending to like me. Whatever you reported back about me to your father, it was enough that he was sure I was a source. And he tried to kill me."

Ash bowed his golden head. "Kami," he said, his voice hushed. "I *do* like you."

Kami did not know what to say, so she waited until Ash

spoke again. "It wasn't all lies, I wasn't pretending. I just did some terrible things. I was wrong and I'm sorry. I'm trying to make up for it now."

Ash must think that Kami was awfully judgmental for a girl who had been making out with him wildly the night before.

Kami gnawed on her pencil in distress at what her life had become. "I know," she said, more gently. "I'm sorry about your dad. And to a lesser but still significant extent, I'm sorry about your mum." She wondered if you could get lead poisoning from excessive pencil biting, and decided to stop.

Kami looked up, disconsolate, into Ash's smile. It was still a lovely smile, but it was more hesitant than usual, and that made it look more real.

"Thanks," he said.

It was comforting, having a guy seem like he wanted to be around her. Kami feared she was setting a low bar here. He'd kissed her, he thought she'd kissed him back, and he was so good-looking that people stopped and stared at him in the street. It was distracting and wonderful, being the sole focus of someone that beautiful.

And he liked her, he'd said so. As easy and reassuring as that. No laying claim to her soul, and no possibility of hatred.

Kami cleared her throat again. "Funny thing," she said, tapping the crackling-thin paper in front of her, curling up like an autumn leaf. "The names of almost every family in Sorry-in-the-Vale are here, sorcerers or not. Except mine."

"It wasn't like that, between your family and mine," Ash said. "There weren't specific trades made, or services done.

The bargain was made a long time ago, that they would guard and serve us. Until the power of the Lynburns was broken, and your grandfather ran away."

"And your grandmother killed him for it," Kami filled in.

Ash looked apologetic. "She would have seen him as a traitor."

Kami's grandfather had died before her father was born. But she'd known her grandmother: Sobo had lived half her life in this small English town, oceans away from Japan. She had made no secret of the fact that she considered most of its traditions insane. Sobo had never known about the magic. But Kami could well imagine what she would have thought of the Lynburns' expectations of their family.

"What was the bargain?" Kami asked.

"Matthew Cooper," Ash began.

"Matthew-the-statue-in-the-town-square-Cooper?"

Ash nodded. "He was an ancestor of yours. He did the Lynburns and Sorry-in-the-Vale a service—I don't know what, exactly—and died doing it. His nearest relative was a man called Glass, and his relatives were rewarded in his stead, given the guardhouse and the Lynburns' protection. The loyalty Matthew had shown was demanded from them in return."

Kami thought of the statue, so familiar to her she had never wondered about it. She was wondering now. She was planning to find out Matthew Cooper's story. But she wasn't planning to relive it. "How times change," Kami remarked. "I don't take well to demands. And I don't plan to do any serving."

"One thing hasn't changed," said Ash. He bowed his

head over his papers again. The light poured in through the ancient window behind him, wrapping him in gold. The only dark things about him were the two hands on his shoulders, as if his ancestors were pushing him into place. "I know you don't have magic anymore. I wanted you to know that you have my protection. If you ever need help, all you have to do is call on me."

Kami was frustrated by the way Ash talked about magic, as if it was the only possible power she could have, as Lillian talked about it. As if without it she was entirely helpless. She knew Angela was ready to guard her; she knew Rusty and Holly would too. Even Jared, whatever else he felt about her, had come to save her on the night of the Scarecrow Trials. She was just as ready to defend them in her turn.

Kami could not promise Ash forgiveness, or friendship, let alone anything more. But this was something she could do. "Thank you," Kami said at last. "You can call on me too." She flashed him a real smile. "Don't be afraid. If something bad happens, I'll protect you."

Ash grinned. Kami wasn't sure he knew she meant it, but he'd learn.

"There's a record here of a woman paying for an extra year of her life," Kami said. "Explain that to me. What kind of spell is that?"

Chapter Six
Faithless Blood

"Lots of people would be grateful for that food," said Holly's mother, rapping on the table by her plate.

Angela or Kami would have had a retort, Holly knew. She imagined snapping out something clever, the look on Mary's, Ben's, and Daniel's faces, how her mother would have been silenced. Her father was on the phone in the corner of the kitchen, but even he would have heard her. Being who she was, Holly muttered an apology and put a forkful of food in her mouth.

"You're not on one of those fool diets, are you?" asked Mum, frowning at her. "You don't want to lose your looks, darlin'." She gave a short laugh. "They're about all you have going for you."

"Yes, sir, tonight," her father said, his mumble into the phone audible in the sudden silence. "Yes, sir. Hallow's Field. I'll be there." He hung up.

Holly tensed at the mention of Hallow's Field, which was one of the fields their family had farmed before Holly's uncle Edmund had run away from Lillian Lynburn and the Lynburns had taken most of the Prescott land back. One of Holly's earliest memories was seeing her father drunk and cursing Edmund's name. None of their family was ever given the chance to forget that the Prescotts had once counted in this town.

Holly looked around at their kitchen, the cracked flagstones, the ceiling with a black cloud pattern of soot in one corner and the brown mottle of rot in another. The Prescotts had stopped mattering years before Holly was born.

Holly thought about Angie's kitchen, which was all shining metal and basically looked as if it was from the future. She cringed at the idea of her friends seeing the inside of her house. Not that that was looking too likely.

Angie and Kami would probably already have drifted away from her if it hadn't been for the sorcerers. And how sick was it to be almost glad there were murderers in town? Holly tried to swallow, but the food was bitter, as if she had picked up a handful of ash from the grate and shoved it in her mouth. She forced it down and pushed her plate away.

"Just not hungry, I'm sorry," Holly said to the scarred surface of the kitchen table. She got up from the table and collected everyone's plates, which was a trick she'd learned years ago. Nobody would stop her if she was doing work they didn't want to do. She kept her head down, bent over the sink. The cold water turned her hands red and raw, and they kept stinging even when she went to her and Mary's bedroom. She changed into her pajamas just so she could climb into bed and stick her hands under her pillow.

There was a little spotted mirror on the wall. Holly could see her reflection in it.

Don't want to lose your looks, Mum had said. As if Holly

could keep them: she could already look at Mum and see how fluffy hair could get thin and pink cheeks turn sunken and pale. Holly wasn't beautiful like Angie. She was just pretty.

It was stupid to think that way. Holly liked the way she looked, mostly: she had fun with it.

Holly thought, suddenly, about calling Jared to take her mind off things. She couldn't call Angie or Kami, didn't have the first idea what to say, and Jared apparently didn't have anyone to talk to either. Holly could sympathize with the urge to leave home.

She doubted that Jared was going to make her feel better. Her hands warmed under her pillow, and eventually she drifted off to sleep.

When Holly woke, she had the disorienting feeling that came from having slept too long or not long enough. It was still night, so she assumed it had only been a couple of hours. She had turned over in her sleep: the first thing her eyes caught on was not the mirror but her sister's bare pillow, a dented silver hollow in the moonlight.

"Mary?" Holly called her sister's name softly, and swung her legs out of bed. The spot in the bedroom floor where the carpet had worn clean away scraped the soles of her feet. She walked to the door, opened it, and looked down the hall, vaguely thinking that Mary must be in the bathroom.

Her brothers' bedroom door stood open, a square of paler shadow cast inside the room. Holly could see both their beds, Ben's neatly made and Daniel's mattress naked, the sheet a ghost draped over the bolster.

Holly spun and ran down the hall, feet slapping against

the tile outside her parents' room. She shoved the door open, words already on her lips about to spill forth, about needing help, needing search parties, needing someone to take over.

Her parents' room was deserted as well, the blankets and sheets tumbled together. One pillow lay pale and lonely on the floor.

Holly went still, her hand pressed against the door. The realization went through her like a stone sinking through cold water: she had been deserted.

Lillian Lynburn had said the Prescotts could not be trusted. Her father had called someone "sir" on the phone during dinner, and promised he would be at Hallow's Field tonight.

Rob Lynburn had called his sorcerers together.

Holly ran back down to her bedroom and knelt on the worn floor, fumbling through her clothes from the day before. When her phone finally slid into her palm, cool against her sweaty skin, she almost sobbed.

"I don't care, Kami, tell me about it in the morning," Angie's voice said in her ear a moment later, husky with sleep. Angie would know what to do.

"Angie," Holly said. "It's me." There was a beat of silence where Holly wondered if Angela might hang up.

"What's wrong?" Angela said, her voice much sharper and more awake.

"My whole family isn't in their beds," Holly whispered. "I think there might be something bad happening at Hallow's Field."

"Then we have to go down there," Angie said decisively. "I'll go wake Rusty."

"I'll call Kami," Holly volunteered.

"We'll meet you outside the field," Angela said, and paused again. This time Holly heard her sharp, hesitant breath. "Holly?"

"Yes?" Holly whispered back.

"Don't worry," Angie told her, and hung up.

Holly felt a little steadier as she called Kami's phone.

"What news?" asked Kami's voice, fearless and curious, and Holly was able to tell her and keep her own voice calm.

Holly told Kami the plan, and was surprised when Kami did not answer immediately. Instead there was only silence, and a quiet creak.

"What is it?" Holly asked, the skin on her shoulder blades crawling, wanting to turn around even though she was sure the sound was coming from the phone.

"Nothing," Kami answered. Her voice was the one that shook now. "It's just that I looked in my parents' room. My mother is gone too."

Chapter Seven
Hallow's Field

Kami could not get the image out of her mind of her father lying asleep, one hand flung across the bed, reaching for her mother who was not there. Kami could not believe her mother had gone.

She put her head down against the night wind and charged on. She was farther from Hallow's Field than the others. The wind tossed her hair into her eyes and screamed in her ears as she ran. She almost didn't notice the rattle and hum of the motorcycle on the cobbles until it turned into a screech beside her. The motorcycle wobbled into her path, and she looked into Jared's face.

"You're going to Hallow's Field on your *motorcycle*?"

"Want a lift?"

"No," said Kami. "I mean, you're going into a situation where something really bad might be happening, and you've decided to make sure they can hear you coming? Better hope being a tavern wench works out, because you, sir, will never be a ninja."

Jared's bike was resting at an angle, the heavy metal frame leaning against Kami's body. He was looking up at her, his gaze steady and his voice less harsh than usual.

"Come on," he urged. Kami could not tell if it was a challenge or a plea. "Come with me."

Kami wished for the thousandth time that she could read his mind. She thought of her mother, who had lied to her all her life and left them all tonight. She felt as if she could not trust anybody in the world.

She said, her voice a whisper, "I don't want to go with you."

"Fine," Jared replied, leaning away and kick-starting his bike.

Kami walked on. By the time she reached the place outside Hallow's Field where they had agreed to meet, her hands and feet were numb with cold. She walked through a ditch to reach the chain-link fence where the others stood. The ditch water bled slowly through the canvas of her shoes.

The fence cut up Hallow's Field into a hundred steel-framed triangular pictures. Kami could only catch glimpses of chaos in the night: flickers of fire, silhouettes of people, sharp bursts of laughter, and sounds she couldn't identify. They didn't even sound human.

Hallow's Field was not surrounded by fences on all sides: there were barns at the far end, and on the side of the field that ended in the looming shapes of barns ran the dark scribble of a blackthorn hedge.

Holly, Angela, and Rusty were huddled together by the fence, on the opposite end of the field; Jared stood a little apart from them. Kami only caught a glimpse of Holly's face, but she was pale as moonlight.

Ash and Lillian weren't here yet. This meant the only one here who could do magic was Jared, and he'd known he was a sorcerer for about a month.

"Let's go take a closer look. We need to see what Rob is doing," said Kami, and set off at once so that no one would have a chance to stop her. As she circled the perimeter of the field, she kept seeing flares of orange light and hearing more of those sudden awful sounds. Kami kept her head down in case she was captured in a brief moment of light. She was aware someone had caught up with her when a shadow spilled into one of those flashes of light from Hallow's Field and across her path.

Kami crouched even lower, seizing the chain link of the fence in one hand and Jared's T-shirt in the other, bringing him down to her level.

"I'm not going back to discuss our options," she told him.

He kept his voice low, matching hers. "Who asked you to? Telling each other to do the sensible thing is not really the basis of our relationship." He was close to her and almost smiling, his focus entirely on her despite the horror beyond the fence.

Kami recalled vividly how she'd thought it was him kissing her. She had to stop hoping like this. It was humiliating, and it hurt too much. Kami let go of his shirt and turned her face away. "I wasn't aware we had any sort of relationship."

Kami walked on. After a moment she heard the rustle of Jared's footsteps coming after her. She crept along a line of thornbushes and saw a throng of people standing silent up ahead. She and Jared crouched down by the bushes and waited like the crowd, shivering in the cold dawn, as light bled into the world.

So they could all see what the sorcerers had done.

The sorcerers were gone. The field of winter-dry grass was painted with slick red blood, the ground carved with dark lines and symbols cut deep into the earth, and in the blood and symbols lay the huddled shapes of dead animals. It made Kami think of what had happened to Nicola, and it made her sick for a whole other reason: this field was so utterly transformed, turned into a gory nightmare. Rob Lynburn had taken a piece of her town and made it his.

The people standing in front of the gate to Hallow's Field, Kami was almost sure, were not those who had been running through the field casting spells and shedding blood. There was the mayor, Chris Fairchild, and his wife, Jocelyn, and several people who Kami knew were on the town council. There was her headmistress, Ms. Dollard. There was Mrs. Thompson, who Kami knew was a sorcerer, but who looked as if she might be about to have a heart attack.

There was her own mother, shivering in her winter coat, sleep-tangled bronze hair spilling over her shoulders. Mum looked tense, every line of her body straining. She looked as if she expected something more.

And more came.

Rob Lynburn came striding down from the hill where the thornbushes grew wild, forming a dark background for his shining gold hair. He was alone, his sorcerers apparently dismissed now that they had done their work. That made sense: people would be more afraid if they didn't know for certain who Rob's sorcerers were.

"I called you all here to make an announcement," he said, his voice ringing out in the cold morning air. "Sorry-in-the-

Vale is going back to the old ways. Sorcerers are going back to the old ways. I will be the Lynburn who rules in Aurimere, and this town will be protected, blessed and full of power again. And power has a price. The price is blood."

Kami thought of what the Lynburns had asked from their town. The assembled people watching him looked scared, but Kami noticed that none of them looked surprised.

There was a sudden loud crackling, like several small bones snapping all at once, from Hallow's Field. Kami flinched, coming up against the hard line of Jared's chest. For a moment she saw nothing in the field but the nightmare she had seen before, but then she tilted her face up. A mass of clouds was eating the blue-gray of the sky. The clouds were suddenly touched with orange and scarlet, as if the sun had blazed into the sky.

It wasn't the sun.

Down in the still-wet blood of Hallow's Field, there was a new fire kindling. The smell of smoke hit them, thick and almost sweet. Kami felt Jared's body tense for a spring.

She grabbed at him with no hesitation for once, seizing at his wrists, her head banging against his collarbone, her whole body involved in a fight to keep him down and still, keep him safe. He was so much bigger than she was that it was like trying to wrestle down an animal.

Kami let go of one wrist and seized his shirt again, using her leverage on it to swing herself back to face him. Then she took his face in both hands, tight jaw against her palms, her fingertips slipping against his scar.

"No," she commanded softly.

Jared stilled, his body relaxing enough that Kami felt

able to let go. Then her eyes stung as the smoke hit, tears abrupt and hot on her cheeks.

Hallow's Field was an expanse of seething flame, the blood and the dead lost in the fire. It licked red tongues through the wire fence and swallowed the thorns that were encroaching on the fields with a roar. Sweat ran down Kami's face, mingling with the tears. The fire did not catch on the thornbushes that lay outside the field, did not spread along the dry grass to the surrounding fields. The fire simmered behind its fence like a creature Rob had caged.

Firelight cast patterns on Rob's pleasant, handsome face. He moved forward slowly to where the little throng of people stood. Everyone scattered except for one lone figure in her winter coat. Kami's mother tilted up her face and looked at Rob. Kami could see the effort it cost her not to back away.

Rob smiled at Kami's mother as if she was rather sweet, as if he didn't know her at all. "In the old days, the town would offer up a sacrifice on the winter solstice for the coming of the new year," said Rob. "So you have a choice to make, and after that the rest will live. You'll live charmed lives, sheltered and guarded, under a real sorcerer's rule."

"The rest will live," echoed Kami's mother, her voice frayed with exhaustion. "So, you mean one person will die."

"If you all want to die," said Rob, "I'll be happy to oblige you."

Kami's legs ached from crouching, her hands ached from her grasp on Jared's shirt and his wrist, and her eyes hurt as she tried to watch her mother.

"I trust you're all going to be sensible," Rob said, in a

terribly reasonable tone. "I will be waiting to accept your tokens. I'll be watching for the signs." He vanished as Lillian had once, in a sigh of wind and a blink. He left Hallow's Field burning.

Jared pulled away from Kami as soon as Rob was gone, rising to his feet. Kami stood up too. She looked across at the crowd by the gate, and saw them all recognize Jared. She saw her mother, looking at her.

Kami had to look away. From the opposite direction, she saw the others coming, Lillian and Ash at their head. They were walking at a fast clip, Lillian zeroing in on Jared because Lynburns were the only people she ever really saw. "Who did you see?" Lillian asked.

"Rob," Kami said. "And the people here. He summoned them so they could see what he would do."

Jared nodded. "So he could issue his ultimatum. The town goes back to the old ways, or else."

"My family," Holly said uncertainly, and everyone turned to look at her. Angela shoved her shoulder in front of Holly's, glaring indiscriminately, and Holly went on: "They were all gone when I woke up. I hoped, but—they're not at the gate."

"We know Rob was collecting sorcerers," Lillian said crisply. "Your family came at his call and did what he wanted them to do."

So it was true: Holly's family were all sorcerers and would come and kill on Rob's command. Kami watched Holly take a deep, shaky breath.

"Forget him," Jared said tersely. "What are we going to do?"

Lillian eyed the people at the gate, their scared faces, and then looked away from them to survey the burning field. "I don't have to do anything," she answered. "I'm the Lynburn of Aurimere, and magic has come back to this town. The sorcerers are all going to come to me. Then we'll meet my husband and his traitors before the town. We will crush him."

Chapter Eight
Past Hearing

"We're getting out of this town," said Mum.

She'd run home, dragging Kami along as if she was five years old. Kami was still out of breath. Ten had hunched in on himself and tears had instantly sprung to Tomo's eyes as they watched their mother going crazy in front of them.

"Mum, you're scaring them," Kami said.

Ten and Tomo sidled toward her.

Mum was throwing her clothes into a suitcase on the bed. The whole room was a tornado. She stilled and looked at Kami. "They should be scared."

"Claire," Dad said from the doorway. He walked toward Mum and turned her, hands on her shoulders, to face him. "Claire. Stop."

"Jon," Mum snapped back. "There isn't any time."

"You're scaring the kids," said Dad. "You're scaring me. Leave town? You were the one who always wanted to stay in this town. It was your dream."

Mum was trembling under his hands, though she hadn't trembled in front of Rob Lynburn with a field of blood and fire behind her. "I've been dreaming too long," she said. "Now we have to survive."

Kami wanted to tell her father what was happening, but Tomo was leaning hard against her legs. None of them had ever seen their parents act this way before: Kami could not desert her brothers. She sat down on the floor and Tomo climbed into her lap as he had not done since he was four years old. Ten leaned heavily against her shoulder, face bent to Tomo's head, and Kami felt anchored to the floor, helpless under the weight of those she loved.

"Claire, what is going on?"

"I don't deserve for you to trust me," Mum said rapidly. "I know that, and I'm sorry. I'm going to explain. But we have to get out of here quickly. Let me call Helen and tell her we're coming to stay."

"I can't go," Kami called out from the floor. "I'll stay with Angela and Rusty."

"No!" Tomo sobbed, clutching her as if she was trying to go right now.

"You're coming with us," said Mum. "The Lynburns can rot in hell for all I care, every one of them. Rob told me the link was broken—you're safe now—"

"Been having a lot of private conversations with him, have you?" Kami snapped.

"If someone doesn't tell me what's going on right now—!" Dad shouted as Kami had never heard him shout before. Still leaning against her, Ten flinched and made a low sound.

Dad's eyes cut away from Mum, toward Ten. He let go of Mum's shoulders and walked over to him, kneeling down and giving him a hug. His eyes met Kami's, and Kami nodded.

"Let me call Helen," Mum pleaded.

"Okay," Dad said reluctantly. Mum went over to the bedside table, autodialed Helen's number on the cordless phone, and left it on speakerphone so she could keep packing.

Kami rocked Tomo and thought. She couldn't go to London: if she could get away, her family couldn't follow her. Her parents would have to save Tomo and Ten. She was still thinking when she heard Aunt Helen's voice in the quiet. "Hello? Helen Somerville speaking."

"Helen, it's Claire," said Mum, and suddenly she was crying, in great hungry gulps. "The Lynburns are back, really back, the way they used to be in Grandma's stories. They already killed a girl—I thought it was just one of them, one of the young ones run mad, I thought it would all stop and it wouldn't be so bad. I thought there had to be some way to get back our lives. But they want blood, and we have to escape."

It was terrifying to see Mum break down at last, knuckles white on the phone, telling Aunt Helen that nightmares from their childhood had come true.

There was a pause.

Then Aunt Helen said, in a cheerful voice, "Well, I'd love to come see you, Claire, but I'm not getting any time off work until Christmas."

Mum's breath caught, her whole body going limp with something that looked like despair.

Kami held Tomo closer and glanced at Dad. Dad's eyebrows were drawn together in a frown. He stood up, pushing Ten gently toward Kami, and took the phone out of Mum's lax hands.

"Helen?" he said. "Helen, it's Jon. Can you hear me?"

"Hi, Jon," Aunt Helen replied. "Of course."

Dad let out a breath he'd been holding. "I don't really understand what's happening, but Claire is very upset," he said. "She says that she wants us to leave town, that there's something dangerous going on. What's all this about the Lynburns?"

The room was warm with the light of full morning, creeping inch by bright inch across the carpet. This was Kami's home, where she expected to be safe. Now, everywhere she looked, her family was afraid.

Aunt Helen's voice came through the phone again, so happy and normal that it made Kami's insides clench. "I'm glad you're getting on so well with the new neighbors. I can't wait to meet them myself."

Rob wanted the whole town to be afraid, but he didn't want them to get help. Magic was connected to nature, sourced from it and influencing it, so Kami didn't think he would have been able to put a spell on the phones.

It was the voices of the people in Sorry-in-the-Vale Rob must have twisted and warped, so that they literally could not speak against him, not in a way anyone outside their town could understand.

Dad hung up the phone and stood staring at the dead device in his hand. Then he lifted his eyes to his wife's face. "What's happening?" he asked, his voice full of tightly leashed calm.

"You have to tell him the truth," Kami burst out. She could not bear seeing her mother lie to her father again, not this morning, not on top of everything else.

"I will," said Mum, clasping her shaking hands and pressing her knuckles to her forehead. "I was going to," she added. She looked at Kami, white-faced, uncertain that she would be believed, and looked at Dad in the same way. "When we were kids, I thought you heard all the same stories I did. Nobody talked about the Lynburns much. It was just something you *knew*."

"*What* was something you knew?" Dad asked. "Claire, *what?*"

"That they were sorcerers," whispered Mum. "That they killed your father, Jon."

"My father?" Dad said in an incredulous voice.

"I thought you knew, and when I realized you didn't—I loved you so much," said Mum. "I loved Sorry-in-the-Vale so much. I wanted it to be different; I wanted the town to be wiped clean of all the old stories. I wanted it to be the way you saw it. I didn't know how to tell you the truth, but I hoped you would never have to know as well. The Lynburns' power was broken before we were born. They weren't killing people anymore. I thought I could forget the old stories, that they didn't really matter."

Kami could not read her father's expression. He looked the way Mum had said she wanted Sorry-in-the-Vale: wiped clean. He looked as if he did not know how to feel and thus felt nothing at all.

"But the Lynburns still scared me," Mum said. "They weren't killing anybody then, but I didn't want them near me. I didn't want them near you. So when Rosalind Lynburn said she'd go after you, I told her I'd do whatever she wanted: I told her I'd do a spell. I didn't know, I never dreamed it would hurt the baby."

Dad looked across at Kami and, with love and fear, said her name.

"I'm okay," Kami said quickly, for both of them. "I'm all right."

Her mother and Rosalind had magically created a link between them, so that Rosalind could still see Sorry-in-the-Vale after she was gone. It had turned into an entirely different link between their children. It had made Kami different, she knew that: the girl with the eyes that stared at nothing, the girl who talked to someone who wasn't there. But it wasn't like her mother thought, being controlled by a Lynburn sorcerer. It had been Jared, who she had always known better than anybody else.

Dad looked searchingly at Kami and, apparently reassured by what he saw, turned back to Mum. "A spell?" he repeated. After all that had happened, Kami saw he still did not quite believe.

Mum saw it too. Her face changed from misery to something like distraught elation. She had been lying to Dad since they were teenagers, and now the lies were finally being stripped away between them. "I'll show you," she said, and took his hand. "Come on then. I'll show you."

Kami stayed with her brothers as her parents went out the door of their house. Her mother was leading her father as though he was newly stricken blind, stumbling through an unfamiliar world.

Sitting on her parents' rumpled bed by the open suitcase, Kami called Angela, to see if she could talk to *anyone* on the phone. She was relieved to find that she could.

Angela said that Rusty had tried calling their parents. She did not elaborate on that. Kami did not ask her to.

"So by now, everybody knows there is no help to be had outside," Kami said thoughtfully. "Which means people are going to run. Either away, or to Rob, or to Lillian."

Angela paused. "A few people have come to Lillian," she said slowly. "She was right when she said people would turn to Aurimere. The mayor's here."

Kami looked out of the window to where Aurimere stood, gold towers against the pale haze of a winter sky.

"You said a few people?" asked Kami. "How many exactly?"

"Less than a dozen," Angela said, and they were both quiet for a moment.

Kami wished fiercely that she could be there, taking it all down, the first time in memory that the townspeople had come to Aurimere to hold council with their sorcerer. Even if there were so few of them, she wished she could be among them. She looked at Tomo, tucked in beside her, and Ten sitting at her feet. She couldn't leave them. "Where are Jared and Ash?"

"Ash said he was going to do research," Angela said. "I think Jared went with him. I haven't seen either of them in a while, but I don't think either of them left."

Kami was glad Jared had gone to Aurimere at least. "Okay. Call me if there's any news, all right? And tomorrow we meet at Rusty's gym. Lillian doesn't want us? We'll do this by ourselves."

Kami hung up and called Jared's number. She received the automatic message that it was turned off. Kami very carefully did not curse in front of her little brothers. She wished there was something she could do, right now.

Ten cleared his throat, as if he was an adult at a business meeting, and said, "Can you maybe explain stuff to me?"

Kami had an idea. "How would it be," she asked, "if I wrote it down, so you could read it and understand it, the way you do your encyclopedias?"

Ten tilted his head, and she saw him get it. "Like one of your newspaper articles."

"Exactly like that, yes."

"I don't read!" Tomo announced semi-hysterically, as if this was the absolute last straw. "Ever."

"I'll explain it to you," Ten offered. When Kami stood, hefting Tomo's weight as best she could, Ten reached up and grabbed Tomo's hand.

They went into Dad's office, because Kami figured that was the place Ten would feel most reassured. Dad's stuff was lying around in piles. The background picture on his computer was one of them all the Halloween before last, when Kami had dressed up in spectacles, with a notebook and a blue shirt with an *S* on it, to be Superman and Lois Lane's superpowered reporter daughter. Ten had been Albert Einstein with a shock of cotton-wool hair, and Tomo had been a fireman.

Kami opened up a blank document and started typing, Tomo in her lap, Ten with his sharp chin digging into her shoulder.

From the study window, Kami could see the glimmer of fire that was Hallow's Field, still burning, casting an infernal glow on the clouds above the town. When scared people looked out of their windows, trying uselessly to call for help, they would see their home touched by hell.

Kami realized that until now, she had imagined that normal life would somehow go on. She had thought secrets should be told but had not calculated the cost of the telling. Now their voices had been twisted so they could not call for help, and how could they know what else Rob had done to make sure none of them would escape? Kami had always thought of Sorry-in-the-Vale as a little confining, had wanted to burst past its limits into a wider world. Now their town, from the woods to the cliffs, was their whole world: nobody could pass these limits. All the stories had come true. All the secrets were out and hunting them like monsters through the streets. And their town had transformed, through terrible alchemy, from gold to something dark. Everything was changed.

"You're not taking my voice away," Kami said aloud, and began to write.

Chapter Nine
Waiting to Answer

"I wish all the sorcerers in the world had just one throat," Angela announced. "So I could punch them in it."

Holly looked up from where she had been staring at her own hands.

They were all sitting in the parlor of Aurimere, and it was terrifyingly fancy. Of course, that didn't faze Rusty, who was apparently sleeping on the red sofa with the weird canopy, or Angie. She was sitting in the corner of the sofa and utilizing her superpower of glaring at everyone in the room.

There were not that many people in the room. There was Mayor Fairchild and his wife, and Lillian Lynburn wasn't even being nice to them: they weren't sorcerers, so she was talking to them as if they were children. There were a few more people who Holly thought were sorcerers: a lady who worked in the bank; Mavis, who had been a few years ahead of Holly in school; the two Hope brothers who owned the big Hope farm. A few more people whose faces she knew but whose names she did not. Eight possible sorcerers, all told.

Not enough to fight Rob's army of blood-shedding shadows. Not anything like enough.

"It doesn't seem like there are . . . a lot of people here," Holly said in a low voice.

Angela frowned. "Kami said Mrs. Thompson was a sorceress, and she didn't seem to be on Rob's side, so where is she?"

Holly stared.

"Mrs. Thompson owns the sweetshop," Angela supplied.

"I know she runs the sweetshop, she's my great-aunt," Holly said. "My great-aunt Ingrid is a sorcerer?"

Of course it wouldn't occur to Angie that the sweetshop owner was someone's aunt. Angie's parents were basically on holiday here.

And practically all of Holly's relatives were sorcerers. Her parents, her sister, and her brothers, they'd all gone off to Rob. They'd had a hand in creating the nightmare that was Hallow's Field.

Holly had never given much thought to whether her parents were good or bad people. She knew that their lives were lived in a tired groove of bitterness, retracing their past wrongs over and over until the present was nothing but an old track worn dark.

She had never thought about where that bitter path might lead.

"Maybe they're protecting you," Angela said suddenly. "Your family." Holly started: she hadn't thought anyone was paying attention to her.

"They're probably just scared," Holly said. "Who wouldn't be scared? And if that guy—Rob Lynburn—if he offered my dad a way to be better than everyone else, to be important . . . My dad would really like that. I don't know.

Maybe they're all just scared. I wish I could help them, but I'm scared too."

She had woken up all alone. Her parents had taken her sister and her brothers. Rob Lynburn had come recruiting, and he must have left her out because she was already close to Kami, the source he hated. Holly had come that near to evil.

"Everybody who is not sure of their power needs to come down with me to the Crying Pools," Lillian continued. "Those who see gold in the water are sorcerers."

Lillian stood from her chair and walked through the people crowding around her like a queen deigning to mingle with her subjects, not looking behind her because she assumed they would follow where she led. She left Chris Fairchild standing behind her, the mayor looking as if he felt useless but did not even dare to feel furious about it.

When Lillian passed Holly, she paused.

"Are you coming?" asked Lillian, entirely ignoring Angela and Rusty. "Your family did leave you asleep when Rob called the sorcerers to his side, which goes to show Rob doesn't think you would be useful. But perhaps he was basing that on the fact that you already seemed allied with my son and nephew. It might be worth a try."

"I've looked at the Crying Pools," Holly told her, staring at the ground. "I won't be useful."

Holly could feel the weight of Lillian's gaze on her, though she did not look up until she heard the click of her boot heels moving away.

"What a shame," said Angie. "Imagine the glory of being Lillian's lackey."

Holly was able to look up then. She saw Angie looking at her, and felt the way she used to when she had Angie's attention: glad to have it, and steadier because of it.

"How are you doing?" Angie asked awkwardly.

Holly tried to smile. "Not so great," she answered. "Can we—can we get out of here?"

She did not want to stay here in the sorcerer's house, stained with blood and gold, thinking of power and how her parents had been tempted by it. She was scared. She wanted no part of any of this: she had often wished she were not a Prescott, but never more than she did now.

"Of course," said Angie.

* * *

Angie's living room was almost as intimidating as the parlor at Aurimere. It was white and clinical as a doctor's office, if said doctor's office had a fur rug on the floor and a sofa with gold curly legs.

Rusty was in the kitchen making tea and snacks. Angie was prowling about the room like an unhappy cat.

"I'm sorry," Angela said at last, and sat down beside Holly. "I don't know what to say to make it better. But I'm sorry."

That already made it better: that Angie, who never pretended, was concerned. It made Holly feel special, in a way she never really had before. She saw Angie's hand waver for a moment, then move toward Holly's: she was glad for a moment.

Then Holly remembered and flinched. Angela withdrew her hand.

"Can we just get it over with?" Angela demanded. "I

want to be friends with you again, without all this weirdness. If you think I'm disgusting or something . . ."

Holly looked at Angie then, stricken. "Oh no," she said. "No."

"Then can I just say," Angela began, and stopped, then started again. "I don't want to say I'm sorry, as if a guy hitting on a girl is a compliment and a girl hitting on a girl is an insult that should be apologized for. I won't try anything again. I obviously picked up cues that were not there; I don't have any experience and I'm sorry that—"

"Cues?" Holly asked. She felt cold suddenly, as if she had been turned to ice and might shatter.

"What?" said Angela.

"You thought there were cues?" Holly asked. Her voice sounded cold too. "You mean you thought there was a chance I might like you back . . . that way?"

There was a silence.

Angela said in a level voice, "I made a mistake."

"Yes, you did!" Holly stood up, looking at anything but Angie. "I have to go home."

Home might still be empty, or it might have her family in it, her family with blood on their hands. Holly was scared to go home. But she couldn't stay here. The whole world had become terrifying and hostile; Holly felt like it was closing in on her like a trap with cruel teeth, and the only way to survive would be to lose some part of herself.

* * *

It was night, and the terribly few people who had come to Ash's mother were mostly gone. Aurimere was silent. The sound of a door opening behind him made Ash start and twist around in his chair. As usual when he saw Jared, he got a sinking feeling. Every time was like the first time Ash had ever seen him: every time he felt the same horror. Another young Lynburn, when Ash had thought he was the only one, and this one was already everything Ash's father wanted. This one was already a killer.

Jared leaned against the doors of the counting room, head tipped back against the carvings of fire and water.

"So you're back," Ash said. "I thought you were never going to darken these doors again."

Jared smiled, the scar by the side of his mouth tightening. "Don't worry. I'm not here to stay."

"But you're always welcome," Ash told him. "My mother's made that very clear."

Jared's smile spread. Of all the painted Lynburn faces in the gallery, Ash had never seen one that looked as distant as his brother's.

"The heir of Aurimere," Jared said, his voice mocking. "Don't tell me you bought that. Imagine me ruling anything; imagine anyone trusting me with anything that mattered. It's a joke. Your mother is just trying to punish you." He left the doors and strolled over to the table. He pulled out a chair and reversed it, straddling it, leaning his arms along the chair back with his chin on his arms.

"You think?" Ash asked.

"I do," said Jared. "Why, Ash. Don't tell me you ever bought me as a real rival."

Ash's father had told him to watch Kami, and she had responded to the attention until Jared had arrived on the scene. His parents had spent all their time talking about Jared until his father left. Jared was the focus of everyone's attention, and Ash was out in the cold.

"Kind of funny," Jared observed.

"What's funny?" Ash asked, wondering if he could edge his chair away without Jared noticing.

"That neither of us even knew the other one was alive," Jared said. "And yet you were always trying to be the good one. And everyone always knew I was the bad one."

"Trying to be the good one?" Ash asked. "By—by almost killing someone for my dad?"

"Yeah," said Jared. "Isn't that what you were trying to do, be good?"

Ash hadn't thought anyone would be able to understand that, when he barely understood himself how he'd gotten so twisted up. He'd never thought anyone would understand, least of all Jared.

"The Lynburns," Jared continued quietly. "Aurimere. They're what matter to you. You're better than me. You were born to all this. Of course you're going to have Aurimere. I don't want it. I'd ruin it. I ruin everything I touch." He slanted a look at the Lynburn coat of arms, and apparently saw something different than Ash saw, because he smirked and added, "And let's face it, the place is pretty screwed as is."

Ash had no idea how to deal with him. "I don't understand."

"We're not in competition," said Jared. "We don't even want the same things. There's no reason for us to be at odds. There's every reason for us to work together."

Ever since the night in the woods when he'd disappointed

both his parents, no Lynburn had given Ash the slightest sign they thought he was worth bothering with. Even though Jared made a two-legged table look stable, his offer was tempting. "What did you have in mind?" Ash asked warily.

Jared's focus on Ash tightened, eyes narrowing, so Ash felt as if Jared had leaned closer even though he had not. "That ceremony with the Crying Pools Aunt Lillian was talking about," he said. "Is there a book about it? How's it done?"

"As far as I know, it's pretty simple." Ash tried to make out the expression on Jared's face, but he got nothing. Ash's reflection in Jared's pale eyes looked back at him, worried and hopeful. "Are you thinking of going to my mother and getting her to do the ceremony?"

"Would she have to help me?" Jared inquired. "Does it have to be just one person doing the ceremony and one person helping?"

Ash hesitated.

Jared blinked, slow and considering. "I was thinking, what if both of us did the ceremony together. And we didn't tell Aunt Lillian until it was done. Might do her good to get a surprise."

His mother had said she didn't think Ash would survive it. Ash wanted to prove her wrong, but he could not stop fearing she was right. "You don't technically need another sorcerer to help," he offered, tentatively. "Mum helped Dad, but she did it alone. There are just a few words you need to say; most of the ceremony is about what happens when you go into the pool. It's a test. It's more than that. It's a trial—

it's about being strong enough to reach another place, from which you can access more power."

Ash looked again at their coat of arms. Fire and water, Aurimere and the sword, and a drowning woman giving the lie to their motto, *We neither drown nor burn.* "There's a way to open a channel of magic between us, so we can share power," said Ash. "That's what Mom did for Dad. We could do it. If we trusted each other enough."

"We shouldn't decide right away," Jared said. "It's a serious enough undertaking. We should both think it through."

"Yeah." Ash nodded. "That makes sense."

Jared reached forward and took one of the papers from the table, flipping the worn-soft square of ivory paper casually between his brown fingers. "What are those words you need to say?"

Ash told him. Jared nodded, seeming mostly absorbed in reading the paper in his hands. "There's someone here called Lydia Johnson who gave a lot of money for a love spell. Can we actually do those?"

"Not love," said Ash. "If an attraction's possible, we can direct and intensify it. But it won't last."

"So some long-ago Lynburn cheated the woman," Jared remarked. "Aren't we a charming family? Personally, I'm amazed the townspeople never barred all the doors and burned Aurimere to the ground with every last Lynburn inside."

Ash stared. Personally, he was amazed by how crazy Jared was. The question about love spells made an awful suspicion occur to him. "What about you?" Ash asked. "You said that

Aurimere and the Lynburns were what mattered to *me*, and that you and I didn't even want the same things. So what matters to you? What do you want?"

Jared's smile made Ash flinch. "Nothing I can have," Jared told him. "Thanks for all the help, Ash." He swung out of his chair, the piece of paper fluttering to the floor. Ash stooped to pick it up and it occurred to him that, crazy or not, Jared was the only member of his family who had reached out to him at all since that night in the quarry.

"Jared," he called out.

Jared was already at the door, but he stopped and turned his head.

"I just wanted to say thanks," Ash continued awkwardly. "Good talk. I will think about it."

Jared stood framed by wood carvings of fire and water, as if choosing between the devil and the deep blue sea, and the first feeling that Ash could empathize with crossed his brother's face.

For an instant, he looked guilty.

"I'll never take Aurimere away from you, Ash," Jared said. "I swear. You can believe that." Then the door carved with fire and water closed behind him, and Ash listened to his footsteps slowly fade away down the stone halls of home.

Chapter Ten
Past Saving

The kids were back in bed by the time Kami heard the creak of the front door opening, and instantly afterward the loud sound of her father's voice.

He sounded furious in the same frightening way he had before.

"You just wanted to protect me, and protect our children, and protect the town."

"Yes," said Mum.

"So you told lie after lie, all for the best, until you had told so many lies you didn't know how to begin telling the truth."

"Yes," Mum said again, desperately.

"I could have forgiven you for any of those lies," Dad said, though he didn't sound forgiving. "But there were so many of them. You didn't know how to begin telling the truth? I don't know how to begin trusting you again. There was no time in our lives when you weren't lying to me. There's nothing to go back to."

Kami crept down the stairs, trying to walk softly and sidestep every creak, until she was in position to look down into the hall. She could see her parents' shadows, black against the yellow wall, and how far apart they stood.

"There was nothing you could have done if I had told you," Mum said, low. "I did wrong, but I did it because I love you and I love the kids."

"It wasn't your choice to make!" Dad said. "They're not just your kids. They're *our* kids. That's what it meant when we got married, that we promised to make those choices together, and I always have."

"I know you gave up a lot to come back to Sorry-in-the-Vale when I told you I was going to have Kami," Mum told him unsteadily. "And you never threw it in my face, until now."

"That's not fair."

"I wanted to make it up to you, I wanted to make things right for you," said Mum, her voice changing, becoming more like her usual voice, trying to be calm, trying to explain matters. "So I did a spell, and it hurt Kami. After that I was sure I could never tell you any of it. I was sure you would never forgive me."

"Well then," Dad said. His voice had changed too: it was very soft. "At last we find something we can agree on."

They went into the kitchen. Kami heard the clatter of their movement, the absence of noise that was their furious silence. Her hand was still locked around the banister, gripping the wood as if there might be some comfort there. As if wood and stone were what her home was made of. She thought of Aurimere House, where Angela had said people were going to Lillian, where there might be answers.

Angela had said Jared was there too.

No. She wasn't going to do it. She was going to go back

to bed and sleep, and in the morning she would be in control of herself. In the morning she would fix this.

Kami pried her hand off the banister. She walked slowly back up the stairs and into her room, shutting the door behind her with finality, as if she could make the world outside stop. She lay down on the bed, still in her clothes, and closed her eyes so she could not see the fires burning. Scarlet traces lingered in the darkness behind her eyes. Falling asleep felt like giving up, like she could not bear her own thoughts a moment longer and was snatching at oblivion.

She didn't get oblivion. She dreamed instead of water and gold, drowning and burning, and not caring. She dreamed that Jared was back in her head, where she could be utterly sure of him. Everything else was chaos in her dream, and it did not matter. She was happy.

Kami woke with a violent jolt that snapped her into awareness, curled up in her sheets with every muscle tense and aching.

She got out of bed to close her window and found herself just kneeling instead, her whole body shaking. She laid her face down on the icy cushions of the window seat and reached out, hand on the windowsill. As if there was anything there to grasp but the bitterly cold night air.

Kami had never been like other people. She had never had to cry herself to sleep alone. It was overwhelming to realize that there was not going to be any comfort ever again. She was going to spend the rest of her life living the way other people did, in terrible everyday loneliness, and she did not know how to bear it.

She wanted to make any bargain to have him back.

Kami rose after a long dark while and slipped down the stairs and out the door as quietly as she could. Then she began to run, along the curve of the woods to where the path led straight up to Aurimere.

The windows were all lit up, and the hall was so bright that for a moment when the door opened all Kami could see was someone tall, and light on fair hair.

Ash said, sounding surprised but pleased, "Kami?"

"Is Jared still here?" Kami asked.

"No," Ash answered, after a brief pause. "But he's all right. Actually, we had the first good conversation we've ever had. What would you think about us doing the ceremony together?"

"The Crying Pools ceremony?" Kami asked. "The one Lillian said was dangerous?"

"Yeah," Ash said. "I mean, we both know it's a big decision. But it's something to think over. It might make all the difference to the town. Look, do you want to come in?" He stepped a little aside. The night air was pulling frost-tipped fingers through Kami's hair, but she stayed where she was.

"Did Jared say that? That it was a big decision?"

"And we both needed to think it through," Ash said.

"Think it through?" Kami repeated, above the sound of the wind. "Jared? Don't you know him at all? If he sounds reasonable, or sensible, or capable of any sort of rational thought, it means he's lying through his teeth! What did you tell him about the ceremony?"

They stared at each other for a moment of horrified silence. "I told him how to do it," Ash said at last.

Kami turned and ran away from the lights of Aurimere,

down the dark path into the woods. Behind her she heard Ash slam the door of the house and run to catch up.

* * *

The tree branches were limned with ice: it made the whole wood look as if it was made of moonlight, branches shining like icicles in the night. Everything was sharp silver and darkness. These woods had been Kami's once: in these trees she had seen her thoughts brought to life in real and vivid color. They were not her woods anymore.

Kami went crashing through the debris of dead leaves and fallen tree trunks, scrambling and sliding. A screech and the flutter of ghost-pale wings against the sky made her jump and glance up. She didn't break stride until she was in the clearing with the Crying Pools, panting. She grabbed a willow to hold herself up. She leaned her face against the trunk, feeling it scrape against her cheek, and stood staring out at the stretch of water and grass.

The grass was broken and dead around the pools, like a metallic spiderweb splintered and scattered in shards over the earth. The branches of the willows by the pools were bare, their outlines reflected in lacy shapes in the frosted mirrors of the pools. The little hollow was utterly silver and silent. Kami thought for a moment that all was well.

Then she saw the crumpled shape by the edge of one pool. She ran to kneel in the icy grass and touch the worn surface of Jared's leather jacket.

Kami let out a sob and saw the dragon's-smoke cloud of her breath drift away into the air. Standing by the willow, white and stricken, was Ash.

"The ice on the pool isn't broken," she said, and heard her own voice break.

"It wouldn't be," Ash replied. "The ceremony is about becoming one with the elements, controlling nature. If he went into the pools, he should have gone in without a ripple. Or without breaking the ice."

Kami thought of the way Jared had always been drawn to these pools, how when they had found out the truth about what their link was he'd gone diving in one of them. He'd broken the surface of the pool then. He had been human enough to do that, then, and she'd had to save him.

"How can we stop him?" Ash whispered.

"I intend to start by saying 'Screw this,'" said Kami, and cast about for a stone in the woods. Ash watched her in obvious confusion, but she ignored him and found a stone. She hurled it into the frozen pool with all the force she had.

The ice shattered, turning into drowning glints of silver in the black water.

The night water was opaque: Kami could not see Jared or anything else, though she knelt by his jacket again and shoved her hands into the water up to the elbows. It was so cold it burned, and she had to pull her arms out, gasping with pain.

"Kami," Ash whispered. He sounded horrified. His voice also sounded as if it belonged in this night world, natural as the sound of wings and birdcall, while hers had disturbed the quiet. When he moved forward and toward her, she saw how he seemed to fit into the woods, slim and pale as the wintertime trees.

"He's in there," Kami whispered back.

"Yes, he's in there," Ash said, and crouched down across the pool from her. "But you can't reach him."

"I can reach him anywhere," Kami told him. "And you're a sorcerer. Do something! Do magic."

"You're going to have to be a little more specific than that!"

Kami glared at him. "You said this was about—about becoming one with the elements. But he hasn't stopped existing. He's in there. He's just on—on a different elemental wavelength. Plane. Something like that."

In the shadows moving behind the whispering leaves, in a place seen through a glass darkly, Jared was there. She had been able to reach him across an ocean: she had to believe she could find him now.

"You don't understand," Ash said hopelessly.

"I understand this," Kami returned. "Think of where he is, conjure it up, bring it closer. Open a door for me, or I swear to God I will break through a wall." She stood up and reached a hand across the pool to Ash, whose fingers closed around hers, unexpectedly strong.

His eyes went wide. "What are you going to do?"

"I'm going in after him," Kami said. "Don't let go of my hand." She took a firmer hold on his hand, and jumped into the pool.

It was like taking a tumble into the night sky. She felt as if she was falling through fathoms of airless darkness, lost beyond recall.

Ash's hand stayed tightly clasped with hers, though it made every muscle in her arm scream to hang on. She struck out with her free hand, blackness all around her, skin burning with cold and lungs burning from lack of oxygen. This was a nightmare eager to swallow her whole, but if Jared was here, some part of her could survive. She was not going to give up until this place surrendered what was hers.

She reached out again and again, fingers finding nothing, and then she clawed through nothing. She kept searching: she'd pulled him out of this pool once, he'd saved her from drowning once. Jagged pieces of memory slid through her mind, and she felt that if only she could put them together, she would understand how to get to him.

Except that she did not know how. All she knew was that she was not giving up. Darkness was blotting her out, but she made the thought of finding him her last light and chased it until even that was winked out and lost.

Kami could feel her fingers again when she felt another hand brush hers, and knew whose it was. She held on with all the strength she hadn't known she had left, entwined her fingers with his, clinging so hard that they would be drowned or saved together. She hung on to him and hung there in space, numb and almost content.

Then she was drawn up through the water, inch by painful inch. When she surfaced, her lips opened and she breathed in mingled air and water. She choked and held on to both boys' hands so fiercely her fingers felt as if they might break.

Ash was saying something, murmuring words of horror and relief, as he helped Kami out of the water. She knelt in the cold dirt and felt Ash's hands through the soaked material of her shirt.

"Help me," she rasped, pulling their white linked fingers apart and plunging her now-free hand back into the water.

Ash reached into the water again too, grabbing fistfuls of

Jared's shirt. Together they dragged him out of the pool and laid him on the moonlit-white broken grass.

Jared lay still as the dead. He should have been dead, Kami realized.

The tiny gold lines of his eyelashes were kissed by frost. His hair in her lap was glittering with ice crystals. But he was still holding on to her hand, grasp sure and strong.

"Jared," Kami said, desperate and commanding.

Jared opened his eyes suddenly. They were paler than she had ever seen, white and treacherous as the winter ice she had shattered to get to him.

"Jared, can you hear me? How long were you down there?"

Jared's lips moved, shaping her name. Drops of water landed on the silvery lines of his face. Kami could not tell if it was lake water dripping from her hair or tears.

She bent over him as he shook in her arms and started to breathe like a human being again, in shuddering gasps as if he might live.

"You can't keep acting like this," Kami told him fiercely. "You cannot continue to be this stupid."

Lightning flashed overhead like an answer to her, that he would keep being this bitter sorcerous stranger, that perhaps he had never been anything else.

It bleached the whole world white, the pools turning into diamonds. The drops of water on the planes of Jared's face, on the pale line of his bared throat, gleamed like broken glass.

Kami covered her eyes with her trembling hand and thought: I can't keep acting like this. I cannot continue to be this stupid.

PART III
PLOTTING A COURSE

. . . mystery down the soundless valley
Thunders, and dark is here;
And the wind blows, and the light goes,
And the night is full of fear. . . .
—*Rupert Brooke*

Chapter Eleven
A Drop of Blood, a Single Tear

Kami and Ash helped Jared back to Aurimere as early morning flooded the sky with pale, sickly light, making the woods and even Aurimere look gray as ashes.

Lillian opened the door. When she saw Jared propped up between them, wet hair sluicing tracks like tears down his face, Kami saw her go as white as Jared.

She opened the door wide, holding it with fingers gone white too. They were across the hall and halfway up the stairs when she spoke.

"I've changed my mind," Lillian said, still at the open door. Her back was to them. "I do not want either of you stupid children attempting the ceremony. You're all too young and too criminally foolish to be of help to me. I can do this myself."

"Mum," Ash said from Jared's other side. Kami couldn't see his expression.

"No, Ash," Lillian snapped. "Don't argue with me. That's the least you can do. It's decided, do you understand me? It's done."

They put Jared into his room. Ash went to get some of his own clothes. While he was gone, Kami wrestled Jared up onto his pillows and dragged off his soaked T-shirt. He leaned heavily against her, and she tried to steady him, one hand on the nape of his neck and one against his stomach, feeling the muscles there clench. He mumbled something into her hair. It took her a moment to recognize her own name.

"What?" she whispered back. She wanted to hold him, but he wasn't a part of her anymore. She couldn't keep pretending he was.

He murmured, "Make it stop."

Ash returned. Kami smoothed a sheet over Jared's shoulder before she left; it was the last gesture she permitted herself.

Kami texted Angela and rescheduled the meeting at Rusty's for the next day. She went home and found her father sleeping on the sofa. She walked upstairs in the sleeping hush of her home and climbed into her cold bed. When she woke, it was evening, and she called Ash. He said that Jared's room was empty; the bed did not even look slept in, as if he had never been there.

Kami sat looking at the phone in her hand. Lillian's voice echoed in her mind, saying *It's done.*

* * *

On Thursday morning Kami walked her brothers to school with her father. Dad had to pry Ten's hand out of his.

"You're not going in?" Dad asked.

Kami hesitated, because "I'm skipping school" was never a good thing to say to parents. Though this was an unusual situation and it was possible Dad would write her a note saying "Excused due to sorcerers." She looked up at her father.

He was young for a dad, and had always looked young to her before, carefree and easygoing. Today his face seemed older. Kami wondered if she wore her own dark night the same way.

"Were you hoping to talk to me?" Dad said before she could think of how to answer his first question. "I'm sorry, honey. I can't talk to you right now. I just don't know what to say."

It had not occurred to Kami before that her father might blame her, too, for keeping the secret from him. The possibility of that, of being locked away from his love, shocked her so much she could not speak.

Dad nodded at her as if they were acquaintances who had met in the street; then Kami watched him walk back toward home and the woods. All the trees were bare and lonely as abandoned bones. She waited until he was gone, then set off for the High Street, and the rooms above Hanley's grocery shop where Rusty held his self-defense classes.

Rusty's gym did not appeal to her the same way her headquarters did. It consisted of two small rooms, painted an unsightly shade of turquoise, which you reached by walking up small dark stairs leading from the grocery store. Rusty claimed the ladies of the town often paused in their shopping and took trips up the stairs to look through the door, which was half glass and wire mesh, to admire his manly form.

Right now it was a bright square in the dark, the lights on inside. Kami had walked briskly through the streets, able to nod to people as she passed and act normal with no conscious effort. She was surprised to find she could not stand the idea of facing her own friends.

She sat down at the top of the stairs and cried instead, thinking of her mother and father and her home, that she had never known how true the word *broken* could be for a home, how a home could be left useless and in pieces. She cried thinking about Jared under the ice, and cried for how alone she felt.

She cried quietly, hands pressed to her eyes, and as she cried she was almost relieved. Here she was, lonely and miserable, and she was still going to go into the gym and do what needed to be done. She had wondered who she was without Jared, stripped of all her supports and forced to stand on her own. She had worried that she would break if her heart broke, but she wasn't broken. She had lost everything, but she was not lost. It seemed a worthwhile thing to know.

Kami started at the sound of the door below slamming. She wiped her eyes hastily on her sleeve, but the thunder of footsteps up the steps was too fast for her: she had barely managed one swipe before Rusty was kneeling on the step at her feet.

He was the usual Rusty, a gym bag slung over his shoulder, hair rumpled and wearing a pink T-shirt that read I'M TOO PRETTY TO DO MY HOMEWORK. His expression was different, though.

"Kami," he said, and his voice sounded different too. "Are you crying?" Rusty knelt there looking up into her face, hazel eyes clear and serious. He lifted his hand to her face, and his fingers captured a tear.

"I was just—" Kami batted him away, embarrassed. "It's nothing. I'm all right."

"You're not all right!" Rusty said. "You're crying. Come here."

"No, really," Kami said, pushing him gently back. She smiled at him, and rubbed her sleeve across her face, dabbing at the corners of her eyes with one sleeve edge. "I'm fine. It's okay. You don't need to make a fuss. We should go inside."

Rusty kept hold of her shoulder, his move to take her in his arms cut off, but apparently not quite ready to let go.

Kami turned her face away, sliding the strap of her schoolbag back onto her shoulder. "I can't believe I'm saying this, but . . . ease up, Rusty."

He stood and she lifted her face to his. Her smile was more natural this time. Rusty didn't smile back. "Fine," he said. "You're fine. Everything's fine. Fine."

He strode up the steps past her and swung open the door with enough force that it was still standing open when Kami followed him. There were no chairs in the room, so everyone was sitting around on gymnastic mats. Ash's eyes were on the door; he and Holly both looked slightly concerned. Angela was sitting up and trying not to nap on the mats at least, but she was wearing a pair of sunglasses and smiling an ironic, scarlet smile. Jared was leaning against the wall.

Kami took a deep breath and pulled herself together. Rusty crossed the floor in one swift movement.

Kami knew, in a vague way, that Rusty was tall and strong. She was so used to the fact, and so used to him flopping about in paroxysms of idleness, that she never really thought about it. Now, though, she saw as he approached Jared that he was actually taller and broader across the shoulders than Jared.

Jared tilted his head, as if he was noticing that too. He looked slightly interested in what was going to happen next.

"I've actually been waiting a long time to do this," Rusty announced, and punched Jared in the face.

Ash and Holly jumped. Angela sat up straight and pulled off her sunglasses, lips parting in a startled grin.

Jared staggered, but the wall held him up. He looked up after a moment, and his mouth flickered into a bloody smile an instant before he launched himself at Rusty.

Jared and Rusty were off the mats and on the floor almost at once. The crack of flesh and bone meeting wood made Kami clench her teeth. Jared flinched every time just before one of Rusty's blows hit, but then he threw himself at Rusty in return, a vicious whirl that Rusty had to expend all his energy holding off. Kami did not think Rusty had an instant to notice that Jared was afraid.

Jared tried to bash Rusty's head open against a wall. Rusty threw him up against the door, so fast that Kami had to sidestep and so hard that she was afraid they would break the glass.

Then Jared was on the floor again, and Rusty managed to pin Jared's wrists over his head on the mat. He knelt on his legs and shook his head like a disappointed grandfather when Jared snarled at him. Jared sank his teeth into Rusty's wrist and managed to roll free and to his feet, winding back his fist. Rusty punched him in the stomach and Kami saw Jared's minute flinch again.

Kami cast her schoolbag to one side. "Angela, help me!"

she yelled. She leaped on Rusty's back, seizing his hair and pulling his head back. "Stop it. Stop it! I'll hurt you—you know I can."

Angela was at Jared's back before Kami had finished speaking, grabbing for his wrist, ready to bend it past the point of pain. Jared dodged away from her, stumbling into the door in his haste. His shoulder knocked against it hard and he winced, baring his bloodstained teeth. "Don't touch me," he said, his voice thick.

"Don't worry," Angela returned. "Rusty, cut it out, what are you thinking?"

"I was thinking that he made Kami cry."

Kami abruptly let go of Rusty and gave him a shove. "No, he didn't."

"You were crying?" Jared asked. His voice was thick with blood and shaken with pain so Kami could not read it, but she thought it had changed.

"It's nothing to do with you," Kami snapped at him, and glared at Rusty. She was feeling uncharitable in every direction.

"But why were you—"

"What did you do?" Angela demanded of Jared.

"I didn't do *anything*!" Jared said. "All I've been trying to do is what she wants!"

"My freaking hero," Kami snarled.

Jared sent her a brief bitter glance. Kami returned the look with interest, then looked away, pressing her hand to her forehead as if she could push through her skull and put all her thoughts in order. She had goals she needed to achieve;

fighting amongst themselves was not going to accomplish anything.

"You did say," Rusty pointed out with a virtuous air, "that you wanted me to teach everyone how to defend themselves."

"Is that what you were doing?" Jared asked, swiping at his bloody mouth. "Teaching?"

"You have to use a firm hand," Rusty said earnestly. "That's how you learn. I'm very dedicated to my craft. And I was not planning on the lesson getting so out of hand. That was your fault. You have absolutely no concept of any sort of fighting technique. You kept trying to bash me with stuff. This is why I never go for blonds. They are all vicious creatures."

"I *do* have a fighting technique," Jared informed him. "It is a little-known discipline known as 'winning.'"

"How about we try—"

"How about you try shutting up, sitting down, and listening to me?" Kami asked. "Nobody is allowed to hit anybody until you've all heard my plans."

"You're not the boss of me," Rusty muttered.

"You're strangely mistaken," said Kami. "I am too. I set up *The Nosy Parker,* I discovered the sorcerers, and I started the investigation, and now you're part of my team. Or you're not." She cast Jared another darkling look. "Any arguments?"

"Actually, I've got lots," said Jared. "A splendid variety. Take your pick. But about that, no."

"All right," Kami called out. "Glad that's settled. Thank you all for coming. Let's discuss our plans."

Ash still looked apprehensive about all the violence, but

he raised his hand and contributed: "I thought my mother was handling things from now on."

That was what the whole town seemed to be thinking: that Lillian would do it for all of them. Angela said that Lillian had even sent the mayor home like a little boy. Kami had no clue why the idea of placing your life in a sorcerer's hands wasn't terrifying to anyone else.

"Good point," said Kami. "Lillian has made it pretty clear that she doesn't want our help. But we're not going to sit around and do nothing while all this lasts."

Ash raised his hand again. "Have you ever sat around and done nothing in your life?"

Kami grinned at him, and was rewarded with one of his wonderful smiles. "Sounds boring. What about life, liberty, and the pursuit of adventure?"

"The pursuit of happiness?" Ash said.

Kami told him, "Same thing." She surveyed the room. Everyone seemed ready to listen. "The sorcerers use blood, hair, and possessions to do spells. They personalize the spell: they make the spell stronger. And they can protect people. Ash told me that Lillian used Rob's and Rosalind's hair to protect Aurimere House from them."

"If they can't use magic against us," Angela clarified, "we can fight them. And we can win."

Kami beamed at her. "Exactly."

"Just one small problem," Angela said. "I don't mean to cast a dark shadow on all your hopes and dreams, except of course I do because that is who I am. I'm a dream ruiner. We can't exactly chase people around with scissors trying to snip off their hair. Nor is leaping on people and attempting to suck their blood likely to be welcome, unless someone has some very disturbing fetishes."

Angela leaned in toward Holly and snapped playfully; Holly recoiled as if Angela was a snake. Angela did not stop smiling, but her smile turned dark. "As you see."

Kami gave up lecturing the group from above, and went to sit on the practice mats close beside Angela. "Don't be silly," she said. "I don't want us to chase people with scissors. And I don't want us to bite them. That's assault. All I want to do is steal their stuff."

There was a pause.

"Comparatively, it's legal," Kami said defensively.

"Stealing in the name of justice is okay," Jared put in. "We'd be like Robin Hood. Steal from the rich, punch them in the face. I'm pretty sure that's how the saying goes."

Kami automatically looked at him when he spoke. His mouth was cut and his smiles were always small and almost secret anyway, as if he wasn't planning to share. She wasn't sure if he even was smiling, but she had the urge to smile back. She didn't: she looked away.

"Rob and Rosalind have both left stuff in Aurimere we can use. I have a list of all the people we know are sorcerers, and all the newcomers to Sorry-in-the-Vale. And we have to watch for the others." Kami stopped speaking and surveyed the room. "So to clarify: the plan is espionage, theft, and violence. All in?"

Everyone indicated that they were.

"Okay, then we can start the self-defense training," Kami said. "We can't all do magic, so Lillian thinks we're useless. What we need to do is learn to protect ourselves and others, and prove her wrong. So everybody's going to get taught a little self-defense. Angela, you take Holly."

Angela gave Kami an accusing look. Kami ignored it: she thought Holly and Angela could use the chance to talk.

"Jared," said Kami. He glanced at her. Every time she looked at him, all she could see was how he had looked by the broken ice of the Crying Pools. She saw the lightning filling the water, and his white still face.

"Rusty's going to teach you," she said. "I pick Ash."

* * *

"I don't want to hurt you," Ash said.

"You're not going to hurt me, I promise you," Kami encouraged. "But it'd be nice if you'd just try. Look, I'm just standing innocently around in a lonely, dark alleyway. Come on up behind me and grab me."

Kami stood with her back to Ash and after a moment she felt him take hold of her shoulder and her waist. It was potentially the most gentlemanly grabbing ever. It was more like ballroom dancing in which Kami seemed to have gotten accidentally turned around.

Kami efficiently elbowed him in the stomach, grabbed his wrist, twisted his arm up, and stopped with the hard edge of her palm laid against the warm skin of his throat.

Ash looked down at her, his face dismayed and open. He looked vulnerable. It was terribly appealing, even though she knew it was at least partly a facade.

"I'm sorry," Ash said. "I'm not very good at this."

"It is so unfair that you got the nice one," said Rusty.

Kami grinned, shook her head, and asked without thinking, "Want to switch?"

Jared went still. Rusty glanced down at him in alarm, waiting for yet another dirty trick. Jared just turned his face and looked at Kami from where he lay on the floor.

"I bet I can get Ash to hit me," he suggested.

Rusty rolled off him and sat crouched on the mat, wiping his forehead. "You are extremely annoying, I have to grant you that," he said. "It's a rare gift. Go ahead and try. That means I can have Cambridge."

Rusty sent Jared a sweet smile. Jared ignored him, rolling over on the mats and pushing himself to his feet in one movement. "Come on," he said to Ash, jerking his head in the direction of the door and walking into the next room.

Ash cast a doubtful look around, but finding no help offered, he went warily in after Jared.

"That was quite a display," Kami told Rusty.

"Are you overwhelmed by my rugged masculinity?" Rusty inquired.

"Yes," Kami said. "Obviously. But aside from that."

"No, no, keep going on about that," Rusty urged, and went over to the water fountain in order to splash his face and duck his rumpled dark head under the jet.

Kami crossed her arms, narrowed her eyes, and watched him. "If I want someone hit," she said, "I'll hit them myself."

"Noted," said Rusty.

Kami hesitated. "Are you all right? That wasn't like you."

"Maybe, Cambridge," Rusty suggested, strolling back to her from the water fountain, "you don't know me quite as well as you think."

Chapter Twelve
A Drop of Blood, What You Hold Dear

The other room was much smaller than the first one. There were no mats.

Ash found himself staring at Jared. His mouth was bleeding; he had almost thrown his life away yesterday and now he seemed exhilarated, as if next time he planned not just to throw his life but to hurl it away with great force. Ash had no idea how to react to him.

"You shouldn't have come after me," Jared said.

"Believe me, I wasn't going to," Ash replied. "I had no idea what you were planning to do. It was Kami who put it together."

Jared glared at him. "So now I'm going to live. And maybe I'll take Aurimere from you after all."

"You don't want it. You said so."

"But I might want to spite you," Jared spat out. "Aren't you angry? I mean, for God's sake. Look at me. I threw my own father down the stairs. I broke his neck. I lived on the streets for one summer, like so much garbage. My mother wanted to leave me there. And *your* mother thinks I would be a better leader than you. She thinks you're that worthless. She thinks you're more worthless than worthless."

Ash struck out. He just wanted to make Jared stop, that was all. He felt sick when the pain exploded in his knuckles.

When Jared smiled, his teeth were stained with fresh scarlet. "Don't you hate me?" he demanded. "I'd hate me."

"You just tried to drown yourself," Ash said. "You seem to hate yourself plenty already." He thought of Jared lost under the ice, took a deep breath, and dropped his fists. "But I don't hate you. I'd like it if we could figure out a way to work together."

"Well." Jared raised an eyebrow. "That's what we're doing, aren't we?"

Ash felt extreme foreboding. "By, uh, hitting each other?"

"No," said Jared, and smirked. "Though I'm liking that part, aren't you?"

"Not if by 'liking' you mean 'enjoying in any way,'" Ash replied.

Jared smiled again, mouth closed so Ash could no longer see his bloody teeth, and leaned back against the wall.

"I'm on her side," said Jared. "If you're on her side too, then we're already working together."

It wasn't what Ash had meant or what he had been hoping for, but it was the closest he and his cousin had ever come to having a moment of peace. There was no need to ask who Jared was talking about, or why Jared had been so keen to hit him.

Kami smiled at him, glanced in his direction all the time, had chosen to train with him, agreed to work with him, and agreed to watch his back. She might have saved Jared, but she barely looked at him.

Kami had picked Ash.

* * *

Kami and Rusty had been practicing throws for half an hour while Holly and Angela tried and failed to complete any sort of self-defense move.

"How about you attack me," Angela suggested in exasperation. "And I'll show you how it's done." She turned around, presenting her back to Holly, and Holly hesitated, her eyes a little wild.

"Just put your arm around my neck," Angela began.

"You don't have to say it like—" Holly started.

Angela turned on her. "Or how about this?" she asked. "How about you stop acting as if I'm contagious?" She wheeled around and picked her sunglasses and her bag up off the floor, then stormed out in a whirl of black hair and red silk.

Kami noticed Jared and Ash at the door of the next room, watching Angela go and looking baffled. They seemed even more puzzled when Holly covered her mouth with her hand and rushed out as well.

"Good practice, everyone," Rusty said at last. "Light on the actual learning, heavy on the emotional catharsis, and thanks to Jared I think I need a rabies shot, but them's the breaks." He started stacking the mats in one corner of the room.

Kami picked up her bag and made her way out the door and down the stairs, where Ash caught up with her.

"What was all that?" Ash asked.

"None of your business," Kami said firmly.

"It sounded like—" Ash stopped, and glanced over his shoulder up the stairs.

Kami followed his gaze to Jared, coming after them. Jared gave a tiny nod, confirming that it had sounded like that to him too.

"Wow, Angela and Holly," Ash said, sounding awed. "Hot."

"Excuse me, what is wrong with you?" Kami demanded. "Other people's sexuality is not your spectator sport."

Ash paused. "Of course," he said. "But—"

"No!" Kami exclaimed. "No buts. That's my best friend you're talking about. Your first reaction should not be 'Hot.'"

"It's not an insult," Ash protested.

"Oh, okay," Kami said. "In that case, you're going to give me a minute. I'm picturing you and Jared. Naked. Entwined."

There was a pause.

Then Jared said, "He is probably my half brother, you know."

"I don't care," Kami informed him. "All you are to me are sex objects that I choose to imagine bashing together at random. Oh, there you go again, look at that, nothing but Lynburn skin as far as the mind's eye can see. Masculine groans fill the air, husky and—"

"Stop it," Ash said in a faint voice. "That isn't fair."

Behind them, Jared was laughing. Kami glanced back at him and caught his eye: for once, it made her smile, as if amusement could still travel back and forth like a spark between them.

"Ash is right, this is totally unfair," Jared told her. "If you insist on this—"

"Oh, I do," Kami assured him.

"Then I insist on hooking up with Rusty instead of Ash. It's the least you can do."

"Ugh," Ash protested. "You guys, stop."

"She's making a point," Jared said blandly. "I recognize her right to do that. But considering the alternative, I want Rusty."

Ash gave this some thought. "Okay, I'll have Rusty too."

The sound of the door opening behind them made them all look up the stairs to where Rusty stood, with one eyebrow raised.

"Don't fight, boys," he remarked mildly. "There's plenty of Rusty to go around."

Ash looked mortified. Kami burst out laughing.

"So," said Ash. "Can I walk home with you? Sorry if you'd rather I asked Rusty."

Kami glanced at Jared. He seemed unaffected by the question, as if he hadn't even heard it. She appreciated that Ash had asked if he could walk with her, rather than if he could walk her, like she was a poodle. And it had been so simple for her today, being able to look at Ash and smile at him. There was no pain in this: surely it was healthier.

She reached the bottom of the stairs. Ash held out his arm, and Kami took it.

* * *

It was evening, and there was a bite in the air that sank down to the bone. The dying light overlaid the fields with silver, as if it had already snowed. Kami was sure it was going to.

Ash offered Kami his leather jacket as they walked. She accepted because it seemed only sensible: all she was wearing was a short-sleeved black knit T-shirt with a red heart pierced by an arrow on it. As she put the jacket on she thought of trying to climb inside it while she kissed him. She held the collar of the jacket closed, high, to hide her burning cheeks.

Kami wondered if he was going to try to kiss her again. Did she want him to kiss her? Maybe she did. Maybe it was just about comfort in a time when her town and her home were falling apart.

She was concentrating so hard on looking away that she didn't see much until she felt Ash tense. Then she focused on the street in front of her, the row of homes, with their windows squares of silver and on their doors . . . streaks of blackness, gleaming darkly.

"What's going on?" Kami demanded.

Before Ash could answer, she remembered, and then she was running faster than Ash could follow her, down that winter-pale street and onto her own road lined with the silvery skeletons of trees.

Her gate stood before her, sturdy-looking and familiar and sweet, and before the gate she saw a dark figure stooping.

Kami stepped forward, and the shadowy figure looked up at the sound of her coming. In the moonlight her mother's face shone, and her mother's hands gleamed with the same darkness that had touched every door in Kami's town.

I trust you're all going to be sensible, Rob had said. *I'll be watching for the signs.*

Blood marking their homes, the sign of submission Rob

had asked for. The sign that the town would cooperate with the sorcerers' demands.

"Don't," Mum said, her voice shaking. "Don't look at me like that. This is for your brothers."

Kami's voice tore, as if it was a piece of paper in her mother's shaking hands. "You think this is the way to protect them?"

"I don't know any other way," her mother whispered. Her mother had already sacrificed one child to a sorcerer. A little blood on the gate should not have been a surprise.

Kami opened the gate, shoving past her mother and running inside the house and up to her room as if nightmares were chasing her. She felt as if she had been marked instead of her home: she felt weak for wanting something from magic, for not being able to stop wanting. She lay in bed until house and night were still around her, and then she crept softly downstairs and began to fill a bucket with water. The moonlight alchemized the water from the faucet into a bright white stream.

Kami looked out the window and saw someone at her gate. Fear touched her for a moment, but then she recognized the face.

Her father.

She turned off the taps and walked out of her house, carrying the bucket in both her hands so it would not spill. Silently they washed the blood away from their gate together.

Chapter Thirteen
At Your Gate

Sorry-in-the-Vale was a frequent tourist destination in the summer, which meant Kami knew the places in town where strangers were likely to go. And nobody could be invisible if they wanted to buy milk or stamps.

After school on Friday, Kami made sure everyone was in position. Angela kept sending her text messages of bitter complaint from the gift shop.

Kami herself was turning loitering into a fine art at the post office. "I always wondered what it would be like to work behind the counter here," she told Mrs. Jeffries, being energetically charming while keeping one eye out the door. "I want to write an article about it, in fact."

Mrs. Jeffries patted her dark hair. "I do like that paper of yours."

"I would call it . . . 'The Secret Lives of Postmistresses,'" Kami said.

"I don't know about that," Mrs. Jeffries told her doubtfully. "Sounds a little saucy to me."

"Oh no," Kami assured her. "Mine is a worthy publication. Completely lacking in sauce." She spotted her quarry coming down the High Street, letters in hand, and texted a group message requesting immediate assistance. "So could I possibly come behind the counter?" she asked.

"Weeeeeell," said Mrs. Jeffries.

Kami jiggled the gate invitingly, and Mrs. Jeffries swung it open. At the precise moment Kami slipped inside, the phone in the back rang. Mrs. Jeffries gave Kami a questioning glance, and Kami nodded encouragement.

Mrs. Jeffries went to answer the phone, while Kami spared a moment to hope Holly could keep her occupied long enough. Then the door of the post office swung open, and the stranger came in. She was tall, with hair so red it was almost vermilion. She had clear green eyes and Kami decided as soon as she saw her that her name must be Carmen or Veronica. Some classic evil name.

Carmen/Veronica gave Kami a skeptical look. Kami drew herself up and tried to look like a youthful but dedicated postmistress. "New here, are you? Welcome to Sorry-in-the-Vale," Kami said. "I'm Mabel Jeffries."

"Indeed?" said Carmen or Veronica.

"And you are?"

"Ruth Sherman," said the woman, handing over her letters. Kami was tempted to keep them, but Ruth Sherman— shame about the name, possibly her evil sorceress title was Ruth the Ruthless—had propped her handbag up on the counter and was watching her carefully.

Kami stuck on stamps and deposited the letters in the postbag with an innocent smile, resolving to fetch them out when Ruth was gone. The door jangled and Kami was relieved to see Jared burst into the room. Ruth turned at the sound, and obviously recognized him. Or rather, recognized a Lynburn when she saw one.

"Staying with friends, are we?" Kami asked loudly, to attract her attention. "Enjoying yourself?"

Jared sidled up. He was not very good at sidling; he was more of a loomer.

"I plan to," said Ruth.

Kami gave up on conveying messages to Jared with her eyebrows at the same time Jared gave up on subtlety. Instead he just knocked Ruth's handbag onto the floor.

"Oh no," he exclaimed. "Clumsy me."

Kami clicked her tongue against her teeth. "I am so sorry," she said. "What must you think of us? Those stamps are on the house. I mean the post office." She spoke very fast, because she'd just heard the click of Mrs. Jeffries hanging up the phone. Jared rapidly stuffed the contents of Ruth's bag back inside and thrust the bag into her arms.

Then they both stared at her intently and expectantly.

Ruth Sherman raised her eyebrows at them and backed out of the post office.

"Who was that?" Mrs. Jeffries asked, bustling out from the back just as the door swung shut after Ruth Sherman. She started at the sight of Jared, still crouched on the floor. Then she did a rapid scan of her post office. She instantly caught sight of the lone lipstick rolling on the floor.

"The poor lady must have dropped that," she said, and undid the gate, stepping out to get it.

Jared put his hand on it. "No."

Mrs. Jeffries stared down at him. "What do you mean . . . no?"

Jared and Mrs. Jeffries stared at each other, neither breaking eye contact, in a perfect deadlock.

Then Jared smiled at her. "I mean," he said with conviction, "it's mine."

"It's what?"

Jared stood up, pocketing the lipstick. "I know," he responded. "Everyone tells me I'm more of a summer."

Mrs. Jeffries continued to stare.

Jared continued to speak. "I'm going to go now. Me . . . and my lipstick."

Since the gate was already open, Kami seized her chance to escape. "I too will leave. I have soaked up so much post office ambiance today already!"

Mrs. Jeffries visibly gave up on the youth of today with their random comings and goings, and even more random cosmetics.

Kami and Jared escaped out into the chilly brightness of the wintry air, sunlight pouring on them clear and cold as if through a crystal.

"Good save," Kami told him. "I mean, it's going to be all over town by nightfall, your reputation is ruined, but it was a noble sacrifice."

"That's me," said Jared, and tossed her the lipstick. Kami caught it in both hands. "Chivalrous."

"Oh, chivalry," Kami said. "You get it from those old books of yours. Alice Duer Miller said chivalry was 'treating a woman politely / As long as she isn't a fright / It's guarding the girls who act rightly / If you can be judge of what's right.'"

"You be the judge of what's right," Jared said. "If you like. I wouldn't know."

Kami glanced over at him. "You do okay."

"However, you're not allowed to judge my books," said Jared. "I am not the one who has actually read a book actually called *The Bride of the Cursed Emerald.*"

"Quality literature," Kami told him, used to defending her mystery novels. "Turned out the butler did it. With the cursed emerald as a murder weapon. But the bride still loved it. The emerald, I mean, not the butler. Nobody loves a butler."

It was ridiculous how simple it was to talk to him now that they had something to laugh about and an adventure behind them. It was such a relief to have him with her, and not to hurt any longer.

Kami could not help resenting him in the midst of happiness: that he could take it all away.

"Do you hate me?" Kami asked, without planning to. "I mean—do you?"

She forced herself to look at him as punishment; he had stopped walking and was facing her. He looked stricken, as if she was the one who had hurt him.

"Sometimes," he said in a low voice.

"All right," Kami said, and clenched her hand around the stupid lipstick. "Well—I have to go home now. Thanks for all your help."

* * *

Kami was taking her time walking home. This morning she had seen her father come out of his office again, his door open enough to show a mess of blankets on the sofa, and her mother was already gone. Maybe to the bakery. Maybe somewhere else.

For the first time, Kami could almost understand her mother's fear. If the truth didn't help anyone, and love didn't last, what was there left to struggle toward?

The path home was a gentle curve. Kami followed it, and did not look up to Aurimere. She looked at the woods lining one side of the way instead, and thought of warnings passed down in the form of stories about never straying into the woods.

As if staying on the path meant you were safe.

"Kami," said a voice behind her, proving her point, and Kami squared her shoulders and turned to face Sergeant Kenn.

He was a stocky, gray-haired man of about fifty, who wore horn-rimmed glasses. He had patted her hand and given her cups of tea when he talked to her about finding Nicola Prendergast's body. It had been his scarecrow that tried to kill her on Halloween.

"I'd like a word with you, young lady," he said.

Kami stifled a desperate urge to laugh. She kept walking, hastening her pace. "I don't think we have anything to say to each other."

He hurried up alongside her: she could hear his slight out-of-condition pant in her ear. "I think we do," said Sergeant Kenn. "You were spotted up at Hallow's Field, you know."

Kami kept walking, her head down. "And if I was?"

"You don't have magic anymore," the sergeant said. Despite everything, hearing him say "magic" made her want to laugh again. It was all so strange and horrifying: she almost

139

could not believe any of it. "You might be wise to stay out of sorcerers' affairs. Let the Lynburns settle it."

"Is that your considered opinion, as an officer of the law?" Kami inquired. "Is that what the law is about—the strongest people having what they want, and the weakest submitting?"

Kenn paused. Kami spied her house and walked faster.

"This isn't a town like any other town," he said. "If your grandfather had done his duty, if your mother had told you the old stories, maybe you'd understand better. Sorry-in-the-Vale used to be a lucky place to live—*blessed*, you might say."

"Oh, I wouldn't."

"People were saved from accidents that would have killed them anywhere else," Kenn continued. "Harvests were saved because storms didn't touch us. Things are all shaken up now, but back then, the sorcerers' way was a good way to live for everyone. The sorcerers' laws are worth following."

"Tell that to Nicola," said Kami. There were trees converging on the path now, branches in her way, pine needles on the cold earth. There was no way to get away, or to be safe. Not really.

"I'm telling you," Kenn said in her ear. "I'm hoping you might be sensible. Lynburns should stick together. Rob Lynburn wants his boy to join him."

Kami took a swift, deep breath. "Which one?"

"It's Jared whose source you were, ain't it?" Kenn asked, the country burr in his voice making her want to laugh again, it was so homey and familiar, and this was all so nightmarish and bizarre. "You might still have some influence over him, I thought. I've always had a fondness for you; Rob would go easier on you if he thought you'd talked Jared around to his side."

It might have been flattering if he'd been asking Kami to use her feminine wiles to turn men to evil. But no, it was about being a source, and the link that meant she might still have some pull with Jared. Jared, who hated her.

"Like you said," Kami told him, "I was his source. I'm not anymore. He doesn't give a damn what I do or what I say."

"Oh now, I wouldn't say that," Sergeant Kenn observed. "I saw him come charging to save you from my little scarecrow. Quite sweet, I thought it was."

Kami swallowed at the thought of this man standing at his window, looking down at her lying in his garden, the shadow of the thing he had created falling on her. "He would've saved anyone," she said. "He'd protect anyone who needed it. But you wouldn't understand that, would you, officer?" She opened the gate she had washed clean of blood, set her feet on the path leading to her door. Surely that path would be safe, if any path in the world was.

It wasn't. Kenn followed her inside the gate, crowding her against it and setting a heavy hand on her arm. Kami put her hand on his chest, pushing him back, but he would not be budged. "If Rob decides not to go easy on you, it won't just be you who suffers for it," Kenn told her. "Your family's not safe. Your home's not safe."

I know, Kami thought, but she couldn't say it. Instead she pulled her arm forcibly away and tried to turn around, and Sergeant Kenn grabbed her elbow to stop her.

Kami brought the elbow he'd been grabbing back hard,

put her whole body weight behind it, and sent him flying over the garden gate, on his back in the dirt of the road. She leaned over her gate and smiled at the ridiculous picture he made, as if she wasn't scared at all. "Stay away from my family," she said.

Then she tried to move and found she could not. She looked down. The dead briars of the roses, usually twined around the top of her gate, were now curling around her arms. She tried to jerk away, but some of the suppleness of live branches had returned to them and they fastened tight as ropes. The briars slithered up along her arms like snakes, and thorns slid deep into her flesh.

Kami looked at Sergeant Kenn and saw his eyes narrow with concentration in his kindly face. She tried to yank the briar out from around one arm with her other hand. The curved black thorns dug thin, deep furrows along her arms, blood welling and the thorns refusing to pull free. A sob rose in her throat that she refused to let out. She could not keep a grip on the briars, blood making her fingers slick.

Sergeant Kenn tried to struggle up on his elbows, but found his arms sunk too deep in the earth.

Kami had just a second to think that that couldn't be right, not when the frost had made the ground hard as stone, when she saw two things. One was dirt crawling over Kenn's legs, every grain of earth moving like a vast army of brown ants to cover him.

The other was the foot landing on Kenn's throat.

Kami looked up at Jared's set face.

"Let her go," said Jared in a measured voice, as the flood of earth moved faster and faster, until Kenn was mostly covered, his scared face framed by dark dirt. "I'll bury you alive by her garden gate. I'll enjoy it. Every time she goes out in the morning, every time she comes home, she'll walk on your grave, and she'll know she's safe."

Kenn tried to say something, but Jared's boot pressing down on his throat made that difficult. All that escaped his mouth was a thick, terrified gurgle.

"The only reason I have not to kill you is if you spread the message," Jared said. "People fear Lynburns? You can fear me. Tell them all: I see any sorcerer near this house, and this is where I put them. This is where I put you. I might give you air. You might be alive for a lot longer than you want to be. Now tell me that you're going to do exactly what I say."

The pressure of his boot must have eased, because Kenn was able to gasp out, "Yes."

The grains of earth rolled into his open eyes, then mingled with the tears to make muddy tracks. "I swear!" he sobbed out. Jared lifted his foot and stepped back.

Kenn rolled over in the clinging earth and crawled on the ground to get away from Jared, crawled on his hands and knees, then staggered to his feet and ran, stumbling and terrified, down the path by the woods.

Jared turned to Kami, and she flinched, then gave a cry as the thorns sliced her arms. Jared glanced at her face, his own unreadable, and took a step toward the gate, approaching her with what seemed like wariness. He lifted his hands over her briar-twined arms, but only the shadows of his fingers touched her.

The briars uncurled themselves, retreating down her

arms, the thorns skimming in the air along her skin but not cutting her again. The briars touched her fingers and slipped off like loose rings. Jared's head stayed bowed for a moment over her arms, bare now but for the blood.

"You'll want to get cleaned up," he said in a quiet voice, and took a step back.

Kami took a step back as well, and looked at his face. There was a nasty gash over his eyebrow, and his mouth was red and swollen, his lower lip cut in two places. "Looks like Rusty did a number on you yesterday."

Jared smirked and immediately winced. "Ash got in a hit too."

"You might want to get cleaned up as well," Kami said. "There's disinfectant and stuff in the house. Want to come in?"

Jared hesitated a moment, and then nodded. He swung the gate open and followed her up the path home.

* * *

Kami carried the first-aid kit down from the bathroom to the kitchen. When she came into the room, Jared was standing awkwardly in the exact spot on the red tiles where she had left him. There was a rolling pin lying on the low oak table and a line of empty plastic plant pots along the broad windowsill. He looked supremely uncomfortable in the midst of all this domesticity.

"You first," Jared said as Kami approached him with the first-aid kit.

"Okay, but don't think it'll get you out of disinfectant," Kami warned. She put the kit on the table and went over to the kitchen sink, where she ran her arms under the tap.

The water ran down her cuts, turning faint pink and swirling down the drain. When she put on disinfectant, the cuts stung but she did not let herself cry. She'd had enough of that. She blinked and focused on Jared instead.

In the sunset-warm light coming through her kitchen window, it was easy to see Jared was thinner than he used to be. The contrast of his appearance with the cared-for, comfortable surroundings of home was too great not to notice. There were shadows under his eyes and his dark-blond hair was longer than usual, curling in on itself at his nape. Something about him reminded her of a stray dog, lean, piteous, and always afraid of being hurt.

Or he was one of the invincible Lynburns, he had almost buried someone alive, and she was crazy.

Kami turned off the taps. When she looked up again, he was much nearer than she'd thought he would be.

"This towel's clean," he offered, his voice still quiet. "I mean, it looks clean."

Kami blinked. "Ah, the 'it looks clean' boy version of hygiene," she said, but her voice came out a little shaky. She held out her arms, wrists up, and then regretted doing it: it was a stupid thing to do.

He reached out and started, with great care, to pat her arms dry. She felt the warmth of his hands through the dish towel, his breath stirring her hair.

She moved incautiously, and the towel touched an open cut. Kami let out a small sound.

"Sorry," Jared said, fast. "Sorry. I'm really sorry."

"It's okay."

Jared looked at her, eyes shading to silver as he stared. "I'm sorry," he repeated.

"Don't think you're getting out of disinfection," Kami warned him. "Could you go lean against the dishwasher or something, you impossibly tall person," she added.

Kami dabbed disinfectant on a cotton ball, and crossed the kitchen floor to stand beside him. Jared slouched down against the dishwasher.

It made her remember the hallway at the Water Rising, shaking in the dark and wanting so badly to be close.

But this was Jared, and that had been Ash.

"That looks nasty," she said, wielding her cotton ball. She dabbed and he drew in a hissing breath. "Was Rusty wearing rings or something?"

"Yes, that's Rusty," said Jared. "Hands dripping with ornate gold rings. His new look, surprisingly pimping."

"You're so clever, mouthing off to a woman who has disinfectant and is ready to use it." Kami dabbed at the gash again, feeling his breath go uneven against her cheek.

"Sorry," she whispered, dismayed that she was hurting him that much.

"There must be some way to magically heal people," Jared said, face turned away from her. "But I'd have to practice on people to find out, and I don't like the thought of getting it wrong."

"Lillian should know," Kami suggested.

"Aunt Lillian is not terribly impressed with me right now."

"That stunt you pulled at the Crying Pools," Kami observed, "was not terribly impressive."

Jared shrugged. "I thought it might work. And I didn't much care if it didn't."

Kami didn't know what to do about it, if he felt like that. She didn't even know why he would.

"It was dumb," Jared said at last, watching her back away. "I won't do it again."

"You'd better not," Kami told him. "And speaking of dumb things. It's not that I don't appreciate the gallant rescue."

Jared crossed his arms. "Do I get points taken off for bad technique?"

"Why were you even there?" Kami asked. "Were you following me home?"

"Are you asking me if I was stalking you?"

"Maybe," said Kami. "Were you?"

"Yeah," said Jared. "Little bit."

Kami had to smile because he was so weird. She could hear her brothers watching television, the sound of her father playing music as he worked. It seemed as if everybody was safe for the moment, and she could just try to work this guy out. "Don't do that."

"I wasn't following you home so I could break into your house and steal your underwear," Jared pointed out. "There are sorcerers killing people in this town. I wanted to make sure you got home safe."

Kami looked down at the first-aid kit. She didn't think there was anything you could do for a split lip, though "don't get punched in the mouth again" seemed like a good first step that Jared had obviously not considered. He kept welcoming pain, as if it was the only friend he wanted.

"Why not just walk home with me? As in, with me aware of the fact that you were there?"

Jared did look at her then. "But I thought . . . ," he began.

Kami saw her mother at the gate, coming home before dark for once. Mum had stopped to stare at the disturbed earth. Kami saw the look on her face, guessed what she might be thinking: that this looked like a grave, looked like trouble and magic on their very doorstep.

"What did you think?" Kami asked Jared. She wanted him to say something, anything, to make her feel better.

He said nothing. He'd been able to say he hated her.

"Why this anxiety to keep me safe?" she demanded.

Jared's lip curled. "You saved me. In the woods. Now we're even."

"I didn't realize we were keeping score," Kami said slowly. "I don't want you to guard me. I'm nothing special. You said that. Didn't you?"

"Yeah," Jared said. His voice was rougher than usual, and she wanted to hit him.

"I'm not your magic link anymore. I'm nothing to you anymore. So leave me alone."

He looked at her, winter in his eyes. He hated her sometimes, he said: she was sure he hated her then.

"Whatever you want," said Jared, and turned away. He paused at the kitchen door. "Thanks for the first aid," he added. "You didn't have to do that."

It was a simple enough thing to say. It didn't change anything. But it made her want to cry. She didn't cry. She watched Jared pass her mother at their gate, and saw her mother turn pale in Jared's shadow.

Kami put her hand in her pocket and drew out the two objects she had in there. She looked at them glitter in the November sunlight: Ruth Sherman's lipstick and the button she had pulled off Sergeant Kenn's uniform when she pushed him away. She didn't need comfort, not from anyone. She had a way to fight.

PART IV
WINTER SONG

I have been torn
In two, and suffer for the rest of me.
—*Edna St. Vincent Millay*

Chapter Fourteen
Call upon My Soul Within the House

Several weeks of attempting to hunt sorcerers had passed when Kami woke and found that the world had turned white. It was as if someone had tipped a layer of powdered sugar over Sorry-in-the-Vale, turning the landscape into a vast wedding cake.

Kami stirred in a warm nest of blankets, blinking at the brilliant pallor of the world outside her window. Her lashes stuck to her cheeks, and her hand was pinned under Tomo's head.

Mum and Dad had spent the night shouting at each other. Tomo and Ten had climbed into Kami's bed and huddled there, all of them listening miserably together.

Kami pulled herself upright in bed. Tomo was sprawled over three-quarters of the mattress, and Ten was curled at the bottom of the bed like a cat. She'd seen other families fighting and breaking apart, but it had never seemed like something that could happen to hers.

There was a trail of footsteps in the snow: a dark line

leading from their doorstep to Kami did not know where. Her mother was already gone.

The creak of the bedroom door made Kami startle. Her father looked in, and Kami saw the crease of worry between his brows ease when he saw them all there. Another thing that shocked Kami was seeing both her parents so scared.

"I'm calling this one a snow day," Dad said. "Come on. Let's all have porridge and honey and hot chocolate, and build snowmen. You in?"

Tomo woke up, flailing wildly like a small windmill that had found itself trapped in a bed. Ten was already uncurling, looking alert and happy.

"Thanks, Dad," Kami said. "But though your offer is generous and chocolaty, I think I'm going to school. Lots of work to get done."

You can't find them, Lillian Lynburn had said. But she was wrong.

* * *

It seemed like everyone had had the same idea as Kami's dad. There were a few kids standing in front of the school, but the school's windows were dark, the doors barred. None of Kami's friends were in sight except for Ash: Kami imagined Angela had taken one look at the snow and decided she was officially in hibernation.

But Amber Green was there, and Kami had stolen one of her pencils. Ash had said he could use Amber's possession to make sure they could see Amber no matter what spells she cast to make herself invisible. Ash had also agreed to help Kami.

"I think your plan is insane," said Ash.

Ash agreeing was really the important part.

"Trailing someone is a classic maneuver," Kami told him. "My plan is elegant in its simplicity. Walk with me now."

Kami gestured to Ash to follow her through the school gates. She walked with him down the path along the wall, ostensibly heading up toward Aurimere, then gestured to him to go down low.

Ash crouched in the icy grass and gave Kami another baffled and pleading look. Kami smiled at him encouragingly and moved back along the wall, keeping low, so nobody would see their heads over the wall as they returned to the school. Just before a curve in the wall, Kami stopped. She could see the gate from here, and see people trickling out.

Ash leaned toward her, his jean-clad knee pressing against hers. "What on earth are we doing?"

"Shhh," Kami reproved him. "The first rule of stakeout is no talking on stakeout! And you're already in trouble for not remembering the second rule of stakeout, which is bring me doughnuts."

Ash subsided into a worried silence, which he preserved until they watched Amber Green and her boyfriend, Ross Phillips, take a left directly from the gate, instead of heading down to Sorry-in-the-Vale and their homes. Kami squeezed herself against the curve of the wall and prayed they would not see her, gesturing for Ash to do the same.

Once Amber and Ross had passed, Ash said, "What if they're just going off to . . . uh, you know. Be alone together." His already cold-flushed face turned even pinker. He was so handsome and so embarrassed it was impossible not to smile at him.

"Then we'll go away very quickly," Kami promised.

"This is how it goes. Shadowing people is frequently the tawdry part of an investigation."

"How many investigations have you actually conducted?" Ash asked doubtfully.

Kami chose not to dignify that with a response. She moved past Ash and followed Amber and Ross, whose path soon diverged away from the wall, the town, and Aurimere. Their course was clearly set west of the town, which was mostly overgrown fields. It was like a moor, crisscrossed with dirt lanes leading nowhere. One such lane led to Monkshood Abbey, the house where Rob's parents had lived, and killed.

Amber and Ross were tiny dark figures in the lane, small shadowy shapes against a framework of pearl-glistening boughs, banks of snow-crowned undergrowth, and snow-lined stiles and gates. Carts or cars had obviously passed down the lane this morning: there were two dark furrows in the pale surface of the snow. Amber and Ross were each walking in one of the lines in the snow when they blurred, their dark shapes suddenly lost to Kami's eyes as if they had been stirred into the landscape like sugar cubes in a glass of hot milk.

Ash cut himself off midswear with a guilty look at Kami, clutched at the pencil, and muttered some other words under his breath.

Amber's form coalesced back into view, blurred at first, then clearer and clearer. Kami could see snowflakes settle, like shining pieces of lace, in the fox fire of her hair.

"Come on," Kami said. "Shortcut." She plunged into the undergrowth, brambles clawing at her jeans. She scrambled over a stile half concealed in the bush, grabbing at the snow-piled wood to boost herself over, and her white woolen gloves were instantly soaked.

The fields stretched wide and far, a pristine blanket of white fringed with the curling darkness of trees on its borders. The sky pressed down low against the earth, a dense layer of pale gray cloud that seemed like a dark, dim reflection of the snow. Cutting diagonally across these fields meant that they would get to a certain turn in the lane before the other two did. She faced an expanse of trackless snow, a perfectly blank page.

Kami began to run.

* * *

Monkshood Abbey was set at the top of a snowy slope, the dark crest on a white wave. The foot of the slope was ringed with fire.

Last time Kami had seen Monkshood, the house had been deserted and the moat had been empty. The only difference now was that the door was not barred, and they watched the beacon of Amber's hair disappear through that door into the dark.

Monkshood seemed to lurk on top of the low hill. It was not built with the towers and wide-open windows of Aurimere. It had been built for the cadet branch of the family, Kami guessed sometime in the Victorian age: it was square and respectable, menacing as well as humble, like the cringing henchman you always knew was up to no good.

Kami bet Rob could not wait to return to Aurimere.

Once past the moat, Ash looked more and more nervous.

Kami was aware there was nothing he wanted less in the world than to see his father. She put out a hand and slipped it in his. Ash's fingers curled gratefully around hers.

"We'll just take a detour around the back and peep in through the windows. See what we can see: see if there are sorcerers there we don't know about yet," Kami said. "Then we'll go."

Ash squeezed her hand and did not answer, but Kami took this as agreement and set off, boots sliding in the ice, away from the fire and toward the house.

Kami headed for the window that Jared had broken last time they were here. She was not expecting to see the window still broken. Beyond the jagged glass there had been an empty room.

"I wonder if Rob has bothered to cast a spell to protect his house from useless unmagical little me," said Kami. "I bet he hasn't."

When Ash did not move to boost her, she got a leg up on the mossy windowsill and did it herself with a grunt of effort. Her palms got skinned as she tumbled in.

"Kami," Ash whispered, from the other side of the window frame. "Kami, you can't—"

"I'm just going to take a look," Kami whispered back.

There was furniture in the room now, a desk, a chair, and a lamp. Kami picked up a pen from the desk and put it in her pocket, because she was now a kleptomaniac for great justice. The door leading to the rest of the house was slightly open, and through the small space Kami saw movement and heard voices. She turned and met Ash's horror-struck gaze through the broken window.

Kami gestured at him to get down. Then she dived behind the desk, curling up small beneath it, her cheek against the floor. She waited, her cheek getting extremely cold against the floor, and listened.

"It's a real shame about your children not having magic, but I know I can count on you and Alison to support me and train the others." Rob's voice was smug and calm.

Kami wondered why the name was familiar for an instant before she realized. *Hugh and Alison Prescott,* she thought. *This was Holly's father.*

"Of course," said Hugh Prescott gruffly. "That witch up on the hill drove my brother away and then blamed us for it. We only want our due."

"You shall have it," said Rob. "And Lillian will pay the price for her mistakes. Everybody in this town is going to get precisely what they deserve. And we know her numbers are laughable. But we want no doubt to remain in anyone's mind. I want a sacrifice, and I want every soul in Sorry-in-the-Vale to offer up their tokens. We want to crush Lillian's people in front of the town, and that is why the young ones need careful training. See to it."

They might have exchanged nods or smiles. Kami heard one of them walk away, his tread heavy, and the click of someone else's shoes on the floor.

"Can I have a word?" a woman's voice murmured. Kami recognized this voice immediately: it was Jared's mother, Rosalind.

Kami watched her tan leather boots cross the floor, heels clicking on the worn wood, closer and closer to the desk. Rosalind walked around the desk, and Kami froze. Rosalind's step halted for an instant, and then she paced her way back across the room and toward Rob.

"You were talking with Claire Glass alone again," Rosalind said, her voice sharper than Kami had ever heard it. "Why is that? It's not like she can help us in any real way."

"That's right, she can't," Rob told her. "She's not like us. You can't possibly imagine she means anything to me."

There was the soft sound of a kiss. Kami made a face: she wished that parents would just plan evil and not have discussions about their love lives.

"Claire Glass behaves the way the people of this town should all behave, that's all," said Rob. "You know we need them all to submit. You know why. There are so many of them—so many sorcerers even—waiting in their homes like scared animals in their dens. All of them need to choose a side. All of them need to choose our side."

"I know." Rosalind took a deep breath. "Tell the others . . . tell Ruth and Hugh, especially, not to go after our family. I don't want Lillian or the boys hurt."

"Nor do I," Rob said. "I will make every effort to spare them. And I know you will do whatever you can to please me in return."

"I swear," Rosalind told him. "Now go."

Kami watched Rosalind's boots cross the floor after him, but Rosalind paused on the threshold. Before she went out, she said, very quietly, "You should leave."

* * *

"I call that a very successful mission," Kami said, safe in the library at Aurimere.

"Aunt Rosalind caught us. I think getting caught is sort of the opposite of success."

"Except now we know she's willing to protect us," Kami said. "Knowing that an enemy has divided loyalties is useful information."

Ash shrugged. Kami was leaning against one of the glass-fronted bookcases. Ash stood by the baby grand in the corner, staring down at the piano keys rather than at Kami. She wondered what it had meant to him, hearing his father and his aunt today.

His golden head lifted. She was surprised to see him wearing a tiny smile.

"Aha," said Kami, her own smile spreading to encourage him. "So you had a little bit of fun being spies."

"Well," Ash said. "Not at the time. But maybe looking back on it. Do you think everyone will be impressed?" He began to play a little tune, the piano keys tinkling.

Kami tapped out a rhythm on the wooden surface of the bookcase. "How could they not be?" she asked.

Ash closed the piano lid with a flourish, crossed the floor, and held out his hand to her. Kami looked down at her tapping fingers as if they had betrayed her and realized she was standing in the exact place Jared had the night he said he wanted nothing to do with her.

"I can't actually dance," Kami objected, suddenly shy. "I mean, I've done it. But people tell me . . . that I shouldn't."

"What do they know?" Ash asked, his hand still out. After a moment more of hesitation, Kami put her hand in his, and Ash pulled her away from the bookcase into his arms.

Ash could dance as well as he could play the piano. He moved in gentle circles across the floor, navigating sofas and chairs with effortless grace. Kami just had to follow his lead. He'd been trained for this sort of thing, she supposed, being the young prince in the castle. Being a fairy-tale prince who could waltz any girl around a room, him all gold and the room all arched stone, the moment perfect no matter who the girl happened to be.

Ash twirled Kami and pulled her back in against his chest. When he dipped her, she had a moment of unease because she couldn't stand up by herself and would have fallen without his arm supporting her. But she looked up into his eyes, soft and sparkling with laughter, and smiled up at him instead.

Ash bent and kissed her. The kiss went through Kami like summer sunlight.

Just then the door opened with a creak.

"Sorry," said Jared. "Aunt Lillian was looking for Ash."

They all stayed still for a little too long. Kami and Ash did not drop each other's hands, and Jared was standing braced as if waiting to be hit.

"Great," Kami said at last, the word falling like a drop of rain into a pool, absorbed into the silence. She tugged her hands out of Ash's and took a step toward Jared; he took a step back, not looking up. "We've found out a lot of stuff we need to tell Lillian."

"She's in the drawing room," Jared said, backing up, and they both followed him. When they got there, Jared opened the door for them.

When Kami gestured for Ash to go in ahead of her, he touched her arm. She turned to him and he gave her a worried glance, as if he thought he had done something wrong but was unsure of what it was. Kami gave Ash a quick reassuring smile, then looked back at Jared, catching a glimpse of his face as he looked down again.

"Hey," Kami said softly. "Is everything okay?" She felt dumb asking. It wasn't like Jared was ever subtle about it when he was upset: this was just him being quiet and not meeting her eyes, a little withdrawn. He was just feeling awkward about interrupting; he wasn't unhappy.

That was confirmed when Jared answered, in a level voice, "Fine."

"Okay," Kami said uncertainly. She lifted her hand to bridge the space between them somehow, and a faint shudder ran through Jared's body. He stepped away from her and into the drawing room, going to stand by the fireplace.

Ash was already sitting on the window seat, his mother standing beside him. He was telling her the story of what they had discovered.

Lillian was listening, a bored look on her face. She was wearing a mulberry-colored shirt that made her hair look lemon-colored in comparison, very much the self-assured lady of the manor.

"Mum, he's training his sorcerers too. He thinks he'll crush us."

"He's wrong," Lillian said. "I'm better than he is. I always was. If he's forgotten that, he's going to get a surprise. And how dare you take a risk like that without consulting me first?"

"It was my idea," Kami said.

"How terribly surprised I am," Lillian remarked.

"And I think," Kami said, forging ahead, "that now we know for sure where their base is, we should attack Monkshood. We're the ones at a disadvantage when it comes to numbers: we need to catch Rob by surprise."

"You need to stop concerning yourself with the affairs of sorcerers," Lillian said. "From what Ash tells me, it was only my sister's mercy that spared your lives."

From Lillian's tone, it was clear she considered this hint that Rosalind was not entirely committed to Rob's course of action the only valuable intelligence Kami and Ash had gathered.

"I'm sorry if you feel I should have consulted you," Kami said, which was a bit of a non-apology, but she doubted Lillian was going to think it over that much. "But I think it's important—"

"I am not attacking Monkshood Abbey like a thief in the night!" Lillian snapped. "Rob betrayed me and broke my laws, and the whole town has to see him punished. I have to do this properly. Of course you do not understand. You are not a sorcerer. This is none of your business."

Kami stared at her. She didn't throw up her hands in exasperation, because she'd never made that kind of gesture in her life and she didn't know how to start, but she wanted to.

"This is everyone's business," she said finally, and turned to leave.

"Don't talk to her like that," Ash said behind her, and Kami appreciated the defense without imagining that it would do much good. She kept walking, down a couple of stone steps through yet another hall, heading through the cold maze of Aurimere until she was out.

She was in the great hall when she heard the footsteps running after her and saw the shadow fall on the golden wall of windows.

"I'm all right," Kami assured him, but when she looked round it was Jared. "Oh," she said. "I thought you were Ash." She bit her lip as soon as she'd said it.

Jared said curtly, "Sorry to disappoint. What do you want?"

Kami blinked up at him. He leaned against a window and she stopped and leaned against it with him.

"Well," she said. "How do you . . . mean that?"

"You told Aunt Lillian that you wanted to attack Monkshood."

Kami seized Jared's arm. "Jared," she said. "Listen to me very carefully. You are not to attack Monkshood on your own."

He looked down at her hand on his arm, fingers clutching the leather sleeve tight. Kami released her grip.

"Why not?" Jared demanded.

"Because there are too many of them," Kami said. "And you would die. And then we would have even fewer sorcerers than we currently do."

Jared nodded and stepped away from her, out of the picture. Kami did not know what made him act like this, as if he didn't care what happened to him and nobody else did either.

She walked away from the window, away from him, and continued across to the front hall and out of Aurimere.

The wind met her on the front steps in a cold rush, and she realized she had left her coat out to dry in the library.

Kami squared her shoulders under her jumper, pulling the floppy green sleeves down over her hands and her cauliflower-shaped knitted hat down to her eyebrows. She began to walk the icy path down from Aurimere.

"Wait," Jared said, close behind her, and she felt his jacket settle warm on her shoulders.

Kami put up her hand and held the collar of the jacket closed at her chin. It hung loose around her, warm inside from his body heat, the leather rough under her fingertips.

He circled around to meet her eyes. "I just want you to know," he said. "I don't care what Aunt Lillian wants. You don't trust me, or you just don't want me bothering you anymore. I don't blame you. That doesn't matter. You can count on me doing what you want. You can be sure I'll take your orders and not hers."

It was beginning to snow again, Kami realized. Faint, almost transparent pieces of white, like ghosts torn into shreds, were drifting and settling around them.

"I don't want to give you orders," Kami said.

She thought they could walk back together, at least for a bit, that perhaps he could explain what on earth he was talking about, but Jared backed off as soon as she spoke. The look he threw her suggested that any attempt to accompany him would not be welcome. He walked away through the falling snow, hunching his shoulders against the chill. All he was wearing was a long-sleeved T-shirt.

Kami wanted to be angry with him, but the emotion

would not quite resolve in her chest. She had been so frustrated with Lillian, had felt like no matter what she tried to do, the sorcerers would make sure she was ultimately helpless, and he had come to her. He could not fix things any more than she could, but one thing he could do was always be on her side. She pulled his jacket closer around herself and walked home warm.

Chapter Fifteen
Wild Night

The snow was melting by the next morning, and school was open. Kami didn't see Holly except in their last class, which was English, where Holly was sitting at a desk with Derek Fairchild. Kami stopped on the threshold of the room, startled: she and Holly usually shared a desk.

Holly was laughing, all curls and lip gloss, casting out so much color and sparkle that it took a moment for Kami to see she looked tired. She shot Kami a glance through her tumbling hair that might have been apologetic.

Kami took a seat on her own and tried to catch Holly after class, but Holly was using boys as bodyguards, and Kami could not get through. She was distracted at a crucial moment by the appearance of Ash.

"Damn it, I lost her," Kami exclaimed as Holly's crowd melted around a corner.

Ash blinked and smiled. "Who were you trailing this time?"

"Holly," Kami answered. "I think—I thought she might need to talk. But maybe she doesn't want to."

"I'd like to," Ash said. "If Holly has left a gap in your

schedule." He inclined his head toward the school doors. Together they went through them and down the steps.

The slate roofs and yellow stone of the town were visible now, wreathed with snow. As they walked through the gates, Ash offered her his arm, and she looked up into his eyes.

The very first time she had ever seen him, she had thought he looked like a dream come true. Now she knew that he tried to live up to everyone's expectations, and that worried her but did not really take away from his charm. It was an amazing relief to know that how you felt about someone mattered to them.

"What did you want to talk about?" Kami asked.

"Anything," said Ash. "It doesn't matter. I only want to talk to you."

All she had to do was smile at him. He wanted to charm her, wanted her to make him feel good about himself and wanted to make her feel good about herself too. She could feel wanted with him: wanted in the right way, and she could want him back the right amount. This was how things should be between a boy and a girl. This was healthy.

"We should probably talk about kissing," Kami blurted out. Smooth. She was so smooth.

"Kissing?" Ash repeated. "I wasn't aware we really needed to have an in-depth conversation on that topic. Since all I have to say is 'Sounds great.'"

"I mean *past* kissing," Kami said. "Specifically, in the Water Rising. We never talked about it, and now that we—I think we should. I know I gave you the impression that I like you. And I do, I do like you, but I wasn't—I didn't—"

There was a reason Kami had not brought this up before, she discovered. She had thought it would be humiliating, but she had not realized she would find it literally impossible to tell Ash what had happened.

The last thing she expected was for Ash to finish the sentence she could not.

"That wasn't me," he said.

Kami swallowed down the tangled debris of words rising in her throat. Then she swallowed again. "I beg your pardon?"

Ash dropped her arm and moved away from her, leaving a cold space against her side where he had been.

"I never kissed you at the Water Rising."

"You didn't?" Kami said.

Ash shook his head. Nothing about his manner was trying to be appealing anymore. He seemed all shut up inside himself rather than reaching out to her. Kami felt desperately sorry for him, for what must have seemed like someone choosing to forgive him. Her smiling and speaking to him after the Water Rising must have made it seem like she had chosen him, wanted to be with him, not that she wanted to stop thinking about someone else.

"So it was Jared," Kami said slowly, and saying the words aloud made them seem real. She had been right the first time, right to trust that she knew him well enough to know him in the dark.

And he had kissed her.

Kami realized that Ash was looking expectantly down at her.

"I'm so sorry," she said in a rush. "I'm terribly sorry, what an awful mistake to make, you must think I'm a complete fool. This is very embarrassing," she added. "I really thought it was you."

Ash's eyes were bleak. "It wouldn't matter who it was," he said quietly, "if you had wanted it to be me. But you didn't, did you?"

Kami opened her mouth, and closed it.

Ash had wonderful manners, almost always. He was too much of a gentleman to leave her scrambling for an answer he already knew. He nodded, and walked back toward the school so she would not have to walk with him. Kami put a hand on the gate, wanting to call after him, but she did not know what to say except that she was sorry again.

The sun was glittering on the lingering snow and turning it to water, washing everything clean.

Jared had kissed her.

She could go home, Kami thought, and get his jacket. She knew his hours at the Water Rising: when he was done with work, she could go return it to him, and maybe they could talk. She had a secret to tell him.

* * *

Holly could not talk to Angie and Kami. She was scared they would be able to see right through her and know the secret she wasn't ready to tell. And she couldn't talk to boys, because they knew nothing: all they wanted was pretty surfaces and nothing underneath.

Being angry at the world made her think of Angie, and thinking about Angie made her miserable. She told the guys she was talking to that she had to go to the bathroom and walked out of school alone, ready to get on her bike and escape it all for as long as she possibly could.

Instead she met Ash, inexplicably walking *back* across the icy gravel of the playground to the school.

"Hi, Holly," he said, unfailingly pleasant, trying to smile at her. Ash was the only one of the Lynburns who had a face that seemed human, handsome but not like a painting or a statue.

Right now he looked as if he wanted to feel better. "You look like you're having a worse day than I am," she said. "Want to go to the pub and have a chat?"

* * *

They had to go to the Water Rising, because the Mist and Bell was closed. There were a lot of people in Sorry-in-the-Vale lying low these days.

But the pub was noisy, as if there were a lot of people in town craving an escape. Not only Martha and Fred but even Jared seemed busy, moving among the customers and working the bar. Holly caught glimpses of manically cheerful faces, smiles stretched too tight, and she focused her smile on Ash.

He bumped shoulders with her companionably. "How are you feeling?" he asked her. His voice was warm and sympathetic, and exactly what Holly did not want. She didn't want to let anything slip: she wanted a distraction.

She slid her fingers over the back of his hand, circling his wrist under his sleeve. Small intimate touches that could be passed off as casual, and thus seemed even more intimate, had served her well in the past.

"I'm feeling fine now."

"Your parents are sorcerers working for my father," Ash said, his voice still gentle, as if he could see that she was in pain. "But your brothers and sister are just like you. They can't do magic. They won't be on the front lines, and they're probably scared."

"Who says I'm scared?" Holly asked. She took a deep swallow of her ginger ale and continued to flirt her fingertips along Ash's pulse.

She knew Ash felt it: it was in the way he smiled and looked down, then back into her eyes. Holly leaned forward. She saw him take in the significance of that move too, but he didn't make one of his own.

So she made another. She leaned forward and pressed a kiss on his lips, light as a casual question, and drew back to wait for his answer.

"I'm glad you asked me here," Ash said. He kept trying to be so considerate, Holly thought in exasperation. As if he cared about her. As if they were on a date.

Holly's smile pulled tight against her teeth. "So am I."

"Because . . . ," Ash said, and looked down at the table. "I mean, I'm sure you noticed that I have family issues as well. I'm sure you've noticed that my family has more issues than the *Times*."

Holly did not laugh. She didn't want to talk about her family, or about his; she didn't want him acting as if she'd asked him out because she liked him. She'd thought that, well, he was a Lynburn, one of the family who had come to town and ruined everything. He'd come very close to hurting Angie once: it didn't much matter if Holly hurt him.

Ash put his free hand over Holly's, and her clasp on his wrist went loose.

"If you want to talk to someone," Ash said, "I'm here."

"I'm sorry," Holly said, standing up. "This was a mistake." She tried to think of a way to tell him that she was leaving because she didn't want to be cruel, because he was better than she had thought he was. Finally, she said, "I don't want to talk. That's the last thing I want." She turned away, heading straight for the bar. All she wanted was to con a drink out of somebody so she could try to forget about how terrible the whole world was, including her.

Holly leaned against the bar. At the same time, Jared came over and dumped his empty tray. There was snow on the ground, but he had the sleeves of his shirt rolled up past his elbows and a couple of buttons undone. He looked overheated and overtired, but aside from that, Holly didn't know if he was feeling anything at all. He wasn't like Ash: he was like the other Lynburns, with faces cold as stone and eyes cold as steel.

There was a splash of what seemed to be lime cordial on his open collar. When he dumped the tray, he pushed his hair back and looked at her. "You look like you could use a real drink," he said indifferently.

"Please," Holly responded.

Jared leaned over the bar and tipped some whiskey into Holly's glass. Holly drank it.

"Thanks." Holly looked up from her drained glass into his eyes. She realized he was looking at her with a certain consideration.

There was no sweet curl to his sullen mouth, no excitement and no nervousness betrayed. He looked just like she felt: as if he would do anything to feel differently than the way he did now. His eyes were beacon-bright. He looked like driving too fast down a dark lane.

Holly met his eyes, and did not look away. Jared put his hand out over the corner of the bar and drew her slowly toward him. She let him do it because nothing about his demeanor suggested that he would care if she pulled away.

"I can't hurt you," she asked. "Can I?"

Jared murmured, as if he was telling her a secret: "You're welcome to try."

Then she was flush against his body, the corner of the bar digging sharp into her back and his warmth going through her, turning into heat.

Jared leaned forward and set his mouth against hers. The kiss turned deep almost instantly, his hands clenched in the curly weight of her hair. The noise and lights of the bar faded away to a buzz in her ears, light dying behind her closed eyelids.

When the kiss broke apart, Holly's mouth was stinging and she was staring up at him.

Jared looked down at her. "Want to go up to my room?"

Holly said, "Yes."

✳ ✳ ✳

Jared didn't kiss her on the stairs or in the hall, didn't touch her hand or even look at her until he had turned the key in the door. Then he turned to her, motions as mechanical as they had been with the key, and Holly stumbled across the floor of the room with his mouth on hers again. She hit the bed on her back, half bouncing and half arching from the mattress into his body over hers.

He had his arms braced on either side of her body, kissing her as if he wanted to drown in it. Holly grasped his arms, fingernails digging into the tense muscle beneath the cotton, and kissed him back. She was writhing on the bed she hadn't seen, encouraging him to drown and take her with him.

He pushed Holly's T-shirt up, making a sound against her mouth that sounded wild. Holly tore his shirt open with shaking hands, steadying them by pressing her palms against his skin and sliding them down the sleek muscle of his chest, the ridges of his abdomen, and against the slight rasp of hair. He kissed her again and again, his mouth a brand on hers.

She made a noise of her own, urging him on, greedy as her hands on his skin, reaching to pull open the button on his jeans, though his hands had not gone near hers. She was desperate to be hurt or used or anything, as long as she wanted it, as long as she could prove it was only this she wanted.

The thought was a cold shock that made her turn her face away, flushed cheek against the heated pillow, and stare at the wall. Messing around with boys was often an escape, but it had always been fun before.

The weight of his body was still pressing down on hers, muscles straining, and she almost turned her mouth back to his.

Jared breathed, "We can't do this." He rolled off Holly and went to sit on the window ledge. Holly pushed herself up on her elbows against the pillows and nodded silently.

"I can't care about you at all," Jared said.

"I wasn't exactly asking you to," Holly reminded him.

His swollen mouth curved. "That's not what I meant."

Holly looked around the small room: one wall stone and the other plaster, a dusty mantelpiece piled with old books. A naked bulb swung from one of the beams and cast yellow light on the tangled sheets and the thin chain around Jared's neck.

"There's this book," Jared said. "And in the book a guy said that he would rather touch someone's hand if she was dead than another girl who was alive. It's creepy. I know that." He was staring off into space, as if at some private nightmare. "Nothing matters in comparison. Nobody is real but her. So it feels sometimes as if nothing else matters at all, including other people. She wouldn't like that. Other people *should* matter."

"I shouldn't have done this," Holly said. "Kami's my friend."

"She won't care," Jared said. "I was in her head, once," and there was feeling in his voice for the first time: longing. "She didn't want to be tied to me, didn't want me hanging on her like a parasite anymore. She said that. And if she didn't want it, I shouldn't have wanted it either, should I? But I did. I still do."

So he loved Kami. Holly had never doubted it; she didn't think Kami had doubted it before the link was broken. But what she couldn't tell from his words, and what she remembered Kami wondering too, was whether Jared actually wanted her, the way any guy might want any girl. The way he'd wanted Holly the first time they had met and moments before on the bed. She didn't know if he loved Kami like that. Maybe it didn't matter, if what he felt was too warped and twisted to be of any use to anyone.

"It must be nice," Holly said tiredly, "to know exactly what you want."

"Not when you know what you want, and you know you can never have it again," Jared told her. He sounded tired too, his voice so worn it was almost soft.

Holly found herself almost wanting to laugh at how badly her attempt at an escape had gone.

"Men," she said. "Always going on about feelings all the time. I have to go." She felt a moment of pride at getting out the clever retort, and she was smiling slightly as she tugged down her wrinkled shirt and opened the door.

She found herself staring down into Kami's startled face. For a moment, Kami looked only startled, her dark eyes bright as if she was expecting something lovely to happen. She had Jared's ever-present leather jacket over her arm, and her free hand was lifted as if she'd meant to knock. Then the light in Kami's eyes dimmed. Holly could see the whole thing through those eyes: the rumpled bed, Jared with his shirt and jeans undone.

Jared was absolutely still, staring at Kami.

Kami was the first one to speak. "I'm terribly sorry," she said, her voice almost ludicrously polite. "I just wanted to give this back. I'll go."

"Don't!" Jared said, his voice too loud, as if giving an order. Holly turned at the sound: he caught Holly's eye, and flushed so red it made his scar burn livid white. He looked away.

"Please don't go on my account," Holly said, and then her attempt to be casual collapsed. "Oh God," she said. "I'm really sorry, this isn't—"

"It isn't any of my business," Kami told her with conviction. "And you have nothing to be sorry for."

"I was just leaving," Holly said. "I'm sorry. I'm going to go now."

Kami's hand went to Holly's sleeve, as if she might ask her to stay. The idea was so hideous that Holly dodged around her and hurtled down the stairs, through the pub and into the street, where she started to run.

Holly didn't even know where she was going until she found herself in front of Angela's house, staring at the blank black windows. Angela wasn't in. Holly didn't want to stop, or admit to herself what she was doing, so she barely halted before the gate. She just turned around and headed for the grocer's shop. Rusty and Angela were always training, and must be doing so now more than ever: Angie must be there.

Holly ran so fast she was panting, and if the pants sounded a little more like sobs as she went, she told herself that it didn't matter. The grocery was dim as she walked through it, shelves stocked with shadows. Holly was relieved when she got to the stairs. She ran up the steps, then stopped dead with her hand on the door.

Through the wire-meshed glass, Holly could see Rusty and Angela sparring on the mats, fluorescent lights giving the turquoise room the appearance of an aquarium in the night. Rusty had his back to her, though she could hear the rumble of his voice. He must have been saying something funny, because Angie was smiling.

Angie was wearing a ponytail, the shining-straight length of black hair spilling over her shoulder. Her mouth was gleaming, her teeth a glint behind the glossed curve of her lips, made up even when she was wearing sweatpants and a tank top. She always looked like a girl in a movie. She made the world act like she was in a movie, everything else going out of focus as the camera slid from the dark fall of her lashes against her cheek to the pale slim line of her neck and the shadowy dip of her collarbone, the soft swell and gentle curve inward of her body under the stretched white cotton.

Except there wasn't a camera, and this wasn't a movie. It was just that Holly was looking.

Holly sat down on the top step and put her head in her hands.

She wasn't sure how long it had been when she heard the creak of the door opening and felt her body tense and then relax as Rusty said, "Holly? What's going on?"

He sat down on the step beside her, big shoulder jostling her as he settled, and Holly looked up at him. Her lashes were sticking together with tears, and in her spangled blurry vision she saw the angled lines of his cheekbones and the sometimes-curling, sometimes-tender line of his mouth. He was like Angie, but he was a guy; a ton of girls in school had a crush on Rusty Montgomery. It would be perfectly all right.

And maybe because of that, and maybe because she was frightened, Holly lunged forward and grabbed Rusty's face in her hands, bringing his lips to hers.

Rusty almost started out of his skin. He grabbed her shoulder and held her back. "Whoa," he said. "Steady there. What are you doing?"

Holly's shuddering breaths turned to real sobs. She couldn't look at him: she buried her face in her hands again.

"Hey now," Rusty said, and patted her on the back in a

slow rhythm. "Easy. No need to get so upset. It's only natural to crave a taste of my sweet, sweet love. You are by no means the first."

Holly hiccuped out a laugh between sobs and between her fingers, and Rusty laughed with her, steady and calm, like the hand patting her back.

"And I am always flattered," Rusty continued, "but I love my sister. Not in an 'I love my sister and I want to make out with her' way, that would be terrible and disturbing, but in an 'I love my sister, and I'm not going anywhere near the girl she likes' way. Be a big mess. Life is hard for me, with all my irresistible sexual magnetism. It's a real problem, almost as bad as the fact that my steps are now the number one crying spot in Sorry-in-the-Vale. I have to maintain control of the situation at all times or my life would devolve into a nonstop romantical frenzy."

Holly tried to swallow her hiccups down. It was ridiculous, how Rusty could sit there at perfect ease, completely aware of how Angela was and not even seeming to mind. Her family would have minded a lot.

"You don't understand," she said.

"You think I underestimate the effect of my appeal on the general populace?" Rusty nodded thoughtfully. "Could be."

"Some people are that way," Holly burst out. "And it's okay. It's okay, if that's how you're born. I know that. But what if you weren't born that way, what if you were just some sort of freak, if you'd been with a ton of guys and you still liked guys and then if you were . . . if you started noticing, what does that even make you? What kind of person can't just choose to be one way or the other?"

"Uh, bisexual people might be the kind of person you're thinking of?" Rusty suggested. "I've also heard it called 'sitting on the fence and admiring the view on both sides.' Holly. Being able to love more than one kind of person, in any kind of way—that doesn't mean there's something wrong with you. There's nothing wrong with you. Well, you are pretty hair-trigger with the whole kissing thing; you should learn to check that kissing is cool in the future. I was fine, obviously, but others have nervous dispositions and might well be taken aback."

He kept talking, rubbing soothing circles on Holly's back, as if what she had said was no big deal at all. He was such a weird guy, so casual about everything: maybe nothing she could say would upset him.

"You don't understand," Holly said, and began crying harder. "I *can't*."

Rusty fell silent. After a moment, he got up and Holly heard the creak of the door opening and closing again.

Holly was not surprised when someone else settled on the step beside her. Angela was careful not to lean against her, but every molecule of Holly's body was aware of Angie's.

"Holly," Angela said, her voice low. "What's wrong?"

Holly looked up again and saw Angie's face this time, not anyone else's, just Angie with her dark intent eyes, looking at Holly as nobody else in the world did, as if she took her seriously.

"You can't tell anyone," she whispered, leaning in closer.

Angela blinked, mouth tipping at one side as if she might be about to make a joke about pinky swears. She nodded instead.

Holly looked at the hands she'd been cradling her head in, her damp cupped palms. There were teardrops glistening on her fingers.

Each of the teardrops burst silently into a point of light, lucent and shocking. Fireworks, contained in the curve of Holly's hand. They were beautiful, but Holly didn't even know who she was anymore.

"I'm a sorcerer," she said, very quietly, as though if she said it in a lower voice, it would be less true. As though it might not change her life.

Angie slid an arm around Holly's shoulders gradually, making sure Holly was all right with it. Holly leaned back in the circle of Angela's arm and closed her eyes.

Chapter Sixteen
A Preference for Breathing

There was a small mirror hanging on the stone wall of the little inn room. Kami looked into it because she had to look at something else when Jared was doing up his jeans. Her face in the glass looked young and small, as if she didn't have a clue about the world, as if life was never going to stop surprising and hurting her.

"Well," she said, smoothing the jacket over her arm and then laying it on the tangled sheets. "Now I've returned this, I'd better get going." She was reluctant to let go of the jacket, her fingers lingering stupidly on its scarred brown surface. "Sorry again." She let go of the jacket and stepped away from the bed.

"Kami," Jared said as he lunged between her and the door.

Kami was forced to look at him. She had to tip her head back because otherwise she was eye level with his collarbone: his shirt was still all undone, crumpled white cotton against an expanse of pale-gold-tanned skin, a thin chain glittering at his neck.

He'd kept wearing the coin she had sent him. By now Kami supposed it was habit. Possibly Holly had grabbed it, the way she had obviously been grabbing at his hair.

"You're in my way," Kami said, keeping her voice level. "I suggest you get out of it."

"I want to tell you something," Jared said.

Kami had absolutely no right to mind what Jared and Holly did, and she was perfectly prepared to listen to what Jared had to say. But was this the time or the place, Kami thought, for a heart-to-heart?

Was this the outfit? She had seen Jared in nothing but his underwear before, but that had been in the darkness of a closed swimming pool. This was an actual room, an actual bedroom with actual lights on. He seemed a lot more naked now, with his shirt pulled open and the blurred touch of Holly's candy pink lipstick on his jaw.

"Kami," Jared repeated. His voice scraped on her name: it sounded like it hurt him to say, but maybe it just hurt to hear. He reached out a hand, fingers curved as if he was going to cup her face. He never touched her, and she couldn't let him start now. Kami took a step back, even though that meant being a step closer to the bed Jared and Holly had obviously been rolling around and around in.

Jared surveyed the place as if he was startled by his own room, the mess of the bed, his reflection in the mirror, and then looked back at Kami. "I didn't mean it," he said.

"You didn't mean what?" Kami asked. She was furious with him: this wasn't the kind of thing you did accidentally.

"What I said to you in the library at Aurimere," Jared said. "After you broke the link."

So he wasn't talking about something that had happened moments ago in this room. He was talking about something that had happened weeks ago.

"You wanted to break the link," Jared said.

"Rob would have killed me if I hadn't broken it!"

Jared bowed his head. "I know. I just meant that even before Rob, you didn't want for me to be dependent on you like that. I was furious with you for breaking the link, for wanting to. I didn't think that you would believe me or care, but it was still stupid of me, and wrong. I'm sorry."

"That's why you said it?" Kami asked.

"I told myself it was best to make a clean break. I didn't want to hang around and have you taking pity on me. I thought it would be best for you. And I was angry with you and I wanted to hurt you. I didn't think I could hurt you, but I tried. I know it was terrible of me to feel that way, wanting to hurt you and wanting the absolute best for you, at any cost, all at the same time. I know that it makes no sense."

It made less sense than anything Kami had ever heard in her life. Everything Jared was saying, about what she had said about the link, it was true but not the whole truth. And why would she take pity on him?

He had told her, in the dark cold heart of Aurimere, that she was nothing special. She had been at her most lost and lonely, and she had carried around with her the lingering fear that it might be true.

He knew her better than anyone.

Now he said it wasn't true. It was like a weight had been taken off her, a stone that had been pressing against her chest so long, she had almost become used to it.

"I don't think you're weak," Jared said. "I want to guard you because you are important to me. Because you are—

God, this is going to sound so stupid, I can never think of a way to say it—you are precious. I can never think of how to describe the value you have to me, because all the words for value suggest that you belong to me, and you don't."

"All right," Kami answered at last. "Thank you for telling me."

He looked up when she spoke and kept looking, eyes fastened on her. She felt his gaze like a pull on her, as if he expected some response. She wanted to say she forgave him, but she couldn't prioritize his feelings over hers, not when he was the one who had lashed out.

"Now you know you can hurt me," she said. "So don't." She waited for him to nod and added quietly, "You're important to me too. I want to be friends again."

"Then that's what I want too," he said.

She had come intending to tell him of the discovery she had made, and to talk to him about the kiss. She could still tell him about the discovery. But she wanted out of this room.

"I have something to show you," she said. "But not here. I'm a little uncomfortable being here—not that I mind, of course I don't—"

Jared repeated after her, his voice flat, "Of course."

"Can I just go?"

"Of course," Jared said again, still standing in front of the door.

"Can I go through the door," Kami asked, "or do I have to execute a super-spy rappelling maneuver and make it out through the window?"

Jared looked torn between a smile and some other expression Kami couldn't read. He didn't move away from in front of the door. "What do you have to show me? Tell me where you'll be and I'll come."

"I was thinking I would be outside the pub," Kami said. She would have settled for the other side of the door. All she wanted was to be out of the room, and he obviously understood the situation so little that he thought they could hang around chatting forever.

Kami moved forward and Jared stepped aside, eyes following her as she went. She reached out for the handle and pulled the door open, and escaped at last.

Outside in the dark street, she lifted her face to the winter-torn sky, the cold wind washing her heated skin, and she told herself that she must be the stupidest person alive.

When Jared came out of the inn, his shirt was buttoned and his jacket was zipped up to the chin, and his face and hair were wet as if he'd run a tap over his head. There were droplets of water running down his brow, and his collar was damp.

"I really am sorry for interrupting," Kami said.

Jared frowned at her. "You didn't interrupt anything." He'd never lied to her when they were linked, but she supposed he was embarrassed.

"So I performed a little experiment," Kami said. "Ash had to have Amber's possession to break her spell. Ash and Lillian had to use Rob's and Rosalind's hair to make their spell work on them. I figured that this spell twisting our voices might not work on a sorcerer. I hypothesized, if you will, that a sorcerer might be able to hear us."

Kami took her phone out of her pocket with a flourish and said, "Look what I can do." She rang a London number and waited a few moments before a voice came on the line.

"Hi, Henry Thornton speaking."

"Hi there," Kami said. "This is Kami Glass? You remember me from when we visited you in London and couldn't help but notice you were a sorcerer. You pulled a gun on my friend and I hit you with a chair."

"Don't call me, Kami." There was the sound of a quick indrawn breath and then the beep of a dial tone.

Kami looked triumphantly up at Jared. "The magic doesn't work on other sorcerers! Henry can hear us."

"Henry, our new best friend," Jared said, circling around her in the nighttime street. "I hope he can put this whole trying-to-shoot-me thing behind us. He doesn't seem that keen to help out."

Kami grinned at him. "Because I have not yet worked my persuasive mojo on him."

"I didn't realize it was a matter of mojo."

"I want to be a journalist," Kami said. "That means I have to coax my sources into trusting me and spilling all their secrets. It's a very subtle, yet effective, process."

Jared tilted his head, a streetlight combing his hair with gold. "I'm looking forward to it."

Kami redialed Henry's number. This time Henry answered after one ring.

"Don't call again. I am not interested in anything you have to say."

"We hate Rob Lynburn too," Kami said quickly. "He tried to kill my best friend. She beat him half to death with a chain. And he's trying to take over our town."

"Isn't that what the town was made for, though?" Henry asked. "Maybe you should all get out of there and leave them to it."

Isn't that what the town was made for?

Sorry-in-the-Vale, where she had been born, where she had run through sun-bright streets every summer. Made to be ruled, made to thrive on blood. "You expect us to run away and abandon our home? You didn't close the door and hide behind it when we came to see you and you thought Rob had sent us," Kami said. "You got a weapon and you came out and faced us. You were ready to fight."

Henry was silent for a moment longer, then said in a low voice, "People shouldn't use sorcery like he does."

"We need you to fight again," Kami said. "Rob is going to sacrifice someone on the winter solstice, and there aren't enough sorcerers to stand against him. We need help."

"I can't exactly call the police," Henry told her.

"Officer, I have a serious magical emergency," Kami said. She was pleased by Henry's quiet laugh. "No. Surely there are other sorcerers you could talk to? People who wouldn't agree with what Rob Lynburn is doing?"

"I don't know that many other sorcerers."

"But you know some."

"Sorry-in-the-Vale," Henry said, and hesitated. "People talk about it like it's a law unto itself. The other sorcerers might want to keep away from it, like they always have."

"But if you talked to them," Kami said. "Lillian Lynburn doesn't want this any more than you or I do. If you could make them understand that there are sorcerers here who don't want to go back to the old ways or the old laws, do you think they might help?"

"I could try," Henry said at last. "We're not a community like the Vale sorcerers, but there are a few of us who try to keep in touch. I can ask."

"Thank you," Kami told him. She hoped he could hear how much she meant it.

"Good luck, Kami," Henry told her. "I really will try."

Kami said to the dial tone, "That's all I ask." She slipped her phone into her pocket and looked up at Jared. "Well?"

He was just looking at her; she couldn't quite read his expression. "'My best friend beat Rob Lynburn half to death with a chain'?" Jared asked. "I thought you said you were going for subtle."

Kami opened her mouth and closed it, so overcome with indignation that she could not speak.

"But you really pulled off effective," Jared added with a grin.

Kami remembered how the feeling that provoked that grin had felt, his amusement rippling through her. She could not help smiling back. "Less of your sass, Lynburn. Nobody likes a tavern wench who gives them backchat. It'll be hell on your tips."

"My tips are extremely good," Jared noted. "Mrs. Jeffries from the post office seems to like how I wear a pair of jeans. Or possibly she's waiting to like how I wear Perfectly Luscious Plum Lip Gloss."

"I think you should try it. I bet it would suit you." Kami hesitated. She'd told Jared about Henry, and interrupted him with Holly. She couldn't think of any other reason to stay.

"Come back inside," Jared said. "It's freezing out here. And as the resident tavern wench, I can score you a hot toddy." He held open the door for her.

"Yeah," Kami said, and smiled up at him. "All right."

"I will, however, be expecting a tip."

"Why is it always saucy o'clock for tavern wenches, that is what I want to know," Kami said, passing into the bright warmth of the bar. Then she stopped so abruptly that Jared walked into her. He jerked back as soon as they touched.

Kami barely even registered it.

Sharing a bench in the Water Rising, leaning into each other whispering and flirting, were Rusty and Amber Green. Rusty, and one of Rob Lynburn's sorcerers.

Chapter Seventeen
The Montgomery Secret

Kami did not know how to tell Angela about her brother's decision to date evil.

The next day, *The Nosy Parker* came out, with the article Kami had written to explain sorcery to her brothers in it. The article did not specifically mention magic, or Rob Lynburn's demands. It talked about Sorry-in-the-Vale being under threat, the temptation to do nothing, and the absolute necessity of standing against evil.

Kami left the table in the front hall of the school stacked high with newspapers, and when she came back with Angela before her first class, the table was bare.

"You realize this means you have to photocopy some more in your free class," Kami instructed Angela sternly.

"I like to think of it as my nap class," Angela said. "I'm a very advanced student, but I've got to keep in training."

"We have to spread the message of rebellion."

"I don't know how you expect me to fight evil while insufficiently rested," Angela complained.

They were walking down the hall together. Angela was swinging her messenger bag and there was a multicolored scarf flying blazing colors from her neck. She seemed, insofar as one could tell with Angela, happy.

Angela changed the direction of her sphinxlike smile suddenly, and Kami glanced around to see Holly approaching in a cloud of bright curls and fuzzy pink jumper.

"Hi, Angie," Holly said, and in a more subdued manner: "Hi, Kami." She fell into step with them, walking on Kami's other side, and said, "I got you some of my parents' things." She pressed a little bag into Kami's hand, like a peace offering.

"Thank you," said Kami.

Her hope that they could leave it at that died when Holly said, "So we should probably talk."

"I have no objection to talking, ever, at any time at all," Kami said. "You most likely know this about me already. But if you're thinking of what I think you're thinking of, we don't really need to talk about it. I mean, it's none of my business. Though I'm sorry about my amazingly awkward timing."

"Don't be sorry," Holly said. "It wasn't anything, I swear. I don't want to have caused any trouble between you guys."

"There's always trouble between us," Kami told her. "But none of it is your fault. We had a talk after you were gone; I think it went okay."

"Oh, good." Holly glanced at Angie and bit her lip. "I wanted to say I was sorry."

"You have nothing to be sorry for," Kami said firmly. "But if you have any free classes today, please photocopy some extra copies of the paper and I promise to love you always and forgive you for any evil you ever do. Some say love cannot be bought, but mine is available at this time for anyone with a good heart and the ability to use a photocopier."

Holly looked uncertain, but Kami kept a stare of laser-like focus on her and she gave in. She dropped the subject, and offered, "I do have a free class after lunch."

"So do I," said Angela, and did not mention napping.

Kami gave her a betrayed look, which Angela deserved for being one of those girls who was willing to go above and beyond in the cause of fancying people and not in the sacred name of friendship. "Also, I have some good news," Kami said, and then saw Amber Green go into the ladies'. "Which I will tell you later! Go on ahead without me!" she finished brightly, and darted after her quarry.

Kami was in luck. There was nobody else in the bathroom. Amber was in front of the mirror applying lip gloss. The little tube clattered into the sink when Kami came in and leaned against the door.

Kami saw her face in the mirror, eyes wide and lips parted. Then her expression shut down, every feature clicking into place and forming a mask.

"Hey, Amber," Kami said. "I want to talk."

Every tap in the bathroom glittered as they all turned at once. A half dozen streams of water were in sudden hissing unison, like a chorus line of snakes. "Well," Amber said, "I don't."

Kami looked at the sinks splashing with water. "Is that meant to intimidate me?"

Over Kami's head, the skylight splintered. She looked up and saw the sudden cracks, reflecting rainbow points, racing to join together and form a spiderweb. Then the skylight imploded, sending shards raining down on her shoulders and hair.

Kami closed her eyes and waited for the glass to stop falling. When she opened them, she saw Amber standing with her back to the sinks, hands behind her back gripping onto the porcelain. Amber was standing in a flood with her shoes getting wet. She didn't seem to notice. She was staring at Kami.

Kami saw her own face in the mirror. There was a cut on her cheek, and the rising red of blood.

"Maybe you killed some animals," Kami said with growing confidence. "But we've known each other since we were born. We sat together in class for five years. You got in trouble for talking during a test once when you loaned me a sharpener."

"I'm *not* your friend," Amber told her sharply. "We were never friends."

"I know that," Kami said. "But you know me. And you're not going to kill me." She took a step forward and Amber's body tensed. The memory of Sergeant Kenn's thorns slicing into her arms came back to her. She could get really hurt if she was guessing wrong. Kami stepped forward again, and Amber's eyes dropped.

"What are you doing with Rob Lynburn?"

"What are you thinking, standing against him?" Amber asked softly. "Don't you realize he can—we can do magic? This town was built for sorcerers to rule. What makes you think you can stand against us? What are you, *stupid*?"

"Is that what you want?" Kami asked. "To rule?"

Amber flushed, color contrasting sharply with the fox fire of her hair. "I'm a sorcerer. I don't want to live in a city, getting sick every autumn because the year is dying and I don't have enough magic to thrive. Sorry-in-the-Vale is where I belong, and it's going to belong to Rob."

"It doesn't have to. What if—"

"What if I said no, and he killed someone I love?" Amber demanded. "Have you even thought about what the cost of standing against him would be?"

"Have you even thought about what the cost of *not* standing against him would be?" Kami asked.

Sorcery had turned the bathroom into its own self-contained pool with the water rising. The broken glass was floating now, so much sharp, glittering debris.

"It's all right for you," Amber said. "Your family were always the Lynburns' pets. What's the plan for you, that you'll just be passed from one Lynburn boy to another as a source? Or are you hoping to become the next Matthew Cooper, and have them both? You'll always have something to protect you. And you're not a sorcerer. Once Rob gets what he wants, once the town is back to the way it used to be, things will be relaxed. The people who want to keep the benefits of Sorry-in-the-Vale will stay, and those who don't will leave. You can go away. But I can't."

Kami thought suddenly of Henry Thornton, skin sickly gray in his London flat, confessing on the phone that he didn't know many sorcerers. Sorry-in-the-Vale offered a sense of community for sorcerers like Amber. It was made for her, in a way. "If you don't want to leave," Kami said, "surely you want this to be a place worth living in?"

"I can live with what Rob wants," Amber said. "It comes with all kinds of advantages for me. There's no guarantee of living on your side. You should think about that. It's less than two weeks until winter solstice, and the other Lynburns are going to lose. There's no guarantee, even for you."

"I'll take my chances. What does Rob Lynburn want with Rusty?"

Amber blinked, then smiled a very careful, cool smile. "Why would you think he wants anything to do with Rusty? He's not magical. Maybe it's *me* who wants something to do with Rusty," she said, a faint touch of slyness in her smile. "He's very good-looking. Perhaps you've noticed that already."

"Jared, Ash, and now Rusty?" Kami asked. "This is a frenzied romantic merry-go-round I'm on in your imagination. I'm kind of flattered. And don't you have a boyfriend?"

Amber had always been that girl, the one who seemed to have been born with a boyfriend. Now that Kami knew Ross and Amber were both sorcerers, the idea that Amber had been born with a boyfriend was disturbingly close to the truth.

Amber shrugged. "Ross and I aren't exclusive. It doesn't matter. He knows how I feel about him. He knows I don't take Rusty seriously."

"You can tell Ross, and anyone else who's interested," Kami said, "that I do. I take Rusty extremely seriously. If anyone has any plans concerning him, if anyone even thinks about hurting my friends, I will—"

"Oh, what will you do?"

Amber's laugh rang out, and Kami saw the pieces of glass actually moving in the water now, like tiny transparent sharks. She was braced, but it was still a shock when it happened: the blast knocked her off her feet. Amber concentrated the cold air from the broken skylight between her palms and aimed it at Kami's chest.

Kami fell backward, lying gasping amid the water and broken glass. Amber's face above her was a haze of red with a pale center. "There's nothing you can do," Amber explained, very softly, and left.

As soon as she could move, Kami got up and retrieved Amber's lip gloss from the sink.

* * *

Kami had already missed her first class by quite a lot, so she figured there was no harm in slinking up to her headquarters. She could sit with her back against the radiator and dry off, and nobody would see her and get upset.

It was a good, solid plan. It was a shame that it immediately collapsed when she opened the door and Jared looked up from his desk. The only thing to do was brazen this out.

"Oi," Kami said. "Did the orders not get passed down to you? Everyone with a free class has to be photocopying the paper. I wish I could get our staff to work more like a well-oiled machine."

Jared said nothing. He just got up from the desk, chair crashing to the floor behind him.

"I see you've spotted that there's something off," Kami observed. "Well, good. I want you all to be honing your observational skills."

He was advancing on her. Kami tried to retreat toward the security of her own desk.

"Uh, but verbal skills are important too," Kami suggested. "So please say something."

"What," Jared demanded, "happened to you?"

"Small contretemps with a sorcerer," Kami admitted. She backed up until she hit her desk, at which point Jared was right there. "Very small," she said, looking up into his still face. "Tiny."

Jared touched her then, the back of his fingers light against her face, just below where she had been cut. "You're bleeding." Then his hand fell away.

"There may have been a limited quantity of broken glass involved."

"Oh God," said Jared, in what appeared to be furious prayer. "Oh God." He moved in closer, as close as he could be without touching her. She leaned against the desk and he bowed his head over her shoulder, turned his face into the curve of her neck. She felt his ragged breath run uneven down the skin at her nape, the brush of his wavy hair against her chin.

"Who was it?" Jared asked. "I'll kill them."

"You are not inspiring me with a desire to give you a name, Captain Murderface of the good ship *Unbalanced*," said Kami. "It was nothing new, just a sorcerer trying to scare me. I can handle myself."

What she'd said to Amber worked in reverse as well. She couldn't imagine hurting someone she'd gone to school with.

Jared seemed to realize she was serious. He took a deep breath, and asked no more questions.

"You can't ask me not to do dangerous stuff," she warned him. His hands were braced on the desk, arms surrounding her but not around her.

"I know that," he said, words falling on her neck like

kisses. "It would be like asking you not to be you. But I'm not with you, and I was always with you before. I keep thinking about something happening to you when I'm not there, when I won't even know about it."

Kami lifted her hand, intending to stroke his hair, but somehow she couldn't quite do it. Her fingers curled, almost touching him. "Sometimes I think about that too," she whispered. She had almost been too late at the Crying Pools.

"I wish," Jared began, and stopped, breathing in. "Do you remember how you used to believe I wasn't real? Sometimes I wish that was true. If I was just a thought in the back of your mind, then I'd be with you, and I'd be better."

In the back of her mind, Kami was aware that what Jared said was irredeemably crazy. But that didn't disturb her like it should have: the only thing that upset her was the thought of how he must feel about himself.

"I'd miss you if you weren't real," she said. "I wouldn't like that. Do you never think about me?"

To her embarrassment, it came out almost like a plea.

Jared moved and the muscles in Kami's stomach jumped as he did so, his breath traveling up the line of her neck, warm and light on the sensitive skin.

He said into her ear, "I think about you all the time."

Maybe, Kami thought, maybe if she turned her face into that whisper, he would kiss her.

Maybe he would if he thought that was what she wanted. But he had been with Holly yesterday, because that was what *he* wanted. She wondered with a sinking feeling if he had kissed her, Kami, in the Water Rising because he'd thought that she wanted him to. If that was why he had done it in the dark. He could need her without wanting her: he could want the link back and nothing more.

Kami did not turn her face toward him. Her fingers stayed hovering over his hair until their breath reached a mutual rhythm but their skin did not touch at any point. "I was thinking about what you said yesterday," Kami said at last. "About me taking pity on you, about making a clean break. And I was thinking—what on earth were you talking about?"

"You told me I was too dependent on you."

"I said *we* were too dependent," Kami said. "I never said *you,* I was never talking about you, I was talking about the link and what I worried it was doing to both of us. That we were all twisted up, like two linked trees that had grown together into weird shapes."

"Too different from other people," Jared said, as if he was agreeing with her but also as if he was aching to go back. Kami caught her breath. "Strange," Jared murmured. "Sick."

"Yes," Kami said, and had to continue quickly because somehow it came out as if she was agreeing to that note of yearning in his voice. "I wanted to know that we could both be independent people. I wanted to know who we would be if the link was cut. But that doesn't mean I wanted you gone. You know how I feel about you." She'd told him, the last thing she had ever said to him, in their own private language, mind to mind: *I love you.*

The thought of how she had said that, how she had come running to the Water Rising last night to find him with Holly, made her insides curdle with humiliation. She didn't want to be that girl, who made a fool of herself over a guy.

They were both so messed up because of the link. What

she felt could be because of the link and because they had lost it. What she knew was that losing him was not a bearable option.

Kami pushed gently at his shoulders, palms against the material of his T-shirt and not his skin, and gave herself the space to slide away and slip behind her desk.

When she allowed herself to look back at him, he was looking at the wall and not at her, the line of his jaw tight. "And what do you think of who I am, now the link is cut?"

"I wish you were happier," Kami said. "But all in all, I think you're okay."

"I'd like to be better," Jared said abruptly. "I'd like to be better, to you. I want to make things better for you."

"That would be nice," said Kami. "However, you could not have faced down the sorcerer with me today."

"Why not?" Jared asked, and looked at her under his lashes. "As long as I was with you, and I hadn't run off to do something suicidal on my own. As long as we were together, wouldn't that be better?"

"Usually yes, today no," Kami told him. "Because it was in a ladies' bathroom, and that would be scandalous."

Jared laughed, and it was on that note that Ash walked in. He looked startled by the sound of Jared's laugh, and a whole lot more startled by the company he had just walked into. "I was just going to get the paper and photocopy it," he said.

"You are a god among men," Kami told him. "And it is excellent to see you, because I have to talk to you."

The necessity to defeat evil trumped social embarrassment. She went around the desk and toward Ash, who was by the door.

"Kami, what happened to you?" he asked.

"That's not important right now," Kami said, waving it off grandly. "What's important is that I was talking to a sorcerer today, and she let something very interesting slip. She mentioned Matthew Cooper. Do you have any records from his time in Aurimere? I remembered he was from sometime in the 1480s; I checked the base of his statue, which says he died in 1485. Elinor Lynburn was the heir in Aurimere then: she was the one who hid the gold bell from the Aurimere bell tower in the Sorrier River, remember?" She glanced back at Jared.

"I remember," Jared said.

"We need to know who the other Lynburns living at the time were," Kami said. "In fact, I want to know everything there is to know about Matthew Cooper."

✳ ✳ ✳

After school, and seven trips to the photocopier to print out more papers, Kami paid a visit to the Montgomerys' house. It was still light outside, the awful glass and steel additions to the white house catching the sun as it sank through the sky. Kami slipped through the gate at the side into the back garden and saw no movement in the windows as she went. She was a little worried that nobody was home.

When she tried the back door, though, it was open, and Rusty was standing in the kitchen with his head in the fridge. He emerged with a packet full of sliced cheese and blinked sleepy hazel eyes in her direction. "Cambridge," he said. "Angela isn't here."

"Excellent news," said Kami. "As I came to see you."

Rusty looked both mildly pleased and mildly alarmed. He

closed the fridge and leaned against the granite top of their kitchen island. "Speak on," he encouraged her. "Cheese?"

"Cheese that comes presliced is like chewy plastic."

"That's true," Rusty said, eating it. "But the alternative is slicing it myself, and that would be a betrayal of my commitment to idleness." He was wearing a crisp brand-new T-shirt, forming a sharp contrast with his dark hair, which was sticking up all over the place. Considering him objectively, Kami had to admit he was adorable.

It really *was* possible that Amber just fancied him, but Kami thought she'd test the waters.

"So, you're dating a sorcerer working for Rob Lynburn," Kami said. "Just thought you should know."

Rusty raised his eyebrows. "Once more a good man is led astray by the undeniable sexiness of evil."

"Rusty!"

"Come on, Cambridge," Rusty said. "You know it's true. There are many examples in film and novels, both the excellent graphic kind and the kind with all the tiring words that you so mysteriously enjoy. You have the valiant hero. And you have the enticing minx trying to lure him to the dark side."

Kami threw her schoolbag on the kitchen island. Rusty gave her a benevolent look and ambled off down the hall to the Montgomerys' freakishly white sitting room. Kami followed, hot on his heels.

Even the scary cubist paintings on the white walls were done in ivory and cream. Kami had to resist the temptation to take off her shoes while Rusty sprawled on the pearl-colored sofa and finished eating his cheese.

"Don't worry," he told her. "Doesn't matter what naughty vixens they send to assault my manly virtue. My strength is as the strength of ten, because my heart is pure."

"Rusty, you idiot," Kami said. "I told you she was an evil sorceress. So you knew all about it and you're not trying to redeem her with your love or anything, are you?"

Rusty held his hand out flat and tipped it gently from side to side. "Eh. Honestly that sounds like a lot of effort."

"Well, what do you think you're doing, then? Spying?"

"I told you, it's the unfortunate hotness of evil. Hotness that burns like the flames of cute, cute hell." Rusty placed his hand on his heart. "But like I said, don't worry. I will overcome temptation, no matter how temptacious."

Kami sat beside him. The material of the sofa was so slippery she thought she might slide right off. "Rusty, this is serious. We're a team: we have to tell each other information like this. We have to trust each other. And 'temptacious' is not a word."

"Okay," said Rusty. "Let me handle this. Trust me, Kami."

Kami glanced over at him in surprise. He rarely used her real name.

He even more rarely looked both serious and alert, but he looked both now, leaning against the cushions and tilted in her direction, his dark hair ruffled against the pale silk cover of the couch. "I know what other people think about me," Rusty told her. " 'That Rusty,' they say. 'Charming and handsome,' they say first, of course—they're not blind. Then they add, 'All the ambition and drive of a chocolate sundae.' "

"Rusty, no," Kami said.

Rusty put out a hand, palm raised, to stop her. "They're

right. That's what I am. Why not? Most things come easy to me, most things come lightly. That's what I come from and how I was made. Russell Montgomery the Third," he added, and grinned at her. "I was exactly the son my parents wanted: no trouble, no demands. Why demand anything when it was all going to come to me anyway? I had this nursery suite in London, it was pretty great. I miss the scheduled naptimes to this day. And then one day I heard this noise through all the doors, this baby screaming her fool head off, and it was Angela."

Rusty used the hand he'd lifted to stop Kami from speaking and made a small gesture; Kami wasn't sure what it meant.

"I had been introduced to Angela before, obviously. They brought the baby to me from the hospital, and there was a christening where she wore this big lace meringue dress and looked alarmingly like a two-month-old bride. We were somewhat acquainted, but honestly I was more interested in my toy trucks and my naptime beanbag. Only she just kept yelling, and it was interesting because I thought it was so dumb. I knew she didn't want anything, because that wasn't how we were brought up—the nanny would have made sure she had all she wanted, though she wasn't paid to fuss. I didn't really get why Angela was doing it, so I went through doors and up stairs until I found her. She was just lying in her crib, because babies are unimaginative like that. And I know people think Angela is pretty now, but none of those people ever saw her as a baby. She was god-awfully hideous. I swear she looked like a bad-tempered mutant tomato, and she was making a sound like a cat being fed into a printer.

"I just couldn't figure it out, you know? Why she was so angry, when everything was fine. I sort of wanted to go away and pretend it wasn't happening. But she was unhappy, I could tell that much. She wasn't ever going to be like me, a content sort of person. She was always going to be raging at the world, and there was only me who would even think about paying attention. So I picked her up and took her back to my rooms and showed her the naptime beanbag, and it was me and Angela from then on. And then Mum and Dad decided to set us up in a house surrounded by all this peaceful pastoral evil, and there was you. You care about a lot of stuff like Angela does, and you don't even have the basic common decency to pretend you don't. Only you aren't angry about how much you care, because you always had someone around to give you all the dumb stuff babies cry for, and your house was— I want to be like that someday, be someone like your dad who can help make something like your house. When I went away to college, it was all fine, everything's always fine for me, but nothing was important. So I sort of slid out, bringing Claud with me, which was a mistake, but I didn't know you were going to have the bad taste to date one of my friends. I would never have invited him to stay if I'd known he was going to grow that goatee. It had a whole other personality. Tiny Even More Self-Important Claud."

"Is there a point to this meander down embarrassing memory lane?" Kami asked.

"Actually," Rusty said, "yes. I was worried about you, when it came to Claud. I'm worried about Angela with this whole business with Holly. I'm worried about you again, with the voice in your head turning out to be this surly guy. I actually wanted to punch someone. I never actually want to punch people.

"So my point is, things aren't easy, with Angela and you. I don't take you two lightly. This is the great exception of my life. I don't want you to interfere on this. I want you to trust me to deal with Amber: she needs someone to talk to, and I think that might come in handy. I also think that she is not going to talk to someone who actually called their newspaper *The Nosy Parker*."

Looking around at the Montgomerys' sitting room, Kami could picture the showcase loneliness of the Montgomerys' nursery. Rusty could not have been more than four when he carried Angela back to his room, recognizing despite the fact that nobody had given it to him that what Angela needed was love. "My newspaper's name is awesome, and that was a very touching speech, Rusty," she told him. "But actually, you haven't been as convincingly louche and laissez-faire as you appear to believe. I knew all this already. On any day of our lives, I would have trusted you with my life. And I'll trust you now." She sat up straight despite the slippery sofa, and looked him directly in the eye, so he would know she meant it.

But the sleepy look of boundless good humor was already restored to Rusty's face, and his hooded lids were hiding whatever expression was in his eyes. "Don't pretend, Cambridge," he said. "You know my beautiful speech has made you see me in a whole new and even more attractive light. You totally think I'm secretly deep now. And you are right. It is true. I have deeps." He slid even lower on the sofa, his eyes falling almost completely closed. "Maybe," he added, his voice almost too casual, "this revelation will lead you to make the sensible decision, and go for me."

"And wouldn't that be a magical thirty-six hours," Kami said. "Before you died of exhaustion."

Rusty did something unspeakable with his eyebrows. "Why, Cambridge, I am *scandalized*!"

"Shut up!" Kami told him. "You know what I meant. Shut up your entire face."

He was still laughing when she left on a mission to find out about Sorry-in-the-Vale in the 1480s. Matthew Cooper's secrets might have lasted six hundred years, but they could not last a moment longer. The winter solstice was only weeks away.

Chapter Eighteen
What I've Tasted of Desire

Kami had never liked Aurimere. There was something about the way she had been insulted and assaulted there a bunch of times that had really put her off. But she *was* growing a little fond of the records room. There was the table full of hidden sorcerous accounts, the wall of gold-clouded windows, and the fact that Ash always came in to keep her company. They had spent the better part of a fortnight in here now, searching for any sign of Matthew Cooper.

The first day she came to the records room after she and Ash had cleared up what happened in the Water Rising had been ferociously awkward. But Kami had persevered, and Ash was lonely enough that he responded to any gesture. Kami thought that was why he had decided to like her in the first place. It was embarrassing and a bit sad to reflect upon how little actual allure Kami had when it came to guys. That Kami Glass, people must say as she went by. About as sexy as a teapot.

Her first piece of luck came when she flipped open a book with the unpromising title *Illustrious Personages of Gloucester-shire* and discovered that the Lynburns considered themselves so illustrious they had inscribed a family tree on the flyleaf.

This one was the oldest of the family trees she had seen. It started with the names of James Lynburn, born 1440, and his wife, Annis, also born a Lynburn. They had had two daughters. One was Elinor Lynburn.

"Hold on to everything," Kami said.

Ash looked up warily from his books.

"I have Elinor Lynburn," she said, tapping the brown writing sprawled on the yellow paper. "She had a sister called Anne. And hold on to everything even harder, because in 1484 Anne Lynburn married Matthew Cooper. And in 1485, Anne Lynburn and Matthew Cooper both *died*."

"So Matthew was a sorcerer?" Ash closed his own book and leaned forward. "He must have been, to marry a Lynburn. We only ever, ever marry sorcerers. And they both died in the battle when Henry VII's soldiers came to Sorry-in-the-Vale."

"But that's just it," Kami said. "I've been researching, and there's no evidence Henry VII's soldiers ever did come to Sorry-in-the-Vale. Nothing confiscated, no lands burned, no record of other deaths. Just that Elinor Lynburn put the bells in the river, that Matthew Cooper died and had a statue erected to him for his courage, and now we know that Anne Lynburn died as well. Nothing but those two deaths, and the lingering story that the Lynburns did something to save the town. It's a mystery, Ash. And I can't help but think it's a clue as well: a clue to how we can protect the town again."

Ash frowned. "They must have done something."

"Must have," Kami said. "And it must have been something big. What did Elinor and Anne Lynburn do, and how was it different from anything any Lynburn has done before or since? How was Matthew involved?"

Ash nodded slowly, conceding her point.

"The Glass family was given our house because we were Matthew's relatives," Kami said. "There haven't been any records to suggest any of my ancestors were sorcerers. Instead, there's been a long history of the Glass family being some sort of special servants to the Lynburns." She wrinkled her nose to express her feelings on that subject.

"The house was a return for special loyalty," Ash said.

"It's not like the Lynburns didn't expect loyalty and service from everyone," Kami said. "Why give us a house, why keep us especially under the eye of Aurimere? You can watch my house from the Aurimere bell tower, for God's sake. They had a reason to do it. I don't think Matthew Cooper was just any sorcerer. I don't think he was a sorcerer at all."

Ash looked thunderstruck. "What could he have done for the town if he wasn't?"

Kami asked, "What am I? Think. Anne Lynburn was a lady of the manor, she wouldn't have been fighting even if there had been fighting, but she and Matthew died at the same time."

Light dawned on Ash. He said quietly, "A sorcerer dies with their source."

"A sorcerer and a source can accomplish great things. Anne and Matthew did. They saved Sorry-in-the-Vale. But they died for it, and the Lynburns decided that sorcerers should stop using sources. They kept the Glass family close because they knew we had the *potential* to become sources, *and they didn't want us to.* Maybe they kept us close because they thought that the time might come when the town would be in enough danger that a Lynburn would have to take a source again."

They both startled when Lillian's voice rang out: "And are you saying that time has come?"

Kami closed her book and smoothed a hand protectively down the cracked calfskin cover. "I'm trying to find out what the past has to teach us."

Lillian was wearing a tan jacket, and her hair was swept up. She was obviously on her way out on another trip to the woods with her new sorcerers.

None of Kami's group was invited on these trips, not even Jared and Ash.

Lillian hesitated for a fraction of a second, but with her it was unusual enough to be notable. "Don't fill my son's head with any wild ideas."

"I can think for myself, thanks," Ash said.

Lillian shot him a disapproving look. "I have seen no evidence of that so far," she observed, and swept out.

Ash and Kami exchanged looks, Ash apologetic and Kami rolling her eyes.

"Amber Green said to me that Matthew Cooper . . ." Kami hesitated, thinking of what Amber had actually said: *Are you hoping to have them both?* "She gave me the clue by talking about sources, and Matthew Cooper having them both. I didn't know what she meant at the time, but—could she have meant two sorcerers to a source? Is that possible?"

"No," said Ash. "I've never heard of such a thing, and how would Amber know something I don't? Look at the evidence. If Matthew had been Elinor's source as well, she would have died too. No, I bet Amber was referring to some ancient unsavory piece of gossip about the sisters sharing. What a family," Ash said, and Kami knew he was thinking of his father and Jared's mother, living together in Monkshood. "I used to be proud of them," he added. "I used to think I could never live up to them."

"Now you get to do whatever you want," Kami commented. She opened her book again, but she did not miss Ash's look, which was intrigued.

The windows by the table only opened onto the Lynburn gardens, undergrowth and tree branches turned into silver snakes by winter, so Kami moved along to the arrow-slit window by the door. She saw bits and pieces, not quite cohering. Sorry-in-the-Vale's ice-touched roofs, the dark spikes of the wood, the black spot on the landscape that was Hallow's Field. The snow would not settle there, as if the ground was still burning. Lillian's fair head, traveling down the road from Aurimere.

Kami paused for a moment and hoped, so fiercely it was like a prayer, that no matter how annoying Lillian might be, she was right, and that she could handle this.

Then, because Lillian might be wrong, Kami returned to her research.

* * *

That evening Kami detoured on her way back home to walk up the High Street and visit the statue of Matthew Cooper. She stood in the street at the foot of the pedestal and really looked at him. The statue had been there all her life, about as remarkable as one of the cobblestones, until now. It was so very old, the name and the dates blurred like the old grave-stones in the little graveyard by the church.

She traced the dates now with her finger, the stone hard yet almost crumbly under her fingertips, like fossilized bread. As she knew the date of his death for certain, 1485, she could make out the date of his birth: 1466. He had been nineteen when he died.

If Matthew had been a source, he must have chosen it as he had chosen his wife—as they had chosen each other.

How could anyone be linked like that and betray each other? Kami could not imagine that what Amber had implied was true.

She stood looking up into the statue's almost-lost face and wondered if he had loved her, his magical wife from the house high above the town. Had he not been able to help loving her because of the link, and was that really love? How had it been, when she changed from being a magical other-worldly stranger to being the very center of his heart? Kami had only experienced it the other way around, from having to losing.

How did stopping loving someone even work? It hap-pened to other people, Kami knew, and thought of her par-ents. Her mother was spending so much time out of the house with the sorcerers that Kami had barely seen and hardly spo-ken to her. Her father was still sleeping in his office.

Maybe Matthew had never found out what it was like to stop loving someone any more than Kami had.

Maybe love lasted forever if you died young.

Kami's morbid train of thought was derailed by seeing Lillian Lynburn walking down the street with a stranger who could only be another sorcerer. He was a tall thin man, dressed all in gray. Kami ducked behind the statue of Matthew Cooper, and concealed by his shadow she watched where Lillian and the man went, seeing them part and him turn up Shadowchurch Lane.

He went up to the Kenns' house, and she saw him stop and take a key out of his pocket.

So he's living there, Kami thought, *and not at Monkshood.* Kami remembered Amber Green, and wondered exactly how many sorcerers on Rob Lynburn's side were not really comfortable being around him. She also wondered what Lillian was doing in the company of someone who was obviously one of Rob's sorcerers.

Lillian looked from left to right, hesitating in the shadow of the church, and then ran, her footsteps hurried and faltering, under the horseshoe shape of the stone entrance to the church grounds. Kami noticed the way she ran, and that her red lipstick was ever so slightly blurred, a tendril of her pinned-up hair coming loose around her ear.

Someone else opened the door of the church, and though the vestibule of the church was dark, Kami saw a glint of black and red tiles, and blond hair. The two golden-haired women drew closer in that shadowy space, with their bright heads bowed and their hands clasping.

The woman waiting in the church was the real Lillian Lynburn, and the woman coming to her was Rosalind, dressed up to look like her sister, Kami realized. Kami was certain Lillian had not mentioned being in contact with Rosalind to anyone.

"You don't understand why you have to give in," she

heard Rosalind say, softly. "You don't know what he's really planning."

"Hush," said Lillian, who was predictably awful at whispering. "You don't know who's listening."

Kami's plan had been to stand hidden and eavesdrop at the church gate, but the sound and sight of the sisters was shut away as the door closed. Kami moved forward, and then she stood in the graveyard and stared transfixed, forgetting all about sorcerers and their secrets.

The wide white stone with the kanji inscribed on it always caught Kami's eye. Now she noticed it even more than usual, because she saw a man in jeans and a black sweater in front of it. He had one arm propped up against the stone, and with his free hand he was hitting the top.

The graveyard in Sorry-in-the-Vale was as small as the church. Not a lot of people were buried there nowadays, but Dad had insisted that Sobo be buried close to where they lived, close enough so Kami and her brothers would see where she rested every day and sometimes say "Hello, obaasan" under their breath as they passed. "Born Shinto, marry Christian, die Buddhist," Sobo used to say when she refused to go to church at Easter. They hadn't had a Buddhist funeral, but Dad had seen to it that Sobo was cremated. They had put her name in kanji on the gravestone because even though they wanted her there, close, like she'd always been, they had not wanted her to seem like just anyone. Of course, the man at Sobo's grave was her father. But he wasn't standing or moving like Dad, and his voice was different.

He was speaking in a furious torrent of Japanese. He and Sobo had occasionally broken out in Japanese to each other when she was alive, and Kami had heard Dad whisper a few sentences of it now and then when they visited the grave together. It had been their private language: Mum and Dad had been young and frantic when Kami was born, too busy to know how to raise her bilingual without excluding Mum in her own home, and nobody had wanted Tomo and Ten to have advantages Kami didn't.

Only Dad spoke it now. Kami knew a few words, but not enough to make out this torrent of furious pain. She found herself trembling as she watched him: he sounded like a scared kid having a tantrum because he could not get his mother's attention.

Kami put her arms around herself and felt her body shaking. Dad hunched over the gravestone and Kami lifted her hand to her mouth, physically silenced herself, as she listened to the raw sound of her father sobbing.

He'd tried so hard not to let them see this. Kami wanted to go to him, but she was scared of him. She didn't want him to be like this, unknowable and terrifying.

Kami did not really realize she was retreating until her hand was on the gate of the churchyard. Then she lifted the latch and saw something that she had never noticed before: the iron was shaped like a small hand, and to close the latch you dropped it into another little hand fixed into the wall.

Kami closed the gate behind her, the two metal hands meeting again, and started down the lane, around the corner. Then she was running up the High Street until she reached the black door of the Water Rising.

She pushed open the door. Inside the pub it was dim and cool. Jared was pushing a pint across the bar to old Mr.

Stearn, whose grizzled bull terrier was sitting patiently by his stool, head drooping in much the same attitude as his owner's.

Jared looked up from the bar and caught sight of her. His whole face used to change when he saw her, as distinctly as the difference between a landscape with light on it and one in shadow. But not now.

"Martha, I'm taking a break," he said.

Martha, sitting at the other side of the bar reading a book, just nodded. Kami recognized the look she bent on Jared, and noted that in the time Jared had been here, somehow the Wrights had moved from fear to tolerant affection for the crazy.

He did that somehow, Kami thought disconsolately, moved in and before you knew it you had moved from a place of "Dear God, I do not even know what is happening" to not wanting it to stop.

She looked around at Martha, and Mr. Stearn and his bull terrier, who fixed her with identical bleary stares. She wanted to scream because her father was breaking his heart in the churchyard.

But that was the thing Sorry-in-the-Vale was founded on: people would let tragedies rain down all around them, and continue with their own lives, refusing to notice.

Kami could not help wondering what most of the people in Sorry-in-the-Vale thought of sorcerers. They must seem absolutely fearsome, their powers unimaginable, like gods. They must seem like a threat that simply could not be faced. It almost made sense that everyone wanted to leave the war among the sorcerers to the sorcerers, and that they were all trying so desperately to pretend they could go on with their ordinary lives.

Nobody seemed to have noticed that Kami was upset, which made her think that perhaps she did not look as if she was falling entirely to pieces. That was good. She had to keep it together, keep everything under control. She stood with her hands in her jeans pockets so nobody would see them shaking, and Jared snagged his jacket from a hook by the door, reached in her direction, and hesitated: she thought he'd been going for her hand, but he tugged at her belt loop instead. Then he looked down at her, their eyes catching. Dismay passed over his face as he obviously realized that the belt-loop thing was perhaps not the casual move he had planned.

"Let's go for a walk," he said, and stepped away to hold open the door for her.

Kami went out into the street. She did not head back down toward the shops of the High Street, but up to where the street tapered into fields and the occasional residential house, gardens billowing out about them like women curtsying in green gowns. There was ice on the ground, lining the wood fences with white, silvering the grass and casting a pale shimmer over everything in sight. It wasn't quite evening yet, the sky the dark solid blue of a dying afternoon, but it was cold.

Kami walked alongside Jared, hands still in her pockets, staring at the ice-touched gold of the pavement. Her throat was aching. It had been dumb to run to him. Jared cleared his own throat, and she looked up to see him watching her.

"Something's wrong," he said at last. "You have to tell me what it is. I can't read your mind anymore."

Kami tried to laugh. It came out a little uneven. "I would have thought that was the upside to not being linked. You don't have to hurt when I do anymore." Kami crossed her arms under her breasts, trying to create some defense against the chill wind.

"I still do," Jared said, his voice low. "I just don't know why."

"I don't know how to talk about stuff like this. I want people to think I can handle myself," Kami told him. "I don't mind anyone thinking I'm crazy, I never did. I just don't want people to think I'm helpless. I want to be the one with the answers."

"Oh, is that all?"

Kami stared, and caught the wry twist of Jared's smile.

"I just wish I had the questions," he said. "I've never felt any need to talk to someone about things that counted, to find out what was wrong. You were the only one who ever mattered, and I always knew."

"And now?"

He stopped walking, turned, and faced her. "You're still the only one who matters. And I have to learn how to ask you. So here it is: I don't care if you don't have the answers. I only want you to talk to me."

Kami looked up at him and he backed up a step. She was angry for a moment, before she saw that he was holding out his hand to her.

She reached out, and when she laid her hand in his she saw him make a visible effort to control the start away from her. He closed his fingers over hers, and helped her up the couple of steps until she was perched on a stile. Jared sat on one of the steps and looked up at her. There was another of those hesitations he always betrayed, then he leaned back deliberately, shoulder pressed against her knees. She felt a little shiver run through both of them.

Talk to me, he'd said. Kami took a deep breath.

"My father found out about the magic," she said. "He found out about my mother lying to him, about all the lies she ever told, and he's so angry with her. I don't know if he's going to forgive her. And if he doesn't—God, it feels ridiculous to say this when an evil sorcerer wants the town to choose a sacrifice in two weeks. People's parents split up all the time. But I feel like if he doesn't forgive her, the world is going to end."

"I'm sure he'll forgive her," Jared said.

"He said that she had told so many lies he didn't know how to begin trusting her again." The words hung trembling in the cold air. Kami wished that she could come up with a reason that Dad was sure to forgive Mum. She had been able to forgive Mum for every lie she had told, but every kid knew their parents lied to them a little, trying to protect them from the truth of the world. Dad and Mum were meant to be equals. Kami was just starting to discover how terrible the thought of being lied to was: Jared had only been able to lie to her for a couple of months.

"He'll find a way," Jared said. "There's always a way. If he loves her, then he'll do anything to stay with her."

"What if he doesn't love her anymore?" Kami whispered. Once she had gotten that out, she was able to tell Jared everything else—what they had said to each other, how scared Tomo and Ten had been, seeing her father in the graveyard today—detailing every crack in her breaking world.

Jared listened, his eyes fixed on her face. "It might be a good sign, that he's so angry," Jared said eventually. "Not—if he was lashing out because of that," he said carefully. Kami's grip on his hand tightened. "Just because he's angry doesn't mean he's stopped loving her."

He hesitated, then added, "The day after you broke the link, I smashed all the mirrors in my rooms at Aurimere. Bedroom, bathroom. One in the hall." He glanced away from her, as if a little embarrassed, and then immediately back. "I didn't say that to make you feel worse. It's just that you're the only emotional frame of reference I have."

"Why would you do that?"

"I had to break something," Jared said. "And I was—I was so sick of myself, thinking about what I'd said to you, thinking about who I was, someone you didn't want."

"That is not what I decided," Kami told him fiercely. "Is that why Lillian threw you out of the house?"

Jared hesitated.

"Come on, I told you all my screwed-up family stuff," Kami said. "You have to tell me things too. You have to talk to me as well: that's how this friends thing works."

Jared's fingers flexed as if he was about to let go of her hand, but Kami kept her grip firm.

"Aunt Lillian asked me to be the heir of Aurimere," he said. "Be the sorcerer guardian of Sorry-in-the-Vale, I guess, like she is. Apparently any Lynburn can be chosen for the job by the current incumbent."

The inside of Kami's mouth was cold. This was because it had fallen open. "What?" she asked, and started to laugh. "What? Your aunt says, 'Please take this magnificent mansion, please be prince of all you survey,' and you say, 'How dare you suggest such a thing to me! Moving to the tavern! Jared out!' *Why?*"

A smile played around Jared's mouth. "Because she can't have been serious."

"Why wouldn't she be serious?" Kami asked. "I mean, I get that you wanted to be fair to Ash, but were you not even tempted?"

Jared looked genuinely puzzled at the thought, as if he was wondering what in the world he was supposed to be tempted by.

"Unearthly power," Kami reminded him. "Untold riches. Great big mansion. Lord of all you survey."

"I knew you wouldn't care about any of that," Jared said. "So what good was it to me?"

Kami had no answer to that question. In fact, she had no idea how to respond to that. Eventually, she said, "What I want isn't the most important thing."

"It's the *only* important thing," Jared answered. "I mean—I know it's crazy. I tell myself that. The world doesn't turn on what you want. I tell myself that but I don't believe it, not really. I know you wanted me to see things differently once the link was broken, but I can't. It is always about you for me." He smiled that wry little twist of a smile again. "Which is why I have made this conversation that should be about you all about my feelings."

"I asked you about them," Kami said. "Jared, you have to stop acting like you don't count for anything now that the link is cut."

He said nothing, just sitting there, still smiling that little smile.

"You leaving Aurimere was pretty noble," Kami elaborated. "I mean, nuts, but noble. It wasn't fair to Ash, you wouldn't be used to punish anyone—not that I think that was Lillian's motivation—and you're out. You don't just turn her down; you leave home to make your point. Not to mention all the attempts to save Sorry-in-the-Vale single-handedly. You're like a honey badger."

"I'm like a what?" Jared started to laugh. "No, I'm not. That's ridiculous."

"Honey badgers are badass," Kami argued. "The honey badger is the most hardcore of all the animals. They break into beehives and they get stung all over. Not because they have to. Just because they think bees are super tasty. Also they have been known to bite the heads off puff adders, collapse from the venom, and wake up from their comas going 'Hey there, delicious snake.' That's how honey badgers roll."

" 'Honey badger' is not a badass name," Jared pointed out. " 'Death ray badger' is a badass name."

Kami hit him on the shoulder without even thinking about it. "Remember when I said you were worthwhile? I meant that. But I didn't mean you had no flaws. You have many flaws. And one of them is not taking awesome compliments well."

"Also, you mentioned being nuts."

Kami smiled. "That I don't really mind."

He sat on the stile steps and looked up at her. The day was dying now, the sky darkening from blue to gray, the ground from silver to shadows. There was only color at the point where the two met, in a leaf-green, rose-smudged horizon. She was struck as she had been before by how much he, a city boy born and bred, seemed part of Sorry-in-the-Vale, eyes like moonlight on the Crying Pools, gold hair turned to shadow and his scar turned to silver.

"I think your parents will work this out," he said. "But if they don't, you'll be okay. I know you. You'll have all the answers in the end, because you always keep searching."

"I know you too," said Kami. "If you decided you *did* want Aurimere, I think Aurimere would be lucky to have you."

If Lillian was the one who got to do the choosing, and not Rob: if Sorry-in-the-Vale was not taken away from them all. If Lillian succeeded. If Henry managed to bring help. Kami shivered.

"I'm sorry. I feel stupid that I keep running to you. I don't want to be dependent on you. I don't want to be dependent on anyone. I want to be able to handle myself."

"Being able to depend on someone doesn't mean you're dependent on them," Jared said. "I mean, I think. I wouldn't know myself, obviously."

"I do believe someone promised me a hot drink and hasn't delivered yet," Kami said.

Jared stood up, steeled himself, and lifted her from the stile, hands on her waist, swinging her down as if she was light. Kami caught at his jacket and found herself laughing again, laughing up into his face, with that rush of feeling that they were in tune again.

She could kiss him now. The thought flashed into her mind like electricity, lighting every nerve ending with an impulse to act. She could use her grip on his jacket to push herself onto her tiptoes and pull his head down to hers.

Only every time he had touched her today, he'd had to

brace himself as if for an ordeal, Kami thought. And he had been doing more than kissing Holly.

Kami remembered when she herself had flinched from physical contact with Jared. He had been only in her mind and nowhere else for so long, it had been strange that he existed in the outside world at all. The fact that he was there to *be* touched was almost frightening.

She had grown used to it, become familiar enough with his face that she could match up his expressions and feelings, until it had become the one face she wanted to see every day. She wanted him to be real, and touching him had become something she wanted to do.

She'd gotten over the first reaction, but he hadn't, and that might be because he didn't want to. Maybe, Kami thought, he could barely touch her because what he wanted was for her to be back in his head, linked and safe and beloved, and not there to touch at all.

She didn't know what he wanted. She didn't even know what she wanted, not for certain.

"Thanks," Kami told him, and let go of his jacket. They started to walk to the pub, close but not touching, and she continued: "Do you miss your family?"

"Uh, no," said Jared. "On account of all the evil."

"I meant your family at Aurimere," Kami said. "They miss you. Your aunt asked me to ask you back. You haven't seemed happy since you left. Do you miss them?"

"My aunt the ice queen and my cousin the bunny killer?" Jared asked. "That family. Do I miss them?"

"Yes," said Kami.

"Maybe," said Jared. "I'm not sure."

"This is just a suggestion, but I was thinking that maybe other people should matter to you. I think that it would be good for you. You could be good for them too."

Jared nodded, a little thoughtfully. She wondered if he was thinking about Holly.

He was wrong about what he'd said. She wasn't going to have all the answers, because there was one question she did not dare ask. Because she wanted to keep him more than she wanted answers: he was the one exception to all the rules she had, and she could not ask him if he didn't like touching her because he wished she was not real. They were friends again, and perhaps that was all they should be.

The kiss had happened, though.

"You said," she said slowly, "that what I wanted was the most important thing. But I don't want you to do things because I want them. I want you to do what you want. So what is it that you want?" she asked him.

He was silent for the space of a few breaths, long enough for her to begin to hope, and then he said, "I want the link back. More than anything in the world."

"I see," Kami said softly. She kept walking beside him, but a little farther apart. The cold air surrounded her on all sides.

PART V
WANDERING BECOMES TOO LONELY

Tell a man to explain how he dropped into hell! Explain my preference! I never had a preference for her, any more than I have a preference for breathing. No other woman exists by the side of her. I would rather touch her hand if it were dead, than I would touch any other woman's living.

—*George Eliot*

Chapter Nineteen
Favor Fire

Ash had been staring at his phone, trying to work up his nerve, for the last twenty minutes.

He was standing in the portrait gallery of Aurimere early on Friday morning, and he felt like all of his ancestors were judging him. Charles Lynburn, 1788, looked coldly out of his gilt frame as if to say that he would have been quicker about making this call than Ash, and when he was alive phones hadn't even been invented yet.

Ash gazed at the floor instead of at the Lynburns all around him and hit the call button. After a few rings, he heard Jared's voice in his ear. "Who is this and what do you want?"

"Is that how you answer the phone to every number you don't recognize?" Ash demanded.

"Ash," Jared said. "Shame. I was hoping it would be a telemarketer. How did you get this number?"

"Kami gave it to me."

Ash heard the indrawn breath at her name, and wondered if it was a means of getting Jared to do what he wanted or a means of getting him to hang up.

Jared didn't hang up.

"Mum takes the other sorcerers out training every morning," Ash said. "I'm not invited." He waited, until Jared said, "Unless Aunt Lillian's soldiers are booze hounds to a man and downstairs in the pub, nor am I."

Ash allowed himself to relax a fraction. He hadn't really thought his mother would let Jared help her, and banish Ash. Not really.

"And yet we're the Lynburns," Ash said. "We're the strong ones."

"Oh, you keep telling yourself that."

All Ash had ever wanted was to be at home and surrounded by his family. Now, under the judgmental gaze of a hundred Lynburns, with a sneering Lynburn voice in his ear, he started thinking about the merits of running away and changing his name. "Ash Smith" had a certain ring to it.

"We're going to have to fight," he said. "So do you want to practice fighting together? Like we sparred together at Rusty's place, but with magic."

He thought but did not say that he had been taught things Jared hadn't, let the offer of assistance remain implicit, and hoped there was no way Jared could guess at his ulterior motive.

"Do I get to punch you in the face this time?" Jared inquired, and before Ash could reply he said, "I'll meet you at the bridge over the Sorrier River," and hung up.

* * *

Ash had only been at the bridge over the Sorrier River at night before. Then the trees had been simply shadows over the thin silver line of the river, wet rocks turned into mirrors by the moonlight. Now the trees formed an arch of brown that looked carved, a curve over the straight line of the bridge. Lingering gold leaves were trembling, fragile, in the air, and clinging to the branches as if they feared the fall to the river.

The river was full, colored gray and brown by the rocks and the riverbed, splashing and churning as it ran its course. Jared was leaning against the side of the bridge, arms propped along the railing, watching the water. He did not look up until Ash was standing awkwardly beside him, and had been doing so for some time. When he did, the look was brief and cold.

"All right, then," said Jared. "Let's see what you can do."

"Um," said Ash.

Jared looked down at the river and smirked. "Little bit of performance anxiety? Can you not do it when someone's watching you?"

"Magic is not a joke!"

"Put up or shut up," Jared said. "I don't have all day."

Ash put his hands in his pockets and stared down at the river. He concentrated on the light in the water, glints where the scarce sunlight touched the currents, and wove them together in his mind.

"When you want to do something magical," he told Jared, not looking at him, "you have to choose a particular piece of nature as your source for the moment: you have to make something a single focus."

Ash took one hand out of his pocket and reached out, palm up, asking the river, and the thread of light on the water that he had made came flying out onto the bridge. It hit his palm with an icy-cool shock and hung taut over the side of the bridge, a transparent glittering rope.

"So then you lasso your enemies?" Jared asked. "You're like Wonder Woman." He slanted an amused gray glance over as Ash made a faint exasperated sound at the back of his throat. "What?" Jared asked innocently. "I am just trying to understand the practical application of this magic."

The rope disappeared in Ash's hand, leaving nothing but sparkling drops in his palm and against the planks of the bridge. Ash felt his temper evaporate with it.

"Let me give you another demonstration," he said, and magically shoved Jared with all his might.

Jared was quite obviously not expecting anything of the kind, and he fell spectacularly, with a yell and a grab at the bridge that missed by a fraction of an inch, and a splash like a white fountain. Ash stepped away from the side of the bridge to avoid getting wet. When he stepped back he saw Jared already struggling to his feet in the surging currents. His hair and shirt were dripping wet, and the river was almost to his waist: he was clearly having trouble standing upright.

The river went pure pale gray and entirely, perfectly flat, like the surface of a pebble worn by years of rushing water. When Jared looked up, Ash saw that his eyes were like pieces of the river, cold and opaque.

He felt the bridge rattle, and looked on either side to see the wooden rails of the bridge peeling gently away, small fissures in the wood becoming cracks that chased each other. The whole thing was going to give way, Ash thought, and braced himself for the icy shock of the water.

It never came. He blinked open eyes that he had not realized were shut and gave Jared a puzzled look.

"There are non-sorcerous people who might want to use

the bridge," Jared said. "I'm all for mindless vandalism, but it seems like a jerk move."

Jared grabbed at the log supports of the bridge rail and hauled himself up onto the bridge. Ash was not sure if he could have done that, and was reminded again of the fact that Jared was obviously a lot stronger than he was, used to taking care of himself.

It did cross Ash's mind that he really might be about to get punched in the face, but Jared didn't punch him. He stood on the bridge, looking as determinedly immune to cold when soaking wet as he had looked earlier, on a winter morning with no jacket, and said, "What's next?"

"You set those scarecrows on fire," Ash reminded him. "Can you set a tree branch on fire? Living branches should be more of a challenge."

Jared looked at a tree branch hanging over the bridge in a slender silver line above the gray water. It burst into flame.

"Okay," said Ash as the fire swallowed the branch at a roar and the crackling, burning piece of wood fell into the water below. Jared walked off the bridge into the woods, flames trailing him like a pet comet. Ash raised his voice. "But can you do it without—and this is really important—starting a forest fire?"

Jared did not answer. Envisioning what his mother would say if he was the accidental catalyst of Jared's burning the town to the ground, Ash dashed after him, scuffing up dirt and pine needles under his feet as he ran. Luckily, it was quite easy to follow the burning tracks Jared left behind him, pine needles glowing like lit cigarettes and then going out.

He caught up to Jared, seeing his turned back and

branches turned into torches, red tongues of fire licking at the pale morning sky.

It wasn't out of control. Not yet.

"Stop!" Ash shouted. He ran at Jared, seizing him by the shoulders and whirling him around to yell in his face. "I said one branch. One! How much fire do you think you can manage before it gets out of hand? You have to stop *now*."

Jared's face was sheened with sweat, and it was gathering at his temples, where his hair was still damp from the river. The fire stuttered and coughed, sounding like his stupid motorcycle, and then all the branches went out.

"This is a lot more effort than it was before," he said, and his voice sounded harsh, as if he'd inhaled some of the smoke curling through the woods.

He didn't know it, but he had just given Ash the perfect cue.

"Of course," Ash said. "You were able to wake the woods when you had a source. You didn't need to focus on any one thing: she was the one thing, and the power flowed through her to the rest of the world."

Jared sat down abruptly on the forest floor, leaning against a tree with his head tipped back and one leg drawn up. He looked exhausted and sick.

"There's no need to remind me."

"I'm sorry," Ash lied, making his voice sound humble the way he did when one of his parents was angry with him. He ducked his head and added, "I can describe it, but I can't imagine it. What was it like, having a source?"

"Ask a fish to describe water," Jared said, with a sharp

gesture at his own wet clothes. "It's how I lived all my life, until now. If you want to understand, I can describe what living differently, living your life, seems like to me."

"All right," Ash said uneasily, not sure how that would help him but not wanting to turn the offer down.

Jared gave him a bleak look. He said, his voice measured and deliberate, "It seems like hell."

Ash made no sound. The smoke from the burned wood drifted up through the bare tree branches, forming strange silvery patterns on the wind, moving gently from side to side, almost uncertainly, as if it was lost.

"Every dark moment you ever had in your life," Jared said. "Every time you were a kid hiding under the covers convinced that nobody in the world existed, that it was just you and the nightmares. Every time you felt alone in a crowd, alone by yourself, forever and essentially alone, and don't pretend there weren't moments like that. Every time you felt worthless, every time you thought there was no purpose to existing, no center to the world and no peace to be found. I never had a single moment like that, I was never lonely a day of my life, until now. Now I feel like the world is hell, and hell is a place where the souls of the damned can still see heaven. Because that's the worst thing of all. And yet I can't look away."

Ash nodded as if what Jared had just said made any sort of sense, and looked somewhat desperately around. There was no help forthcoming from the trees or the drifting smoke.

"But you don't end up—you know, mated for life or anything," he said. He felt like it was important to check.

Jared looked up at him. Ash discovered there was nothing

that felt so epically unjust as Jared, of all people, looking at him as if he was crazy.

"What?"

"Well, I couldn't help but notice you making out with Holly at the bar."

Ash winced at the memory. His dad had said to go make friends with Kami Glass, and he'd done as he was told because he always did what he was told, and Kami was goofy and fun and pretty, and she was always trying to be and do good, and he had started to feel sick about what he was doing. He'd assumed she would never forgive him, and had been amazed when she had.

Except that had been a misunderstanding.

It had hurt, but then there had been Holly, gorgeous and friendly and soothing to his hurt ego. Thinking of how desperate he must seem, turning to any girl who gave him attention, made Ash cringe.

Especially as Holly had been playing some sort of weird game, and had abandoned him sitting at a table so she could make out with his cousin. At least Kami was straightforward: you could trust Kami.

Jared looked up at Ash, and this time it seemed as if he was really seeing him.

"Oh yeah," he said. "Sorry about that. You didn't deserve that." His mouth twisted as if he found the taste of halfway decent words in his mouth bitter and regretted saying them. "Though what you were doing with Holly in that bar at all, when you had Kami dancing with you, I don't understand. Are you stupid?"

Ash was in no way feeling charitable toward Holly, but

this struck him as unfair. Holly was very good-looking, after all, and Jared must have noticed, what with all the kissing.

"If you like Kami better," he began, and Jared cut him off with a laugh, wild and with a crazy edge to it. Ash spoke irritably over the laugh. "I wasn't the one kissing her in the Water Rising. She may have thought it was me, but you knew it wasn't. So if you were kissing Kami one night and taking Holly upstairs a few weeks later, I really don't see how you can take me to task. You're the one getting it all over town."

The look on Jared's face was suddenly a little terrifying. Ash wondered if he was supposed to apologize for implying Jared was loose with his favors.

"Kami thought it was you who kissed her," said Jared, and even though he did not move, for a moment Ash really thought Jared was going to kill him. His face went too still, and his eyes utterly, murderously blank, so pale they almost glowed.

Then Jared tipped his head back against the tree again and closed his eyes.

"Of course she did," he said. "That makes sense."

There was nothing Ash hated more than the feeling he had said the wrong thing. "I didn't mean—"

Jared's eyes snapped open. He was glaring, openly hostile: just another member of Ash's family who hated him. "Why did you call me here, Ash? What do you want?"

Ash searched his mind frantically for the right thing to say, the tactful thing that would please and persuade Jared.

"I—I don't—" he began, stammering like a child. "I want . . . Come *home*!"

Jared's face cleared. He stood looking at Ash, his face a

real mirror of Ash's for once, as utterly surprised by what Ash had said as Ash himself was.

"I thought you'd be glad to be rid of me," Jared said, and laughed unconvincingly at the end of what was clearly not a joke. "You don't even like me."

Ash hunched up his shoulders and stared at the river. "What has that got to do with anything? You're family. You're not actually evil. You don't like me either. You keep hitting me. You're awful to me all the time. But you're meant to— I thought you would stay."

There was a long silence. Ash thought seriously about drowning himself in the river.

"I won't hit you again," said Jared.

Ash felt a hand settle on the back of his neck, too heavy, thumb moving in a small circle. He glanced uncertainly up, and Jared snatched his hand back. He was looking moodily down at Ash, but Ash didn't think the angry unhappiness was actually directed at him.

Ash wasn't an idiot. Jared was weird about touching Mom and Aunt Rosalind; Ash remembered that Jared would let Ash's dad hug him or clap him on the shoulder, but neither of them had him anymore.

"Come on," Jared said gruffly. "We need to get to school."

"Right," said Ash. "Do you have to go back to the Water Rising and grab your stuff?"

"Nah," said Jared. "We can walk together. I won't even be awful to you. Not for the whole walk."

Ash found himself laughing. "It's a fifteen-minute walk."

"About that, Ash," said Jared. "I'm going to have to ask you to move pretty quickly. I've only got so much self-restraint."

Chapter Twenty
My Own, My Only

Kami spent Saturday at Aurimere poring over books and trying to find any further mention of Matthew Cooper or Elinor and Anne Lynburn, or of how Matthew and Anne had died. All she found was a note in the records table about a sacrifice made in honor of the Lynburn daughters.

Kami closed her latest book with a slam. She did not know why the townspeople had not risen up against the Lynburns years ago, frankly. Whatever happened to the folksy and charming tradition of storming the castle with burning torches and pitchforks?

She pressed her face into the heel of her palm, eyes shut tight. They were training; they had collected information; they had collected the sorcerers' identities and their possessions. But they didn't have enough information, and Lillian didn't have enough sorcerers. Winter solstice was coming soon.

"Kami," Ash said, sounding a bit nervous, possibly because Kami was slamming books shut and hiding her face in despair. "I was wondering if I could have a word with you."

Kami lifted her head from her hand and tried to smile across the table at him.

Across the dark shining expanse of mahogany, Ash sat

looking nervous, soft blond hair rumpled as if he had been running his fingers through it in distrait fashion.

The thought flashed through Kami's mind that he was going to ask her out.

"I was talking to Jared yesterday," Ash continued.

Or maybe not.

"Do you know what's going on with him?" Kami asked. "He was avoiding me at school and he's not answering his phone. Do you have any idea what his plans might be? Are they really suicidal or just a little suicidal?"

"I don't know what's going on with him. I'm sure he's fine," Ash said in a way that did not sound like he was sure at all, and that suggested that Ash did know what was going on with Jared. "We were out practicing magic and we got to talking about having a source."

Kami's immediate reaction was to be angry and say that was private, but she told herself firmly that made no sense. Jared and Ash had to practice magic, and the way Jared was accustomed to doing magic was with a source. She should be glad they were working together.

She looked down at the table, at her own hands wavering over her papers. She could feel the blood rising hot in her face. "Oh?"

"The way Jared talked about having a source," Ash said softly, "it sounded nice. Never being lonely again. Having someone to support you."

Kami was becoming familiar with the feeling of desolation that came upon her now, turning her cold even while her cheeks still burned. She wished she had never learned to understand loneliness, and that Ash had not brought it up.

Where are you? she asked Jared in her mind, sending love and loneliness and fury at him, contradictory emotions that she could not express in words. They used to be able to understand each other, even when they made no sense.

Sometimes she could not stop herself from speaking to him like this, even though he would never hear her again.

" 'Nice' is not exactly how I would describe it," Kami replied, and was horrified to hear her voice shake. The corners of her eyes burned, and she was even more horrified to see a teardrop fall onto the brown cover of her book.

"A lot of power comes with being a source," Ash said. "Maybe enough to help turn the tide against my father."

"It didn't help much against him when we had it, and we don't have it anymore." Kami's voice was not friendly. "We have to do without it."

"Maybe not," said Ash.

"What do you mean?" Kami asked. "Is—is there a way to get the link back?"

If they had to reestablish the link to save other people, to save the whole town. If they *had* to.

"Sort of," Ash replied. Kami stared at the closed book and the wood grain in the surface of the table. "You broke the link with Jared," Ash went on, as if she didn't know that. "There's no way to make another link, once broken, without more power than any sorcerer has unless he or she completes the Crying Pools ceremony."

Kami looked up. "He's not trying that again!"

When Ash saw her face, he let out a low exclamation, got up from his chair, and rushed over to her side. He went on his knees on the stone floor beside her chair, fingers light against the side of her face. Ash never had any trouble touching her. His fingers lingered, as if he liked to do it.

"Kami," he said, "you're crying."

"No, I am not," Kami lied. "I got something in my eye."

"You got something in your eye."

"Yes. Possibly a speck of dust," Kami said, and broke down. "All right, possibly my feelings."

Ash smiled a little, sympathetically and tentatively, until she smiled too.

"You don't understand what I'm asking you," he murmured. "It has nothing to do with Jared. He is not the only sorcerer in Aurimere."

"What—" Kami began, but before she could form the question properly in her mind, he had answered it.

"You and I could do the spell together. You and I could save the town together. You could be *my* source."

Every muscle in Kami's body went stiff. Ash registered her reaction: his hand fell from her face, and he seized her cold fingers. He hung on to her hand hard, in almost the same way she had held on to the records table, as if letting go would mean disaster.

"You don't have to worry," Ash said. "I wouldn't be like Jared." He pressed her hand. "I've read up on sorcerers and sources. I'd keep a careful distance and not intrude on you. I wouldn't make demands of you like he did. I wouldn't make you unhappy like he did. This would be a partnership, a good partnership. We would respect each other, and trust each other, and together we could do so much. I can't think of anyone I would rather be linked to than you." His voice went softer on that last line. She looked down into his eyes, the prince kneeling in his own castle, and realized he meant every word.

"Kami," he said, "I know what I'm asking for."

"Ash," she whispered, "you have no idea."

She pulled her hand out of his, trying not to recoil, trying not to pull back too fast and seem too desperate to become entirely separate from him.

"It is the most intimate thing in the world," she said slowly, trying to explain in a way that would not hurt him further. "You could ask me for anything else and it would be less personal, and less private. Anything."

There was even something intimate about speaking of it, her voice suddenly pitched low. She saw Ash flush, and look confused as to why he was flushing.

"You want to touch my soul naked," Kami said. "You want me to touch yours naked as well. I can barely even think about doing it: the idea makes me so scared. I don't mean to insult you. I'm trying to tell you that you cannot understand. You said—you said you wouldn't be like Jared, but you don't understand that either. You think the way he is about me is crazy. You don't see that I'm the same way about him. Neither of us can help it. He did make me unhappy, *and* he made me happy. I did the same to him. He made demands of me and I made demands of him, because that is the greatest demand you can make of someone; we made demands of each other every time we breathed. I could not possibly do that with anyone but Jared. Don't ask me again." Kami took a deep breath, let it slide through her mouth and fill her lungs with air, and reminded herself that she could breathe on her own.

Ash's head was bowed. She wanted to reach out: he was the kind of boy who it was impossible to imagine anyone rejecting, and yet she found herself doing it over and over again.

Kami stood up, pushing her chair back, and said, "I have to go."

* * *

She took a detour on her way home, walking up the High Street and heading for the Water Rising. She told herself that she just wanted to check Jared was there. She found out that she was lying to herself as she approached the statue of Matthew Cooper, a pale gold form in the darkness, and saw Jared coming down Shadowchurch Lane toward her.

Kami's first thought was that he looked terrible. He was wearing only a long-sleeved T-shirt and jeans, which was ridiculous on a winter night. It was worse than that, though. In the half-light cast by a streetlight three dark shop doors away, his face was all set lines, hollows, and shadows.

"I was looking for you," Kami said.

Jared walked closer to her, step by step, but slowly, as if he was being dragged toward her against his will. Kami walked to meet him at the corner: she put out her hand and laid it on the support of the low stone wall.

"Why?" Jared asked, his voice scratchy. "Was Ash talking to you?"

"Actually, he was. He asked me if I wanted to be his source."

Kami saw the way he changed color, the check in his step that was almost a stagger, and she was fiercely glad to know that he and Ash had not discussed passing her from sorcerer to sorcerer like some convenient magical parcel.

"He did?" Jared said. "He asked you that? I'll kill him."

"Don't," Kami said, her voice brittle. She felt brittle all over.

"Kami, please," Jared said. "I know I have no right to ask you, I know how he must seem to you, compared to me. I know you meant to kiss him and not me that night at the Water Rising. I know I'm—I'm different, I'm not right, I want too much from you and I'm asking too much now, but please don't do it."

The yellow light cast by the streetlamp was like the circle from a stone being thrown in a lake, a ring spreading and turning faint as it spread. Jared stood at the wavering edge of light looking at her, his face exiled and haunted, and Kami realized he was begging her.

"How dare you?" she demanded, and her voice was stronger now. "You think I'm going to do that? You think I would even consider it? I told Ash that I would never do it. I meant it. I hate that you act as if you're the only one in this. It wasn't just you who was ripped into pieces. It was never just you, any of it. I miss you too. I think about you too. And I hate it, I hate feeling so pathetic. I wish I had wanted it to be Ash in the Water Rising. But I didn't. I wanted it to be you."

Jared hesitated, moving forward a fraction so the light struck his face and then going very still. She couldn't read his expression.

"You did?" he asked.

Fury failed Kami, and fled. "Yes," she said helplessly, her hands loosening from their fists and hanging empty at her sides. "But that doesn't matter. What do you—"

Jared erupted from stillness into movement so suddenly

Kami almost flinched back, but she did not. She stayed where she was and he reached her in a step, cupped her face in his hands, and kissed her mouth. Kami turned her face up to his, her hands full of the worn cotton of his shirt. She wanted to get a grip on this moment, standing in a circle of light with darkness all around, but with him, with him at last, and hold it tight.

They clung to each other and stumbled against the wall.

"Come here," Jared half gasped. He dropped his hands, but she did not have time to register the loss before they were at her waist, lifting her onto the wall so her face was closer to his. "You are really small," he told her breathlessly, stroking her hair back from her face with hands trying to be gentle and not quite managing it. "I'm always afraid that I'll hurt you."

"What," Kami said, laughing against his mouth a little, incredulous, "you're afraid I'll get a crick in my neck?"

"Well, that is a worry," Jared said, trying for solemnity.

Kami could only see pieces of his face this close up, the gold fringe of his eyelashes, the silver strike of his scar. Then he kissed her again, kisses showered down on her lips, the side of her mouth, her cheek, her chin, his mouth open against the line of her jaw and pressed on her neck as she leaned her head back. She shook under the rain of kisses and slid her arms around his neck, bringing him in closer, the line of his body drawing up against hers.

"Kami," he said, his breath warm on the sensitive skin of her throat. She could feel his heartbeat, she thought, or her own against his mouth.

She opened her eyes and said, "Yes?"

She was almost off the wall, crushed for an instant with the cold stone against her back and his body against hers. Then he stopped kissing her, pressing their foreheads together.

"Are you okay, is this all right?" he said in a whispered rush.

"I don't know," she whispered back, her voice shaking out of control. "Don't stop."

She touched his chest, tentative, her hand light against the flat hard muscle. It came as a shock, for the hundredth time: he was real. She felt his chest lift, fast, as his breathing changed, and touched his collar. She pulled him a little closer, cheek against his cheek, feeling the satin line of his scar, the slight roughness where he had not shaved. Her hand brushed a slender line of metal, and she realized it was the chain he always wore.

Maybe not out of habit after all.

"I'm glad you asked, though," she said. "Asking's sexy."

She laid her palm against the small cool circle of the coin that hung around his neck, and against his warm skin. Her fingers tangled with the thin chain and she pulled on it, turning his face back to hers, catching the tiny sound he made with her swollen mouth.

She smiled, and the sensation of her own lips curling on his sent heat curling through her body. "And you?" she whispered, tucking the smile like a secret against his skin. "Are you all right?"

"I don't know either," he said, and she felt his hand shaking against her face, palm steadying as he rested it against the curve of her jaw. He kissed her, slow and long and trembling, and said against her mouth, "I'm not usually all right. But I—I love you. God, don't change your mind. Don't stop."

"But—Holly—" Kami murmured, slipping out the couple of words against his mouth.

"I *don't care* about Holly," Jared snarled at her, then swallowed, and touched her hair again with that awkward not-quite-gentleness, pushing a strand off her cheek and looking at her with a sort of hungry wonder. "Not like that."

Maybe he was just telling her what she wanted to hear. But it was what she wanted to hear, she found, exactly what she wanted.

She leaned forward and kissed him again. She let go of his collar and touched his shoulders because she couldn't seem to stop touching him long enough to complete a simple task like undoing her own coat.

"Let me," Jared asked, voice hushed, and drew back a little, kissed a place just above the corner of her mouth as he slid the zipper of her coat open. She could feel his hands shaking; the zipper snagged a couple of times, and her breath caught. "Why are you wearing this?" Jared asked in a fraught whisper.

"Golly, I don't know, a winter coat on a lovely December night, what was I thinking?" Kami twined her fingers in his hair, felt it soft and curling loosely at the ends around her fingertips, as if trying to hang on to her. *Yes,* she thought, and wished he could hear it. *Don't let me go.*

Jared laughed, the sound barely louder than a breath in the hushed bright space between them. "Golly," he repeated softly, sliding his hands inside her coat. She felt the warm touch of his fingers through her thin jumper, at the small of her back, pressing her closer. "I'm not used to your English dirty talk."

Kami almost laughed back, but his mouth touched hers, and the laugh was lost.

"Actually," Jared said, and kissed her again, featherlight, "I'm not used to any of this." He caught her open mouth with his, less careful now. "I haven't done it a lot," he added, the whisper scraping his throat and a hint of teeth touching her lower lip, the faint sting sending a shiver coursing through her body. "And I want to get it right."

She did not know her lips had parted with the shiver until the kiss turned deep and her breathing shallow. Every time he touched her, the touch felt new, like something they had just invented together. It never stopped being a shock, that this was Jared. It was always a little scary, even something as small as his fingers stroking the nape of her neck.

He started back slightly, making a low sound that was half hunger, half distress. She looked up at his eyes, almost black, darkness swallowing all but a vanishingly faint ring of silver.

"Jared," she said, and reached out to have him back.

Her fingers trailed light along the line of his collarbone, nails tracing the dip at the base of his throat, and she felt the shudder run through his body. She curled her fingers in under the collar of his shirt and used her hold to pull him in again.

She kissed him and he made another low sound, this one deeper in his throat. Touching him would have been unthinkable a few months ago. She felt almost dangerously happy, afraid at any moment that it was all going to be taken away from her, dashed into pieces before her eyes, that it would turn out to be a horrible mistake.

She felt dizzy and shuddered a little, pulling away from him, but even as she leaned away she could not stop the shivers coursing through her, could not stop kissing him back. A point of cold touched her neck, causing another shiver, and she looked up and realized it was snowing, bright white-feather points against the dark curtain of the night and the spotlight of their streetlamp. Kami felt a brush of warmth against her face and looked down to see Jared brushing a snowflake from her hair. She smiled and closed her eyes against the dancing glints of snow, the melting icy kiss against her skin, and met his warm mouth. They kissed and kissed, shivering and shaking apart, neither of them daring to touch each other anywhere risky, both scared and trying not to scare the other off.

Kami linked her arms behind his back, felt the breadth of his shoulders and the reality of skin and muscle and bone, and thought again, *Don't let me go.*

Chapter Twenty-One
Her Legacy

Kami swung open her gate, and the sound of its creak tore the cool peace of a very silent, very early morning. She followed the crazy paving, gray in the ghost-gray light, to the door of her house. When she walked through to her kitchen, she found her mother there, already swinging her bag onto her shoulder, ready to go out.

Mum looked up. "Kami," she said in a low voice, "where have you been? I thought something might have happened."

Mum's voice sank on the word *something*, as if she had not been able to even imagine what might have happened to Kami, only able to nurse dark and insubstantial fears. Kami looked at her mother, her mother's always-beautiful face above a zipped-up black hoodie and jeans. Her gray eyes looked huge: she looked younger than she usually did, and terrified.

Kami had been so angry with her mother, but looking at her now, she felt the fierce urge to shield her from everything that was making her so scared.

It was strange to feel protective of your own mother.

"I'm sorry," Kami began.

Her mother interrupted: her voice as sharp as one of her culinary knives. "Were you with that Lynburn boy?"

Kami shrugged off her coat and dropped it on a chair. "Yes," she answered, sympathy draining away. "Actually, I was making out with him all night. Tell me, are you going to the bakery or are you going to Rob Lynburn? My Lynburn doesn't have half the body count yours does."

Her mother went even paler. "I'd never betray your father," she said, her voice very low.

"Then what are you doing, Mum?" Kami demanded.

"The Lynburns are mad!" Mum snapped. "They all want a show of submission; they want you to act like their servants. And I'll do it, I'll play the humble villager, if that's a way to keep my family safe. That's all I want, for you all to be safe. That's all I'm trying to accomplish. And you're scaring me, Kami. You're breaking my heart. You have to be more careful."

"We can't let him win," Kami said.

Her mother's eyes traveled over her. Kami knew her hair was tangled and her mouth was swollen, and she knew that her mother thought she was a fool.

"You don't get it," Mum told her. "He's already won. The other Lynburns will accept that. All that really matters to a Lynburn is another Lynburn. It's the others who stand against him Rob will crush. And if this boy doesn't have a use for you anymore, he'll stand by and let you be crushed."

Kami laughed. "You have no idea who he is. He doesn't ever stand by for anything. And he loves me."

She believed it, believed every word, but she felt herself flush as she said it. She'd always known he loved her, it had been the one certainty above all others that had never changed, but she had never said the words aloud and she had never meant them quite this way before. She had said it to him, and she hardly knew what she had meant. They were terrifying words, words to encompass a world.

Her mother looked at her sadly, her mother who men only had to look at to love. She might know better than Kami did.

But all she said was, "I have to go." She pulled up her dark hood, covering her shining-gilt hair and shadowing her pale face. Kami shuddered in the cold air that ran through the open door as her mother went out.

Kami went upstairs and had a stinging hot shower to warm herself and wake herself up. She stood under the water and was terribly, newly aware of her own body, of the paths the drops of hot water were following.

Her old boyfriend Claud had touched a lot more of her body than Jared had tonight, but she had not felt made new because of him. Jared knew her, knew almost all the thoughts she had ever had, every dark fear and bright hope. When he touched her, he knew exactly who he was touching. There was a weight to their touches that made her body seem like a newly found land, with discoveries possible she had not dreamt of. Kami closed her eyes and let the drops of water drum on her eyelids.

She didn't know how much of it was about the link, but he liked her. He loved her: he'd said so, though she would never again be able to know precisely and completely what he meant when he spoke. She just had to trust him, like every other couple in the world.

If they were a couple.

Kami shook her head at herself in the mirror, and the water-black locks of her hair came unstuck from her face and waved around her head.

Kami tried calling Henry Thornton again, but his phone just rang and rang. She chose her outfit more carefully than usual: a royal-blue dress with long sleeves, purple tights, and swinging plastic purple earrings. When she looked in the mirror, she had to shake her head at herself again, bothering about how she looked to a guy at a time like this, but her reflection smiled at her and seemed to regret nothing.

Her father was in the kitchen when she came back downstairs. Coffee was brewing and he was reading *The Nosy Parker.*

"My daughter, reporter of all the evil magical news of the day," he said. "The boys told me you'd written an article that explained some things. I have to say, it makes a lot more sense than what I've been able to come up with on my own."

Kami was aware she should have responded to what he was saying with a smile and a joke, but instead she stood stricken.

He looked so completely normal, her dad, his black hair sticking up from a shower, wearing a shirt that said BABY, I'D DESIGN YOUR GRAPHIC. She could not put the sight of him together with the desperate man she'd seen in the graveyard.

"I—I can tell you things," she offered at last. "Whatever you want to know."

"Your mum thinks it'd be best to lay low and let these . . . sorcerer types work it out," Dad said. "She seemed pretty worried about how much you're involved."

Kami was glad to hear they'd been talking about anything in what seemed to be a civil fashion, but she didn't know what to say. "Yes, I am heavily involved with deadly magical danger" did not seem the kind of thing a concerned parent would wish to hear. She looked over at him and saw he was pouring three cups of coffee. "Is Mum still here?" she asked, hoping this meant something good for them, when the doorbell jangled.

"No," said Dad. "But I am expecting a guest."

He made to slide off his stool, but then the kitchen door swung wide and Lillian Lynburn walked in. She did not bother to close it.

Dad raised his eyebrows. "The front door wasn't open."

"I find things are usually the way I want them to be," Lillian said. "Because I can do magic."

"Can you do *manners*?" Dad inquired. "It's customary to wait for someone to answer the door."

Lillian did not look impressed by the customs of ordinary mortals. She did not look impressed by the kitchen of ordinary mortals either. Rob had been in Kami's kitchen once, and had looked friendly and comfortable enough. Lillian looked as out of place as a character in a fairy tale. Possibly an evil queen, if evil queens had really fancy tweed coats.

"Let me tell you about customs, James," said Lillian. "I am not accustomed to being summoned to someone else's home. You're very fortunate that I came."

"I am indeed blessed," Dad told her. "I am also, by the way, called Jon."

Lillian looked faintly surprised. "Are you?"

"Really?" Dad asked. "Really? I was the only Asian guy who went to our school. I kind of stood out. While you are an identical twin, and I still managed to know your name."

"I'm afraid I don't take your point," Lillian told him. "I

am also afraid that you called me down here to waste my time."

Kami patted Dad on the arm to console him for Lillian Lynburn's entire personality.

"All right, Lucinda," said Dad. "I'll get right to it. I've absorbed that there's a conflict going on between you and your husband, and that you're on the side that doesn't want to hurt anyone."

"I would not go that far," Lillian observed. "Shall we say I don't approve of ritual human sacrifice and leave it there?"

"At last some common ground between us, Leslie," said Dad.

Kami could not quite believe that her father was getting sassy with a sorcerer. She hastily picked up her coffee and hid a smile behind the cup.

"I've also gathered that *my* family has some kind of ability your family might find useful."

"Your family members are sometimes born sources," Lillian clarified.

"Sure, whatever," Dad said. "Lana."

Lillian rested her hands on the belt of her coat. Its ornate gold buckle was in the shape of a woman's face, surrounded by snakelike locks of hair. Lillian's fingers twitched slightly.

"I admit that it has occurred to me that the power a source can lend a sorcerer might prove useful in the battle ahead. Your daughter—"

"We'll leave my daughter out of it, thanks," said Dad. He closed a hand over Kami's when Kami opened her mouth to protest. "But I want to protect my family and my home just as much as you do, Linda. If there is a way that I can help you, I will. How can you tell if you're one of those . . . sources?" He ended the sentence in a questioning voice, as if unsure if he'd gotten the word right.

Lillian gave a brief nod. "I can tell," she said. "If I concentrate." Lillian walked into every room as if she owned it. She walked across this one as if she owned it but was slightly horrified to find herself there, like a queen in a basement. Lillian reached the table that bore their coffee cups and reached over it, framing Jon Glass's face between two fingertips. Her nails were bloodred. She looked into his eyes for a long moment. Kami's father did not flinch, but met her gaze steadily, while Kami held on to his hand. Then Lillian stepped back with a dismissive disdainful gesture that said it all before she spoke: "Seems like being useful skipped a generation."

"So—"

"So you're not a source, and I'm done here," Lillian announced.

"Wait a minute," Dad said. "So I'm not a source, whatever you mean by that. What else can I do? There has to be *something*."

Lillian considered. "Keep out of my way." She headed for the door. Dad abandoned his coffee cup and followed her out, Kami at his heels. "Look. My kids are in trouble, and I want to—"

"Kids?" Lillian repeated. Her ringing tone must have pierced through the walls. As if in answer to a summons, Ten and Tomo were on the stairs, both wearing pajamas and peering down at her.

"Yes, kids, Liz," Dad said impatiently. "The reason I asked you to come here rather than coming to see you."

Lillian was studying the boys. Under her cool, impersonal gaze, Kami could see Tomo's usual eagerness wilting. He backed up a few steps, and shy Ten ranged himself in front of his brother. Kami went to the foot of the stairs so she was in front of both of them.

Lillian's stare flickered to Kami, then away to her father. "Your reasons do not concern me," she told Jon. "I will protect you because you are part of my town, but I have neither the time nor the patience to stand around answering your questions and bearing your insolence."

Anger passed over Dad's face, but he looked at the stairs and bit his lip. "Okay then, Lulubelle," Dad said. "You have a great day."

"That is not my name!" Lillian snapped, finally breaking, and slammed the door behind her.

"Okay, kids, the mannerless sorceress is gone! Go get dressed," Dad yelled, and Ten and Tomo looked grateful to run off. Dad wandered back to the kitchen table and his coffee.

"You are aware she could set your hair on fire just by thinking about it," Kami said casually.

Dad shrugged.

"The sorcerers are the ones with the magic," Kami said. "Nobody knows how to stand against that. When you try . . ."

Kami took a deep breath and walked over to the table. She rolled up both her sleeves and held out her thorn-scarred arms across the table to her father.

Dad looked at them for a moment, then put down his coffee with a bang. He came around the table to take her abruptly in his arms. "Oh, baby girl," Dad said. "Who did that?"

Kami shook her head mutely, face buried against his T-shirt. She was not letting her father go off and get murdered by a sorcerous policeman, or a sorcerous anything else.

Dad rocked her for a moment, almost rocked her off her feet, and pressed a kiss into her hair. "So do you agree with your mum, then? You think we should stay out of this?"

"I can't," Kami said. "I have to do something."

Her dad sighed. "You know, when you were three years old, you got lost in the woods and we found you with your head in a foxes' den. Sometimes I think very little has changed. I mean, you might be a bit taller."

"Short jokes from you, really, Dad?" Kami said into his shirt.

"I don't know what you mean by that, when I am such an ample manly five foot seven," Dad returned. "What are we going to do, then?"

"Well, the thing to do is be sneaky about this," Kami said. "I've found out some names of the other sorcerers, so we know what we're up against. I found a sorcerer in London who might be coming to help the others. And I'm researching something that happened in 1485. An ancestor of ours saved the town, once. And if I can find out how he did it, so can I."

"In 1485?" Dad asked, and she felt him relax at the thought that his kid was only reading records. "Well, uh, I bow to your keen journalistic instincts. But what can I do? How can I help you?"

Kami thought, *You are helping me,* and kept her face

hidden in his shirt another moment. She knew that answer would not satisfy her father. So she said, "I'll let you know."

"Mind you do," said Dad. "And Kami, you promise me: be careful."

"I'll try," Kami told him, and broke away at last. She moved to the other side of the table so she could grab the peanut butter. "Dad," she added, "I was thinking, when all this is over, I'd like to learn some Japanese, if you wanted to teach me." She glanced up from spreading peanut butter on her toast to see her father looking at her.

"Ki o tsukete," he said. *"Kami ga aishite iru."*

Kami leaned her chin in her hand. "What's that mean?"

"It means I always wanted three sons," Dad said. "Really never felt the need for a daughter at all. Three sons would've made me feel all virile."

"Oh, I see," said Kami, and smiled: she knew enough Japanese to be sure he had not said that.

"Well, I have to make sure the pathetic number of sons I actually have are getting dressed," Dad said, and headed for the door. Before he opened it, he looked around and said, *"Arigatou."*

Kami knew the Japanese for "thank you" perfectly well, but she raised her eyebrows interrogatively anyway.

"Means 'get lost,' " Dad explained to her.

Kami stole her father's coffee, smiled against the brim of the cup. "Understood."

Chapter Twenty-Two
His Legacy

Ash was woken on Monday morning by the sound of knocking so loud and violent he thought for a moment that it was a thunderstorm. He tossed in his bed, trying to block out the sound, but it just kept going. Finally he groaned and dragged himself out of bed and his room, lurching toward the noise, intent on making it stop. He met his mother on the stairs. She was in her pink wrap with her hair flying, but she was self-possessed enough to give Ash's ratty pajama bottoms a scornful look before she sailed down the stairs. Ash rolled his eyes and followed her to the front door.

When she opened it, Jared stood framed on the threshold. There was a duffel bag over one shoulder.

"You should have a buzzer installed," he remarked.

"A buzzer installed. In Aurimere?" Lillian asked, sounding as if Jared had suggested performing unspeakable acts with the remains of the Lynburn ancestors.

Jared smirked and said, "Can I come in?"

Lillian, still looking absorbed in her private nightmarish vision of Aurimere with buzzers and elevators, nodded and led Jared into the library. She went and stood looking out the window, wrap pulled tight about her. Ash went to stand by the bookcase where he could see her face and try to puzzle out what she was feeling.

Jared dropped his duffel bag in the center of the floor, then headed for the mantelpiece. Leaning against it, he said, "I thought I might move back in." He said it so casually, after swaggering in as if he had no doubt they would welcome him, or as if it didn't matter much to him whether they did or not.

"Of course you are welcome to move back in," Lillian said. "You're a Lynburn. Aurimere is your home, and is open to you forever."

Jared gave the library, with its carved mantelpiece and tall ebony glass-fronted bookcases, a skeptical slanted look. "See," he said, "that doesn't mean much to me. It's a huge spooky-ass house that must cost a metric ton of money to heat. And I just met you people this summer, and you were strangers, and strangers who were being snotty about the sacred Lynburn tradition. Which appeared to be basically being jerks for hundreds of years and leaving records about it so everyone knows the shame of our jerk legacy. Which honestly seems like a poor move."

Ash refused to let himself smile. He just looked from his affronted mother to his smirking cousin, then decided to stare at the chandelier. It was a series of gold spikes and small glittering lights that combined to look like a shining crown of thorns.

"Only I was thinking that I'd like it, having something like family," Jared said, and looked at Ash's mother. "Some people who matter to me. My mother wanted to leave me in

San Francisco, I know that. But you wanted to take me with you. And you haven't lied to me yet, Aunt Lillian. Besides, you're kind of awful, and I get that. I'm awful sometimes myself."

Mom's face was so expressionless Ash suspected that she was rather taken aback.

"Ash has lied to me, of course, but that's sort of his thing and I also got him to punch me and throw me off a bridge, which counts in his favor."

Jared looked to Ash, apparently for confirmation. Ash made a tentative hand-waving "what he says may be true but please don't think I have transformed into a violent lunatic" gesture.

"And you two could use someone else around. Aunt Lillian, you're too hard on Ash, and he's going to start having the vapors and taking to the fainting couch."

"Oh, thanks," Ash snapped, and Jared grinned at him.

"You can't be mean to him all the time. I want to be mean to him sometimes. We can switch days. I doubt we can get along," Jared said. "But we could rely on each other enough to know that we'll turn on anyone who goes after one of us. And we could have fights and know nobody's going to run away and live in the tavern."

"You can rest assured, Jared," Lillian said, very drily, "I do not ever intend to run away and live in the tavern. Go put your things in your room and we'll say no more about this."

It was not exactly the touching reunion that Ash had imagined. But Jared nodded, scooped his bag off the floor, and headed out. Ash heard his footsteps going up the stairs.

His mother stood at the window with her wrap still pulled tight, eyes turned to her town. "Are you pleased to have him back?" she asked.

Her question startled Ash. He did not recall another time when she had asked him what he felt. The surprise made him actually consider the answer, rather than just telling her what she wanted to hear. "I am," he said slowly. "I mean—I trust him, I think. I want him to be my family. We don't have much family left." He thought, but did not say, that he didn't want it to be just him and his mother and the widening chasm of her disappointment between them.

Mom kept staring out the window, as if she had not heard the answer.

Ash cleared his throat. "Are you pleased?"

"Yes," his mother answered. "What he said, about people who matter to him. That meant something to me. The only people who have ever mattered to me are Lynburns."

"Nobody else?" Ash asked. "Ever?"

"There was someone I thought might matter once," his mother said, and Ash thought about Holly's uncle Edmund, who had been meant to marry his mother and had run away at seventeen instead. "But that came to nothing, and I was the heir of Aurimere. I thought it would be for the best, to keep to ourselves. My pride was hurt, and the Lynburns had to carry on. I let your father persuade me to marry him. I broke my sister's heart. I did worse than that. I knew the man she left with was bad for her, but I didn't think about where Rosalind had learned to believe that she should be punished. I was always making decisions for her. I never worried that she didn't argue with me. I didn't want her to argue. And you see what has come of that. Rosalind went away for years, and now she has left me and Aurimere again.

"Jared came back." His mother's voice sank a little. "My sister might come back too. I hope she will. That's who matters to me, Rosalind and Jared and you."

"Not Dad?"

His mother was silent for a long moment. Then she said, "No. Jared was right about one thing. Nobody is born family. You have to show some loyalty: you have to want to be family. I don't think your father ever did. He wants us to be a different family, like he wants this to be a different town. He's my enemy. And I will fight him."

It had been just him and Mom and Dad for years. And it had never meant to either of them what it had meant to Ash. They had both simply been waiting for their real family to be reunited, and their real lives to resume.

If this was his chance for a family, Ash wanted to be sure it was real this time. "I wasn't sure I still mattered to you," he said. He hated that he sounded so needy when he was telling the truth.

"Of course you matter."

"But you said . . ." Ash's mouth was so dry that for a moment his voice failed him. "You said I was such a coward."

"Standing by, knowing your father was perpetrating atrocities, wasn't very brave, was it?"

Ash bowed his head.

"But that doesn't mean you have to be a coward forever," his mother said. "You stood up against your father in the end. I do not know how to say soothing words to you, Ash. I had high hopes for you, and you disappointed me. But I let you down too: I left you to Rob, like I left Rosalind. If you had gone to Rob, if you had gone from me too, it would have broken my heart."

His mother had never spoken to him of her heart before, and now she was talking about it in a calm, practical voice. Ash wanted to reach out, assure her somehow that he would never hurt her.

"We both want to help you," he offered. "Jared and me."

"Oh, help me." His mother almost laughed. "I do not want either of you to help me. That's the problem. Helping me is dangerous work, and you are both children. Rob almost died completing the ceremony of the pools: he would have died if I had not saved him. And Jared went off to do it on his own, without instruction, without preparation. I do not know how he survived. I thought that I had killed him. You are both so young. I want my other sorcerers to be good enough to stop Rob without either of you."

"How's it going?" Ash asked.

His mother was obdurately silent. She'd said enough when she implied she was struggling. His mother never admitted defeat.

"You know Kami?" Ash said.

His mother raised her eyebrows. "All too well. Her father called me in to see him," she volunteered. "He called me Linda and Lulubelle and a number of other names beginning with *L*. I think the man's mentally unbalanced, although possibly good at crosswords."

Ash suppressed a smile. "Kami was able to get past Dad's spell and get in touch with a sorcerer in London. We hope that he'll bring other sorcerers down to help us."

"The idea of being beholden to a bunch of scruffy sorcerers with no sources to speak of and no place of their own is hideous," his mother murmured.

Ash saw the slight relaxing of her shoulders and realized the extent of her relief. At the same time, he realized the extent of her dread, and how bad the situation must be. They only had one more sunrise, and then the solstice would come: the sorcerers from London had to come too.

Chapter Twenty-Three
The New Sorcerer

"I hate suspense," Angela grumbled. "I wish that Rob and his merry band of evildoers would quit waiting around for the stupid solstice, strike the town with lightning, and prance around the smoking wreckage wearing our entrails as necklaces."

Shockingly, there was no support for Angela's point of view from anyone else in the headquarters. Of course, it was only Kami, Holly, and Angela. Rusty did not count, since he appeared to be actually asleep on the sofa. Kami had tried dropping pencils on his head to test this, and he was now curled peacefully slumbering with pencils in his hair.

Kami had texted for everyone to meet in the headquarters after school on Monday. Jared and Ash were still not here.

"Rob has made a fatal mistake by giving us time to band together and make amazingly cunning plans, which we are doing," Kami said.

She did not let herself think about how little time they had left. She was busy at her desk, separating out all the sorcerers' possessions they had stolen into a dozen even parcels in small brown bags. If a teacher came in, Kami was going to claim it was a craft project.

"Are we?" Angela asked. "We don't even know if these spells work. We haven't tested them out."

"That's why we're going to test them out now. Because we're a team," Kami said. "The six of us."

Angela looked around the room, her lips moving as she counted the number of people there. Her eyes slid along the gray walls and the fake-wood desks as if she thought Jared and Ash might be hiding under Kami's ruler.

"Yes, all right, I take your point," Kami grumbled.

"But I did not make it aloud," said Angela. "Because I hold you in true affection."

She said it mockingly but Kami smiled at her, and after a moment Angela smiled back, white teeth against scarlet lips, the most beautiful girl in Sorry-in-the-Vale by a thousand miles.

The door opened, and Kami saw Ash on the threshold. Jared was behind him, a shadow whose face she could not make out, but she saw how Ash was briefly dazzled and dazed by Angela's smile. She wished for a shameful moment that they had not appeared at that exact time.

Ash nodded to them all and walked in. He smiled at Kami too, his smile as soft as Angela's was bright. "Kami," he said, and she realized he looked happy for a change. "Hey, you look great."

She was in the same outfit she'd worn Sunday, down to the earrings. She'd wanted Jared to see it.

"Thank you," Kami said, the little compliment shoring

up her confidence. She wondered about how Ash and Jared had come in together, apparently in amity. Then she nerved herself, hoping no change showed on her face, and looked at Jared. He was leaning against the wall of the headquarters, the way he always had to lean against something.

He looked more or less the same as ever, in his scarred leather jacket, his smile a twist that could not be compared to Ash's or Angela's. But this was his smile; she knew how it felt from the inside out, and it always made her smile helplessly back.

"At last!" said Kami. "We're going to go down to the woods, and the two of you are going to try and kill or capture the rest of us."

"Sounds like a good time," Ash responded doubtfully.

Jared went over to Kami's desk to examine the tiny pouches: dabs of Ruth's lipstick, a corner torn from Amber Green's notebook, hair from brushes left behind by Rob and Rosalind. The flotsam and jetsam of sorcerers' daily lives.

"One more ingredient before the spell," said Kami. "Come here, Samson."

She picked up her tiny pair of scissors, sharp and glittering in the afternoon light, and Jared leaned helpfully across the desk. It was easy to grab a piece of his hair: one lock curled around Kami's finger as soon as she touched it. The afternoon sun touched it too, turning it into spun gold.

Jared was looking up at her for a change. He said, "Hey there, Delilah," and her scissor blades sheared the lock away.

Kami put the lock into one of her little bags, then tied the bag closed with twine and put it in Jared's hand.

"A drop of blood, a single tear, a lock of hair, what you

hold dear," Jared murmured, and Kami thought she could hear magic crackling behind his words. "Do not touch me. Do not come near."

Light not from the sun passed over his cupped hand, making the bag shine as if it had suddenly become a cache of jewels. Then the bright moment was over, and Jared tossed the bag back over to Kami. She caught it.

"So. Think I can hurt you?" Kami asked, grinning.

He crossed his arms over his chest and regarded her sidelong. "I know you can."

* * *

The woods were alive with ice and fire, the leaves whispering tales to sorcerers. Kami ducked behind a holly bush, its waxy leaves and bright berries providing some slight cover, and watched Jared stalking through the trees. She kept her breathing as quiet as she could, watching him turn his head her way.

Tree branches reached out for her from the other direction, flame sparking along the bark, and Kami had to retreat fast from the cover of the bush, still crouched low on the earth, and made as if to rise as she watched Jared's jean-clad legs approach.

He threw a fireball at her, and Kami held up her little pouch that contained so many stolen relics from sorcerers and one waving lock of Jared's hair.

"Noli me tangere," she said, the words to activate the spell.

The fireball disappeared into a cloud of something paler than smoke, like a puff of breath on a winter day.

Jared came toward her. She ducked back to the ground the instant he reached her side, kneeling to toss him over her shoulder and into a tree. He went flying and hit hard, his head connecting with a loud crack, then slid down the trunk and lay still.

Kami stood up and could not help clapping her hands together.

"Awesome!"

Jared blinked up at her from the forest floor, pine needles in his hair and eyes not focused. "Oh, thanks."

"No, but seriously," Kami said. "This is a teaching moment. Did you see how the fire on the branch flickered out when your head hit the tree? We've got to break their focus on whatever source they are using. And we can already stop them using any magic on us."

She looked around, and was disappointed none of the others appeared to be there to share the exciting discovery.

Jared was being totally unsupportive. "So you're going to be telling Angela to aim for my head?" he asked. "This is terrible news."

"I'll tell her not to kill anyone during our training sessions," Kami told him. "That is a waste of resources. And also personally I would be upset."

"Thanks," Jared said, softer this time, as if he meant it. Or possibly as if speaking louder would hurt his head.

Kami walked over to the place where he lay and looked down at him, a little worried. Winter sunlight was spearing in a line of brilliant white through the trees, and lying on the earth with Jared were brown leaves, dry and curled and crackling beneath her boots.

Jared seemed to have no interest in getting up. He lay there, eyes hooded, almost closed, and his fingers loosely curled in among the dead leaves. Kami stood over him, watching the darkness cast by the branches touch his still face, light striking the small bright scimitar curves of his lashes, painting the shadows beneath in long lines over his cheekbones. A slight pressure made her look down and see Jared's hand had shot out: his fingers were circling her ankle.

"Is this the scene where the dauntless heroine approaches the villain and he grabs her because he's not quite as hurt as he's pretending?" he drawled.

Kami stooped and grabbed his wrist in one clean economical movement, using her grip to flip him over onto his stomach and coincidentally very close to a large stone, half-hidden in the dirt. She knelt lightly in the leaves, knees on either side of his body, and let go of his wrist only to grasp the hair at the back of his head.

"No, this is the scene where the dauntless heroine grabs the sucker who didn't think she was ready for him, and bashes his brains out against a rock."

She used her grip on his hair to gently mimic that movement, not letting his forehead actually connect with the stone.

"I won't give a demonstration that is completely true to life."

"I appreciate that," Jared told her. "Can I— I'm going to get leaves up my nose."

Kami didn't understand what he meant right away, but she got it when he turned over, moving gently so as not to dislodge her. He lay on his back in the leaves again, staring up at her. The winter sunlight poured in cool on his face, shimmered on his gray eyes.

It did not matter what distant iron city had raised him. He had been made by Sorry-in-the-Vale, his bones as much a part of it as the valley and the woods. It was as if she had the whole town spread underneath her. Or the whole world, since right then he was the only part of it that mattered.

His hair, dark gold on bronze, mingled with the scattered gold-brown leaves. There was dirt smudged on the unscarred side of his face, pressed like a gray shadow on the paler hollow of his throat.

She was keenly aware of the warmth of his sides and the lift of his ribs against the inside of her knees, and the fact that she was wearing a dress.

"Hey," she whispered.

She saw him swallow, saw the pulse point at the base of his throat flicker. "Hey," he answered, and the audible rasp in his voice made her smile.

Against her tights-sheened skin, she felt tension pull his body taut and hoped it was a good thing as she leaned forward. The pale light in his eyes made them shine like mirrors, and as her shadow fell on his face his eyes went dark, intent and tender. Her hair swung from behind her ears as she leaned in, just long enough to hang a curtain between them and everyone else.

She leaned down slowly, until his breath was touching her lips, and she felt how unevenly it came. He was perfectly, absolutely still beneath her: if he raised himself on his elbows, lifted his body at all, they would be in dangerous territory.

Kami did not care. She propped herself up with a hand on the earth by his head and let her lips touch his, very lightly, catching his shuddering breath in her mouth.

"Kami!" Holly's voice had never been so entirely unwelcome. "Kami, we think we may have killed Ash."

Kami jerked away at the sound of her name, and by the time Holly's cry was done ringing through the trees she was sitting on the ground a very respectable distance from Jared, knees drawn up to her chest and dress covering the tops of her boots. She felt a little light-headed: she could not quite believe what she had been doing.

"They better have killed someone," Jared said, sitting up and scowling. "Or I will."

She looked over at him and all the dark glowering he was doing, and found herself smiling.

"Come on," she said.

They both scrambled up off the ground and began to make their way through the trees in the direction Holly's voice had come from. The thought did cross Kami's mind that Jared might possibly take her hand or put his arm around her shoulders, do one of the things that said "Yes, together" to everyone who saw you, and to the person you were with, as well.

He did not. When they broke through the trees to reach the bank of the Sorrier River, Kami forgot about that because Ash was bleeding from the ear.

It seemed her friends had figured out about going for the sorcerer's head and disrupting their focus.

"I may have gone ever so slightly too far," Angela admitted grudgingly.

She was standing with her arms crossed, leaning against a tree. In her vivid scarlet-and-cobalt-striped silk top, she looked like an exotic bird that had gotten lost in an English wood and was feeling grouchy about it. Holly was standing by her, being supportive of Angela's assault-related decisions. Which meant it was left to Rusty to administer womanly sympathy. He was kneeling on the riverbank beside Ash, who was sitting with his legs dangling over the water and looking a little forlorn.

"Blondie looks totally fine," Rusty said in his slow pleasant voice. "Aside from the bleeding, that is."

Kami felt Ash could do with a little more sympathy than that. She rushed over and knelt at Ash's other side, Jared following her.

"How are you doing?" she asked Ash, touching the side of his face lightly with her fingertips. There was a trail of blood coming from his ear, but other than that he seemed okay.

"I'm all right," Ash said, sounding rueful. "I don't know why it's always me."

Kami put a hand on his shoulder and rubbed it comfortingly.

"How many fingers am I holding up?" Jared asked. She looked and saw him holding up three.

"Three," Ash said.

Jared frowned. "Oh dear. That's not right. Buddy, I think you need a hospital."

Kami dropped the hand that had been rubbing Ash's shoulder to punch Jared in the shin. "I'm sorry, Ash, he's a jerk," she said. "He's a jerk who is holding up three fingers."

Jared made a relenting sound, half grumble and half sigh, and reached over to help Ash up. "All right, let's get you home," he said, and Kami realized he meant Aurimere.

They were all talking as they left the woods, Angela and Kami about how they could apply this new knowledge to fighting sorcerers, Kami planning what they would tell Lillian, with Jared contributing that they could possibly bypass Lillian and tell the sorcerers she was training, and Holly volunteering to speak to Mrs. Thompson because she was her great-aunt. Rusty was plaintively talking about dinnertime.

Ash had color back in his face by the time they were out of the woods and walking up to Aurimere, but Kami drew level with him so she could check on him anyway.

"How are you holding up? I'm sorry about Jared," she added, loudly enough so that Jared could hear, and he tossed a grin at her over his shoulder. "He is incorrigible," Kami said. "He cannot be corriged. Believe me, I've tried."

"He doesn't bother me," said Ash, easily enough so she thought it might almost be true. "Give me a little time and I'll be fine."

Ash looked sorry as soon as he had said it, and the rest of them went quiet. They had so little time left.

In the silence, Kami looked up the curving path to Aurimere and saw someone coming down it. The sky was darkening and the sun was in her eyes, so at first all her vision was able to resolve was a dark shape. Then the details coalesced: the springy mass of brown curls, the thin serious face, the beaky nose and the glasses perched on top of it.

Henry Thornton.

Kami left Ash's side and ran up the path, not stopping until she was standing just a foot away from him. She saw Henry look at her, going through the same process she had: confusion followed by recognition based on a single encounter, matching her up with the voice on the phone that had begged him to please help, to please try.

"You came," Kami said at last.

Henry smiled, a shy and slightly nervous smile. "I did," he said. "I had to. You—you sounded as if you were in real trouble."

"Oh, we are. Thank you," said Kami as the others drew level with them.

Henry's gaze skittered warily over the faces of Jared and Ash, the Lynburns. Appreciation flickered briefly in his eyes when he saw Angela and Holly, who were sort of overwhelming placed side by side, but his eyes were dragged back to the Lynburns. Kami wondered just what Rob had done to him to scare him so badly.

Ash absorbed the situation at a glance and took charge of it gracefully. "Welcome to Aurimere," he said, extending his hand, making a bloody boy in a dusty road seem like a lord greeting an honored guest. "I can't express how glad we are to see you."

Henry hesitated, but accepted Ash's hand and faintly returned his smile. It was very hard to resist Ash's charm when he turned it full on, Kami thought, even when you knew that he was playing you.

"Hey, man," Rusty said, seeming to note this was an important occasion and giving Henry a sleepy grin. "Who are you again?"

"You must stay at Aurimere," Ash said, sweeping away the awkward pause. "You and everyone you have brought with you. You're all friends of Aurimere now. You're most welcome."

There was a much more awkward pause then. Henry looked at them all as if he was so sorry.

He did not have to say a word. They all stood there on the path to Aurimere, silent and huddled together against the cold realization that Henry had come alone: that Rob was coming tomorrow, and there would be nobody to help them.

PART VI
STORM CLOUDS GATHER

Over the woodlands brown and bare,
Over the harvest-fields forsaken,
Silent, and soft, and slow
Descends the snow.
. . . .

This is the poem of the air,
Slowly in silent syllables recorded;
This is the secret of despair. . . .
—*Henry Wadsworth Longfellow*

Chapter Twenty-Four
Farewell Fear

Lillian took Henry's news without turning a hair.

"I asked everyone I could think of," Henry said, standing humbly by the mantel in the drawing room. "People I didn't know, that my mother had only heard about. Everybody said that Sorry-in-the-Vale makes its own laws and should be left to itself."

"That much is true," Lillian murmured.

Henry looked like a tradesman summoned in to hear the lady of the manor's pleasure. Kami could envision him twisting his cap between his hands.

"All the sorcerers I've been in touch with, we don't have much power. We don't have traditions or official records. There are a few powerful families, but they keep to themselves. We don't have a community of sorcerers like you do."

"Because this community is working out so well," Kami said.

Lillian turned her ice-gray gaze on Kami. "This is sorcerers' business."

"Anything that's my business is Kami's business," Jared said. He was leaning against the wall, and had nodded at

Rusty and Ash to join him; they were standing on either side of him.

Kami had not realized quite what he was doing until she tilted her head and saw him from the angle Lillian was seeing him: he, Ash, and Rusty had formed a team behind Henry, having his back.

"We have no time," Kami said. "We're all in this together, because we all suffer if Rob wins. You're going to have to put up with me. I'm not going away."

Lillian's hair was loose for a change, and she looked tired, eyes sunken in her face. It made her look frighteningly like Rosalind. "Fine," she said. "We have to make a contingency plan anyway."

Ash started. "Mother, what do you mean?"

"If Rob wins," said Lillian. "I'm not saying that he will. Of course he won't. But it is only sensible to have a backup plan. If he wins, I'll be dead."

"Mom!" The word seemed ripped from Ash.

"Don't call me that, Ash," Lillian snapped. "I'll be dead; we both have to face that. Rob crosses the threshold of Aurimere and takes the town over my dead body. That is the responsibility I inherited from my mother; that is the bargain of our town. Before I surrender Sorry-in-the-Vale, I will die. And I cannot allow the only Lynburns left to be Rob and Rosalind. So you and Jared cannot take part in the battle tomorrow. You have to get out of Sorry-in-the-Vale and gather your resources; then you can come back and crush him."

She sat down in one of the high-backed gold chairs, crossing her legs and turning her face away from her son. There was another hush among the group, as there had been when they realized that Henry had come alone. It sank in for all of them that Lillian had basically told them that she believed she was going to lose.

Lillian looked around the room. "Where are the others? The Prescott girl and the good-looking one?"

"Baby," said Rusty, "I'm right here."

Lillian gave him a horrified look, then bent her gaze on Kami, who said, "Holly and Angela are talking to some of the sorcerers who haven't chosen a side yet. You told us that we were excluded from your plans, so we made our own."

Under Lillian's gaze, Kami wished she had sat on one of the high-backed gold chairs as well, though Lillian's head would still have been well above hers, and Lillian would still have been able to look down her nose. However, Kami felt she would have had more dignity than she currently did, sitting small and alone, practically lost in a slightly cracked leather sofa.

Jared broke ranks behind Henry and strode over to Kami, crossing the room under her startled gaze. She thought he was coming to sit beside her, but instead he slung himself to the floor and sat at her feet, one arm clasped loose around his drawn-up knee and his head bent toward her. She could have reached out and ruffled his hair.

Lillian looked both taken aback and displeased. Kami was a little taken aback herself, but she supposed it was a gesture aimed at Lillian, and she touched his shoulder lightly in thanks. "If I said that I was ready to hear your plans now . . . ," Lillian proposed, her face impassive.

"I haven't been holding back to punish you," Kami said helplessly. "We've been practicing how to fight more effectively against sorcerers. I've been trying to find out about Matthew Cooper, and Elinor and Anne Lynburn, because they were able to defend the town once."

"Against some ordinary king's pathetic soldiers," Lillian sneered.

Henry stared at her, as the only one who was unused to Lillian acting as if she lived in the 1700s. Then he looked away, at his own hands, twisting them together against the white stone of the mantelpiece, where flowers and drowning women tangled together in a marble river.

"It was brave of you to come," Kami told him. "Alone, and for strangers. We all owe you more than we could ever repay."

"Let's show Henry to his room," Ash suggested

Henry looked grateful for the reprieve. They walked toward the door, sweeping him away in their rush.

"You could always come back to our place if you don't fancy Aurimere," Rusty suggested.

"That's okay," Henry said, giving Rusty a look of relief that there was another guy around that wasn't a Lynburn. "But, er, thank you. So I gather things aren't going terribly well?" His green eyes, unexpectedly bright behind his glasses, sought Kami's.

"Not terribly," she said. She felt distant, part of her still in the next room with Lillian, remembering her talk with businesslike valor about a last stand. "This is so stupid," she exclaimed. "We can't go out there with less than half the amount of sorcerers Rob has and try to face him down in the town square. We need to take Rob and the others by surprise."

Henry blinked three times in quick succession. Kami

looked away from him, let her eyes slide to where they wanted
to go and catch on Jared's face. He was already looking at her.

"Let's go," Jared said.

Kami smiled back at him, a current of excitement passing
between them.

Ash said heavily, "My mother would never agree."

They all knew it was true. She was set on her sorcerers'
battle, on a display of strength before the town. They had a
better chance with Lillian than without her, and the very few
sorcerers they had would follow Lillian's lead.

"Well," said Kami, "at the very least, we need to make
sure all Lillian's sorcerers have the advantages we can give
them. Holly and Angela are on it, but we need to all be talking to them. We need to give them the bags we made. Ash
should take the ladies, because he's charming."

Ash looked pleased. Jared raised his eyebrows.

"Are you saying that I'm not a charmer?"

"You are very dear to me, but you have all the savoir faire
of a wildebeest," Kami told him.

"A wildebeest," Jared repeated.

"A dashingly handsome wildebeest," Kami assured him.
"Now let's go call on some sorcerers. Bring me a revolution."

She looked away from him and saw Rusty's glance from
her to Jared, alert for a moment. The Lynburn boys withdrew
in opposite directions, while Kami sidled over to Rusty.

"Don't look at me like you know something," she said.
"You don't know something."

"I know many things," Rusty told her. "I am a very great
genius. I'm going to go charm some people too. I may not be
a Lynburn, but I am the most charming mofo in town." He

gave her a hug and said, "Take care of yourself, Cambridge," in an unusually serious way.

For a moment she thought he was warning her about Jared, but then she realized that this could be one of the last times they saw each other. Rusty smoothed a hand down Kami's hair and she hugged him back, and could not watch as he left. She looked away instead, and caught Henry's eye.

"You seem to have a lot of friends," Henry said, a little wistfully. "Must be nice. Being a—what I am—it's hard to get close to people. I always thought that Sorry-in-the-Vale, where magic was an open secret, I thought that it would be amazing. Meeting a Lynburn, sorcerers who can do things like in the stories, I thought it would be like meeting a legend."

"Ah," said Kami. "Sorry about Lillian, then."

Henry smiled, a slight smile that disappeared almost as soon as it was born. "She's a lot better than Rob," he said. "I couldn't believe it when he called me and asked me to come to Sorry-in-the-Vale. I thought he was going to show me something wonderful. And instead he killed a helpless animal in front of me. He told me all magic ended in blood." Henry shivered as if he was back in that night, watching his dreams turn to ash and blood. "I don't want to believe that about sorcery," he said. "I don't want to believe that about myself. I mean, I'm a vegetarian."

Kami laughed quietly, but not to mock him. "I know about magic that is nothing like that," she said. "And I know a few sorcerers. They're just people who can do an extra thing. All right, a high percentage of them seem to be lunatics, but I think that's down to being Lynburns and seriously inbred."

Henry laughed in his turn, a quick startled laugh. "I thought there must be something else to magic besides the blood," he said. "I wanted to prove that there was. And then you called."

"And you proved it," Kami told him, and patted his arm. "I'm sorry about hitting you with a chair, Henry. You're good people."

Henry shrugged, minimally. "I'm sorry for threatening your friend with a gun." He looked around and added, "This is some place, Aurimere. My mother had never seen it, but she and her friend who was a sorcerer, they used to talk about it. Like you'd talk about Camelot."

They both looked around then: at the hall outside the library with its dark carved doors, the glass windows stained crimson and white, and the shining flight of stairs that led up to the ebony- and ivory-inlaid representation of a woman by a pool. It was imposing, terrifying, and sometimes beautiful, but it did not look like a place where good things happened. There was so much of Aurimere, like the sorcerers' magic, that was tainted.

Neither of them had mentioned the fact that Henry might have come here to die, that Rob might have been right after all. This magic might well end in blood.

* * *

Even though she was supposed to call Mrs. Thompson Aunt Ingrid, Holly had always been slightly afraid of her. Not for any reason, just in the way kids are of old people, the span of a whole lifetime stretching between the two points where they stood.

She was trying not to be afraid as she crossed the threshold of the sweetshop where "Aunt Ingrid" worked. She was mostly succeeding, because Angie was with her.

It was much more difficult to be scared with Angela striding at your side. It became less difficult when Holly saw that with Mrs. Thompson was Ms. Dollard, the headmistress of their school.

Holly was okay at school, and actually good at some subjects, but she always felt like Ms. Dollard thought that was a fluke and was studying Holly's clothes to see what she was wearing that was against regulations. Kami talked to Ms. Dollard like she was a friend, and Angie stared through her as if she was a nuisance. Holly didn't know how they dared.

Especially since now it seemed that Ms. Dollard was a sorceress.

"Well, hello," Angie drawled. "Having a little conference about the evil taking over our town? Have the words 'We're totally screwed' come up yet?"

"Angela Montgomery, don't talk like that," said Ms. Dollard. Her dark hair, streaked with gray, was in a short bob, and she wore expensive earrings: she didn't look so different from when they were in school, except that she was wearing jeans. "And don't interfere with things that don't concern you."

Mrs. Thompson—Aunt Ingrid—said nothing, but her eyes on Angie were not friendly. Surprise and fear burst in Holly at the same time: a new feeling, not being scared for herself but very specifically for someone else.

Angie was a stranger in Sorry-in-the-Vale, and she had no magic.

Holly put a hand on Angie's wrist, soothing and restraining and on her side all at once. "Doesn't this concern all of us, Aunt Ingrid?" she asked, using the name very deliberately. "We want to help."

"How can you?" Aunt Ingrid asked.

Angela slipped her wrist out of Holly's hold and strode across the floor. She walked like Lillian Lynburn, but Lillian had magic and Aurimere at her back. All Angie had was defiance of the whole world, but she made it work. Nobody could look anywhere else as she tossed two small dark bags, tied with twine, on the countertop.

"Things from Rob's sorcerers," she said. "Hair, blood, possessions. Anything we could get. You're sorcerers, aren't you? You can use these to protect yourselves. You can use them to fight . . . if you decide to fight. "

"This is for Sorry-in-the-Vale," Holly said. "For the whole town."

"I know that, girl," said Aunt Ingrid. She picked up the two bags and laid them on the scales where she measured out gumdrops and peppermint swirls. "Clever idea."

"Kami Glass's," said Angie, sounding proud. Holly wished Angie had a reason to sound like that, talking about her.

Ms. Dollard smiled at the name and touched one of the bags.

"That girl's a pistol," said Mrs. Thompson. "Seems like all three of you girls are set on getting into as much trouble as you possibly can." She didn't seem angry about it. Holly thought, actually, that it might be the first time Aunt Ingrid had looked at her with some approval.

Holly and Angie exchanged a slow smile.

"I guess we don't mind getting into trouble," Holly said, "as long as we get things done."

* * *

After Kami was done handing out the spelled bags to sorcerers, she went back up to Aurimere and spent hours in the records room reading up desperately on Matthew Cooper, as if there might be some clue hidden in plain sight she was going to find at the eleventh hour. She just needed something to do so she would not go mad waiting.

There were some papers, obviously newer, white instead of yellow and with ink still blue instead of brown, which she had skipped over. She looked at them now and saw the year 1485 written in royal blue across the snowy white. If someone had wanted to preserve the records, and some of the older pages had crumbled or decayed almost past reading, transcribing them made sense.

Kami looked through them, hope surging in her chest, and saw it was just a long list of presents to the Lynburns that seemed to be payment. On the side was written "for the harvest." She had seen that a lot in the records already, gifts given for good weather and luck with the animals and land. This harvest must have been pretty great, because the list of gifts to the Lynburns was long. It ended in "silk for the Lady Anne's shroud, for she is drowned and lost, and will be buried by our farthest wall. Their memories lie under Matthew Cooper's stone and wrapped in Anne Lynburn's silk."

Drowned in the Crying Pools, perhaps? But there was nothing else.

So much for eleventh-hour discoveries. Kami leaned her head in her hand. She'd been certain that Matthew Cooper and the Lynburn sisters had been the key to something. She still felt certain of it, but she did not know how to unlock the mystery. She did not know if she could trust her own instinct, and they were out of time.

The world outside the wall of windows had gone black as ink by the time Jared came up from the town and joined her in the records room. She'd given up on the contents of the records table and was standing at the windows watching the light in the sky die out completely when the door opened, and Jared was there at last. He looked as tired as she felt.

The wall of windows seemed to have captured the lights of the room, holding brightness trapped in its yellow panes like something in a display case. Beyond the windows was absolutely opaque blackness, as if the rest of the world had been cut away.

Kami watched Jared walking slowly across the room to her. It was oddly peaceful for a moment, just to watch him and stop thinking. He'd taken off his jacket and he was wearing a light, pale gray jumper. His eyes looked darker gray in comparison, shadowed and troubled but steady.

Here he was, the one of the younger Lynburn generation who people automatically took a step back from rather than a step toward. Like one of the marble Lynburn busts or one of the Lynburn paintings come to rough, vivid life: her imaginary friend and constant dream come to life.

When he closed the distance between them, not touching her but with his face bent down to hers, she turned up her face to his with only inches and light between them and felt like she had been waiting years for this. Here he was, at last.

"If you want to storm Monkshood Abbey right now, just you and me, I'm in," he said.

"That would be a suicide mission. And before you say it, I know you would go on a suicide mission," Kami said. "And how do I know that? Because you go on them all the time. It's like the Land of Suicide Mission is your favorite holiday destination."

Don't do it anymore, she thought. *Try to be safe.*

Jared's eyes scanned her face. "You don't have to worry," he said softly. "I never wanted to die. I only wanted to be useful somehow. I would have done anything, and I was unhappy enough that I didn't care what happened to me."

"But you do care now," Kami said unsteadily.

"Yes," Jared told her. "I care now."

He touched her then, not to kiss her but to put his hand on the small of her back, draw her in against his body. He was solid against her, lean muscle supporting her weight. Kami rested her cheek against the soft material of his jumper.

"I like your jumper," she said into it.

"You like my what?" Jared asked. Kami tugged at his sleeve in response and he laughed. "In the civilized land of the Americas, we call that a sweater. A jumper is a dress. You might as well have just said, 'Why, Jared, what a fetching frock you're wearing today.'"

"Why, Jared, what a fetching frock you're wearing today," Kami said instantly, raising her head so she could lift her face up to his. "You look ever so pretty."

Jared laughed, a soft huff of breath, and rested his forehead gently against hers. "Your frock's fairly fetching as well."

Kami closed her eyes, embarrassed to let him see she was
happy he'd noticed. "Thanks."

"Not as fetching as mine, of course," Jared added. "I am
the prettiest."

Kami pushed him with no force behind it, because she
did not want him even a fraction of an inch farther away.
"One of the few reasons to be glad you came to Sorry-in-the-
Vale. We live until summer, and you can make your bid to
be Queen of the May."

"Kami," Jared said, "I could never be sorry I came. No
matter what happens. I want you to remember that. I'll
always be glad."

Kami punched him hard enough to make him stumble
back a step and let go of her.

"You jerk," she said.

Jared looked extremely surprised.

"You could never be sorry?" Kami repeated. "You want
me to remember that? No matter what happens? Don't you
dare give me the soldier-marching-off-to-his-death speech.
That's rubbish. Remember this, Jared Lynburn. I will not let
you die."

Jared started to laugh, a quiet but real laugh, tipping his
head back against the golden glass. Then he reached forward,
still leaning against the glass, snagged the material of her
dress at her waist, and pulled her in toward him.

She slid her arm around his neck and felt the curl of his
hair against the nape, the solid press of his body against her,

and thought, *Real, and mine.* It was enough. "I have to go," Kami said. "I should go home."

It occurred to her after she said it that he might ask her to stay. Kami had been stroking his hair; now her hands closed, one on the warmth of his neck and one in the waving ends of his hair, getting a grip on him. Panic and anticipation wound through her, twined. She did not know how to untangle them. The idea was like cupping a burning coal in her hands, shifting it from palm to palm, and yet the brightness of it held her eyes and she could not bear to put it down.

Almost every time he touched her, he hesitated, and she was scared too: she remembered being in the shower thinking about her skin as new territory. She thought about his skin now like a land to be discovered, and her grip on him loosened. Her hands trembled.

"Of course." Jared stepped away from her and made a gesture toward the door. "You should go."

Kami nodded and hesitated. She'd already been gone a long time. She really should be getting home. She went toward the door, and looked over her shoulder to where Jared stood leaning against the window, looking after her as she went. She put her hand on the brass hand doorknob. Then she let go of the metal hand and ran back to Jared, so fast that she almost knocked him backward. He caught her by the elbows and she ignored the fact that gravity had just almost defeated them both, and kissed him until she felt his mouth curve against hers, until she could forget for a moment that the world was closing in dark all around them, that the sorcerers were coming for blood tomorrow. She did not know how he felt, but she knew how she did: she was no longer scared to want him, intensely and absolutely, to keep and to the exclusion of all else. She felt like he had taught her how to want: she had never felt even a shadow of anything like this for anyone but him.

"Remember," she said, "I will not let you die."

Chapter Twenty-Five
Kami's Sacrifice

The sun was setting on the bare branches and frost-touched stones of Sorry-in-the-Vale. It was almost the night of the winter solstice.

Three hours before Rob Lynburn was due to appear in the town square, they were getting into position. Kami had already rung the bell and looked through the windows of the Kenn household and seen that the house was empty. Their garden was up for grabs.

"When you called me and said bring garden shears, I really thought it might be for decapitation purposes," said Angela. "I truly wish that had been the case." Despite her words, Angela wielded the shears effectively, able to reach branches of the fir tree that Kami simply could not stretch up to. Across from them, Jared and Ash, and Holly and Rusty, were, respectively, shearing at a holly bush and a yew tree. They were stacking branches up on the low stone wall to make a screen to hide behind.

Kami had noted that Holly had come with Rusty and Angela, on quite a different path from the one that led to where she lived.

"Did Holly stay with you last night?" Kami asked in a low voice.

"Yes." Angela saw Kami's look. "No," she added very firmly, "it's nothing like that. Things are so bad with her family, and there's other stuff too. I'm just being a friend."

"Okay," Kami said.

Angela's lip curled. "I don't want to be anything besides friends," she stated. "Not anymore."

When annoyed, Angela was not a mistress of stealth. She spoke a little too loudly. Over Angela's shoulder, Kami saw Holly register the words. Kami couldn't quite read Holly's expression: Holly moved toward Jared, handing him another branch with a smile and removing herself from earshot.

Kami could read Angela's expression perfectly well: it said that Kami had been silent for much too long. "Whatever you say, Angela," she said hastily.

Angela narrowed her eyes. "I *don't*."

"I believe you," Kami said, making her voice even more innocent.

"I've been your friend for years with no ulterior motive," Angela reminded her, scowling.

"I don't know that," Kami said. "You could secretly harbor a fevered passion for me. You could have bodacious-asianbeauties.com bookmarked as one of your favorite sites. This could have been your motive for friendship all along."

Angela rolled her eyes. "I first met you when you were twelve. You were not exactly bodacious at twelve."

"I had hotential," Kami said.

Angela pinned her with a despairing look.

"When you see somebody who is too young to be actually hot, but you can tell they're going to be one day? Hotential. Like potential, but hot."

Kami set another branch on top of the wall, this one screening her face. When she looked back at Angela, she saw Angela regarding her with an odd expression on her face.

"What?"

"You always make jokes about your looks," Angela said. "You really shouldn't. You're all right. You know, fairly fanciable."

"I knew it!"

"But not to *me*," Angela said. "Not ever. Not because of your looks, because you are half a ton of crazy in a five-pound sack."

"Ah, but is it a bodacious sack?"

Angela sneered at her. Kami grinned back, and after a minute, Angela's sneer turned into a smile.

"Holly's lucky to have you," Kami said. "So am I."

"I know, right?" Angela asked. "I have no idea how you got so lucky. Speaking of which." Her eyes slid over to the holly bush, where Jared and Ash were cheating by using magic not to get cut by the spiky leaves. "What's going on with Jared?" Angela asked.

"I can't . . ." Kami didn't know how to explain it, hope and fear, wanting and shrinking from touch, kissing and talking about love but not talking about anything in normal, casual ways. She didn't know if she had a boyfriend.

"It's complicated," she said. "But I'm—I'm really happy." It was confusing, but it hurt significantly less than the confusion of him wanting nothing to do with her.

"Well," Angela said, "that's good."

That was when Kami realized that Angela had tricked her into having one of those in-case-we-die moments. She glared over at Angela, who naturally glared back.

She was lucky, Kami thought. Her friends had all followed her lead: she'd said they should hide so they could surprise Rob and his people, try to help Lillian and her sorcerers. They could have done what Lillian had wanted, could have run away.

They'd trusted Kami, even though she didn't know what she was doing. She couldn't let them down: she couldn't let any of them die.

* * *

Both of the adult sides followed the rules. They came when the last light of the sun had died, Lillian's people sweeping down from Aurimere and Rob's coming from Monkshood in the west. They had to take Shadowchurch Lane to get to the square, and that was a bad moment: Kami and her friends crouched in a huddled row behind makeshift screens of foliage sheared from their enemy's garden, which seemed all at once utterly fragile and foolish.

She saw Rob's profile through a framework of leaves as he passed, his pale blond hair and his carved Lynburn features. In some ways the Lynburns all looked like variations on a theme, different expressions of personality set in the same ivory and gold.

Rob looked like the nice one. His face as he went by was set in pleasant, determined lines, like a good man set on a worthy task. It made Kami's very bones feel cold, as if they had been turned to iron inside her skin.

Rosalind followed Rob, hair floating, eyes fixed on Rob's back. After her came the stolid profile of Sergeant Kenn, the ice-and-copper face of Ruth, the sorcerer living at the Kenns', the fox-colored haze of Amber Green's hair, the dark head of her boyfriend, Ross, following behind. One sorcerer after another after another, moving in single file.

There were so many of them. Kami had known the number of sorcerers, but now, seeing them—there were so many.

They stood together in the town square. And Lillian came walking down the High Street, fair hair shining like a helm, not standing at a man's back but striding in front of her followers. Kami had never actually liked Lillian, but she admired her for a moment with all her heart, and then her heart sank.

She looked so gallant, so much the leader of a forlorn hope. Even with Henry added to Lillian's army, Rob had so many more people, it made Lillian look pathetic. They were ranged on either side of the town square, a stretch of gold cobblestones their battlefield, and Rob lifted a hand to the single streetlight.

It made a popping, splintering sound and blinked out. Darkness descended. The stars, clear in the sky, pulsed white and strong. There was a line of faint luminescent green along the horizon, and it illuminated the square enough so that Kami was able to see the glimmer of Lillian's and Rosalind's hair, separated by a wide stretch of blackness.

She was able to see the glint of teeth as Rob smiled.

"Lillian," he said, "where is my sacrifice?"

"This town does not live by the old laws anymore," Lillian said. "It lives under my laws. Because it is my town. If you want it, you have to take it from me."

Kami jumped as she heard the crackle in the night, the hungry sudden hiss.

A flame leaped from the broken streetlight, brighter than the bulb had been, a red pillar on top of what looked like a metal spike. The flame rose high and dangerous, the curling scarlet tongue at its tip painting the sky with its own colors. Leering faces in orange and blue surfaced and sank in its heart.

Everyone could see Rob's smile now. He said, gently, "Then I will."

Both sides moved, inevitable as two opposing tides. Ruth Sherman of the crimson hair and fierce face was the one who joined battle first. She was almost close enough to touch Ms. Dollard, but not quite, when she passed a hand through the air, pale in the fire-tinted darkness. Somehow that gesture turned the air twisted and sharp, made a slice of night into a knife.

It cut Ms. Dollard's throat.

The blood was nothing but a slender black line across her neck for an instant. It didn't look deep, didn't look serious, and then there was a dark gush over her white blouse. There was a spray of blood, ebony in the night, an obscene splash of darkness against the golden cobblestones.

Ms. Dollard toppled, and Lillian lunged forward. She raised her hand and Ruth staggered back as if she had been slapped.

Mrs. Thompson stepped forward, a small bag Kami

recognized clasped in her hand, and when Mr. Prescott raised his hand against her a wind rose and then died as she spoke. Mr. Prescott looked stunned.

Lillian looked stunned too, but she caught on fast. She stooped to where Ms. Dollard had fallen, picked the bag out of her hand and held it fast. She spoke the words of a spell, lost in the howl of wind and the hiss of flames, and magic died all through Rob's ranks. Lillian and her sorcerers began cutting through them: Kami saw one of Rob's sorcerers fall, then another. Her plan was working, small successes won at every turn.

Unfortunately, Rob was quick on the uptake as well.

"Burn those," he ordered, and the bag in Lillian's hands burst into flame. Then he lifted a hand and Lillian stumbled. When she looked up, her lip was split and her teeth were stained with blood.

All at once the square was a maelstrom, people throwing themselves at each other, people standing or cringing back, people falling. The square was filled with dark figures and chaos and blood, all of it lit with the writhing red flame of Rob Lynburn's torch.

There were so many more of Rob's sorcerers, and their magic was powered by blood. It was like seeing people try to fight against knives bare-handed. It was so much worse than Lillian must have thought, so much worse than Kami had feared. This wasn't going to be a brave last stand, wasn't going to be something that would decimate the enemy even if it led to defeat.

This was going to be a slaughter.

Kami pressed her hand to her lips so hard she felt her

teeth cut the inside of her mouth. It did not look like joining in the fight would make any difference at all.

Except for the fact that they would die too.

Kami remembered, clear as if she was hearing them all over again, Lillian's words to her son. *You and Jared cannot take part in the battle tomorrow. You have to hide. You have to run.*

Maybe, Kami thought, thinking it and hating to think it, maybe Lillian had been right.

The movement at her elbow made Kami jump. She heard stirring in the garden, in the dark cool space where they were hidden, a whisper in the grass that was someone crawling past Angela toward her.

"Kami," Ash's voice said, so low she almost couldn't hear him. "I don't know if I'm being a coward, but I can't help but think we have to run."

Kami lowered her hand from her mouth, rubbed both her clammy palms against the knees of her jeans.

"You're not being a coward," she replied at last. "It's what your mother would have wanted."

Ash did not move. Kami could not summon the words to say that they all should.

She had not seen the shadow behind Ash until Jared moved forward, lunging the same way Lillian did, and caught Kami's face in his hand, capturing her windblown hair against her jaw and around his fingers. They looked at each other in the firelight broken with the pattern of leaves. Jared's eyes were longing and intent, as if he had only this one moment to memorize her face.

He placed his other hand, briefly, on the back of Ash's neck.

"Both of you go," he said.

Then he was on his feet and racing across the dark garden to Shadowchurch Lane. The ghost of his warmth lingered on Kami's lips, but he was nothing but a shadow lost in shadows.

"Okay," said Kami to the friends clustered around her, hushed and fraught in the silence. "Okay, whoever wants to run should run, but if you don't want to run you should fight."

Silence stretched between them all. Then Angela rose, cat-silent with her hair a darker flutter against the dark sky, and of course Rusty went after her. Both of them went onto Shadowchurch after Jared, and Kami saw them run into the town square.

It was like a little piece had been cut from hell and thrown in the center of her town. And there were people she loved in the chaos of flickering firelight and spilled blood. She had sent them out there. Angela turned like a dancer on the stained cobblestones and kicked Sergeant Kenn in the head from behind. Rusty and Amber Green stood staring at each other across a small flame-lit distance, and then Amber's boyfriend Ross threw a ball of fire from his hands at Rusty. Rusty had to throw himself on the stained cobbles to escape it. Even then Kami was sure it scorched through the ends of his dark shock of hair.

Angela wheeled on Ross, shouting *"Noli me tangere!"* so his fire died in his hands, and springing at him. Kami saw Mr. Prescott lift his hand in Angela's direction: the air coming at her turned into something that glittered, sharp and terrifying.

Holly charged through their screen of branches, leaving

a mess of broken twigs and crushed leaves in her wake, and hurtled in between Angela and her father.

Kami and Ash ducked to make sure they were not seen, both of them on their hands and knees in the dead grass and cold earth. She had waited to see if he would run, but he hadn't. She looked at the desperation and the red shimmer of reflected flame in his eyes.

She looked again over the broken branches. The glass shop fronts on the High Street were all shimmering walls of fire, and the side streets black slashes.

Crimson-haired Ruth did her trick of turning the air into a knife. Jared made a casual gesture and knocked it away, so that it became a whirl of shining sharpness that dissolved into night; then he knocked her away with another gesture and without another look. He stalked through the sorcerers as if he hardly saw them, toward his real objective.

Rob Lynburn saw Jared coming toward him through the burning night air, and beckoned.

Kami reached over to touch Ash's hand where it lay on the ground clutching the grass. His skin felt ice cold. "Ash," she whispered.

Ash tore his eyes away from the square where Lillian was lashing out and dodging away, her sheet of hair a silver banner flying against the dark as she went down.

Kami met his gaze and swallowed down her fear, determinedly fought back her furious, terrified instinct to recoil. "I'll be your source," she told him. "Do the spell now."

Chapter Twenty-Six
Cruel Bonds

The words of the spell fell on Kami like shards of glass. They rained down around her, cold and sharp, and she could not get a grip on any of them: she knew doing so would hurt her too much.

It felt wrong and unnatural, like being stripped naked and stitched to someone else, someone fighting just as much as she was, cringing where every inch of exposed skin touched.

She had never felt someone touch her mind who didn't want to, who she viscerally did not want to touch it.

She found herself clutching Ash's hand for comfort, and bizarre and unreasonable though it was, he clutched hers back, fingers pressing down to bone even as they struggled frantically away from each other in their minds.

A phrase she had heard or read somewhere drifted through Kami's mind: Take this cup from my lips. What was in this cup was too bitter: every sense she had told her it was poison, and she could not make herself swallow it.

Jared was out there. Angela was out there, and Holly and Rusty. She had to help them.

Kami thought, with terrible clarity, the last thought she

would have to herself: *This is the worst mistake I will ever make.*

She stopped struggling against the spell and let herself be drawn into hideous closeness. Two people made into a ghastly parody of one creature, something that should be displayed in a nightmarish carnival.

Jared didn't say it would be like this, Ash told her, outrage and anger and betrayal that wasn't hers in her head like an invading army. *The way he talked about it, it was different. I don't want this!*

Kami wouldn't talk to him like that. She couldn't. Not yet.

She dragged herself up until she was sitting, and opened her eyes. The world was still the same world of fire and darkness and horror. It was she who had changed, and that could not matter now.

"You're the one trained in magic," she said, her voice a thread of sound. "You have to be the one to use the power."

"I can't," Ash choked out. "I don't know how—I'm not—"

He was even less used to this than she was, Kami reminded herself. She had catapulted them both into this and she was the one who had to control it, whose responsibility it was to deal with the situation.

She took a deep breath, her throat sore as if she had been crying, and tried to think clearly. It seemed impossible to create any order in her torn invaded mind, but she refused to let it be impossible. There was magic in the midst of the chaos. It was like trying to capture a storm of knives in her arms, but she forced herself to think of the suffering and magic as separate. She wanted to give the magic to Ash. She thought about opening her arms to him, about offering what she had so he could use it.

Ash took the power carefully, like something they were trying to pass with hands that were shaking, and which they could not drop. Kami felt his surprise and the first, tentative feeling of pleasure behind the terror and panic. He had not expected so much power, or that it would come so easily.

Jared had never really valued or understood the power. Kami had not felt anyone exulting in magic before, or been able to see someone who knew how to use magic take hers and craft something out of it.

Ash's hand uncurled from hers, and he rose to his feet.

A light rose on the tops of the winter-stripped trees, white as moonshine and so bright, like a star fallen from the sky and going nova. The light placed a shimmering halo on Ash's hair and, so crowned, he stepped over the wall and the broken remnants of their screen, and into the town square.

The square was filled from edge to edge with white light: it looked iced, every cobblestone shining. The shadows and firelight had both been chased away, and the chaos had gone with them. Everyone was still, watching Ash walk into the sudden peace he had created.

Rob's hair looked snow white as he turned his head to look at his son. "So you were too much of a coward to pay the true price for power," he said. "Instead you've enslaved yourself to get a quick fix. I see you've entirely given up on making your parents proud, Ash. Maybe you knew all along that you were not capable of doing so."

"Maybe," Ash said. "But now your odds look a lot worse, don't they, Dad?" He lifted a hand to where Sergeant Kenn and Rusty stood, still wreathed in magic though they had both paused in their fight. Kami took deep slow breaths, crouched on the ground, trying to ignore her own existence and become just a conduit to the magic.

The haze of magic wrapping around them dissolved, and Rusty moved, punching Kenn in the face. Angela dived to his side. As the fighting started again, Ash did not go straight for Rob or to Jared's side. He looked to his mother.

Magic was behind the look, and people were thrown out of his way, the crowd parting like the Red Sea. Lillian was facing three sorcerers at once and not doing badly, though there was a deep bleeding cut on her face and a vivid scarlet splash in her silver-fair hair.

Mrs. Prescott was coming at Lillian from behind. She was Holly's mother. This was a real and terrible fight; Kami knew they might have to kill someone, but she could not see any way to murder her friend's mother. She could not, and through the new painful pathways of her heart to a strange land she felt Ash could not.

He lashed out at Mrs. Prescott, not to kill but to stun. Kami could sense the power flooding from her to him: she was able to see herself as divided from Ash in a way that she had never been able to definitively divide herself from Jared. She could see how she could withhold the power, and how she could choose to give.

Kami gave all she had, felt like nothing but a channel for magic, the focus so everything living could give the sorcerer magic. Jared and Lillian were both approaching and Rob was fending them off rather than attacking. Ash had felled three sorcerers in less than a minute.

Rob could see where the real threat lay. He swerved to face Ash, and Ash hesitated to attack his father: Kami felt his love and fear combined, choking him, stopping him in his tracks.

He lifted his little bag like a shield and said, *"Noli me—"*

Rob cut through the spell before it was even complete, and cut through his son too. Kami felt Ash's agony blaze through her. He fell to the cobblestones, twisted and bleeding. Lillian screamed like a Valkyrie who would have a death for a death, and went for Rob at the same time Jared did. Ash tried to lift himself from the blood-slick stones. He lifted a hand, his magic spiraling out from him, to help them.

It did not matter how little practice she had. Ash looked like he might lose consciousness at any moment. Kami had to join this fight. She climbed the wall, and saw Rob note her, take in his wife and his sons arrayed against him, and weigh the odds.

"Come on!" Rob said, his magic cutting a swath of silence through the air like a whip. "I do not intend to risk any of my sorcerers. We can get as much magic as we need, and they can't." He threw up a hand and Jared went slamming into the foot of Matthew Cooper's statue.

Kami ran, though her legs felt unsteady. By the time she was in the square, Rob's followers were leaving. Rob was not. He was standing by Lillian, tilting her chin up in one hand.

"You know I could beat you," he said, "if I was willing to sacrifice a sorcerer or two. But it's not worth it to defeat so humiliatingly feeble an enemy."

He stroked Lillian's hair. It was one of the only gestures of affection Kami had ever seen between this married couple.

"You thought you would at least have a glorious last stand, didn't you, Lillian? But you're just going to be crushed. You're nothing. And now everybody knows it. Now every soul in this town will surrender to me. All this display was for nothing. I can make a sacrifice in the spring equinox just as well. I will have my sacrifice, and this town will submit." He spread out his arms to the square, to the statue and the sorcerers. To anyone watching, the gesture must have looked like victory, and he like a conqueror.

Kami turned away. She knelt down at the foot of the statue where Jared lay, and looked anxiously down at him. He was lying still, but his chest was rising and falling steadily: his head was turned to one side. When Kami laid her hand gently against his cheek and turned his face to hers, she saw the trail of blood on his temple.

There must be some way to magically heal people, Jared had told her. She had the power to try it now: she wanted to try, to assure herself that she could handle this magic, and that it would help. That she had been right to do this.

Kami drew on a little of the magic. It was wrenchingly uncomfortable to be connected to someone else when she was looking down at Jared, trying to reach him. She had to concentrate on his cut, and how she wanted it healed, his pain eased, wound closed: she could not let herself think about him. Kami had her fingers curled just above the wound. She felt the warm flutter of his breath, evening out against the inside of her wrist.

Then she reached out and touched his temple with her fingertips, very lightly. The blood came away on her hand, and underneath the skin was whole. Kami looked up and saw that Rob had left the square. Nobody was there but Lillian and her sorcerers, Ash and Kami's friends, and the bodies on the cobblestones.

Lillian had Ash's head in her lap, his blood on her hands. His eyes were open. Kami could feel his pain through their connection.

"Mother." Ash's voice was soft. "It's not true."

"That he would have won?" Lillian asked. "That you had to chain yourself to a source to give us the smallest chance? Of course it's true. He's right. He is the one with the power." She shook off Ash's gentle hands, as she had tried to step away from Rob's cruel ones, and stood up, leaving Ash lying in the bloodstained square. "But not for long," she added.

Lillian beckoned to the five sorcerers still standing, turned on her heel, and left the square. She was not walking up to Aurimere, Kami thought in a dazed way. She was heading out to the woods, as if any of the sorcerers could possibly be ready for another practice session.

Ash looked at her across the square. Kami could feel his uncertainty and discomfort, could feel someone else's feelings, hideously distinct from hers. He felt everything in a different way than she did: they barely saw the same color when they looked at the sky.

"Rusty," she said. "Angela, Holly. Help Ash, please."

Kami felt Ash's relief, saw Rusty going toward him at once. She wanted nothing but the best for Ash, wanted him healed and saved. Kami looked away from him and into Jared's still face.

She did not want Ash anywhere near her.

PART VII
IN THE BLEAK MIDWINTER

The strength and splendour of our purpose swings.
The lamps fade; and the stars. We are alone.
—*Rupert Brooke*

Chapter Twenty-Seven
The Lady of Aurimere's Error

The others took Ash to the Water Rising, the nearest place that had certain beds and an almost-certain welcome. Kami stayed where she was, kneeling on the cold stone of the square, waiting for Jared to open his eyes. When he did, the sky was lightening from black to steely gray, and she still wasn't ready.

Kami was holding his head in her lap. His lashes stirred and his eyelids lifted: he looked up at her, eyes a lighter, softer gray than the sky. His eyes warmed when he saw her.

With him looking at her as he always did, she felt for a moment as if she was not changed. Then his eyes went flat and his muscles went tense. He said, "Watch out," and rolled off her lap and into a crouch, ready to leap.

Kami looked up and saw Mr. Prescott staggering toward her with fire building in his cupped hands. She reached out a hand and thought, *Stop*—and Mr. Prescott went down again.

Kami had an instant of horror when she wondered what she had done. Then she saw who was standing over Mr. Prescott, a piece of wood from their broken screen of briars and branches in his hands. It was her father. He stood staring down at her, the blood on her hand and whatever wild changed look she had on her face.

"Dad," she whispered.

He looked sick. "Kami."

His eyes traveled over the bloodstained cobblestones, to where Ms. Dollard lay. The slow-dawning horror on his face was terrible to watch: it was like seeing through his eyes, seeing a nightmare. Kami got up, wobbling a little, and ran into his arms. Dad smoothed her hair, murmuring comfort into her ear that seemed meant for both of them.

"Thank God you're all right," Dad said softly. "Thank God Lillian came to me."

Kami felt as if his warm breath, running along the nape of her neck, had suddenly gone ice cold and sharp. She shuddered involuntarily, and the shudder took her a step away out of his arms.

"Lillian?" she asked. "When?"

Dad blinked. "Just now. She came to the door and told me you needed my help."

"Why would she—is Mum at home?" Kami demanded. She found herself trembling inside, as if tiny slivers of ice were racing through her bloodstream, making every cell shiver with dread.

Dad reached out and took hold of Kami's shoulders in a gentle grip. "Don't worry," he said. "Your mother isn't there, but Lillian offered to stay while I went to you. She's waiting downstairs, and your brothers are safe in their beds. There's nothing to be afraid of."

Dad thought Lillian was on their side and could be trusted. Dad had not seen Lillian's face tonight when Rob had told her she was nothing.

"Dad," said Kami. She was able to control her voice

somehow, keeping it steady because she had to, because she could not be sure something was wrong. But she could be sure of one thing.

"We have to go home now."

*　*　*

Kami had been walking down this street all her life. She had always taken for granted that family and peace could be found at the end.

She had never had a homecoming like this, running desperately with her father ahead of her, Jared racing at her heels. The early morning made everything look alien, clouds muffling the dawn: bands of sickly yellow edged with gray thrown over their little garden, over the crumbling roof tiles.

Dad was trying to open the door as Kami flew down the path. His hands were shaking so hard that he could not get the key in.

Kami fished out her own key from her pocket, the pink plastic daisy swinging from it looking pathetic and ridiculous, as if it belonged to a different girl in a different life. She forced her hands to keep steady, as she had forced her voice in the town square, and opened the door.

The hall was still and quiet, the red tiles shadowed. The door to the sitting room was standing open. It was still and quiet in there too. Lillian was gone.

Dad ran up the stairs, hoarsely calling the boys' names. Kami ran behind him, breaths like sobs tearing in her throat. Dad ran into Ten's room, so Kami ran into Tomo's.

Tomo's bed was a rumpled mess, sheets trailing on the carpet, toy trucks idle on the motorways of his blankets and parked in the high hills of his pillows. It was empty.

"Tomo." She said his name when she'd meant to scream it. "Tomo!"

Then she wrenched her eyes away from the bed and ran across the hall, into Ten's room, where Dad stood. His face was blank, as if he could not understand the horror he was suddenly living through.

This bed was empty too. It made Kami's eyes burn, looking at those sheets. Ten always made his bed, small hands smoothing out hospital corners, the most conscientious kid in the world.

"Kami!" Jared shouted.

Kami turned. Her eyes were stinging and her legs numb as she stumbled down the stairs. The light and darkness in their hallway were wavering and blending in her vision. Everything looked sinister: Kami could not help but think of the phrase "seeing things in a new light," and wonder why there was no phrase for seeing things in a new shadow, realizing how dark the world could become.

Jared was in the kitchen. His eyes swung to her, alert, then back to the door of their closet. "I heard a noise," he said quietly.

Kami crossed the kitchen floor in an instant, Jared at her shoulder. She opened the closet door with a jerk. Tomo tumbled out, tear-streaked and terrified and whole, into her arms.

"Kami!" he exclaimed, his hands scrabbling at her clothes as if he was a small frantic animal, clawing to hold on. Kami clasped his head, silky hair against her palm, pressed it down to her shoulder, used her free arm to hold his body tight, tight against hers. He was too heavy and too big for her, and it did not matter at all.

Dad burst into the kitchen and Tomo burst into tears. Their father put his arms around Kami and Tomo for a moment; then Tomo transferred his grip from Kami to Dad, arms winding around his neck. "Tomo, Tomo, I've got you, I'm so sorry, you're safe now," Dad said, like a prayer, like a promise. He touched Tomo's hair the same way Kami had, trying to soothe him and hang on to him at once. "Tomo, I'm so sorry," Dad repeated. "But you have to tell us what happened."

Tomo let out another gulping sob. Kami had been hanging on to his fingers for reassurance, but now she squeezed them, pleading.

"Ten needs you to tell us."

"He came and woke me up," Tomo forced out, voice pitifully small between sobs. "He came and he said that . . . that the lady was scaring him. He put me in here and he closed the door after me and I heard the lady and him, th-they were t-talking. He s-said to the lady that I must've gone after Dad."

Tomo burst into another fit of sobs. Kami thought of Ten standing in their kitchen lying for his little brother, when Ten always went scarlet at the least little fib, and wanted to cry too.

Dad tightened his arms around Tomo, pressing a kiss to the side of his face.

"What else did she say, Tomo? Where did she take your brother?"

"I d-don't know!" Tomo wailed. "She just said he had to come with her, she said she needed—she needed—"

"A source," Kami whispered.

Matthew Cooper's blood, given the house and kept under

the Lynburns' eye, in case a time ever came when they would be desperate enough to need a source again.

Dad's eyes met hers, over Tomo's head. "A source," he said, his voice controlled, trying to understand. "Like—like you are? What does that mean for Ten, Kami? You're all right, aren't you?"

"I'm all right," Kami told him, more forcefully than she would have done if it had been true. But she couldn't lie to him about Ten.

"But I was . . ." Kami looked at her hands instead of into her father's eyes. She glanced at Jared over her shoulder, met his gaze, and looked back down. She rubbed at the inside of her wrist, pulse fluttering under her thumb. "I was never forced to be a source, not by Jared. We were—we were in it together, always. He wasn't using me as a way to get power. I knew that. I wanted to be—close." She pressed her thumb down on her wrist, feeling her pulse pound as if it wanted to break out of her body. "When you don't want to," she whispered, "it's different. We have to save Ten."

Dad nodded. "Would she have taken him back to Aurimere to do this . . . spell?"

Kami thought of the way Rob always spoke about sources, the way Lillian had never actually suggested that Kami become her son's source. She thought of the relentless pride of the Lynburns. And she remembered how she and Ash working together had only been able to hold off Rob's people for a while. Another sorcerer, with less power than Ash, with an inexperienced child for a source, would not guarantee them victory.

Kami thought of all the contingency plans Lillian might have had her sorcerers practicing, out in the woods. "She didn't go to Aurimere," Kami said. "Lillian took the other sorcerers out to the Crying Pools, to do the ceremony. She wants them all to do it. And when they do, she'll have one of them make Ten their source."

In Lillian's desperation, because of her overwhelming arrogance, because she had good intentions, she thought it was all right to take Kami's little brother. She thought she had the right.

"Dad," Kami said, holding Tomo's hand, "you have to stay here with Tomo. I have to go get Ten."

"I forbid you to leave this house," Dad told her, his voice angry enough that it made Kami swallow. "One of my kids is already in danger. You two both have to stay here. *I'm* going."

"Dad, no," Tomo begged.

"Dad, no," Kami echoed desperately. "They're sorcerers, Dad. And I have magic again. I have the best chance of saving him. It has to be me."

Dad's face went colder suddenly, black eyes sharp and dangerous. He looked to the kitchen door. Kami followed his gaze and saw the others standing there, Rusty, Angela, and Holly having joined Jared and looking relieved to see Tomo.

"Your mum told me you couldn't be his source again," Dad said, with a motion of his head toward Jared. "So where did you get magic, Kami? What did someone do to you?"

"No, Dad, you've got it wrong," Kami said. "It's not like that. I asked Ash to. I wanted to. I *chose*. And that means I can save Ten. Please, *please* let me go."

Dad shut his eyes and buried his face for a second against Tomo's hair. "Okay," he said at last. "Okay. But I'm trusting you, Kami. Get him back safe." He unloosed an arm from around Ten and drew Kami in to him, to them both, so Ten's hot cheek was pressed against Kami's forehead. Kami could see the glitter of Dad's eyes and realized that her father was about to cry.

"Get yourself back safe," he whispered, and then he let her go.

* * *

Morning had not come to the woods yet. Light was brimming and refracting at the edges of the wood, outlining the shapes of the trees and trimming branches with diamond points. There was no warmth on the forest floor they were racing over, nothing but cold gray shadow laid across the dead leaves, fallen boughs, and Kami's band of friends racing through the winter wood.

Their breathing and their crashing footsteps were almost the only sounds she could hear, a tiny moving island of frantic noise in the midst of a spreading sea of silence.

Kami could feel Ash's helpless dismay and guilt at what his mother had done in her head, from the little room in the Water Rising where her friends had left him so they could come to her. Even though it wasn't his fault, the fact that he was there in her head was like someone touching an open wound. Even though it wasn't his fault, she found herself almost hating him.

She knew he could sense that. She could not quite bring herself to care; she was too consumed by panic and fear and she did not have the energy to block it off from him. Kami's vision blurred, leaves and earth nothing but darkness under her feet, and her foot slipped beneath the moss.

A hand caught hers, grasp firm. Kami looked up and saw Jared looking down at her. Angela's shoulder supported her on the other side, giving her a moment of warmth. She did not fall. She kept running, until they were so close to the Crying Pools that Kami could see the change in the light, the trees thinning and the cool sunshine pouring into the hollow.

Then Henry Thornton blundered into her path. Kami walked right into his chest. She glanced up into eyes gone dark and wild behind his glasses and felt the frantic grip of his hands on her wrists.

"No," he gasped at her. "Kami—oh no—"

Kami set her hands against his chest and shoved. "Out of my way."

Henry staggered back and she was almost past him, when he grabbed her hand. His fingers bit into her skin.

"Don't look," he said.

"Let go!"

Jared launched himself at Henry, breaking Henry's grip on Kami and backing Henry into a tree for good measure. Jared's fingers twisted in Henry's collar, almost throttling him, face very close to his. "Don't touch her."

Henry stared into Jared's eyes, then turned his face away as if he could not bear to look at him. "None of you should see," he said in a low voice. "I didn't—I didn't know what was going to happen."

Kami took a step, not toward the space beyond the trees where the light changed, infused with the shimmering, shifting quality it gained when it hit water, but toward Henry.

"To my brother?" she asked, her voice shaking with terror. "Has something happened to my brother?"

"Come on, buddy," said Rusty. "Tell us."

Henry did not lift his eyes from the leaves. "Lillian met us holding a child's hand," he said. "I didn't know who he was. I didn't know what she intended for him. Things like sources, like the ceremony of the pools, they're stories to me, and Lillian came with a child saying we had to risk it. He looked so frightened. They all looked frightened. I didn't know what was happening at all, but I couldn't do it. I went away. I meant to come and find you all."

Kami found she couldn't move. She looked at Henry, no urgency in the way he stood, showing no sign of alarm even with Jared's hand at his throat. He looked exhausted past the point of fear.

She lifted a hand to stop Rusty, Angela, and Holly from going toward the pools.

"But you didn't," she said. "You didn't come find us, did you?"

"I made it out of the woods, and I went toward Aurimere," Henry said. "And I saw strange things going on there. I was worried. I thought Lillian would know what to do."

His voice shook. Kami saw him trembling under Jared's hands and shot Jared a meaningful glance. Jared stepped away, but Henry didn't move. He just stayed against the tree, his gaze on the ground.

"So you came back to the pools," Kami said slowly. "But when you met us, you were going away *again*. You were running away."

"I—" Henry's voice cracked, and he stopped.

Kami's limbs felt heavy with dread. What Henry had seen was so bad that he did not want to move and could barely even speak. She didn't want to see it. She wanted to stay where she was, where she would still be able to hope that Ten was just beyond the last trees.

She forced her feet into motion. One step, and then another, over leaves turned gold by winter, lying curled and dead. The crackle of the dry leaves beneath her feet sounded like harsh whispers.

Kami took the last few steps, into the light.

Branches raked the sky, stabbing accusing fingers toward the morning. On the other side of the Crying Pools, along the banks, there was a gleam of frost, a glittering promise of cold to come. The pools looked turquoise in the pale light, opaque as precious stones. The morning sun made the winter air above the pools shine, creating glints of light in the air like the traces of frost on the ground.

Jared had said once, about the Crying Pools, *There are people down there who want me to stay with them.* He had sunk beneath the water, and she had pulled him out.

Nobody had pulled out Lillian's sorcerers.

There were people in the Crying Pools now. Kami could see them, not down in the depths but floating on the surface like so much rubbish. Some were spread-eagled on the water, limbs stretched out, hair and clothes trailing. Some were curled in on themselves like dead leaves. The trees stood like witnesses all around. They were all of the sorcerers who had followed Lillian into the woods and to their deaths. Mrs.

Thompson, the Hope brothers. Every adult sorcerer who had fought on their side and for their town lay in the still water.

Horror rang through Kami's mind, her own and Ash's both, like a scream in a cave that echoed and echoed its own echoes, repeated by the stones, going on forever.

"I don't think Lillian understood how dangerous it was," Henry said, his voice soft as if he hardly dared disturb this air.

Kami turned and looked at her friends, standing ranged behind her. Rusty looked gray, as if he was about to be ill. Tears had made shining pools of Holly's eyes.

I knew, she thought. *I knew Jared would have died if I hadn't come to save him. I should have tried harder to tell Lillian.*

But would Lillian have listened? And even if she had understood the danger, would she have cared?

"She seemed so desperate," Henry said, and Kami saw the guilt she was feeling reflected on his face. "Nobody wanted to argue with her."

No, Kami thought. She was the Lynburn of Aurimere: they never had.

Henry's voice sank even lower. "And there was the little boy."

"Ten," said Kami. "Where is he?" she demanded. "Where's Lillian? What has she done to him?"

Henry looked scared to reply, and Kami remembered him saying, *I saw strange things going on at Aurimere.*

She turned her back on the Crying Pools and plunged back into the woods, not running anymore but walking at a relentless pace, marching to find out the full terrible truth. She heard her friends following her, but she didn't look back at them. Once she was out of the woods and on the curving path that led up to Aurimere, she saw.

Aurimere stood golden on the hill, dominating the town as it always had.

It was wrapped in a crown of fire.

The line of flame wrapped around the crest of the hill, crimson light filling the windows of Aurimere so the house was watching the town with eyes suddenly turned red. It was like a flying scarlet flag of victory.

A fine investigative reporter she made, Kami thought. She didn't ask herself the right questions, let alone anyone else. She hadn't thought about why Rob had spoken to Lillian the way he had, when he'd been leaving to escape and not leaving because they were powerless. She'd just assumed he was gloating.

Rob had known Lillian all their lives. He had known what she would do, how she would use up all her magic so her spell on Aurimere would fail, and he could cross the threshold and have the manor for his own.

He knew what Lillian would do, and he had taken the opportunity she had given him.

"He sent sorcerers down to the woods," Kami whispered. "After Lillian's were all dead."

"I saw them," Henry whispered. "But they didn't see me. I didn't know what to do. I couldn't have fought them. And Lillian, she seemed like she had gone mad; her sorcerers were dead. If we had started throwing fire or anything else, someone could have hurt the child. That poor little boy. He saw them all die. He saw the sorcerers coming for him. He never cried; he just stood there watching.

"Rob's sorcerers took him. They took Lillian. They took them back to Aurimere. I didn't know how to stop them, I didn't know what to do, and so I did nothing. I'm sorry."

"It wasn't your fault."

Kami's voice sounded distant to her own ears. She believed what she told Henry. There was nothing he could have done but die too, and so many people were dead already, but she could not seem to access the belief on any real level.

She wanted someone to blame. She wanted to hate Lillian, who had stolen Kami's brother and got all her sorcerers killed, but she could imagine Lillian's despair. Lillian was a prisoner in her own home now. Ten was a prisoner with her, and Kami knew why Rob would have wanted to take a child, a source, when he hated all sources, when he wanted to wipe all sources from the face of the earth and when he also wanted a child of the town delivered up to him.

Rob wanted her brother for his midwinter sacrifice.

Kami stood still in the shadowy curving road and watched the flames burn around Aurimere. She had been so sure she could act, that somehow she could make a plan and carry it out and stop all this.

Fire cast shadows, Kami realized. There were reflected tongues of brightness and streaks of blackness cast across Sorry-in-the-Vale, swallowing it up in darkness and fire.

The sorcerers had taken back their town.

She hadn't been able to do a thing.

Chapter Twenty-Eight
Laugh at the Night

Kami's father did not blame her. He did not ask a single question when she told him about Ten, only drew her close and rested his cheek against her hair. "I'm glad you're safe," he said.

It had been a silent unanimous decision to come to the Water Rising. Kami's home did not feel safe any longer. Tomo seemed glad to be somewhere else, or just glad to be with her and Dad. He was sleeping in the parlor, head pillowed against Dad's chest. If Dad even shifted position, Tomo whimpered in his sleep.

Kami was thankful he was sleeping, because it meant he had stopped asking for Mum. None of them had any idea where she was.

Henry had taken a room and disappeared in there. Holly had gone back home, to see if her parents had returned or whether they were installed at Aurimere with Rob. Angela and Rusty had gone with her.

"We'll be right back," Angela had said, holding on to Kami's hands. "Holly won't stay with them. She just has to see."

"Of course," Kami said.

Angela had held both her hands, which had felt intensely strange as a gesture from undemonstrative Angela, and looked into her face. "Rusty can go with her," she'd offered at last. "I could stay."

"No," Kami said. "I have Dad and Tomo and Jared here. I'm fine. You should go."

Angela's eyes had searched Kami's face, Kami didn't know for what. She had to turn her own eyes away from that gaze.

"I'll be right back," Angela promised, and gave her a swift ferocious hug before she went, Angela's hair and perfume blocking out all the rest of the world for a moment.

Despite how numb Kami felt, it was a comfort. She closed the door of the inn behind the three of them, Holly looking anxiously over her shoulder at Kami as they went down the street, and turned back.

The people in the pub had not asked any questions. The townspeople appeared to be steadfastly ignoring the fires burning around Aurimere.

Walking past one table, Kami heard Mr. Stearn say "Lynburns" and stopped to hear the end of his sentence. "Settled it among themselves," he said.

Kami opened her mouth to speak and found she did not know what to say. There was too much: her brother, the sorcerers in the woods, how she had allowed her mind to be invaded for nothing at all. Mr. Stearn stared up at her, eyes bleary and defiant, as if he expected her to argue with him. She passed on to the bar, which Jared was leaning against, talking quietly to Martha Wright.

"If you want," Martha was saying, in a low voice, "if

things are bad with your folks, we have your room upstairs. Just like you left it. Your brother can stay too. As long as you need."

If things are bad with your folks. As if Jared had been grounded over his motorbike, when people were dead.

"Do you want to know what happened?" Kami asked.

Martha looked at the bar and not at her. "What can we do?" she said in return, very quietly. She didn't mean it as an offer, that much was clear. She meant she was helpless. She meant they were all helpless.

"Thank you," Jared told her seriously. Martha looked up at his face and smiled before she hurried off to the other side of the bar.

"You've got a fan there, Lynburn," Kami observed.

"It's my aristocratic bone structure," Jared said. "Women of all ages are enslaved by it. My cheekbones command, and they obey." His voice was flat, his fingers tracing the whorls and lines of the old wood that formed the bar. Kami could not force a smile, not even one as feeble as Martha Wright's.

Ash was in her head, inescapable as water when you were drowning. He had no idea how to shield his emotions from her. She felt the cold weight of his presence even though he was wounded in bed, and felt like she could not breathe and would never be able to again.

"Come here a minute," Jared said. He headed across the room to where there was an alcove, formed by a large diamond-paned window that was set deep in the wall and that opened onto the Wrights' tiny yard.

Kami followed him and leaned against the wall on one side of the window. Through the small faintly green panes she could see the dusty gray of concrete, the steel gray of rubbish bins, and the crimson gleam of reflected fire. She realized she was too much of a coward right now to look at Jared.

She knew how he'd felt about their link. She'd known what her being Ash's source would do to him. She'd done it anyway.

She'd thought she had to do it, and it had been her choice to make.

Except that she was so tired, and she knew what it was like, to feel as if he hated her. She didn't know if she could bear it again.

"How are you?" Jared asked, voice pitched low, as if he was trying to be gentle.

Kami was startled enough to look up into his face. He was looking down at her already. She did not know what he was thinking and never would again, but she remembered with exquisite clarity how he had looked when he hated her and he didn't look like that now. The once-cruel curve of his mouth was now a line that trembled a little out of shape when he saw her face. "I don't know," Kami said. "I can't think about it, about Ten. I can't think about it yet."

"Because you don't know what to do," Jared said.

"Yes," Kami agreed, feeling shock wash over her because of how exactly right he was. That all this could have happened, and she had been helpless. "With Ash wounded, and Lillian gone, if we do something before we're ready and Ten gets hurt . . ."

"But you *will* do something," Jared said. "You'll work something out. You don't have to know what to do right away. It's all right not to know."

Kami laughed and the laugh caught in her throat. "It doesn't feel all right."

It felt like she was drifting, floating as helplessly as the sorcerers in the Crying Pools. If she didn't know what to do, if she didn't have a plan, then everything was a mess and she could do nothing but be at the mercy of her own feelings, terror and longing and panic dragging her down.

She couldn't be like this.

"It is all right," Jared said. "It's going to be." He lifted a hand but did not touch her, fingers tracing the curve of her cheek in the air. She could almost feel his skin against hers. She wanted to turn her face into his hand but could not bring herself to make that move: he had not really touched her, and maybe he did not want to.

"Don't hate me," she said in a low voice, and turned her face away, resting her cheek against the glass.

"What?" Jared asked. He spoke loudly enough so that she looked up at him again, and saw his face had gone colder, scar pulled tight and eyes like white ice with black water rushing beneath.

"I know that you said—that you were begging me not to, with Ash," Kami told him unsteadily. "I know I said I wouldn't do it."

"But you *had* to," Jared snapped, staring at her.

"I know I had to!" Kami snapped back. "But I knew how you would feel about it. I did it anyway."

"You assumed I would hold it against you," Jared said. "That's what you think of me."

That was what she thought of him, and she was right. He'd told her as much, told her that he wanted the link back more than anything in the world. She knew what it was he valued. The bleak look on his face made the words die on Kami's lips, turning them into silence and a sigh.

"I broke the link with you because I had to, and you hated me for that," she said at last.

"No, I *didn't*." Jared's voice was so intense, Kami thought that if they had been alone he would have shouted. "I thought you wanted to break away from me, and I didn't want to go crawling back to you, so I lied to you and insulted you. I hated you for wanting to break away, but—but you know how I feel about you. I could never hate you for long."

It was like they were in different worlds entirely, trying to tell each other about what they saw.

"I didn't want to break away from you," Kami said at last. "And I don't want you to hate me. I thought you did once, and I can't bear anything else today. I can't bear even the smallest thing."

"You don't have to. I was wrong and I was lying to you, but I'm not lying now," Jared told her. "It's all going to be all right. I'll get Ten back for you. You'll make a plan for Sorry-in-the-Vale. And you don't ever have to worry about what I feel. The way I feel about you won't change. You can do whatever you like to me. You could turn this town to dust, burn the woods until they were cinders, you could cut out my heart. It wouldn't matter. It would not change a thing."

"What if I ate a baby?"

Jared's mouth curved up at the corners, slow and not cruel after all. "I'm sure you'd have a good reason," he said. "Such as, babies are delicious."

Impossibly, Kami found herself smiling. It was a strange

small miracle. Everything was still completely terrible, but she was able to look up at Jared and smile, as if their worlds overlapped just enough to give them this small warm place to stand together.

She reached for him. He withdrew, a tiny, almost imperceptible flinch away from her, only a fraction of an inch, but it was enough. She let her hand fall by her side. "What if I wanted to rule the world?" she asked lightly. "I might desire to sit on a throne of skulls and be the universe's dark queen."

"I'd totally help you with that," Jared told her. "I am so willing to be a minion, you have no idea. I will throw people into aquariums full of mutant octopi and sharks with lasers on their heads on command." He moved a little closer to her, as if to make up for before, for not wanting her to touch him. "I do understand, Kami. I could never blame you. Don't worry about that."

Kami gave a small shrug. "So I'll just worry about everything else then."

"I'm not," said Jared. "Rob's an idiot. He thinks that this town belongs to him, that he can control it? He thinks that the people in it belong to him? He's underestimating Sorry-in-the-Vale. He's always underestimated you."

"And you," Kami said.

She had meant it as a statement, not a question, but Jared answered almost casually, "I belong to you. He has no idea what he's up against. And that will get him in the end. I believe that. Everything's going to come right for you."

"And you," Kami said again.

"If everything's right for you," Jared said at last, "everything's right for me."

The door of the Water Rising opened again, and Kami saw Holly, Angela, and Rusty. A weight of anxiety Kami had not even realized she was carrying eased off her shoulders. She was able to smile over at them.

Holly beamed back, and even Angela betrayed relief. Kami had not guessed quite how badly off she must have seemed, or how worried they had been. They all went to the parlor together, and the mood was a little giddy as well as desperate.

"This place is starting to feel like a home away from home," Rusty said, settling on the sofa. "We come here, we discuss evil sorcerers, we eat packets of peanuts. It's a soothing and familiar routine. Or it would be if people would just bring me some peanuts."

"I will actually stuff peanuts up your actual nose," Angela informed him.

"You're so cruel," Rusty complained. "My own sister. Why are you so cruel?"

"Some would say it's part of her charm," said Holly.

They were all together, Kami thought, and they were going to pull together, and not be in opposition anymore. That was worth something. No, that was worth a lot.

She sat down in a fragile wooden chair by the fire, because it was the closest to the sofa where Dad was sitting and Tomo slept. She gave Dad a faint smile and reached out her hand across the distance between them. He clasped her hand in his.

Jared knelt down on the floor by her chair. "I'm just going to see if Martha needs help with Ash," he said quietly.

She looked down at his face, that planed, cool Lynburn

face glossed with gold by the fire. His eyes were touched by firelight too, lit up and warm when he looked at her.

Kami smiled at him. "I'll be here."

Jared got up. "I'll be thinking about you."

He went out, and after some time while they all sat around and tried to talk their way to a solution, Ash came downstairs and stood by the fire, not kneeling but looking down at her with concern. He looked pale, and he was walking unsteadily, but he was walking.

"How are you?" Kami asked him.

"Can't complain," said Ash. "How are you holding up?"

"Oh," Kami said, acutely conscious of her own emotions because she knew Ash could feel them. She could feel that he agreed with her, that things had to be controlled and smoothed over, and this genuine accord made their situation seem more bearable. "I'm holding on."

Ash put a hand in the space of the wooden frame of her chair back, and touched her lower back. It was a gesture of support, nothing more, his fingers spread out warm on her skin and his honest wish for her well-being spreading warmer all through her.

It was possible for a moment to believe that Jared was right, and all would be well.

Chapter Twenty-Nine
The Lost Love

He'd lied to Kami.

Jared had been careful not to say anything to her that wasn't true, but he had left her with a false impression about where he was going to be and what he was going to do, and that was as good as lying.

He didn't know how much time he would have before someone noticed he was missing. He was hoping it would be all night, but he couldn't count on that.

So there was no excuse for him to be standing in the dark of the High Street, looking in through the window. It made no sense. He was going to get caught.

It was strange and terrifying, being able to lie to Kami. He'd been so sure, when he lied to her last time and told her she was nothing special, that she could see right through him.

This time he knew she'd believed what he had wanted her to believe.

He hoped that he had helped her feel better: it was a selfish and awful hope. He should just want her to feel better without caring who was responsible for it. He did want that, wanted her happy, but he could not untangle that from wanting to be the cause of her happiness.

He did not know where that left him, except standing in the dark, staring in at her.

The pocket shutters that folded into the window casements were spread out but still hanging open so a large slice of the room showed, a white wall painted over with warm yellow light, a shadowed angle where the wall and ceiling met. Angela and Holly were on their feet, a blur of swinging hair and long legs in his way. Angela returned to the sofa and Rusty, and Holly followed her, and finally Jared could see.

She was sitting by the fire, turned away from the window. Turned toward Ash, leaning in his direction. The swing of hair that was just one brown shade away from black had come untucked from behind her ear, casting a shadow on her gold-touched skin, against the curve of her jaw.

She was smiling. Her mouth was almost always a slight curve, and though her smile was shadowed today it was still the brightest thing in the room. She was like that, always: the vivid point in every room. He thought that was why he had never been able to truly believe she was imaginary.

She had always seemed like the real one. She would be all right. He'd told her that, and he'd meant it. She'd get her town back, and put her family back together.

And the last link between them was broken now: the last couple of days between them did not matter anymore. She'd felt still tied to him because he was the only one she had been tied to, but now she was tied to Ash. The link was new, but Jared knew what it would become.

Ash was a good person. He would do the right thing for her, be what she wanted, not helplessly want to make too many demands.

Jared could be nothing to her now: Kami was free of him at last.

He looked in the window for one instant longer, even though he knew there was no way to memorize her. She was always changing, not like other girls, who looked like pictures. She was more like a river, all constant motion.

There was never going to be a time when he could think, Yes, all right, enough. So he turned away, because he had to, and turned to Aurimere.

It was easy to see in the dark. The flames around it were still burning.

* * *

By the time he was halfway up the hill, the heat of the fire felt as if it was scorching Jared's skin. Standing on the crest of the hill looking into the flames, he could barely see Aurimere at all. The house was hidden by fierce light, the fire crackling like harsh laughter.

Sweat stung at his hairline, burned in his eyes like tears. There was no way through the fire. Unless you were a sorcerer.

Jared concentrated on the fire the way Ash had taught him. It felt different from regular fire, like running your hand over a tire and knowing it had been mended. Magic had been used recklessly to make it. He could put this whole fire out now, and Sorry-in-the-Vale would be glad.

He didn't. Somebody in Aurimere would be bound to notice. He created an opening for himself, like pushing a door ajar. A shadow fell across the fire and he walked in it, through to the other side.

Once inside the fire, he could see Aurimere, the sheer

walls turned silver in the moonlight. There were yellow lights in the windows.

There were invaders in Aurimere.

Jared asked the night to cover him, and it did, loaning him a little of its darkness and wrapping him in shadows so that when he passed by windows all the people inside saw was night. He moved around to the garden, the crumbling wall where he and Kami had talked once, and found the back door under one of the eaves, the one that had a door handle shaped like an iron hand. The small hand, fingers curved, was moon-silvered and moonshine-cold against his fingers. He felt as if there was a cool press on his hand for a moment, before he released the handle and slipped in the door.

The corridor was shadowy, the only lights coming from somewhere up the stairs and far away. Jared was glad: he didn't want to see Aurimere overrun, not all at once.

He tried to walk softly, because the high ceilings and stone of Aurimere carried echoes.

He remembered how alien it had seemed, this echoing chilly place, when he'd first come. But he'd missed it while he was living in the Water Rising. He hadn't realized Aurimere meant something to him until he found how much he hated having it taken away.

Maybe it was just that, chilly and strange as it was, it reminded him of Aunt Lillian.

He couldn't lie to himself. This mission wasn't just for Kami. He was coming to get Ten, but he wanted to save Aunt Lillian as well.

Aunt Lillian had stolen away Kami's little brother, like an evil sorcerer in a fairy tale, as if a sorcerer had to be something the whole town was afraid of. As if his family hadn't done enough to Kami's family already.

Aunt Lillian had more than proven Kami's mother's point. No wonder Claire Glass wanted her daughter to stay away from him.

And Jared still wanted to save her. Maybe to save her so he could murder her himself, he was that furious with her. But he remembered the night he had moved back into Aurimere, when he had woken to a feeling like someone stroking his hair, very lightly so he would not wake. Except that if you slept on the streets for any length of time, you learned to always wake when someone was touching you.

He hadn't woken fast, or in alarm. It was like he knew even in his sleep that he was safe, that he was being watched over, and that meant he stirred more slowly than he would have usually.

That gave whoever it was time so that when Jared opened his eyes and lifted himself from his pillow, all he saw was a crack of light made by the not-quite-closed door.

Maybe he had not quite closed the door himself when he was going to bed. Maybe it was just a lingering remnant of a dream about family, turned into a memory by his sleepy mind and wishful thinking, and nothing real at all.

He was still going to get Aunt Lillian out.

Aurimere had no place to keep prisoners: no dungeons or crypts to use in a pinch. Jared's guess was that Rob would've put his wife in her room and sealed the door.

He slipped up the stairs by the library, past the marble bust of a Lynburn, silent as a shadow. The night was still wrapped around him, a kind cloak, though glints of moonlight off furniture and glass tore at it.

He reached the second floor, crossed to the wing where Aunt Lillian's room was, and had to flatten himself against a wall as two sorcerers ran by. They rushed heedlessly past where he stood in the shadows, shoes clattering on the marble floor: one was a girl who looked younger than he was, hardly more than a child. Her face was familiar, as if he'd seen her in school.

Jared felt the shadows cling to him as he left the corner, the night of Sorry-in-the-Vale telling him that he could not remain hidden long.

He paused and looked at himself in a mirror as he passed down the hall: it had an ornate gold frame and the glass was speckled. His face faded in and out of vision, his hair a gleam in the dark. He looked like the ghost of a Lynburn, still walking Aurimere's halls.

There was a little table below the mirror, with a lamp on it. The lampshade was fringed with points that glowed in the moonlight. Jared's eyes went to their light: they were seed pearls. Seed pearls, caught in the hollow of paws belonging to some very small animal. The lampshade was hung with paws and pearls.

This crazy house, Jared thought, and almost smiled.

His quiet progress down the hall was stopped when he came in sight of Aunt Lillian's door and saw his guess had been right.

The door was closed. He couldn't see Aunt Lillian.

But he could see his mother, standing in front of the door.

She was looking at it as if there was some riddle inscribed on the dark wood, as though if only she could make out what it said, she would know what to do and how they could all be happy.

Jared didn't know if she was a guard, or if she had simply come to visit her sister. But he remembered that once she had protected Aunt Lillian from Rob. Once, she had even protected him.

She stood hesitating and trembling in front of the door, her streaming hair a cascade of moonshine. Jared wondered how long she had been there; it could have been hours.

He walked softly until he was standing very close to her.

Then he pulled the shadows away so they were standing face to face.

Jared smiled at her, baring his teeth. "Hi, Mom."

*   *   *

His mother started backward in surprise and hit the wall, holding up a hand as if to ward him off. It made him sick to see her flinch, always had, but this time Jared bit his lip and looked away, and did not back down. Her intake of breath was shuddering and sharp, echoing in the hallway louder than her whisper: "What are you doing here?"

"I missed you," Jared said. "Come on. What do you think?"

His mother pressed her hands together briefly, as if she had to pray for an instant. "If you go to Rob, he'll forgive you. He wants you."

"Is that what you want?" Jared asked.

His mother's hand fluttered to her throat, a gesture reminiscent of a bird startled out of a tree. "I don't know what you mean."

"You hate me."

"I don't," his mother said, sharply. "I don't—hate you."

"Well, you don't want me around, do you?" Jared asked. His mother looked at him in the same blank way as she had looked at the door, as if he was a riddle she could not figure out and had given up trying. "And you certainly don't want Aunt Lillian around, do you?"

"Lillian's my sister," Mom snapped, claiming Aunt Lillian apparently as easy as claiming Jared was impossible. "I don't want her hurt. I don't want anything bad to happen to her at all."

Jared felt his lip curl. "But you want her husband."

"He was mine first!" Jared's mother said. "He came to me, all through our childhood. *I* was the one he told about my parents killing his. *I* was the one he told about his plans to get justice. *I* was the one who understood him. Lillian never did."

So Rob had laid the guilt of murder on another child's shoulders. Because to Rob and Rosalind both, killing regular people wouldn't have mattered. But killing Lynburns, especially to defeat other people, well. That was a real crime. That had to be avenged.

Jared was used to hating his mother and feeling painfully sorry for her. He crushed both feelings down.

"I bet she didn't," Jared said. "But Rob will either reconcile with her or hurt her. And you don't want him to do either. So why not let me take her away?" He hoped that his mother would assume he meant "and then we will never come back," rather than what he was actually thinking: "and then Aunt Lillian will take back Aurimere and murder Rob."

"Just open the door, Mother," Jared said. "That's all you have to do."

"You can't open the door," she said in a rush. "There's an alarm spell, and a spell on the lock as well. Two different sorcerers did the spells. You can't concentrate on opening the door, because you'll set off the alarm. And if you concentrate on silencing the alarm, you won't be able to open the door."

"Won't I?" Jared asked. "You're forgetting I'm a delinquent." He concentrated on the alarm spell and reached forward, stomach lurching as his mother shied away from him and stared at him with wide horrified eyes. "I would never hurt you," Jared whispered, and slid the earring out of her ear.

He unwound the wire and slotted it into the lock, listening for the click of the lock giving, the satisfaction of the handle turning under his palm. The door fetched up against an obstruction: Jared put his shoulder to it, hard, and heard wood splinter. The door swung open; splinters the size of daggers lay scattered across the floor.

Jared slanted a look over at his mother. "Look, Mom. Just like magic." He stepped over the splinters and stood by the gauze-draped bed. Aunt Lillian lay there unconscious. Her face was slack and defenseless, robbed of character.

Jared heard the sound of an indrawn breath and turned to see his mother at the doorway.

"She looks like me," his mother murmured. It seemed an absurd thing to say about her identical twin, but Jared looked at Aunt Lillian, so terribly vulnerable, and saw what she meant.

He also saw Aunt Lillian's fists, closing on the material of the bedclothes, trying to fight her way out of unconsciousness. "Don't be ridiculous," he said, walking over to the bed and pulling Aunt Lillian up into his arms. "You two look nothing alike."

Aunt Lillian was tall, and had some muscle, and her body was limp with unconsciousness: she was rather a heavy armful. But Jared found himself tucking his chin protectively on the top of her head. It didn't matter that the muscles in his arms burned holding her. She was a welcome weight.

"You're very strong," his mother murmured. "Like your father."

"Which father would that be?" Jared asked. It was a casual enough question, meant only as an insult flung back at her in return. But his mother looked at him silently, her lips parted, and it became more than that.

"Oh well." Jared would have shrugged if not for the burden of Aunt Lillian. "If you don't know, I guess I never will."

"Rob wants you," she said again.

"It doesn't matter," Jared told her. "I don't want him." He walked toward the door carrying Aunt Lillian. His mother retreated before him, her eyes wary as the eyes of an animal that has been incessantly hurt and cannot trust again.

"You don't need him either," Jared said. The words burst out of his throat. "Come on, Mom. Come with us. That's all you need to do. Just leave him: just walk away."

His mother shook her head, and it seemed to Jared that perhaps she couldn't leave: perhaps so much of her had grown around Rob that she would have to tear herself away and break in the process.

"All right," he said. "Tell me where Tenri Glass is."

His mother shook her head again, but this time it was instant and vehement. "No. Rob would be furious."

"And he won't be furious about Lillian?"

"You don't understand," she said. Her voice echoed down the corridor in a way that made chills run down Jared's spine.

"You're all mixed up about that girl," his mother continued. "You always were. You were forever insisting that she was real."

"You swore to me that she wasn't."

"I was telling you the truth!" His mother's eyes glowed, the eyes of something hunted in a wood. "She isn't real. You have to see that. The people who can't do magic, who aren't connected to the earth, they aren't real. Not the way we are."

Jared looked into her eyes and said, "She was always more real to me than you." If he hadn't had Kami in his head to turn to, he wondered, would he have turned to his mother? Would she have loved him, if he had?

"Where's Ten?" he asked. "I'm coming back for him. The only thing you can do is help me not get caught when I do."

His mother trembled.

"Or do you want me to get caught?" Jared asked.

"No," his mother said, the word less than a breath. "I want you safe. The child is in the attic."

"Thank you," Jared said. He walked down the corridor with Aunt Lillian cradled in his arms. He left his mother behind.

His tread walking down the stairs was heavier, and the shadows could scarcely wrap around both of them. Jared was sure someone would hear, or see, but he kept walking and no one did. He walked into the Aurimere garden and out through the fire again: it parted easily as if it was glad to have them free. And then they were past the fire and away from Aurimere, safe in the cool dark.

Jared laid Aunt Lillian on the ground. Her hair spread out like a river, locks forming silver tributaries in the dark grass. She stirred and muttered something, sounding imperious and lost at once.

"God, Aunt Lillian, you idiot," Jared said, stooping over her and brushing back the hair from her face. "What did you think you were doing?"

She lay there, silent and safe. Jared settled shadow over her like a blanket and turned back to the leaping flames, leaving her hidden in the friendly dark.

✳ ✳ ✳

Aurimere was less welcoming this time, as if the house was angry he had been stupid enough to return. The reflection of the fire cast evil red glints on the glass, as if behind every window there were watching eyes narrowed in laughter. Jared touched the walls as he went by apologetically. The firelight made them look like real gold.

He went to the same door, slipped up the same stairs, but this time when he reached the second floor he kept going. The next flight of stairs was dark and familiar to him: when he touched the banister, he felt the carving in the wood that formed flowers in running water, twined in a drowning woman's hair.

Jared had to open a few doors before he found the stairs that led to the attic: he had not gone up there often. The door that led up to the attic was painted white. It had a round doorknob.

The ordinary door actually gave Jared pause, but he did not pause for long. He walked up the fragile wooden stairs, and when his foot hit a step he called on the air to muffle the creak. He called the darkness to wrap around him.

Shadow and silence, silence and shadow, every step. Nobody would see or hear him coming.

When he reached the attic, he looked around and saw oriel windows that the moonlight was shining directly through. They looked like huge pearls, softly glowing in the dark walls.

For a moment everything seemed to be shadows and silence, and Jared thought he had been wrong. Then he heard the low murmur of Rob's voice and knew that his mother had betrayed him after all.

He walked through the dark, toward the sound of Rob Lynburn speaking. He opened one door, begging the hinges to stay quiet, and crossed a dark room. There was light seeping in from the cracks of the closed door across the room. Electric light, slipping easy and yellow as butter under the door, and the murmur of Rob's low pleasant voice. Jared would have liked to fight him, but there was Ten to think of. He had to wait Rob out.

"I thought you would be pleased," his mother's voice said.

Jared concentrated on the door, pleading for quiet, begging with the air not to carry sound, and it swung silently open, just a few crucial inches. There was furniture in the room beyond, swathed in white sheets. It looked like an entire sofa set had died and been wrapped in shrouds.

He looked around the door and saw Rob standing over his mother, so much taller than her that he appeared to be looming. Neither of them was looking at the door.

Jared took a chance. He pulled the shadows close, so close that the darkness faded and moonlight spread into the corners of the empty room where he stood, and he could hardly see. He went down low and crossed, in two swift steps, to behind the shrouded couch.

Once crouched down there, he told himself he was an idiot. His mother had told Rob where he was headed. She had not given a second thought to betraying him. He should not dream of trying to help her.

"There's just one thing I don't understand, Rosalind," Rob said. He put a hand against her throat, gently turning her face up to his. "When exactly did you see Jared?"

The lightbulbs in this room were not shaded but set in clear glass casements, and the naked electric light sheened his mother's lashes with gold. It seemed like a gold shutter obliterated the color of her eyes for a moment as she blinked. "I—I don't understand."

"Before he took Lillian?" Rob inquired. "Or after he took her? She's my wife. She's valuable. You should have known that the thing to do was instantly raise an alarm."

"He would have fought," Jared's mother said with commendable speed. "He's unstable. I've told you that. I thought you wouldn't want to risk your sorcerers, I thought it would be better to catch him by surprise."

"You thought it would be better to lose Lillian than risk sorcerers who aren't even Lynburns?" Rob asked. He was caressing his mother's tumbled hair, hands and voice steady, kind. "Oh, Rosalind," he said. "Try again."

She retreated back into the safe territory of incomprehension. "I don't understand."

"I don't believe you," Rob told her. The tone of his voice

was so reassuring. "Rosalind. Fool me once . . . and you did, didn't you? Now you've let me down again. The others, they're mistaken, they're being stupid, but at least when they see the light I'll know I can trust them. How can I fight with you at my back when you might change your mind at any time, Rosalind? How can I trust you? I simply can't."

His voice was like a lullaby. It was hard to make out the actual words and not respond to the tone: Jared saw his mother straining in toward Rob, face open and eager to make it up to him. "You can," she assured him. "Rob, I'm sorry. I love you. You have to believe me. I love you. I love you."

"Shhh," said Rob. He laid his cheek against her shining hair. "Hush now. I believe you. I do." Jared hardly saw him move, in the shadowed space between their two bodies. He was aware of Rob's hand going to his belt, but it seemed like a meaningless gesture until he saw Rob's arm go back, saw the clean purposeful thrust. "I have only ever loved one woman," Rob told her gently. "And it wasn't you."

His mother drew in a startled, shuddering breath.

"You're no use to me, Rosalind," Rob explained, still kind and reasonable. He drew out one of the Lynburn daggers, its gold blade drowned in slick blood, and stepped back, letting Jared's mother slide to the ground.

It had all happened so fast that Jared had not quite believed it was happening. Now it was done, and he had not done a thing.

There was blood spreading across his mother's torso, turning the pale material of her dress dark. His mother's cheek was resting against the floorboards, and their gazes met. The light was dying in her eyes, a candle guttering under one last too-violent breath.

Her outflung hand was lying under the sofa. Jared reached out to touch it, he hardly knew why, to save her when it was too late to save her or to comfort her when he'd never been able to comfort her.

They had never been able to save each other.

He could not quite reach: their fingers did not quite meet.

She breathed once more, the sound halting and sticky. She did not breathe again. Her eyes were still open, staring at Jared, but they were dull as glass with the light gone out behind it.

Jared crouched on the floor looking into his dead mother's eyes, until the sofa crashed into the farthest wall.

"Hello, son," said Rob.

Jared didn't get to his feet: he just hurled a handful of air at Rob, like a storm thrown from his palms.

Rob did not even raise a hand. He just glanced at the air and it obeyed him instead. He had Lynburn blood on one of the Lynburn daggers. His mouth shaped a faint sneer. "Really, Jared," he said. "Be more intelligent."

But Jared had something else. He had a strand of Rob's hair, found in his hairbrush at Aurimere, saved for this occasion. *"Noli me tangere,"* said Jared, and his spell knocked Rob across the room.

It gave him enough time to run, and he ran. He ran for the attic door and blasted it open with a spell. Ten Glass sprang up, pieces of door scattering at his feet. He looked so small, wide-eyed and terrified, and Jared was so scared he would fail him.

"Ten," he said, "get out of the house, get to my Aunt Lillian. Go fast. Go now!"

Ten stared at him for another instant and then obeyed, charging past Jared and Rob, making for the stairs.

Rob was already on his feet. He lunged for Ten, and Jared launched himself at him, feeling the strand of hair go up in smoke in his hand.

Rob sneered. "What are you going to do now?"

"I'm sure I'll think of something," Jared said between his teeth, and lunged for Rob's dagger.

He grabbed the blade, slicing open his palm and knowing his blood was mingling with his mother's, still warm on the cold gold. He gripped the dagger and threw himself at Rob again, knocking him back, not caring about keeping his own balance. They hit the floor. Rob used his weight to pin Jared to the ground. Rob was bigger and stronger. He grabbed Jared's free wrist and Jared could feel the power behind his grip, trying to wrench his arm out of its socket.

Jared bared his teeth at him in a grimace and sank the dagger into Rob's shoulder. It was all he could reach. His stomach turned at the sound and sensation of the blade cutting through a body, through gristle and meat.

Rob had put this knife through his mother. Jared sank it in up to the hilt, and twisted.

Rob let a pained hiss leak out between his locked teeth, his big heavy body suddenly heavier on Jared's. Then he got in Jared's face and pressed a kiss on his cheek. "My boy," he breathed into his ear. "Who knew Rosalind would be the one who had my real heir? Nothing stops you, does it? And you already have the taste for blood."

"Whose boy I am seems to be up for debate," Jared remarked breathlessly, tugging at the blade. There was so much blood on his hands, it was difficult.

"Oh, look at you," Rob murmured. "A real Lynburn. You breathe and the house listens. If I'd had the raising of you instead of Ash, I know what you'd be. I don't have any doubts."

Jared did not have any wish to hear about Ash's inherent goodness, or think about how much better he would be for Kami. He felt dizzy with rage and the desire to shut Rob up. The world was going black, splattered with scarlet.

This wasn't rage, he realized, his thoughts surfacing from drowning darkness. Rob was sucking the air out of his lungs. He was suffocating. "What do you want?" he gasped out.

"You on my side," Rob said. "You by my side."

Every breath cut Jared's throat, as if he was swallowing razors. "Oh yeah. Sign me up for evil." He grinned wildly up at Rob, even though his sight was going dark: Rob's face dissolving away from him, everything turning formless and strange. "Give me a weapon and put me at your back. You can totally trust me. I swear."

He laughed, the sound almost a whine, and Rob laughed with him, full and hearty. Jared tried to get hold of the dagger, of his magic, of anything, but the world kept up its slow terrible slide away.

"You don't understand what I'm really doing yet. You don't understand anything yet. But you will. All you need is a little training," Rob said soothingly. "Like a horse. You simply need to be broken."

Jared twisted underneath Rob in one last desperate burst of strength, not fighting anymore, just trying to get away. He couldn't. He was losing the fight; he was losing the world.

Distantly, as if it was happening to someone else, he felt the dagger slip out of his hand. He felt Rob's hand, still horribly gentle, stroking his hair.

He heard Rob's voice, low in his ear.

"I know just the place for you."

* * *

Jared woke up with his legs jammed between a wall and his chest. His head was pounding, and his cheek was pressed against another cold wall. He felt himself gasping as he surfaced into consciousness, remembering suffocation even though his lungs were expanded again, air coursing through them as it should.

The air smelled stale. It smelled of something else as well.

He couldn't focus on it. He couldn't focus on anything, fire or earth, wood or water. He was trapped, in an enclosed space he didn't know where, in a little pocket locked away from magic.

Jared dragged in another breath of air and tried to force himself to be calm. His legs were trapped. He couldn't move them, so he tried to move his arms.

One of his elbows met stone. His other elbow met something else, something that felt like a coatrack: cloth and a frail structure behind it.

Jared looked to his side, and felt the breath dry up in his throat.

There was scarcely any light in the confined space. What light there was was faint but not dim enough that Jared couldn't make out the shadowy form that sat beside him, back against the other wall, knee to knee with him, head bowed.

There was so little light that everything looked gray, but Jared knew the fragile remains of the boy's skin really were gray. His chin rested against his chest, but Jared could see the withered side of his cheek, the shadowed hollows of his eyes, or the sockets that might once have been his eyes.

His clothes were worn and old, rotten in places but mostly preserved in that dry air. It was clothing from decades ago.

The hair hanging in that drawn gray face was dry and pale, curling the way dead leaves curled, so pale it looked bone white in this light.

It made Jared think of Holly's blond curls. It made him think of Aunt Lillian.

Edmund Prescott, the boy Lillian would have married. Except that he had run away when he was seventeen.

He had disappeared, and left Rob to marry the heir of Aurimere.

Jared wanted to scream, but he found himself just gasping dry air and staring down at his hands. There was so much blood on them, dark in the gray light. His own, his mother's, Rob's: there was no way to tell, and it didn't seem to matter.

Rob had left a boy here to die, alone in the dark, once before.

Jared closed his eyes and pressed his face against the cold wall. A terrible sound rose helplessly, low in his throat: he clenched his hands against his knees and would not look at all that remained of Edmund Prescott.

He found, after a long dark moment, that there was something he could focus on after all. There was Kami: not in his head, not in any way he could reach. But he could hold on to the images of her, all the memories he had. He could string instants of remembered light up against the enveloping dark.

His breaths were the only sound in that tiny space, walled up alive with the dead.

The swift impatient movement of her hands when she talked and wanted to be writing. The curve of her mouth, the vivid flash of her eyes, and the smile that could leap across a room at you. The steely grip of her hand, in lake water colder than death, the promise in that grasp that she would not let him go.

Another dry desperate sound broke from Jared's throat. He leaned his forehead against his bloody hands, and waited in the dark.

* * *

It was a couple of hours before Kami noticed. The conversation kept starting and fading away, every plan petering out but none of them willing to give up. There had to be some way forward that was not a dead end.

Eventually, though, she went out to the front of the pub. Martha was closing up, wiping down the bar. People were standing by the door in a loose cluster, aware that they should go but terrified to leave.

And Jared was nowhere in sight.

"I thought Jared might be helping you," Kami said. Dread was already rising inside her, building slowly.

Martha shook her head. "I think he's with young Ash."

"He's not," Kami told her. "Ash has been in there with us for hours."

Martha stopped wiping the bar. She looked up, and her and Kami's eyes met. Kami whirled around and ran up the stairs, to Jared's old room above the pub, to every one of the bedrooms. She flung open doors, telling herself that Jared had been through a lot tonight, they all had, he might just be resting, and her own frantic heartbeat called her a liar.

When Kami went back downstairs, she found the others in the bar, talking to Martha. Everybody was there but Tomo, who must have been left sleeping in the other room. She felt Ash's feelings before she saw him, hurt and tiredness pierced through with agony, canceling out everything else.

They all turned to her as she came in, even Dad.

Kami held on to the bar to keep her balance and began, even though she didn't know how to finish. "Here's what we're going to do."

The door of the Water Rising slammed open.

Lillian Lynburn stood framed in the doorway. Her hair was wild over her shoulders, tangled up with the lights of burning fires and the coming morning. Her face was white as a dead woman's.

Her hand was in Ten's. Kami's little brother stood there, trembling but safe. Kami had not realized, until she felt like her heart would break under the sheer weight of her relief, how very afraid she had been for him.

Dad crossed the floor in two steps, took Lillian Lynburn by the shoulders, and shook her.

"How dare you?" he demanded, and the townspeople scattered away from them, wearing the same expression they would have worn if Dad had tried to fight a lion in the town square. "Is this your idea of protecting the town? Is that how you want people to think of you—as a witch who steals children?"

He let her go and knelt down by Ten, clasping Ten's face in his hands, kissing his face. A violent tremor ran all through Ten's body.

"I'm—" Lillian swallowed, a dry sound. "I'm sorry, Jon."

Dad stood, Ten's hand in his now. The people around them looked amazed: he still looked fierce. "You'd better be. If you ever touch one of my children again, I'm going to kill you. And if you expect us to follow you, you're going to have to change."

Lillian had no response for that. She was looking past Dad, at Ash. All feeling seemed to drain out of her, standing there gaunt in the shadows. Her eyes were so pale they looked like winter ice instead of blue, the winter ice of the pools where all Lillian's sorcerers had died.

"Mom," Ash said, and Kami felt his resolve snap in her mind, knew that he could say no more.

She was the one who had to speak.

"Lillian," she said, "tell me where Jared is."

When Lillian answered, her voice sounded distant, as if she was making a proclamation. As if she was a specter or a banshee calling out tidings of death.

"He went to Aurimere alone," Lillian said. "He got me out. He got the boy out. He saved our lives, and he paid for our lives. I woke outside the house with the child calling me to part the flame and let him through. We waited out in the dark for as long as we could, but Jared never followed us. The boy says Rob caught him, which means that he is in Rob's grasp now. He is past all help. He is lost."

Of course he'd done that. How could she, who knew him so well, not have known what he would do? What else would he have done but the most heroic and crazy thing possible? And he had succeeded. He had saved someone he loved and someone she loved, brought them out from under the shadow of death. He was gone beneath that shadow now, vanished into the sorcerers' manor. Lillian was saying that she would never see him again.

Darkness rose up before Kami's eyes, as if she was going to faint, but she refused to faint. She felt Ash's feelings course through her as his gasp rang through the room. He stumbled toward his mother and almost collapsed headlong into her arms. Lillian stood still for a moment, then her hand rose in a stiff jerky motion and she began to awkwardly stroke his hair.

The winter wind blew through the open door, cutting through the shadows, swirling around the people clinging to each other. Everyone was linked, Kami saw, everybody holding on to somebody, and it occurred to her that even if nobody had been willing to fight Rob, nobody had offered up a victim to him either. Nobody had offered the tokens of allegiance Rob had asked for. The people of Sorry-in-the-Vale had not surrendered yet.

Kami let go her death grip on the bar and walked over to the window. She looked out at the frost-touched town and at Aurimere in the distance, swallowed by flames.

"He's not lost," Kami said. Her voice was steadier than she'd thought it would be. "I won't let him be lost."

Acknowledgments

Many thanks to my lovely editor, Mallory Loehr, Rusty fan extraordinaire; Michael Joosten; my wonderful copy editor Deborah Dwyer; Casey Lloyd; Jan Gerardi; and the whole great team at Random House Children's Books.

Thank you very much to Kristin Nelson and everyone at NLA for everything, forever.

Thank you to Venetia Gosling and the team at Simon & Schuster UK—especially for taking so much cover trouble! And to Kathryn McKenna and Sophie Stott for combining their publicity powers.

And thank you to my amazing foreign publishers, one and all.

Thank you to Delia Sherman and Malinda Lo for help with rooooooomance at crucial points, and to Cassandra Clare for magicked telephones. Thank you to Holly Black for being my first reader for this book, and also the first reader (and judicious cutter and rearranger) of the Kiss Scene of Doom. Thank you to Robin Wasserman and Maureen Johnson for general Robinitude and Maureeniness, and to Cindy Pon and Paolo Bacigalupi and Josh Lewis and Theo Black and Cristi Jacques for plotting like fiends.

Thank you to Ally Carter and Jennifer Lynn Barnes for letting me write outside even though the temperatures were "dangerous" and my behavior was "reckless and unsafe . . . again . . . oh, Sarah, why. . . ."

Thank you to Karen Healey and R. J. Anderson for reading *Untold* super early and still sending me squee.

Thank you to the Book Club, especially Stefanie for telling me she wanted to read this early!

Thank you to my whole family, especially my sister Genevieve "Secret Publicist" Rees Brennan.

Thank you to all my friends: in Ireland, in England, and in America, and the best one who came back to Ireland while I was writing this . . . even if she's in Vietnam by the time it comes out!

Thank you especially to Natasha for still living with me, and occasionally yelling "Why does Jared have to be this way?!"

And I hereby acknowledge every one of the lovely, lovely readers who suffered over the ending of *Unspoken*. I'm so happy you read it. I'm so sorry I hurt you.

(Not that sorry.)

(Secretly a tiny bit glad.)

(Thank you so much.)

They've lost a battle, but the war is just beginning.
Can Kami save Jared before it's too late?

The legacy continues. . . .

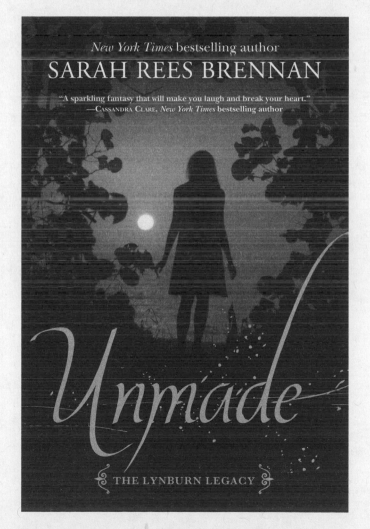

FROM

Unmade

Kami Glass was standing too close to the fire. The magical flames scorched her face, so hot that though her eyes stung and her vision swam, there was no possibility of tears.

Aurimere House, the golden manor from which the Lynburn sorcerers had ruled her town for centuries, was surrounded by a ring of fire that never spread too far or burned completely out. The flames ebbed and flowed like a wicked orange sea, separating her from the house.

There's nothing in there for you, said Ash Lynburn, one of the few good sorcerers left alive and the one sorcerer who was connected to her, mind to mind. *He's gone.*

You don't know that, Kami told him.

I do know that, said Ash. *And if you would admit it, you know it too. He's not in there. He's not anywhere. He's dead.*

Ash's emotions coursed through her, sinking into her every pore. The connection between them was like adding a drop of ink to a glass of water: everything that had been clear becoming distorted. There was no way to separate the two of them, no matter how different they were or how poorly they mixed.

Kami didn't want to be connected to Ash, and he didn't want to be connected to her. They had linked because they had to, because as source and sorcerer together they had magical power that could be used to save their friends and protect their home.

They had been linked for over a month now. They were getting used to it, but it wasn't getting any easier.

Kami had always wanted to be in control of herself; she had never wanted anyone else to try to control her. Ash did not mean to, but his cautions and misgivings were constant obstacles in her path. She felt fenced in on every side.

Worse than that, she felt Ash's misery and despair, heavy as an anchor around her neck. He had no hope, and she did not have hope enough for both of them.

What was she supposed to say about Ash's half brother Jared, her first source, the one she had loved, the boy she had been linked to for so much of her life? "He's not dead! And we're still dating!"?

She wanted to believe that if Jared was dead, she would know. He had been so much a part of her all her life. Even if they had been separated, surely something would have told her that he was completely lost. It did not feel right that magic should be stronger than her own painfully stubborn, painfully clinging heart. She should *know*.

I knew, said Ash. *I knew my father would make Jared pay for defying him. We're Lynburns. We do not forgive. We never permit a second sin against us.*

She refused to surrender to despair, even in her own mind.

I'm getting a little tired of hearing all these mystical

pronouncements about Lynburns, Kami said, and tried to show Ash nothing but determination. *"We are creatures of red and gold," "We do not forgive," "We do not need hearts," "Our family motto is 'Hot blond death . . .'"*

We don't say that last one, said Ash, both bemused and amused. The emotions ran through Kami, sweet but alien, more strange than pleasant.

I admit I may have made that last one up, Kami said. *But I stole the last piece of toast at breakfast yesterday, and you didn't say "Lynburns never permit a second sin" and stab me in the hand with a fork. Even Rob is not consistent all the time. We don't know what he did to Jared. We don't know anything. Jared could still be in there.*

And how would you suggest we get in there to find him? Ash asked.

Kami had been trying to think of a plan to do that for weeks, long before her mother's words had sent her running up to Aurimere as if she could plunge through the flame and rescue Jared, weeks too late.

All her plans had been ridiculous, the laughable imaginings of a panicking child. Or perhaps that was just how they appeared to Ash. Kami was slowly losing her grip on how to differentiate between her darkening view of the world and the shadow through which Ash saw things.

She felt Ash's regret, sympathetic but chilling, like a cold hand placed kindly on her shoulder. She tried to pull herself together the only way she knew how.

I have a plan to get in, she told him. *This is fire. We can go to our school and steal all the fire extinguishers there: we can put it out enough to get in.*

It's magical fire, said Ash. *That's why it never burns out and never spreads. Fire extinguishers aren't going to work.*

He had vetoed every one of her plans.

Lucky for you, I have another scheme. First I need a hundred ducks, but after that it will all be pretty simple.

What do you need the ducks for?

I'm going to put a whole bunch of them in a giant catapult and launch them over Aurimere, Kami said. *This will create a distraction. My message will be: Look at all the ducks I give.*

Ash's amusement sang through her body as a laugh would have sung through her ears: appreciative but humoring her too.

Jared would have said, *I'm in. What's our next move?*

Kami turned her face away from the fires around Aurimere and looked out on the town. She told herself the fire was too hot, and that was why her eyes were stinging; that the smoke had got into her throat, scorching it, and that was why it ached. She lied to herself because she did not know how she would put herself back together if she fell apart.

Sorry-in-the-Vale from this vantage point was all gold angles, roofs and spinning weathervanes under a sky pale and sick with long winter. She thought about Jared, his face that was all angles and harsh lines, one cheek marked with a long white scar and eyes the color of the sky above their town. He looked cruel until he smiled, and all his smiles were small and brief.

She had always thought that Jared looked like he fit into the town and the woods around it, maybe because he was one of the sorcerers this town had been created for and ruled by for so long. Maybe because she had always thought he looked like home.

"Didn't you love him?" her mother had asked. "Didn't you kill him?"

Ash, the constant unwanted guest in her heart, said, *You're not the only one who misses him. He was my brother. I barely got the chance to know him and now he's gone.*

She was not the only one who missed him, but she was the only one who could not accept his death.

Kami had tried to go on with her newspaper, had tried to cope with being linked to Ash and her mother being more and more under the sway of Aurimere. She had tried to carry on, and she had kept hoping.

Everybody was always telling her she was wrong: Angela and Holly with their quiet sympathy, Ash with the sharp grief that cut into every hope she had, and now her own mother in simple words, in the cold light of day.

Jared Lynburn is dead.

The crackling of the fire stuttered and hissed. Kami spun around to see the fire had parted, like water parting at a god's command, to make a passage from the door of Aurimere House to the road that led into Sorry-in-the-Vale.

Kami watched Rob Lynburn come out of the great doors of Aurimere House, over which was written the legend YOU ARE NOT SAFE. He looked around with a smile, lord of all he surveyed.

Until his eyes fell on Kami. His genial beam flickered for an instant and then steadied. He simply smiled and let his gaze pass over her, as if she was a part of his town and thus a possession, something utterly insignificant over which he had absolute control.

His sorcerers followed him in a procession down the road to Sorry-in-the-Vale.

The last one was scarlet-haired Ruth Sherman, one of the sorcerous strangers Rob had called to enjoy the magical benefits of his town, the power that his sacrifices would offer. She was wearing her hair loose, trailing like a comet's tail, and in the wake of that scarlet trail, the circle of fire closed with a sound like a whisper in a hush.

Get everyone, Kami told Ash in her head. She felt his dread as well as her own, drowning out all courage. *Come quickly. I don't know if they killed Jared, but I think they are going to kill someone else.*

* * *

Kami followed where Rob and his sorcerers went, down the broad golden expanse of Sorry-in-the-Vale's High Street. Inn, sweet shop, grocer's, gift shop, the little café where they sold scones and lemonade, and just before the church, the town hall.

It was only a small building, though it was one of the oldest: four hundred years old, Cotswold stone. Kami remembered the details about it because one of the Somervilles, her mother's family, had built it. Under the eave of the low roof, almost hidden in shadow, were golden words: MUNDUS VULT DECIPI.

It meant: *The world wants to be deceived.*

The Somerville who had built this place had known about sorcerers, Kami thought. He had seen the town turning a blind eye and letting the victims be sacrificed.

There were people filing into the town hall.

Kami had not seen this many people in weeks. At the beginning of Rob's bid for power, everyone had pretended life would go on as normal. Everyone had talked a little more loudly and brightly than before, and continued determined on their course, thinking the sorcerers would sort it all out. Now that Rob had won, the streets were emptier, voices were fading into silence, and the shelves at the grocer's were half full and never restocked. When Kami passed by the windows of houses, she saw curtains moving and glimpsed scared faces hiding as soon as they were seen.

This was why Rob had waited. This was how Rob had got them to cooperate. He had known that people could not last long under the silent remorseless pressure of fear, that they would give up anything in hope that the fear would end.

This many people meant that Rob had called them here together.

The hall had a wide black-painted door, its handle twined with wrought-iron weeds, as though it had lain once at the bottom of a lake. Kami saw it fall shut behind the last of the crowd, and she ran up the steps and closed her hand around that wrought-iron handle.

Kami pushed open the door and saw a table, spread with white, saw the glow of light through stained-glass windows land on long golden knives. She saw the man, bound and gagged, on the altar.

Kami charged over the threshold. Ruth Sherman placed herself between Kami and the pale altar, her red brows raised.

"No sources allowed," she said, and knocked Kami back across the threshold, flat on the stone steps.

Kami had been able to fight sorcerers better once, before they had all fed their power with blood: when she had been linked to Jared, and the magic had flowed easily between them.

Now invisible blows and kicks rained down on her, as if the very air was assaulting her, telling her, "You are not welcome here."

Kami, we're coming, said Ash.

I have some advice for you, said Kami. *Come faster.*

She was curled up like a worm, so she turned, jackknifed on the stone, and grabbed Ruth's foot, pulling her weight out from under her. But the air that had hurt Kami caught Ruth and held her in place as if by invisible supporters.

Kami thought of standing outside Aurimere, watching the windows flicker orange and being unable to see inside. She thought of the bloodstained floor in the attic.

Ruth Sherman's hair burst into flame.

Kami shoved her into the street and ran inside the town hall.

It was too late. It had probably been too late by the time Ruth tossed Kami like a rag doll onto the stone steps.

Kami had seen this before with a slaughtered fox, seen the stained tablecloth and the candles. She had even seen what the knife could do to a person.

But she had never seen the whole ritual as it played out. She had never seen Rob Lynburn's golden head, limned by the stained-glass windows as if he was a saint, bent over his work. She had never seen the golden knife drowned in someone's lifeblood, running like a dark red river over the shining carved surface of the table.

She wrenched her gaze away from Rob. She looked at the white altar turning crimson, and into the slack face of the dead man.

Chris Fairchild, the mayor. Kami had seen him talking to Lillian once, and she had not appeared to be paying much attention, but at least she had been talking to him. Kami had never seen him do much, but he was their only symbol of leadership besides the sorcerers.

The magic is greater, her mother had said, if the sacrifice is willing.

Rob had talked to the mayor, and the mayor had promised him a sacrifice. He had given himself up for the town. Rob Lynburn had killed him, cut him open with his golden knives, and all the sorcerers' power was increased with his blood. The power came to Rob through the Lynburn blade, and then he would spread it to his followers like a king distributing largesse.

But not all these people were Rob's sorcerers. Kami looked at the faces of the people watching, and saw they looked sick but not surprised. Kami's guess had been right. Rob Lynburn must have summoned the people of Sorry-in-the-Vale to come see this.

Most of the town had not come. Most people must be hiding in their homes, turning their faces away. But enough people had obeyed. There were ordinary townspeople in the town hall, and they had just sat and watched this horror come to pass.

Kami scanned the faces of the audience, recognizing them, burning into her mind who had been there. She saw Sergeant Kenn, a policeman she would once have trusted to keep her town safe, standing in front of the altar and guarding his leader as he killed. She saw Amber and Ross, two kids from her class, sitting with the sorcerers and absorbing the power. She searched, with a fear that made her vision swim as if she could protect herself from seeing, for her mother's face in the crowd.

Claire was not there. She had not submitted to the sorcerers in this. It was the only mercy Kami could find on this cold morning.

Kami stood in the aisle between the half-full rows of seats, and looked once again at Rob Lynburn.

She concentrated, drawing together the magic she had but could not always command, and all around Rob the stained-glass windows exploded into glittering, sparkling fragments so tiny they looked like dust that shone. They fell all over the stone floor, and the chilly light of day illuminated starkly what Rob had done.

"Murderer," Kami called out. "That's what he is. That's what you all stood and *watched*. He won't stop. He won't stop unless we stop him."

Everyone turned to face her. Rob's gaze on her was steady. He looked amused.

Someone grasped Kami from behind, put a hand over her mouth, pulled her close and held her tight to his chest.

She knew who it was, knew it wasn't an enemy and didn't attack, because of the voice in her head.

Kami, please, please stop, Ash begged her.

She was a better fighter than Ash, but he'd caught her by surprise and was holding her locked to his chest, using his desperation to save her.

Over and above that, worse than anything, were his feelings pouring over her and crushing her: desperation to save her, yes, but despair too, utter lack of hope, consuming fear of his father, and the powerful, terrible urge to flee and hide. Kami tried to fight free of him, body and mind both, but it was so hard.

Rob came walking toward her down the stone aisle. Kami felt Ash tremble against her, felt his horror and fear and love for this man. He removed his hand from her mouth and put his other arm around her, less restraining her than clinging to her now.

She refused to tremble, even when Rob stopped in front of her and stroked her cheek, lightly, with his knife. She felt the hot smear of the blood and the sharp edge of the blade.

Kami raised her chin and glared at him.

"Don't kill her yet," said Rob in a casual voice to his followers. "She's got herself linked to another one of my sons. But I already cut one son loose from her, and I'll free the other. After that she will be beneath my notice, and you can do anything you want."

"Oh," said Ruth, magic turning her blackened hair red again, like a sea of blood drowning out ashes. "I will."

Rob turned away from Kami and Ash toward the townspeople sitting in the hall.

"You did not offer me a winter sacrifice on the day appointed," he said. "Your sacrifice was late. I hope that I have taught you all a lesson, and I will expect evidence that you have learned. I want you all to give me tokens to show that you have submitted. And at the spring equinox, I want you to choose me another sacrifice."

There was a murmur of dismay from the crowd, as if they had honestly thought that one death would make them safe. Kami heard a sob, wild and loud, and saw Chris Fairchild's wife collapse into a neighbor's arms. Rob looked around, mouth curved as if smiling at a private joke.

"One more sacrifice. One more season. Then I promise you on my word as the Lynburn of Aurimere, there will be peace for Sorry-in-the-Vale."

Rob and his sorcerers left. Ash hung onto Kami, his heart beating a wild frantic rhythm against her back, even after they were gone.

Kami heard the whispers of the people around her, rising up to the low ceiling, slipping out of the broken windows, saying that they had no other choice, that everything would be all right, that there would be advantages, that the old ways were the best ways, that they could not be held responsible. She saw women taking their hair down, about to snip it off as a token for their sorcerous leader. Nobody was looking at the dead man on the altar.

She did not have to listen long, because finally the others arrived, all of them running, sunshine-haired Holly, tall, dark, and terminally idle Rusty, and Kami's best friend in all the world, Angela. Holly was trembling. Even Rusty did not look his usual unconcerned self.

Angela took one look at the altar and curled her scarlet lip.

"Goddamn sorcerers," she said. "It is the goddamn weekend."

A few people looked outraged by Angela's flippancy, but

Holly smiled a tiny smile. Angela did not notice anyone's reactions, because she was busy making threats.

"Ash, let go of Kami this minute or I will punch you in the face."

Ash let go of Kami. Kami punched him in the arm.

"I didn't know that *all* my choices were punching," Ash said, rubbing his arm.

"Don't ever grab me like that again," Kami told him. "Or your whole life will be punching."

She crossed to the stone steps where Angela stood, and Rusty made room for her beside his sister, so she could lean into Angela a little. Angela glanced down at her face.

"What is it?" she asked. "Is it this, or is there something else as well?"

"My mother," Kami said quietly. "She told me something about Jared today."

Angela grasped Kami's hand and held it tight. That gesture, and the look on Holly's face, let Kami know that they had already expected to hear news of Jared's death. They were both utterly unsurprised.

She looked at Rusty. He was frowning slightly, biting his lip. He looked conflicted.

"Cambridge," he said, "can we go somewhere and talk?"

Kami followed Rusty down the steps and away from the building that bore the words that promised all men would welcome deceit, the building where people she'd thought she knew had watched a man die.

Rusty was moving fast, as Rusty, lazy as he was sweet, hardly ever did. Kami could barely keep up with him.

"What's this about?" Kami asked.

Rusty glanced over his shoulder at her. There was something apprehensive about his look, as if he was not quite sure she would still be there. Or as if he was not quite sure he wanted her to be.

"You're going to be angry," he predicted.